Praise for Silvina Ocampo:

'Few writers have an eye for th‹
still see the everyday marvellous.
cannot think of a single writer wh.
has chronicled both with such wise

‹ge,

Alberto Manguel

'Silvina Ocampo is, together with Borges and García Márquez, the
leading writer in Spanish'

Jorge Amado

'She lived a little in the shadow of her sister Victoria on the one
hand and of her husband, Bioy Casares, and Borges on the other.
She was an extravagant woman when writing her stories, short and
crystalline, she was perfect'

César Aira

'Ocampo wrote with fascinated horror of Argentinean petty
bourgeois society, whose banality and kitsch settings she used in a
masterly way to depict strange, surreal atmospheres sometimes
verging on the supernatural'

Independent

'Ocampo mixes unembellished narration and dark, fantastic
elements into a heady cocktail'

Lit Hub

'Why has Ocampo remained a hidden treasure to English readers?
... She stands alongside Tanizaki, Dinesen and others as one of the
most imaginative and innovative short-story writers of the
twentieth century, and among the finest practitioners of the genre
in any language'

Asymptote

'Ocampo's technique is beyond all reproach ... sometimes we have to stop and reread a sentence, as if our disbelief has been suddenly tickled awake. This is a reaction we have to many of her stories: do we wake or dream?'

Guardian

'Iconic ... a writer of powerful imagination, drawing on paradox and ploy, perpetual subterfuge of the expected. Her world is peopled with the fantastic, the innocent perverse, the strange or numinous in everyday life. Time is a rubber band and, in a single sentence, ghosts and alternative worlds superimpose'

Granta

THE IMPOSTOR
AND OTHER STORIES

SILVINA OCAMPO (1903–1993) was born to an old and pros-
perous family in Buenos Aires, the youngest of six sisters. After
studying painting with Giorgio de Chirico and Fernand Léger
in Paris, she returned to her native city – she would live there
for the rest of her life – and devoted herself to writing. Her
eldest sister, Victoria, was the founder of the seminal modernist
journal and publishing house *Sur*, which championed the work
of Jorge Luis Borges and Adolfo Bioy Casares, and in 1940 Bioy
Casares and Silvina Ocampo were married. The first of Ocampo's
seven collections of stories, *Viaje olvidado* (Forgotten Journey),
appeared in 1937; the first of her seven volumes of poems,
Enumeración de la patria (Enumeration of My Country) in
1942. She was also a prolific translator – of Dickinson, Poe,
Melville, and Swedenborg – and wrote plays and tales for
children. The writer and filmmaker Edgardo Cozarinsky once
wrote, 'For decades, Silvina Ocampo was the best kept secret of
Argentine letters.' *Silvina Ocampo: Selected Poems* is published
by NYRB/Poets.

DANIEL BALDERSTON is Andrew W. Mellon Professor of Modern Languages at the University of Pittsburgh, where he chairs the Department of Hispanic Languages and Literatures and directs the Borges Center. He has written seven books on Borges, the most recent of which is titled *How Borges Wrote*. He has edited numerous books, including *Voice-Overs: Translation and Latin American Literature*, and has also translated books by José Bianco, Juan Carlos Onetti, Sylvia Molloy and Ricardo Piglia.

HELEN OYEYEMI is the author of seven novels, including *White Is for Witching*, which won a 2010 Somerset Maugham Award; *Mr. Fox*, which won a 2012 Hurston/Wright Legacy Award; and most recently *Boy, Snow, Bird*, *Gingerbread*, and *Peaces*. In 2013, she was named one of *Granta*'s Best Young British Novelists.

JORGE LUIS BORGES (1899–1986), a giant in Latin American letters, wrote numerous books of poetry, fiction and essays, and was a prodigious translator of authors such as Kipling, Woolf, Faulkner and Poe. He was a regular contributor to Victoria Ocampo's journal *Sur*, and a frequent dinner guest of Silvina Ocampo and Adolfo Bioy Casares. Over one of their legendary conversations, the three friends came upon the idea of editing *The Anthology of Fantastic Literature*, which was published in 1940.

THE IMPOSTOR
AND OTHER STORIES

SILVINA OCAMPO

Translated from the Spanish by
Daniel Balderston

First published in Great Britain in 2021 by
Serpent's Tail,
an imprint of Profile Books Ltd
29 Cloth Fair
London
ECIA 7JQ
www.serpentstail.com

First published in the United States of America in 2015 by
The *New York Review of Books* as *Thus Were Their Faces*

10 9 8 7 6 5 4 3 2 1

Typeset in Garamond by MacGuru Ltd
Printed and bound in Great Britain by
CPI Group (UK) Ltd, Croydon, CR0 4YY

The moral right of the author has been asserted.

A CIP catalogue record for this book is available from the British Library.

ISBN 978 1 78816 879 3
eISBN 978 1 78283 884 5

CONTENTS

INTRODUCTION

WHAT WE have in Silvina Ocampo is a writer of the Big Bad Wolf school. In 1979 her forty-two-year body of work was denied Argentina's National Prize for Literature. "*Demasiado crueles*" (far too cruel) was the verdict of that year's panel of judges.* It wasn't Ocampo's poetry the judges were talking about—she'd won notable poetry prizes in previous years. Perhaps her alternately burning and freezing dislocations of perspective are slightly more orthodox in the realm of poetry, where to some extent we half expect to lose our footing and find something startling in the gap between verses. In Ocampo's poem "A Tiger Speaks," having briefly surveyed episodes of interaction between humankind and other species in the first stanza, the tiger begins her second stanza with the remark: "We never managed to agree / about man's true nature."† The tiger's tone awakens ominous awareness of a class of gaze that passes over the deeds of human beings and finds little humanity in them. It could be that poetry is more readily accepted as a natural vessel for long-distance dispatches of this kind, no matter how precise or orderly the poem's technical form. Short stories tend to be received quite differently: certain structural assurances are demanded, some guarantee

---

* "In an interview with Patricia Klingenberg in March 1980, Ocampo reported that she was denied the National Prize in 1979 by judges who felt her stories were '*demasiado crueles.*'" Quote from Cynthia Duncan, "Double or Nothing in Silvina Ocampo's 'La casa de azúcar,'" *Chasqui: revista de literatura latinoamericana* 20, No. 2 (November 1991).

† *Silvina Ocampo: Selected Poems*, selected and translated by Jason Weiss (New York: NYRB/Poets, 2015).

that if and when an event or an idea throws us off-balance, by the end that balance will be restored, or at the very least the tools for its restoration will be within reach. And so "far too cruel" was the verdict on Ocampo's short fiction, some of the best of which is collected in this book. It's true that aside from their narrative technique of tripping you up and leaving you on the floor, Ocampo's stories narrate the inner lives of heartless children, half-mad lovers, and assorted others who lean out of the pages to speak to us with all their anomie showing. Here's the narrator of "Friends," for example, sardonically noting the external resemblance between a surfeit of grief and a light smattering of gaiety: "Nearly the whole town was in mourning; the cemetery looked like a flower show, and the streets sounded like a bell-ringing contest."

As readers of Ocampo we follow the first Red Riding Hood, bypassing that initial pretense of going among the leaves of a book or a forest in search of kindly, tidy wisdom from the type of grandmother nobody ever really had. No, there are voices we follow knowing full well that we'll be led astray. I'm tempted to call Ocampo's readers Red Reading Hoods, but I can well imagine your scorn. In her stories characters negotiate the entrapments of time, which rewards relentless determination, or at least doesn't punish it. In "Icera," a small girl from a poor family decides not to grow any bigger than the biggest doll in the doll department of a toy store near her house; her efforts to keep her material wants small face a setback after Icera's four-inch growth spurt, but that addition of four inches to her height is the full extent of her physical growth between preadolescence and middle age, and we leave her being packaged up happily in a blue cardboard box intended for the transportation of an expensive doll. The narrator doesn't invite us to wonder at or worry about this turn of events; there's a level on which Ocampo's stories are matter-of-fact reports of the everyday traffic (outgoing) between the mind and the world.

Ocampo airily collaborated with her immediate contemporaries, co-editing anthologies and writing a short, charmingly off-kilter murder mystery called *Where There's Love, There's Hate* (1946) with her husband, Adolfo Bioy Casares. Bioy Casares is the author of one of the twentieth century's most ingenious and affecting works of fabulism, *The Invention of Morel* (1940), and part of the fun of reading a book co-authored by this superlatively well-read couple lies in trying to guess which parts were written by Bioy Casares, which parts were written by Ocampo, and which parts were written by one impersonating the other. Her novella *The Topless Tower* (1968) is an adventure diligently narrated by Leandro, a boy who finds himself trapped in a painting. Being trapped in the painting isn't his only problem; his intellect frequently gets ahead of him and even as he describes his surroundings and encounters he underlines certain words that he uses but doesn't yet understand ("lugubrious," "macabre," "cynical"); these notations serve as reminders to look up the meanings later. Here Ocampo's fondness and flair for nonsense literature in the vein of Lewis Carroll is palpable. (*Through the Looking-Glass, and What Alice Found There* is, after all, a book-long chess game.) There are few other writers who can apply such abstract mischief to narrative without stripping it of its human flesh. If Ocampo's solo fiction continues to elude canonization within Argentine literature, it will be because the tradition that Ocampo seems to work within is that of the visionary whose sensibility crosses plural borders.

Like Emily Brontë, Ocampo was a younger sister whose literary vision takes its own unruly path away from that of her elder (in Ocampo's case this elder sister, the revered writer and critic Victoria, was her first publisher). Love is as fearsome in an Ocampo story as it is in *Wuthering Heights*; emotion has a way of sealing us into a charmed circle that makes us incomprehensible to everyone who stands outside it. This kind of circle shrinks and shrinks until even the beloved is impossible to read clearly, and then finally we're unable to even pretend to understand our own thoughts. At times Ocampo's characters speak to us as if under the influence of a truth drug that won't permit them to simplify the expression of their motivations. In "Autobiography of Irene," a malicious act is motivated by panic—how else can a teenage girl govern a tempestuous inner life that turns her regard for a beloved teacher into something that feels life threatening, an emotion one could drown in? "[One] day, crying because I already knew how mistaken and how unfair I could be, I made up a slander against that young lady, who had only wanted to praise me." We also see a similar blurring of psychic attack and defense in "The House Made of Sugar," in which, having ignored his wife's superstitions, a man watches the logically impossible repercussions of his actions drain the stability from his marriage with a petulant malevolence that may remind you of a small tyrant who punishes her parent's disobedience by holding her breath until she loses consciousness. At the end of that story we can only agree with the narrator's summation: "I don't know who was the victim of whom in that house made of sugar, which now stands empty." From time to time a form of comic relief is derived from Ocampo's invitation to view love, romantic or otherwise, from a position of amused disgust—in "Lovers," a heavy date for two of Ocampo's characters consists of the joyless, mechanical overconsumption of cake accompanied by "shy conversation on the theme of picnics: people who had died after drinking wine or eating watermelon; a poisonous spider in a picnic basket one Sunday that had killed a girl whose in-laws all hated her; canned goods that had gone bad, but looked delicious." In "The Guests," a gift box is found to contain "two crude magnetic dolls that couldn't resist kissing on the lips, their necks stretched out, as soon as they were within a certain distance of each other."

Like William Blake, Ocampo's first voice was that of a visual artist; in her writing she retains the will to unveil the immaterial so that we might at least look at it if not touch it: "there are voices that you can see, that keep on revealing the expression of a face even after its beauty is gone," the protagonist of "Autobiography of Irene" tells us. Blake began with drawing, but just as she tells us in her own words, Ocampo was a painter, an increasingly frustrated student of the cubist Fernand Léger ("Nothing interested Léger except the design of his paintings") and then the proto-surrealist Giorgio de Chirico ("I fought with Giorgio de Chirico and told him he sacrificed everything for the sake of color"), until she turned to writing as her own particular means of transforming reality. I consider this when the imagery in Ocampo's stories slides between the concrete and the abstract, recalling Blake's spectral embodiments, the ones that rise and float and walk alongside solidly hewn stars and beasts with the look of living stone. When I read "Visions," a short story of Ocampo's in which a bedridden woman awaits death (or recovery), I see Blake's brutal light, rays that blast through all other colors to center and re-center his paintings and illustrations. "Beauty has no end or edges. I wait for it," Ocampo's narrator says. Either this presence called beauty has an innate power to change us as it approaches and recedes, or it is our own functional creation, an ever-shifting evocation of those moments beyond language when we get closer to and beat an abashed retreat from whatever it is that drives consciousness. Always within reach, yet always mysterious, is this essential self, leading Ocampo to end her own preface to this book with the question: "Will we always be students of ourselves?"

In his preface to this book, Borges writes that Ocampo "sees us as if we were made of glass, sees and forgives us. It is useless to try to fool her." I agree that Ocampo sees, but the all-consuming grudges held by her characters create an initial difficulty in discovering just where her mercy intersects with her clear sight—in "The Fury," a girl who receives a fish and a monkey as conciliatory gifts from her tormentor simply allows the poor creatures to starve to death. Here gentleness is merely a prologue to some truly dark deed or other. In "The Clock House," the role at a party of a hunchbacked man named Estanislao goes from guest of honor to victim—it's impossible to conclusively decide whether or not the child narrator is feigning incomprehension of Estanislao's fate or is genuinely innocent. Either way we readers are brutalized by the educated guesses the narrative leads us to make. The party guests propose that Estanislao's suit be ironed with its owner still in it; this occurs, and the commotion of this event is described in the vaguest and most chilling of terms: "Nobody was laughing except for Estanislao." After that our young narrator N. N. steps back and will not share in the resultant vision. Elsewhere Ocampo demonstrates that she understands, alongside

Emily Dickinson, that "The heart asks pleasure first / and then excuse from pain," but this doesn't prevent her sharp commentary on the eager adoption of strategies to excuse ourselves from pain. The narrator of "The Prayer," a story of deadly weakness, notes the prevailing mood at the funeral of an eight-year-old killed by another eight-year-old: "Only one old lady, Miss Carmen, was sobbing, because she didn't understand what had happened. Oh my God, how miserable, how lacking in ceremony the funeral was!"

I think what Ocampo understands is that so many of our cruelties and treacheries are born out of a sort of rapt distraction; our memories don't work very well and we try to kick-start them with reenactments, or new and wholly unnecessary treacheries that present themselves to us as reenactments. In "The Mortal Sin," a household servant named Chango bids his employers' young daughter to look through a keyhole into the next room, where he'll show her "something very beautiful." The girl does as she's told, and what she sees is made ghastly by the insistent voice of a man in the next room, speaking with "a commanding and sweet obscenity: 'Doll, look! Look!'" In this way the girl is made fully conscious of her gaze being manipulated for the pleasure of another, a pleasure that's utterly indifferent to her own dissent. "I feel such sorrow when I think how horror imitates beauty," the narrator tells us. "Through that door, Pyramus and Thisbe, like you and Chango, spoke their love through a wall."

These stories seem to agree with Lewis Carroll's White Queen that it's a poor sort of memory that only works backward, after all. And the further back we look, the less time we have left to see. Even worse, no matter how long or faithfully we look along that line, it doesn't go back far enough, there's still something, something big that we've all forgotten—we can't remember what exactly we're all supposed to be to each other, what we have been, what we can be, and that makes us rough playmates. The living appall us; how can we be at peace with them when they insist on standing so insistently between us and our ghosts? As Armando Heredia explains in the story "The Impostor," it would be better if we were less careless with the influence we exert upon each others' experience of the boundaries between life and death: "our lives depend on a certain number of people who see us as living beings. If those people imagine that we are dead, we die." If Armando is right, then on a moment-to-moment basis the terms of the continued existence of any individual are far more fragile than we dare to feel. And like those of Ocampo's characters who make it to the end of the story without having been murdered by a thing as simple as a velvet dress, or strangled by a grip as powerful as the eddies of an infernal whirlpool, there's something to be said for counting yourself lucky to be a survivor of yesterday, today, and maybe even tomorrow.

—HELEN OYEYEMI

PREFACE

NOT WITHOUT some feelings of reticence do I write this preface. An old, yet ever new, friendship binds me to Silvina Ocampo, a friendship based on the shared memories of certain neighborhoods in Buenos Aires, of sunsets, of walks across the limitless plains or along a river as quiet as the land, of favorite poems: one based, above all, on the understanding and kindness that Silvina has never failed to show me. Like Rossetti and Blake, Silvina has come to poetry by the luminous paths of drawing and painting, and the immediacy and certainty of the visual image persist in her written pages.

The range covered by her spirit is much greater than my own. The joys provoked by music and color, paradises barred to my memory as well as to my curiosity, are familiar to her. I would say the same of the things of nature: flowers, vague names when I come upon them in Latin and Persian verses, signify something precise for Silvina, something precise and beloved. The universe I live in is opaque because it is purely verbal; in hers, the senses take part in all their delicate variety. Our literary preferences do not always coincide. I am moved by the epic, she by the lyric and the elegiac; she is not drawn so much to the *Chanson de Roland* and the harsh sagas of Iceland as to Baudelaire, a poet I venerated in my youth, or to the idylls of Theocritus. She also likes the psychological novel, a genre whose slow pace I reject out of laziness.

It is strange that it should be I, for whom telling a story is the attempt to capture only its essential elements, who should present to English readers a work as wise, as changeable, as complex, and at the same time as simple as this collection. I thank the gods for this happy fate.

In Silvina Ocampo's stories there is something I have never understood: her strange taste for a certain kind of innocent and oblique cruelty. I attribute this to the interest, the astonished interest, that evil inspires in a noble soul. The present, we might say in passing, is perhaps no less cruel than the past, or than the various pasts, but its cruelties are clandestine. Góngora, who was a normal man and a fine poet, makes fun of an auto-da-fé performed in Granada because it offered the modest spectacle of only one person burned alive; Hitler, an atrocious man, preferred the anonymous horror of the secret death chambers to the spectacle of public executions. Today, cruelty searches out the shadows; cruelty is obscene, in the original meaning of the word.

Silvina has a virtue that is frequently ascribed to the ancients and to the peoples of the Orient, only infrequently to our own contemporaries: clairvoyance. More than once, and not without feelings of apprehension, I have felt hers. She sees us as if we were made of glass, sees and forgives us. It is useless to try to fool her.

Silvina Ocampo is a poet, one of the greatest poets in the Spanish language, whether on this side of the ocean or on the other. The fact that she is a poet elevates her prose. In other parts of South America, the short story is usually no more than a simple sketch of daily life or a simple social protest, or often an unhappy mixture of the two; among us, in Argentina, it tends to be the product of an imagination granted the fullest freedom. The book I am introducing is a clear example of this.

Groussac and Alfonso Reyes have renewed the intentionally verbose and sententious Spanish style with the help of the precision of French; Silvina Ocampo has understood their lesson and has constantly improved upon it in magical works.

—JORGE LUIS BORGES

AUTHOR'S INTRODUCTION

AM I AN outsider or a liar, a giant or a dwarf, a Spanish dancer or an acrobat? When you write, everything is possible, even the very opposite of what you are. I write so that other people can discover what they should love, and sometimes so they discover what I love. I write in order not to forget what is most important in the world: friendship and love, wisdom and art. A way of living without dying, a way of death without dying. On paper, something of us remains, our soul holds on to something in our lives: something more important than the human voice, which changes with health, luck, muteness, and finally, with age.

What will be left of us in this world? Sentences instead of voices, sentences instead of photographs. I write in order to forget scorn, in order not to forget, in order not to hate, from hate, from love, from memory, and so as not to die. Writing is a luxury or, with luck, a rainbow of colors. It is my lifesaver when the water of the river or the sea tries to drag me under. When you want to die you fall in love with yourself, you look for something touching that will save you. I write to be happy or to give happiness. I, who am unhappy for no reason, want to explain myself, to rejoice, to forget, to find something others might find in Ovid in my unhappiness or in my other self.

Palinurus exists in writing, and sleeps in my heart as if in the blue water of the sea. Andersen's mermaid has a beautiful voice I never heard. When I call on the Guardian Angel in my language, he is more beautiful than life itself.

Sometimes you can tell the truth about little things only by not writing. On a white sheet of paper I have been sketching a hand for some time; it is my hand that sketches words. I have loved painting since childhood.

Writing is having a sprite within reach, something we can turn into a demon or a monster, but also something that will give us unexpected happiness or the wish to die.

I studied painting with Giorgio de Chirico in Paris. I came to know the trials of artists, and the joys; I submerged myself in colors that reflected my soul or the state of my spirit. Also in Paris, after feeling that Chirico had given me all that he had to give, I went to Léger's academy: an enormous garage converted into a huge hall full of studios, where the students went with their paintings and their canvases, paper and pencils, and where a sad-eyed nude model sat on a platform, waiting for someone to sketch her. There I excelled as a student. Léger congratulated me, but that was not enough for me. I have retained his preference for design, even if his designs are inferior to those of any other painter's. Nothing interested Léger except the design of his paintings, lost among endless colors and brushstrokes that no other painter could imitate.

I fought with Giorgio de Chirico and told him he sacrificed everything for the sake of color. He would answer, "What else is there besides color?" "You're right. But color disturbs me. You can't see the forms amidst so many colors."

That is how I started to grow disillusioned. I drew away from a passion that was also a torture for me. What was left? Writing? Writing? There was music, but that was as far beyond my reach as the moon. For a long time I had been writing and hiding what I had written. For so long that I suffered from the habit of hiding what I wrote: as if God could heal me and give me a piece of good news that never came. The world is not magical. We make it magical all of a sudden inside us, and nobody finds out until many years later. But I did not hope to be known: that seemed the most horrible thing in the world to me. I will never know what I was hoping for. A beggar who sleeps under a tree without anything in the world to shelter him is happier than a famous man, a man known for his charm, for his talent. What matters is what we write: that is what we are, not some puppet made up by those who talk and enclose us in a prison so different from our dreams. Will we always be students of ourselves?

—SILVINA OCAMPO
Buenos Aires, 1987

THE IMPOSTOR
AND OTHER STORIES

THE IMPOSTOR

IT WAS suffocatingly hot. I reached Constitution Station at four. The books tucked into the straps of the suitcase made the suitcase even heavier. I stopped to finish a strawberry ice-cream cone next to the stone lions that watch over the stairs at the entrance. The train wasn't leaving for twenty minutes. I wandered around the station for a while, looking at the shopwindows. In the bookstore I noticed an Eversharp pencil that was very cheap; I bought it, along with a bottle of pink pomade. I don't use pomade but I thought it might come in handy in the countryside on windy days. I saw my curly hair reflected in a window. Vague memories of my first suffering at school flooded my memory.

I had forgotten something, something very important. I looked at my wrist to make sure that I was wearing my watch, looked at the handkerchief in my lapel pocket, the Scottish wool scarf wrapped around the straps of the suitcase. I had forgotten the bromide tablets. Before and after exams I suffer from sleeplessness, but maybe the sun and air of the countryside would calm my nerves better than a sedative, as my mother told me when she was saying goodbye. She couldn't bear that a boy of my age was taking medication. However, I had forgotten something, something much more important than the bromide tablets. I had forgotten my algebra book; I felt regret when I looked at the sphere of the clock above the platform (its perfect roundness reminding me of the most beautiful theorems). I regretted this because algebra was my favorite subject.

When I got on the train the attendants hadn't yet finished arranging the seats. They were raising the windows vigorously, cleaning with big feather dusters that stirred up clouds of dust and flies. The car was full of smells, of a succession of waves of hot air. The burning light of day was resting in all its blue brilliance on the glass, on the metal handles, on the motionless fans, on the leather seats.

I chose a compartment, and a few minutes later a woman and a very young girl sat down. They were carrying a basket and a bouquet of flowers wrapped in newspaper. I pretended to read my book as I watched my neighbors who, after carefully placing the flowers in the rack above, just as carefully opened the basket and took out of box of *alfajores*. While eating, they spoke in low voices; without a doubt they were speaking about me, because the girl, who was not as disagreeable as I had judged on my first impression, was looking at me out of the corner of her eye, with an imperceptible movement of her eyebrows as if asking a question.

The lady, leaning toward me and offering me an *alfajor*, said to me in a conspiratorial tone, "They have caramel. If I'm not mistaken, you are Jorge Maidana's son."

Unsure of myself, I accepted the *alfajor*. The lady didn't wait for my answer.

"We were as close as brother and sister." Wiping her lips with a paper napkin she continued, "Time, and somewhat unfavorable circumstances, sometimes separate childhood friends. You were just a boy; you surely don't remember those days in Tandil, when we all got together for Carnival and Holy Week."

In a maze of memories I saw the Tandil Hotel, painted green, with lots of little tables in the hallway, hammocks, huge boulders in the garden, shadows, the infinite sun of space, mixed with the indelible smell of perfumes sprayed during Carnival, incense, and the sad jasmine flowers: in that confused Eden, a lady dressed in a kimono covered with vines had initiated me in the forbidden ascent of some mountains.

I nodded.

"What beautiful memories!" the lady continued. "I was a newly-wed. Your mother accompanied me to the carnival ball. In the afternoon, like two butterflies, we played tennis. We went together to the Stations of the Cross."

The girl was looking at me. The lady was sighing slightly, waving a handkerchief, mopping her brow, and then, as if wishing to change the subject, asked, "Do you like reading? That's what I've always said: on trips there's nothing like taking a book. Are you going far?"

"To Cacharí," I answered unenthusiastically.

"To my hometown! Cacharí, Cacharí, Cacharí."

I looked at her with surprise. She went on, "Don't you know the legend? Cacharí was a terrible Indian chief. Near the town he was killed by the army, a century ago. He fell wounded and for three days and nights cried, 'Cacharí, Cacharí, Cacharí ... here is Cacharí.' Nobody dared approach the place where the Indian was dying. They say that even today when the wind blows at midnight in the winter you can hear Cacharí's cry. Are you going for your vacation? By yourself? Can I ask where you're staying?"

"The Swans Ranch."

"But isn't that rented out? Who's there now?"

"Armando Heredia," I answered impatiently.

The lady whispered the name several times and finally asked, "Armando Heredia, the father?"

"He is eighteen," I answered, looking out the window.

"Is he already eighteen?"

I looked at her with hatred: first she asked me whether Armando Heredia was the father, then (in hopes of unnecessarily prolonging the conversation) she acted surprised by my saying that he was already eighteen.

"How time flies!" the lady sighed, once more, pressing the folds of her white muslin lapel against her voluminous breasts. "The Swans is a sad ranch. The house is abandoned and there are more bats than pieces of furniture. But it's normal: a boy your age is not scared of things like that. It's hopeless. I always hold that friends are like family. Parents may draw apart but their children will become close again. Is Armando Heredia a classmate of yours?"

"I don't know him."

"You don't know him! They say the boy is somewhat crazy. They say that he blinded a horse because it didn't obey him: he tied it to a post, hobbled it, then burned its eyes with Turkish cigarettes. But there's no need to get carried away with such stories."

I nodded my head. The girl was delicately tearing apart one of the *alfajor* wrappers. Her hands were thin; her fingers nervous. In her eyes there was a shy sad beauty that captivated me.

The train stopped and I took advantage of an opportune moment: I poked my head out of the window as if someone would be waiting for me, rushed off, climbed down, and walked a ways along the platform. The heat of the afternoon was at its most intense. I felt the burning sun on my head. In a corner, in the shade, four or five men were waiting as if hypnotized. A white cat was sleeping on a bench in the waiting room. When the train started again I heard the monotone of the insistent voice, "These trips in the summer are so long. I only go on them because I have to. I had to take Claudia to the eye doctor. She is going to get glasses."

She took some dark glasses out and, after examining them, added, "She doesn't want to use them. She says that she can't see the words in the newspaper or the stairs, and that the weather looks stormy and sad through the dark glasses."

The girl thrust her head back in a birdlike movement, revealing her round neck. Her eyes moved, restless, from one side to the other, staring absentmindedly at me. I thought that she was right to not want glasses. What would be left of her face without the brilliance of her glance? What would speak in her? If she had been covered with dark glasses I would never have dared to believe that she was looking at me.

I looked out of the window again. No lightning bolt, no sunset, no comet could justify my long contemplation of this lady. The countryside, fervently monotonous with its yellow and green grass, spread out with its repeated sheep, its horses and cows.

My traveling companions still had not allowed me to think.

What would that remote ranch be like, its name that of a bird that only existed for me in the lakes of Palermo Park or the verses of Rubén Darío? What would Armando Heredia be like? When his father described him to me I felt some affection for that boy, so solitary and mysterious, whose indifference worried the entire family. This much was also true: I felt a mixture of admiration and repugnance toward him.

How the imagination can forge something from a name! While the clouds and the animals in the sunset passed by, I imagined him as tall, broad-shouldered, dark, cruel and sad, mannered and impolite, and always smelling of alcohol.

"How can a boy who graduated from school in Europe and was going to be a doctor, a boy with such talent for music, suddenly shut himself in an abandoned ranch, with the company of bats and frogs? Why has he secluded himself at that ranch? It's not to study, or to cultivate the land, or to raise cattle," my mother exclaimed one day, scandalized. But could it be that Armando Heredia was more sensible than the rest of his family? The tenant at the ranch had let him have the ranch house; no matter how small, why not enjoy the country property, since their financial situation did not allow them to go on vacation anywhere else?

Armando Heredia seemed to me to belong to the race of heroes (seeing a cloud I imagined his daring profile): he had not given in to his family's rage. He had dared to give up everything for nothing. Nevertheless, I was not so sure that that nothing was really nothing.

In the windowpanes I saw the reflection of a cloud and the horizon that made the sun look squat and almost purple. I also saw my ruddy brow, thinking: I am a shameful ambassador, sent by my father's friend. I am shy and not that sharp: What influence could I have on the humor of a boy that I'm only acquainted with through vague, contradictory bits of information? "All you have to do is to keep on studying," Mr. Heredia had told me, while smoking a cigar in my father's study. "Show him your friendship if you feel any. I believe in the usefulness of example: no advice could be better. I couldn't ask you, no, I dare not ask you, to take advantage of a possible friendship, tearing out a secret from his heart in order to share it with me. I fear that the mystery of his hiding himself away has to do with a woman or a vice. I repeat: all you need to do, my friend, is to study and take advantage of the healthy air of the countryside. The house is abandoned, but for a boy your age that is not an inconvenience, it's a source of entertainment."

Through the window I admired an endless lagoon in which some sleepy flamingos were resting like flowers. I thought of the coolness of a swim and after staring at the monotony of the water I returned to the earlier thread of my thoughts. My father, who holds Mr. Heredia in high esteem as one of his closest childhood friends, seeing the possibility of a bond of friendship between his friend's son and me as the means of regaining a relationship interrupted years ago by the inevitable circumstances of life, had recommended that I proceed with extreme care, behaving wisely and with my most subtle intelligence, so as to befriend Armando Heredia and be a positive influence on his difficult character. Such hopes were confusing to me.

If I didn't like Armando Heredia, if he didn't like me, how would I endure those two or three weeks of utter solitude in the countryside? At the very least, would there be a radio at the ranch, a bicycle, a horse?

Night fell, the sky emptied. I leaned my forehead on the cool glass: I felt feverish. There was a moment of joy when we saw the first llama and the first rhea lit up by the monstrous lights of the train. I read for a while. I felt as if I were alone and in a sense I was. My conversation partner had fallen asleep; the girl, leaning back in her seat with her eyes closed, was trying to imitate her. I saw that her mouth made the shape of a proud heart. I saw that she had a pinned a small pendant with blue stones onto her dress; the stones spelled out a name: María.

The lights were coming on when the train stopped at the Cacharí station. Armando Heredia was not waiting for me, but instead there was a ranch hand with a hoarse voice, his face hidden in the darkness, and the wreck of a carriage.

Dogs barked. In the darkness of a very large house, of mostly hallways and intertwined vines, Armando Heredia appeared, holding a kerosene lantern in his hand. Thanks to the circumstances our meeting was providentially natural. A gust blew out the lantern. We went into the kitchen to find another one. In the next room, the sour voice of a woman protested about the lantern wicks. They had all burned out that day. Armando Heredia took a gas lamp down from the ceiling and using that light led me down another hallway. We reached a long room; some of the floorboards had collapsed.

"This was the dining room," Heredia told me, lighting up his own face with the lamp. "Everything here in this house was and is no longer, even the food," he added, pointing out a platter with smoked meat and yellow lettuce leaves.

Some people we see for the first time suggest false memories—we think we've seen them before and have no doubt that they resemble other people whom we met at a café or a shop. Heredia wasn't at all as I had imagined him, but he resembled someone I knew. I searched my memory for names, places; I associated him with a bookseller on Corrientes Street, with a math teacher. While I observed the movement of his lips, I lost all hope of figuring out the resemblance. I felt humiliated by my forgetfulness.

"If you want to go to your room before dinner, follow me."

We traversed more hallways and came to a bedroom with a very low ceiling. The windows were of different sizes; the base of the furniture was carved with images of some kind of monster, with double mermaid tails—I could scarcely see the figures by the quivering light from the lamp on the night table.

"In this closet there is a hanger, the only one. It's mine," Heredia said, showing me the half-open closet door in the darkness. "Can you see the drips?"

With interest I inspected the darkness.

"These pots," he continued, kicking one of them, "are intended not only to catch the water when it rains but also to produce sleeplessness and unexpected music. I can attest to the fact that each drop that falls in these pots makes a sound that is slightly different from the one before and the one after. I have heard more than five hundred different kinds of rain in this room."

I thought of telling him, "You are very fond of music." But instead I attentively asked, "Does it rain a lot?"

I washed my hands, took some things out of my suitcase, brushed my hair. Then we sat down to dinner in near darkness.

The merciless sun lit up the sky and a thick wooded area, the tops of the trees clearly coming into outline against the white clouds. A burning wind was blowing across the dry grass. That was the abandoned ranch. Above the roof of the house stretched a eucalyptus tree; some wildflowers grew on the roof. Vines devoured the doors, the eaves of the porches, the window railings. I had seen something similar in a film. A house full of spiderwebs, the doors falling off their hinges, with ghosts.

Except for Heredia I hadn't seen anyone since my arrival. Breakfast, served in the kitchen at seven, was quite frugal. I tucked a bit of cracker and some sugar cubes in my pocket, and ate slowly.

The silence astonished me as if it were something completely new: it seemed oddly terrible and loud.

"It's been a while since I've been in the countryside," I exclaimed, as if responding to a question that no one had asked. "The air and sun bewilder me."

Armando Heredia was walking beside me, kicking the grass. Three dogs were following us.

"Monotonous things are the hardest to get to know. We never pay enough attention to them because we think that they are always the same."

"What is monotonous?"

"The countryside, solitude."

We were uncomfortably silent.

"Why is this ranch called the Swans?" I asked, trying to escape the silence.

"Because of the swans in the lagoon," he said, signaling with his whip toward the woods.

I felt as if I were blind: during the day, the intense light, and at night, the darkness, both obscured my vision.

"Did I tell you that everything has disappeared from this ranch?" he went on. "Everything except for the bats, the spiders, the reptiles, you, and me."

At that very instant, as if illustrating the end of his sentence, a snake slipped through the grass. I jumped back. Heredia asked, "Are you scared?"

That phrase might have offended me, but everything seemed too unreal. I answered, "Everything that is slimy scares me: a fish, a toad, soap when it comes apart, any of those little frogs that come out when it rains."

He offered me a cigarette. We stopped. While he was lighting a match and we protected the flame with our hands I observed him carefully. He was leaning against the trunk of a tree. I examined his black trousers, his worn leather belt, the bluish handkerchief around his neck, his serious, almost Greek profile (that reminded me of the illustrations of statues that fill Malet's history textbook). Again I tried to associate his face with others, without luck.

"Could we go see the lagoon?" I asked. Afterward, I added with real curiosity, "And why aren't there any swans? Did they all get killed by hunters?"

"Nobody hunts swans, but my maternal grandfather had them all killed. He thought they brought bad luck. Everyone in my family believes he was right. Death rectifies many things; in my grandfather's case, it transformed his superstitions into noble, carefully considered attitudes, making his manias seem admirably consistent. My aunt Celina, the youngest of his daughters, who was in the habit of going to the lagoon with the grocer's daughters, got gravely ill one

December day. They said she had gone swimming in the lagoon; she came back home barefoot, her clothing soaked. For forty nights and forty days she trembled with fever in the iron bed where I sleep now, and no one at the time knew that in her delirium she saw the huge swans in the lagoon pecking on her head. "There they are again. They're coming back," Aunt Celina shouted. My grandfather asked her, "Who is coming back?" She answered, "The monsters." "What monsters?" "The big ones with black heads." Her illness lasted for two years. It took a while for my grandfather to figure out who the black-headed monsters were. When he found out he had all the swans killed. Not long after, Aunt Celina died of a heart attack. They say that around that time they found the last swan in the lagoon and that my grandfather strangled it with his left hand. The whole story gave the ranch a bad reputation. My mother refused to come back. She adored Celina. My father, even though he has never spent more than a week here, feels a romantic connection to it. The tenant who rents the fields didn't want the house. That's understandable as his is better. The only ones who stayed here were the old servant, the woman who cooks for us and does the laundry; her husband, who was the oldest employee at the ranch and who has some sheep and some horses; and their grandson, Eladio Esquivel, who is twelve."

"But are they all invisible?"

"If they were silent it would be better," Heredia answered.

"I haven't heard them."

"Today they went to Tapalqué for a wedding. They will come back this evening. They prepared some soup for us—an inedible soup. We will roast some meat on the coals. There's quince jam and cheese."

The description of the lunch whetted my appetite. I took a bit of cracker from my pocket and ate it while looking at the symmetrical rows of trees.

I felt sleepy, sleepy and hungry. It was the burning hour of the siesta. I went into a sort of pantry that smelled of soap and *yerba mate*, where there were flies buzzing around. The shutters were closed. A cool pleasant breeze caressed my brow while my eyes adjusted to the darkness. On the floor, I saw two empty boxes and three bags: one, with uneven bulges, contained the crackers; another, in the shape of a pillow, was full of some sort of bran; the third was almost empty and held dried corn. On the shelves, in a corner, I saw some yellow soaps and a broom; in another corner, some quince jam in a jar and some more on a plate; on the far shelf, three bottles of dark wine, an old seltzer bottle, and a strange object that caught my attention. To see it clearly I climbed onto one of the boxes, then gently took it down. It was a blue porcelain vase with pink ferns in the shape of a basket; a cupid with its mouth open held the top in one hand and a garland of flowers in the other. At some friend's house I had seen a vase with the same design, maybe in a cabinet or in a centerpiece. I left the repulsive object on the shelf; it was covered with spiderwebs and dust. I got down off the box and looked at the jam on the plate. I was hungry but I didn't like quince jam. Resigned, I picked up the plate and devoured the jam.

Our horseback rides delighted me: I waited for them eagerly at day-break, when the birds first sang. Heredia had lent me some riding chaps and a pair of rope-soled sandals. With an incomparable feeling of exultation I crossed the lagoon and saw birds' nests shaped like baskets floating on the water. In a field I found a dark, shiny partridge egg the color of chocolate, and another huge rhea egg.

From the back of the kitchen the voices from a radio could be heard, filling the empty house with echoes. I understood why Heredia had lamented that the inhabitants of the house were not so much silent as invisible. "Other people's radios are aggressive," my friend said while he was taking off his boots to put on his sandals. We went out on the patio. It was nighttime. The moon made a deep impression on me. At that time, not from his way of speaking or from his words but rather from his way of boldly distributing the silence, I experienced the startling revelation of Heredia's intelligence.

We were riding through the fields. I asked Heredia who owned the woods and the houses that we could see in the distance. He explained patiently, "Those woods belong to Rosendo Jara. He has sheep. Those belong to Miguel Ramos, the owner of the store. He has a herd of cattle and a son who breaks horses. That one farther off where you can see a windmill belongs to Valentín Gismondi, a man who is poorer than the others. He has a daughter named María."

Our friendship slowly progressed as we gradually began to let each other into our confidence. I spoke of my antipathy for my older brother, the silly attitude my mother took with regard to such a natural feeling. Blood ties didn't exist for me. Wasn't it enough that we were brothers? Did we have to be friends? Heredia understood me. He spoke to me about his father: "He can't stand the fact that I'm here. He suspects that I am hiding something from him. Can't a person live without hiding a secret from his father? Supposing that he investigates and discovers it—it would still be a secret. Nobody can know me. One day he suspects that I am in love, another that I am drinking. Perplexing him amuses me."

"That's unkind," I said unenthusiastically.

"Why is it unkind? Silly people need to be punished. If I were to take him to a ranch house built of mud, without shutters, maybe even without windows, and showed him a girl like María Gismondi, who smells of smoke but abounds in virtues; if I were to tell him 'This is my girlfriend,' he would treat me like a criminal."

"And is that your situation?"

"No, not at all. I wanted to show you my father's silliness with this example. He is a monster. I have sometimes thought..."

I felt the passing of time, its essence in its repetitions. Remembering the present stretches time out even more. I remembered the smell of the rain at the end of the day when Heredia, without explanation, would disappear from the ranch. I would hear his horse gallop off on the dirt road, or would see a cloud of dust that drew farther away with the carriage.

I thought: He returns who knows when, at an hour when I am deep asleep. I hear the sound of his boots on the flagstones in the corridor. He knocks on my window to wish me good night. I hear him in my dreams. While I sleep, time interrupts its conventional rhythm. In lonely places sleep gets bound up with reality. It is like the imitation of a very long life, with its memories. I have been living at this ranch with Armando Heredia for five or six days and yet it seems as if I have been living here in this house for my whole life, that I have always heard this rain, that I have always seen the sunsets, that Armando has always knocked on my window to wish me good night in the middle of my dreams.

We reached the end of the property on horseback and swam in a round watering trough, what they call an Australian tank, that was in the middle of an old orchard. The water only reached our waists, but I felt more pleasure that I did when I swam at the YMCA or at the beaches at Olivos on the River Plate. We happily splashed around in a couple of feet of water. Birds flew down, their wings brushing lightly against the water, and swiftly soared back into the air. While we were getting dressed beneath a willow, the shade of which sheltered us, our conversation moved toward mutual trust.

"At first, when I decided to stay here, my father thought I was crazy," Heredia told me. "When he finally realized there was no use arguing, because even though he didn't give me a cent I insisted on staying, he asked, as a last resort, that I go to Buenos Aires to consult a doctor. I accepted. I suffered from insomnia and from frequent headaches. My meeting with the doctor—Dr. Tarcisio Fernández, a psychoanalyst—was comical. He himself had ordered me to be absolutely frank, which is why I insulted him during the meetings I had with him at his office. Later, he himself advised my father to let me come to the countryside and asked me, not expecting that I would listen to him, to write down my dreams. He took a blue leather-bound notebook out of a drawer in his desk, saying as he gave it to me, 'This little notebook is for you to record your dreams.' Reconciled, we said goodbye. I promised to obey his request. I wanted to satisfy his childish fancy, I assure you, but I can't, I haven't been able to—I don't dream. Do you have many dreams?"

"Yes, but about absurd things of no interest; many times I believe that I am thinking, yet I am dreaming. I turn into another person: I dream about people, places, and objects that I have never seen. Afterward, when I can't link them to reality, I forget them. I remember that in one of my dreams I fell asleep out of boredom. No doubt they are inherited dreams."

"Tarcisio Fernández would find this very interesting," Heredia exclaimed. "I would like to dream, even if those dreams couldn't be reconciled with reality. Not dreaming is like being dead. Reality loses importance. I think about Jacob's dreams, about Joseph's, about Socrates's, about Coleridge's dream that inspired him to write a poem. Sometimes I wake up with the feeling that my memory has a blank page in it; nothing seems to be imprinted on it. I would commit a crime if that crime allowed me to dream. Maidana, please, tell me one of your dreams. If I were you, condemned to dream about people and places that I don't know"—he interrupted himself for a moment to tighten the strap of his sandal—"surely I would enjoy it. I would devote myself to looking for those places and those people."

"I couldn't do that because I don't have a good memory for faces. I barely recognize people I've seen many times in my life. In a dream I have fewer chances to remember them."

"Tell me some of your dreams," Heredia insisted.

"Right now I would have to make them up. I don't remember any."

Eight in the evening, alone, I wandered through the fields. I wanted to see the birds by the lagoon flying to their nests at sunset. When I crossed a barbed-wire fence I cut one of my fingers. I looked around for a leaf to wipe off the blood but didn't find anything except wild mustard and the thistles by the road. I reached the lagoon.

I leaned against the reeds, out into the water, to wash my hands when I saw a strange creature crouched on the ground. At first I thought it was a sheep that was lying down, one of those sheep, like lions in some paintings, with a man's face. I drew nearer, pushing the reeds aside. It was a man, his hair down to his waist, who was sitting in the water, weaving a sort of cage made out of the reeds, something that would doubtless serve to trap birds. I drew near. I spoke to him. He didn't hear me. In the harsh silence, a sound came from his lips like the song of the finest bird.

Heredia ate little. He didn't drink wine; he never smelled of alcohol. He was kind to animals. His behavior was correct. I was fond of him. The slanders were unfair: I thought about these things while gazing at the bitter branch of waxy leaf nightshade, covered with red fruits, that I held in my hand.

Heredia sometimes would interrupt our dialogue; he would pull leaves from the trees, put them in his mouth, and chew on them.

"My father has sent me a letter, announcing the visit next week of one of his friends." He took the letter out of his pocket and smiled strangely. "He is sending him," he continued, "to spy on me. I don't intend to tolerate any of his intrusions: with a single shot I will kill anyone who tries to intrude in my private life."

"Do you have a revolver?"

"No, but I know someone who could lend me one."

"You would go to jail."

"I don't care about going to jail. Anyway, isn't this a sort of jail?"

"If you like—"

"If I like?" he interrupted suddenly. "Maybe it is, maybe it isn't."

It was raining. As Heredia had predicted, the drops fell into the containers that were spread around my room, falling with rhythmic sounds and such a range of tones that it was impossible not to listen to them (the way you listen to some songs without wanting to).

Why didn't Heredia ever take me to the town of Cacharí? The day that I decided to get a haircut, why did he decide on a trip to Azul so that I, quite unwillingly, had to travel by train? Why didn't he allow me into his room, which was at the opposite end of the house? Was he hiding something from me? My friendship with him, was it all an illusion? I was asking myself these questions when Eladio Esquivel, the housekeeper's grandson, looked into my window and said, "There is mail for you." Beneath a hood that had been improvised out of sacks to protect him from the rain, I saw the boy's smiling face for the first time. I thought, "What a mania I have for finding resemblances among people!" I thought of my father's face when he was ten. I opened the envelope. I read the signature, hoping not to be happy in vain. I read it with surprise. It was a letter from Mr. Heredia, whom I had completely forgotten. I felt a bit disturbed. I couldn't identify the Mr. Heredia I had met in Buenos Aires with the father of Armando Heredia. If I had obeyed my first impulse I wouldn't have read the letter. Perhaps I would have thought how it is impossible to be innocent in others' eyes. Curbing my disgust I started reading. I can't repeat the content exactly but the meaning was more or less this: After asking me what sort of reception I had had at the ranch, whether I was enjoying myself, whether I was hungry, whether life in the countryside agreed with me, he brought up his son, begging me for any news about his behavior, physical appearance, etc. The letter, written in a paternalizing and querulous tone, displeased me. The script was large, slanted, and pretentious. I have some knowledge of handwriting analysis. I reflected for a moment on the main traits of the script. I discovered in it his cowardice and vanity. When I raised my eyes, Armando Heredia was facing me. Like a shadow he had entered my room, like a shadow I saw him enclosed in the doorframe through which the greenish and blue luminosity of the rain filtered in. Ever since my arrival at the ranch I had not felt any guilt about my behavior: Armando Heredia hadn't asked me anything; for this reason, I didn't feel obligated to tell him about my conversation with his father, nor had I even felt the need to reflect on these things. But standing before him with a letter that seemed to reveal my treachery, my face concealed in the dim light, I felt a deep pang of guilt. Heredia took a few steps back before coming forward again: the light shone in his eyes. I followed the direction of his gaze: it traversed the letter and the irrepressible blush of my face.

"So you are in correspondence with my father?"

I waved the sheet in the air and answered, laughing, trying clumsily to put him at ease. "He has written me these lines. I was trying to analyze his script."

"You should analyze your own script to discern what sort of a spy you are." When he uttered these words, Heredia took a pitcher that was sitting on the table and threw it against the wall. The water spilled out like a huge flower. "My father is a fool, but you are a hypocrite. You have come to this ranch under the pretext of needing rest, of studying for your next exams; you neither rest nor study. But you aren't very good at spying anyway; for that you would have to be intelligent."

With those words he slammed the door shut and stormed down the hallway. I listened to his metallic steps beneath the sound of the rain.

In my heart, did anger or remorse win out? Anger turned into resentment would be painful; remorse turned into surprise would be more bearable. I prepared my suitcase. I strapped my books together with the leather straps. I was worried about many things: How would I get to the station? What would I say to Mr. Heredia and my parents in Buenos Aires? Where was my scarf? I opened the shutters. It was pouring rain. I went into the kitchen. Nobody was there. I sat down on a bench facing the door. The smoke from the wet wood made my eyes fill with tears. The housekeeper took her time coming and when she saw my suitcase asked me if I was on a trip. I told her I hoped to leave that very night. I found out the train schedule. I asked her whether the carriage could take me; she couldn't promise anything.

The rain abated. The sky cleared up. I left the suitcase in the kitchen and went out on the patio. I walked into the woods. I was surprised again by the sameness of all the paths through the eucalyptus and the Australian pines. One of the dogs was following me. From the first moment of my arrival it had followed me; in the morning it was always waiting for me by my bedroom door. It was black, woolly, and shy. They called him Carbón.

The rain, a fine drizzle, barely broke through the foliage. The earth in the eucalyptus grove wasn't damp. The layers of leaves trapped the energy of the sun's rays, and in the rain gave off heat and an intense odor. I sat down at the foot of a tree where I could watch the entrance to the house. I thought sadly about the pleasant and unpleasant aspects of my stay. About how little I had studied, about Heredia's insults, about the seeming indignity of my attitude, about the horseback rides, about the swims in the Australian tank, about the death of the Indian Cacharí, when I was disrupted from my thoughts by Carbón, who ran barking in the direction of the house. Later, I saw a car pull up. A man got out, then another. They entered the house. They came back with the housekeeper and her grandson. They tried to lift a very heavy bundle out of the car. I stood up, hoping to see more clearly. I understood that it wasn't a bundle or a crate: the men were respectfully moving a dead body from the car.

With the sense of unreality that one feels after having spent a sleepless night, I followed the housekeeper through the corridors. Armando Heredia was summoning me. For the first time I entered his room. Terrified, I stopped at the door. Armando was lying down, a handkerchief over his forehead. Out of the corner of my eye I saw a basin on a chair next to his bed. With a weak voice I heard him babble, "They told me you were about to go. Maybe I overstepped, maybe I made a mistake. I am violent."

"Are you better?" I asked, nervously interrupting what he was saying. "What happened?"

"I was on my way to town. Instead of walking around the border of the pastures, the way I usually go on rainy days, I took the road. The mud was as slippery as a floor of soap-covered stones. Suddenly my horse slipped, got frightened, and fell into a hole, next to the ditch by the road. I didn't feel anything. Some neighbors who were passing in a car picked me up and brought me back here unconscious."

"Were you hurt?"

"A little, on my head, on my hip, on my left arm," he said, trying to sit up in bed.

He pulled up his sleeve showed me the deep wound on his arm.

"I don't understand how I got this," he muttered perplexedly. He added, "Some stone or the edge of the ditch."

Heredia needed painkillers and antiseptic. I rode to town to find some. I dismounted, tying the horse to a post, and entered the pharmacy. I took advantage of this pretext to visit Cacharí and get away from the ranch for a while. After buying the medicines, I wandered around the town. Clouds of dust constantly rose up: a fine dustlike sand swirled in the air. A row of phoenix palms ran down the middle of the main avenue where I walked. I went into the store and bought a *mate* made of porcelain with the inscription FRIENDSHIP and a pack of cigarettes.

Sitting at the counter, in a pose of sweet indifference, was the girl I had traveled with a few days before. She was resting near a bottle, staring at me. I leaned one arm on the counter and looked at her with adoration. I said to her in a low voice, "Waiting?"

Without taking the hint and without ceasing to stare at me, she changed her posture, took a package and a bottle full of vinegar that the storeowner had given her, and hurriedly walked out the door. Disappointed, I left the store to follow the girl. She had disappeared into the sunlight and the silence. I walked past the square shadows of the houses to my horse, mounted, and rode back with a single hope: the hope of seeing her.

The cries of the cowhands passing with their herd grew louder, then disappeared in a tumult of moos. Armando Heredia could now sit up in bed: the swelling in his arm had gone down. We had renewed our friendship. One day we were talking and laughing about our dispute as if it had happened to other people. For the first time, I stopped to look around the room—the curtains, along with some pieces of furniture, made it dark, blocking the poorly placed windows and the windowpanes of the door; all of the room's angles were askew and it was far too long; its whitewashed walls revealed dark dirty colors here and there. The bed was made of iron and had a little oval landscape above its frame showing a boat with sails unfurled and a blue sky with clouds. The chairs were worn out with use. The chest of drawers, a very tall and desolate ruin, had a broken mirror. The bedside table was gray; it was missing a drawer (in the gap I could see some books, a bottle of aspirin, a green pencil, and a penknife). An almanac from 1930 was hanging on a nail on the right wall and on the wall next to the door there was a reproduction of a painting that must have been by Delacroix. I walked closer to the painting to inspect it: in the dense green of a tropical landscape a tiger was attacking a jaguar.

"I have seen a fight like this," I said aloud.

Heredia couldn't hide his disbelief. Immediately he wanted to know in what circumstances and where I had seen it. I didn't contradict myself. I gave him an unsatisfactory explanation but felt that after listening to me Heredia held me in higher esteem than before.

My conscience was torturing me. If not to lie or to satisfy my vanity, why had I told Heredia that? If I confessed to him that when I saw the reproduction of the painting I had the certainty of having once watched a tiger fight a jaguar, and that when I examined my memory and having tried to talk about it I had understood that that memory did not exist, that in the course of my life I had never seen such a spectacle, not even at the zoo, not even in my childhood or while playing with my toys, what would he think of me?

That's what I was thinking when I saw Eladio Esquivel in the hallway, turning the crank of a well to raise a bucket full of bottles from the bottom where they were kept very cold. When I saw the smiling face of the boy, my memory filled with confused images again. Why did everything remind me of something else? Claudia or María (the girl I had seen in the train), Armando Heredia himself, the repulsive porcelain basket with a cupid and a garland, Armando Heredia's bed, Eladio Esquivel, the reproduction of the painting... I remembered some verses I had read in an English anthology:

I have been here before,
But when or how I cannot tell.

I also had the impression that I had seen all of this before, but without the ecstasy of love, which would be the only thing that could justify it.

I thought about the transmigration of the soul. I remembered some phrases I had read of ancient Indian philosophy: "The soul dwells in the body like a bird in a cage." "The body takes a long journey and when it gets sick, the soul, which bears it, also finds remedies for it, but when the body perishes the soul abandons it, as if the body were a wrecked boat, and finds another to govern as before."

I studied Eladio's face again: I saw on his head a tight dark turban that looked like the velvety flower that my mother, in a garden in Olivos, had called rooster's crest.

I asked Esquivel, "Don't you remember having seen me before I came to this ranch?"

Looking at me with his enormous eyes, he responded, "I have a lousy memory."

"I also have a lousy memory for faces, but this isn't about that. Don't you think you've met me before? Isn't there something about me that you recognize?"

With a curious look he gazed at my face, my hair, my forehead, as if recalling something. He shook his head and said without conviction, "I don't think so."

I answered, "I saw you in India, more than a century ago. You took off your humble turban to bathe in the waters of the river that night. Later you stole pieces of silk from a store and when you died you were reincarnated as a bird." Then I recited these words in a loud voice, " 'The soul cannot die: it leaves one dwelling place for another. I remember you; I was at the siege of Troy, my name was Euphorbus, son of Pantus, and the youngest of the Atreids pierced my chest with his lance. Long ago, I recognized my shield on the wall of the temple of Juno in Argos. Everything changes; nothing dies.' Like Pythagoras, I believe in the transmigration of the soul." Eladio Esquivel stared at me patiently. "At the age of twelve I knew by heart, in Greek, the apology of Er, son of Armenius, who saw the soul of Orpheus transformed into a swan; that of Thamyris, turned into a nightingale; that of Ajax, turned into a lion; that of Agamemnon, turned into an eagle."

The rosy clouds assumed the annoying shapes of angels and altars. Above the grass, the remains of the mist dispersed. In the faint light of the woods, slow, blind Apollo appeared, the horse with a star on its forehead. It was the first time I had seen a blind animal. I prepared this phrase to tell Heredia: "A person who is capable of talking, of understanding, of reasoning, even if he was born blind, can come to know the world of forms and colors through words, through thought; but a blind animal, what secret labyrinths can it know, a prisoner of its movements, like an automaton? What hands, what kind voice will reveal the world to it?" I said, "Animals are the dreams of nature."

Apollo approached slowly, stopping in front of us. A bluish faint light, opal-like, illuminated his dead eyes. He looked like an imperfect statue of stone or of stained plaster. The whole visual world, which frightens horses, had disappeared from his life, along with all pleasure. I felt that my transparent face gave away the horror: I remembered the words heard on the train: "He blinded a horse because it did not obey him. He tied it to a post, hobbled it, then burned its eyes with Turkish cigarettes."

Between us the following dialogue unfolded:

"Poor animal, why don't they kill him?"

"He's still useful for plowing."

"They make him work? He must suffer a lot."

"How can you tell?"

"He barely moves. I have seen him wander slowly, with such indifference!"

"Indifference isn't suffering."

"It's worse."

"Perhaps. But Apollo is not entirely indifferent. You will see."

Heredia lit a match and put it near the horse's nostrils. The horse started, raised his neck, stood on his back legs, then dashed into the trees with the splendor of a mythological figure.

"What is happening to him?"

"He went blind in a fire. He was hobbled and couldn't get away. The heat of fire drives him mad. With Eladio we have fun: we light a bonfire in the corral, lead Apollo inside, then mount him in turn to see which one he can throw off first."

Heredia promised that the next day we would have fun with Apollo. I accepted with a feeling of disgust. I thought, smiling hypocritically: Every friend, sooner or later, reveals to us some unexpected defect. Heredia was revealing my cowardice, or rather the fear I felt of appearing cowardly.

In the distance, among the trees, Apollo had recovered his melancholy indifference.

We were talking with Heredia in the shadow of a phoenix palm.

"On February 28th my father's friend will arrive," he told me; later, leaning on the trunk, he looked at the foliage and continued. "I associate palm trees with the sea. In the sky where the foliage of a palm tree is I always imagine the blue line of the water. I associate palm trees with the sea, as I associate the arrival of my father's friend with a crime: the crime I will commit."

"What is the victim's name?"

Heredia pronounced a name I had never heard before.

It was about six in the afternoon. We were riding horses. At the edge of the woods there were birds flying, making deafening sounds. We were going to town to pick up the mail. We took the shortest path, through the pastures at the edge of the ranch. Heredia stopped when we saw a carriage, which had crossed three or four gates, before it reached the last one. He muttered, "Let's take our time. I don't want to run into those people."

A few yards later, in a dense forest, there was a shack with two enormous fig trees.

"Why don't we hop off for a while? I think there are figs," I said joyfully.

"In the shack with the rocking chair there are never ripe figs."

We neared the place without dismounting from our horses and entered the woods through the shack with crumbling walls. We came up to one of the fig trees and picked one or two figs, still green, then threw them away.

"This is where Juan Otondo lived. He chewed on bones. One night he disappeared. They stole everything that was in his hut except for that rocker"—he showed me the remains of a rocking chair, with holes in the wicker and broken slats. Then he added, "People here are afraid of it because it moves by itself."

Amazed, I gazed for a while at that wreck of a chair that rocked slowly even in the slightest breeze.

"Are you afraid?"

"Somewhere I have seen this rocker before."

At that moment, when I heard my own words, I felt the terror of the supernatural.

"You keep coming back to your theories of reincarnation! Poor Eladio, he can barely remember what he did yesterday and you want him to remember his past lives," Heredia exclaimed, tearing off a fig and throwing it at the rocker. It moved again.

"What I think seems like madness, but when I see that rocker, when I remember it, I understand many things—"

"Are you finished with your rambling?" Heredia shouted at me. Then, inviting me to follow him, he lashed my horse.

My thoughts wandered and I couldn't sleep. I was thinking clearly but that clarity was murkier than what I had been thinking before. I could explain everything, but after this latest revelation I felt a fresh discomfort. Now I realized that that mysterious collection of objects and people which reminded me of others, and which had given me the disturbing impression that my whole existence was made up of memories older than my life or of confusion and forgetfulness...that whole collection of objects and persons had peopled my dreams. I had always dreamed about unknown persons and objects, which is why my dreams always disappeared from my memory. For this reason, and due to the amazement the discovery of that world had caused me, I could now remember those dreams with extraordinary precision.

Tortured by the infinite size of my past dreams, I delved into the labyrinth of my memory. Now I could explain everything. The porcelain basket that I thought I had seen at my friend's house; Eladio

Esquivel, who reminded me of a portrait of my father; the fight between a jaguar and a tiger that actually already existed in my memory—all were mere subterfuges I had used to explain to myself my obsession with similarities, to pardon my forgetfulness, and, perhaps unconsciously, to avoid a supernatural explanation. What I could never have suspected was that the unknown images in my dreams would one day appear in reality and that the repulsive form of that rocker would begin opening up the inexplicable explanation of a mystery. I who had always boasted of the perfect equilibrium of my nervous system now felt disturbed. Trembling with hatred, I remembered Heredia's disdainful attitude, the words he pronounced—"Are you finished with your rambling?"—when I tried to explain these things to him. The pain that hatred can cause, although sometimes fleeting, seems endless when accompanied by the most sincere of feelings.

I couldn't sleep. It must have been about five in the morning. I could hear the breathing of the dog lying by my bedroom door. I got dressed. I opened the blinds. The first light of dawn was visible on the horizon. The timid cry of a bird could be heard. A pale light filtered through the foliage and fell onto the damp grass. I walked into the woods where the night was dying very slowly. I took the path that would give me the best view of the horizon. I reached the gate. I waited there for the sun to come up, as if I needed that occurrence to return to the ranch house. With minute slowness the first light spread across a still-starry sky. How repulsive dawn seemed to me! Some dirty clouds, the dark and light blue parts of the night lowered onto the yellow fringe of the future day, forming a greenish middle fringe. The songs of the birds stopped and started. The light was emerging from the earth in thick waves. Then, suddenly, bits of sun began to appear, taking a long while to rise completely. I inhaled the rough fragrance of the grass. Carbón was chasing some reptile; he stopped, moved the foliage with his nose, panted. We went back to the house. I could hear some paces on the flagstones of the hallway. Heredia appeared by the final column.

———

We went to the ruins of the shed to find some tools to repair the broken seat of the carriage. On a huge sack there was a black cat sleeping. Heredia looked haggard. He feverishly searched for a hammer, some nails, and pliers. I admired his quickness, his skill.

"It's important to finish right away," he said, while hammering in the last nails.

"Why?"

"I have to go to the market. They've asked me to buy some colts."

"Can't I go with you?"

"We won't both fit in the carriage. A neighbor is going with me."

It was two in the afternoon. The sun was burning above the corrugated iron roof of the shed; Heredia climbed into the carriage and struck the horse with his whip, then disappeared in a cloud of dust.

I went back into the house, choosing a few of the less tedious books in my room to study. I wandered around outside, looking for a pleasant shady place in the trees, then lay down on the ground to read. Some little feathers, some seeds, soft leaves, insects were falling from the foliage. I managed to read three chapters of the history book, but the horseflies and the mosquitoes started to attack me. The more I killed the more numerous they became. I sat up, got on my knees, then finally stood up, ready to conclude the battle. That was when a huge bee appeared, resting on the trunk of a eucalyptus tree. I took off one of my sandals to squash it. It was an immortal bee—nothing could hurt it. After being hit three times it flew around me, came into the folds of the handkerchief I had tied around my neck, and buzzed violently inside. Terrified, I untied the handkerchief then threw it as far as I could. The bee remained motionless and triumphant on a blue stripe. When I cut a branch of the tree so as to try to scare the bee away I saw a name carved onto the trunk: María Gismondi. Then I went back to inspect the ground but the bee wasn't on the handkerchief but on my foot. I prudently waited for it to fly off. But my nightmare wasn't over: my right foot was sinking into an anthill that was hidden by the leaves. The ants climbed up my leg.

A warm night, along with the moon and fireflies, welcomed my solitude. I had just eaten and was taking the dogs out for a walk. I passed by the eucalyptus tree and asked myself uneasily who could have carved María Gismondi on it. I thought about Heredia's penknife. I thought of Claudia, the girl I had seen the day of my arrival and several days later at the store in Cacharí. The day I saw her on the train, wasn't she wearing a pin with the name María spelled out in stones? Maybe her name was María Gismondi? Could Heredia be in love with her? If so, why didn't he tell me? I slowly walked through the Australian pines; in my mind I identified the girl on the train as María Gismondi.

In purple letters, like amethysts, I saw her name on the tree: María Gismondi. Could she be the girl I had seen in my dream? Now I could remember her. Was she the one? I had loved her because one must always love someone. I had loved her without remembering her. I realized that the regret I felt when I was with other women was because of her. In other eyes, I had looked for hers; in other lips, her lips; in other arms, her arms.

I remembered a dream: In winter, in a sparsely furnished room with shadows like those in a church, I waited for something, not knowing what, sitting on a bench (the hard bench of a train station). A dark light filtered in through the long skylight windows, filling the room with mist. My heart was bursting with hope. I was waiting for someone. I stood up anxiously, looked through the panes of the lowest windows. In my dream I could feel that the face and body of the young woman who was approaching me depended on me. I didn't wait long, but I could have waited an entire lifetime. I heard her steps on the stones. Then she suddenly appeared, motionless, in the doorway, beautifully severe. Conscious of her imperfections,

I nevertheless adored her, while a gleam in her eyes suggested that she reciprocated my feelings.

"Are you waiting for someone?" I asked quietly.

"No."

"Are you alone?"

"Yes."

"I suspected that someone was waiting for you outside. I would like to talk to you."

"Not here; I can't."

"Where then?"

"I don't know."

"Listen to me. We should talk seriously."

"How else could we talk?"

"With you, there's no other way. With my arm around your waist I want to feel your heart beating in each of your words."

"Which side is the heart on?"

"On the left."

"Is it on the left for everyone?"

"Yes, but don't make me suffer. Why do you ask me such things?"

"Sometimes I want to put my hand over my heart and I don't know which side to put it on."

"When do you want to put your hand over your heart?"

"When something makes a big impression on me or when I feel sick and my father doesn't believe me."

"Why doesn't he believe you? Do you lie to him?"

"Yes."

"Why?"

"When I tell him the truth he gets angry."

"What truth?"

"I don't know; I've never been truthful with him."

"How do you know that your father gets angry when you tell him the truth if you've never been truthful with him?"

"Because sometimes he suspects the truth and then I want to die."

"What does he suspect?"

"That I don't tell the truth."

"What truth? I want to know."

"I don't know."

I drew near the young woman's face. It felt as if something bound us together. I couldn't stand the idea that life kept secrets from me. Aware that I would lose her by doing so, I kissed her desperately on the lips. When I opened my eyes I could see the flowers on a skirt. I wasn't kissing her lips; I was kissing a coarse fabric. The young woman had disappeared.

"But her lips aren't like those flowers. Her lips are like real flowers," I said, sobbing.

The leaves of the vine, which usually hopped around like birds in the wind, didn't move outside. It was hot, and no air entered my room through the door or the open windows. I picked up the poncho from my bed, as well as a pack of cigarettes and a box of matches from the table. Near the house, among the branches of an old laurel tree, where there was the fresh dark vault of a second sky, I found a place to sleep. The stars shone through the spaces among the leaves. Heredia passed by and stopped to see what I was doing. I told him that I was going to sleep outside and he said he wanted to copy me. He went into the house and came back with a pillow, a water bottle, a glass, a pack of cigarettes, and a flashlight. I spread the poncho out on the grass. Heredia put the pillow near the trunk of the laurel and we lay down to sleep. But sleep is not obedient. We began talking and smoking. From time to time we were quiet. Through the foliage we looked at the depths of the sky and listened to the beating wings of a bird.

Heredia was talking to me; I don't remember his exact words, but in each of them I felt that he was going to reveal a secret to me: the secret that I was waiting for. I remember the last words I heard before falling asleep; it was no doubt the preamble to a confidence: "But do you swear not to tell anyone?" When I woke up I didn't know where I was. It was broad daylight. As soon as I got my bearings I looked for Heredia. I looked for the pillow and flashlight; they were gone. I got up. I didn't know what time it was; no birds sang; it seemed to me that everything I had seen, the place, the people, the animals, weren't real. I wandered through the ranch house with the sensation of being a ghost living among ghosts.

I thought that I shouldn't see her, out of loyalty, caution, tact. Nevertheless, I decided to go to Cacharí. It was the late-afternoon hour when girls walk arm in arm along the station platform. There were people, animals in cages, waiting for the train. I paced up and down the platform a few times, stopped at the waiting room, studied the schedule, and at last sat down on some boxes to smoke a cigarette.

Two girls passed by, their fingernails polished; four short girls with very black hair passed by. Then María Gismondi passed by, alone, a slight smile lighting up her lips. I approached her.

"Forgive me, miss, but I must ask you a question."

Looking off in a different direction, she answered, "Go ahead."

"You won't be angry with me?"

She stared hard at me without answering; I continued, "You have two names, don't you?"

"No. I have three names: one is a nickname that was made up by one of my girlfriends; another is the name that my grandmother gave me that nobody knows how to pronounce; the other one is the true one and the one I like the best. Which do you prefer?"

"The true one."

"It's my godmother's name. She is a healer, everyone visits her; she heals the sick. Maybe you're sick?"

"Not yet."

"There are a lot of people here who are sick with rheumatism. They called me once to take care of one patient. But the train is coming..."

With an explosive shriek the train entered the station. The girl ran through the cars looking for something. I followed her from afar. A guard greeted her and gave her a big package of a triangular shape. The package no doubt weighed quite a lot as the girl placed it on the ground. I rushed up and asked almost into her ear, "Would you like me to carry it for you?"

She accepted, smiling.

"It's a sewing machine. It's quite heavy."

I lifted the package. It was wrapped in cardboard, wood, and newspaper.

"I have to carry it to the carriage. My sister is waiting for me across the street."

We walked out of the station. It was night by now. The carriage wasn't there.

"The horse escaped with the carriage," she exclaimed, almost crying. "What shall we do?"

Night reached out dark as a cliff, but beyond the clouds, from time to time, the moon was shining.

"Let's leave the sewing machine here," I said, while I hid the package beneath a bush and began to look for the carriage and the horse. At first nothing could be seen.

"I am afraid," said the girl. The trembling tenderness in her voice seemed to love me.

I drew near and took her hand.

"Don't be afraid."

I closed in and put my arm around her waist, but her body seemed ungraspable, like the night. There are moments that happiness makes almost eternal; it seemed to me that while we embraced time would never end. The moon suddenly lit up our shadows and there, just a few yards away, was the carriage.

"There was no reason to get so upset," I told her, intimidated by her seriousness.

"I wasn't upset because of that."

"Why were you upset, then?"

"I am sad."

"Why are you sad?"

"I don't know. Every time the train goes by I grow sad. I feel it here," she said, taking one of my hands and holding it to her chest.

"Can you feel it beating? Sometimes I think that my heart will break when I hear the racket of the locomotives."

"Has it always been like this?"

"Always. My godmother, who is a healer, tried to cure me."

"Will I see you again?"

"At the house where I live."

"Where is your house?"

"Behind the bakery over there," she replied, pointing to the horizon. "There is a garden with a diosma and a fuchsia."

After helping the girl into the carriage, I lifted up the package. I heard the crack of the whip and then, like a huge sheet, silence covered all of the images.

We were saddling the horses. I asked Heredia, "Is there a healer who lives in town?"

"I think so."

"I would like to see her."

"What's going on with you?"

"I have headaches."

"And do you believe in healers?"

"Why not?"

"Let's go. I will accompany you there."

I hadn't expected him to accompany me. It was an opportunity to find out whether María Gismondi was the same girl I had met.

In Cacharí, after finding out where the healer lived, we neared her house, which was surrounded by poplars as described to us. After tying the horses to a post, we knocked on the door. We waited for a long time. Then a woman with indigenous features appeared. I leaned over toward her while Armando asked her solemnly, "Ma'am, are you the healer?"

"Yes, gentlemen, I am the healer. Would you like to come in?"

We went into a damp room that had a very tall armoire, a cot with an embroidered bedspread, and a chair.

"Who is the sick one?"

"I am," I answered, looking all around with curiosity.

"Sit down," she said. "Where does it hurt?"

"My head."

"Where?"

"Here." I showed her the area on my forehead that hurt.

"You have come too late," she answered, opening the door and looking at the sky. "You will have to come back another day, at four in the afternoon when your body's shadow is a yard long."

Someone was whispering far away in the fields. Purple and pink lights fell like flowers from the trees. I approached the little wall around the well. At the very bottom I could see the water reflecting me—the image I saw was strange. I felt afraid: the fear that children and dogs feel before a mirror.

We were at the bank of a river I was seeing for the first time. We had ridden fifteen miles on horseback. It was a cool spot among the reeds. The poplars cast gentle shadows over the water. We unsaddled and lay down to rest.

Heredia spoke to me of his memories of travel, of his studies in Paris, of his childhood on the beaches of the Mediterranean, of his arrival in Buenos Aires. He spoke to me about his first visit to the Swans, about how the countryside had won over his heart from the first moment. I listened to him, feeling his lack of sincerity. Why did he profess this love for nature if the only thing that attracted him was a woman?

When I asked whether the buying of the colts had been satisfactory, I took a chance and said that I had seen María Gismondi's name written on the trunk of a tree at the ranch. As if he hadn't heard me, he told me about a series of unrelated failures. I insisted, "Who could have written the name of the very person I would like to meet?"

He asked me, pretending to take no interest, why I wanted to meet her.

"I've seen a portrait of her."

"Where did you see that portrait?" Heredia asked brusquely, standing up.

Wavering, I answered, "I don't know."

I remembered the absurd print of the fight between the tiger and the jaguar; now the situation was even more difficult because I had no idea how to explain a lie that so angered Heredia.

"Have you been snooping through drawers?"

"I haven't been snooping anywhere," I answered angrily. "In a very dull dream I saw María Gismondi's portrait. I'm sorry for my boldness."

"How could it matter to me whether you have seen a portrait of María Gismondi? What matters to me is your snooping around."

"I told you that I haven't been snooping anywhere: I saw it in a dream," I shouted loudly.

Heredia cracked his whip above the grass.

"It's not such a big deal," he mumbled absentmindedly. "How sensitive you are!"

"It's the second time you have called me a spy."

I tried again to explain to him that it was a matter of dreams. I made a list of objects and people that I had met in dreams before meeting them in reality; I described them in great detail. I told him about several dreams, with no luck; they were vague, monotonous, and had no fantastic virtues. They were dreams that served as the basis for deeper reflections—only to me were they real. If I had told him a nightmare, perhaps the truthfulness of my tales would have been revealed with sumptuous precision. But I could only recall gray, blurry details in my memory. Why should Heredia care about the porcelain vase, the rocker, Esquivel's face? How could I use these images to testify to the truthfulness of my assertion if he had never paid much attention to them and was unable to recognize them?

Heredia accepted that I hadn't been snooping around the house. By evening we were reconciled. Lighting our way with a lantern, we climbed a narrow green staircase and into the attic to look for a whip. Among broken wood, dusty drawers, and the whistling of bats, we advanced in the cluttered darkness. Heredia wanted to show me a jewelry case and a trunk where various old family keepsakes were stored. He wanted, with some ill will, to show me the awful palace of the bats. After hanging the lantern on a nail, we sat down on some drawers and opened the old wooden jewelry box, which was inlaid with painted designs.

"My mother," Heredia told me, "was the only heir; she never had the nerve to look at these things. By now any sentimentality has turned into indifference. I suspect that she doesn't even know what's in this attic. Out of habit, she doesn't want to return to this ranch."

"But these things are valuable!" I responded with feigned seriousness, believing that Heredia disapproved of his mother's behavior for sentimental reasons.

"Not necessarily. Those that were valuable I had sold in Buenos Aires. The inkwell that was inside a crystal box, with gold carvings around the edges, the ivory-and-lace fan, the monogrammed silver *mate*, the ebony picture frame that preserved a bouquet of flowers made from the dirty hair of my ancestors, all of those things I have already sold. The most ridiculous objects make antiquarians happy. I found a tiny wooden box with mother-of-pearl inlay and a hole where a key could be hidden. I found it underneath one of the floorboards. It took me some time, fool that I am, to realize that the key wasn't the right one to open the box. It was a music box. When it was wound up the top lifted and out came a moth-eaten bird less than half an inch long. The bird sang and furiously beat its green wings. That was my first discovery in this attic. Do you know how much I got for that toy? One thousand five hundred pesos. Now I know the value of things."

"Have you spent many days up here?"

"Many," he answered. "I thought that I would never finish looking at everything: the portraits, old letters, receipts from stores, bits of trash."

Heredia took out a bundle of portraits from the box while I stared with amazement at that spiderweb filled place that had appeared in so many of my dreams. We heard the whistling of the bats crossing the attic in enormous shadows.

"If these portraits were objets d'art, I would be a millionaire!"

Heredia passed me some portraits to look at. They were from all sorts of different periods. None of them interested me.

"Here's the whip," Heredia exclaimed. "It's worthless, but still it's always better than a branch of privet. Let's go."

He took the lantern down and for a moment we could see clumps of motionless bats. Heredia handed me the lantern.

"I will take one of these creatures to Eladio so he can crucify it and force it to smoke," he said, carefully capturing a bat.

At that moment a gust of wind blew out the lantern. Fear paralyzed me. Going forward in the darkness, surrounded by bats and frogs, seemed impossible to me.

"Let's get closer to the staircase," Heredia said.

"I can't see anything," I responded without moving.

"I'm like a cat: I can see in the dark."

He approached the door without stumbling. I felt something brush against my cheek, something cold, rough, and quick.

"A bat!" I cried.

Heredia's laugh—cruel, hoarse, penetrating—wounded me like an insult.

We heard some shots from the end of the garden.

"Máximo Esquivel's out shooting," said Heredia. "When he turned thirty my grandfather gave him a revolver. He shoots at a target on Sundays."

"Who is Máximo Esquivel?"

"Eladio's father. He doesn't live here. Sometimes he comes to visit his son."

We walked toward the shooting and Heredia shouted, "Máximo, don't shoot!"

Heredia asked for the revolver. He aimed at a dove that was sitting on a branch but didn't pull the trigger until it started to fly. The wounded dove fell to the ground and died at our feet. Heredia passed me the revolver. I aimed at a hawk and when I fired I closed my eyes; the hawk, shrieking, flew in circles for a while. Then it followed us to the ranch house.

On Heredia's bedside table I saw a portrait: I thought it was María Gismondi. Heredia was putting on his boots. I was waiting for him so that we could go riding. After he walked past me I looked at the portrait. Against a gray background, the face, lit up and veiled with gentle shadows, seemed to indicate a total lack of character. This defect was perhaps due to the girl's unnatural posture. The only expressive detail was the set of retouched lines and shadows that made up her hair, which was as straight as rain. Like a thick veil, it concealed both sides of her face, cropping the oval shape with soft, glossy light. I felt a deep sense of relief: we were not in love with the same woman. On the face of the photograph, in a slanted and very delicate hand, there was a name with a flourish after it. When Heredia returned, I asked him, "Why don't you ever want to talk to me about María Gismondi?"

"I don't understand," he answered.

"Since she interests you so much, why don't you talk to me about her?" I insisted.

"Who said that I am so interested?"

"It seems so to me."

"Why?"

"Because you have her portrait, because you are constantly pronouncing her name."

"That's a portrait of my sister," he said, showing it to me. "Look." With surprise I read the signature: Carmen Heredia. "But by what right are you asking me about such things?"

"Because of our friendship."

The conversation, which seemed about to degenerate into a dispute, was interrupted by the happy arrival of Eladio Esquivel. The horses were saddled.

"María Gismondi will come this afternoon. I promised her some photographs of her family and a medallion I found in an envelope that had her name written on it. She is a shy, guarded girl. Finding you here would raise her suspicions. I invited her to come today because the caretakers are going with Eladio to Azul. I ask that you shut yourself in your room or go out in the country before seven this evening and not show yourself again until nine."

With those words Heredia revealed to me the secret that I had awaited for so many days.

At quarter to seven it was very hot. I decided to shut myself up in my room. I took off my clothes, lay down on the bed, and studied for about half an hour. I was sleepy and thirsty. I got up, looked out the window. Nobody was there. Absolute silence reigned in the hallways of the ranch house. It occurred to me that without disobeying Heredia's orders I could go (without any risk of meeting anyone) to the pantry to get something to drink. Two or three squeezed oranges, like the ones my mother squeezed, would quench my thirst. I cautiously opened the door. With the thrill thieves must feel when they are about to commit a robbery, I slipped through the hallways, entering the pantry without running into anyone. I chose the oranges; they were hard as rocks. With some difficulty I found a knife in the dining room, though it wasn't sharp enough. I looked for another one and then, just at the moment I was crossing the hallway between the two rooms, I thought I heard a noise. I silently approached an inner window with red and blue panes; I couldn't see anything; the window was too high. Moved by curiosity, I stood up on a chair. What would Heredia have said if he had found me at that moment? Was I doing anything other than confirming the accusation that had so hurt me? Although it might cost me my life I had to see María Gismondi. Through the panes I saw the ramshackle and dark living room of the house. We never spent time there because it was damp and quite dirty. Despite its ruinous state, it possessed a certain stylish class: on the ceiling there were garlands of flowers on the moldings, and the proportions of the windows echoed its former splendor. I saw Heredia alone, facing the door, with his arms resting on the back of a chair. I stayed there for a long time looking at him, with the hope (which he must have shared) of seeing María Gismondi come in; but the light went out and night surrounded the half-open door.

María Gismondi did not appear. I looked at my wristwatch; it was nine o'clock. I could come out of my hiding place and find out what had happened.

Later, during dinner, when I was sitting across from Heredia, our conversation was unexpectedly strained: I didn't have the nerve to ask him anything, and he didn't tell me anything.

I was trying to study, but the letters of the book, red as fire, danced before my eyes.

"You have sunstroke," Heredia said.

He recommended that I lie down. I took some aspirin. The housekeeper brought me a pitcher of orange juice and, on a plate, some slices of raw potato that she placed on my forehead because, according to her, they cure sunburn.

I drank the warm, sweetened orange juice that Eladio served me in a glass. A burning wind, like the wind of the desert, blew in through the window. I asked Eladio to close the blinds, the shutters, and the door, to let me sleep, but in the closed room the violent light persisted. I realized that I was feverish. Trembling, I got up to get some water. I went to the bathroom. I fainted on the tiles. Eladio and the housekeeper picked me up without my knowing it and helped me to bed.

A long hallway appeared at the end of my dream. The hallway of my school that led to a huge theater where the teachers gathered to give oral exams. The questions they asked me were easy, but I couldn't answer them because my tongue was paralyzed. The public, in the galleries, began to whistle. Afterwards, a huge crowd came in through the doors, shouting, "We want to see the dead body!" They began breaking the chairs, the tables, and the books that I was studying. I saw myself in a mirror: huge drops of sweat were falling from my forehead and running down my cheeks. I woke up, my pillow soaked.

We were playing cards on the patio. I couldn't concentrate on the game, thinking to myself: We can live with someone for days on end, sharing meals, excursions, conversations, coming to feel a deep intimacy, and yet not know that person at all: my friendship with Heredia proved it.

What were we playing? I think it was whist. I could see clearly how passion was destroying, devouring the soul of that young man, forcing him to scorn and abandon everything in life, to dissimulate and lie.

That was why Heredia ate so fast, pretended to have business with the neighbors, hastily sold the objects that had belonged to his grandparents; why he had abandoned his studies and shut himself away in the lonely countryside; why he insulted me; why he was unhappy and looked down on his father. It all made sense!

Heredia was nervous.

"Tomorrow at six," he told me, once again showing his trust in me, "I have to meet María Gismondi at the shack with the rocking chair. She will arrive on horseback. Sometimes she rides to her cousins' house where they're teaching her to sew; to get there she has to cross the pasture by the shack. We will meet as if by accident at the hour of the siesta. I will leave my horse in the field and she will hide hers in the woods; there are many hiding places in those woods. We have everything planned. If they find her, she will say that she was gathering figs; if they find me, which is very unlikely, I will tell them that I was helping her gather figs."

"What a wonderful place for a date!" I exclaimed, with an absurd tone, as if I were adulating him.

"It's not what you think," Heredia answered. "When you want to meet up with someone, the lonely countryside doesn't exist. Not even nighttime gives refuge to lovers here. That burning desire one feels to be with a woman in the first moments of love—nature never wants that to be satisfied. One has to seek out the horrible siesta hour, ruined places lit up by the pitiless sun. If I could ask her to return to this house, like the other evening, that would be better."

"The other evening?"

"Yes, the other evening, when I gave her the pictures and the medal."

His answer surprised me. So María Gismondi had come to the ranch house, had come inside, and I hadn't seen her? While I was mulling this over, I said, "I would like to see that shack again."

"Let's go," said Heredia. "I'll make use of the trip to find a place where I can hide with María."

I left my horse tied to a post on the road. I crossed the barbed-wire fences and reached the shack. I told myself: To think that the day before, during our visit, I had imagined that we would only look for a hiding place for Heredia and his girlfriend. It was risky. I thought about all of the dangers it implied. What if Heredia came with the dogs? The dogs would surely find me. What if María Gismondi had the power of second sight so frequent among women? What if she suddenly told Heredia, "There's someone here. I feel someone here." What if Heredia, to calm her down, should look all around? What if he were to find me after a long search and kill me with a single bullet? But I remembered that Heredia didn't have a revolver; he didn't have firearms; how could he kill me? He would make me feel terribly ashamed if he struck my face with his whip. I approached the fig trees; I pulled off two figs and ate them.

Through the broken roof of the shack there was a hole where I could spy. Climbing up would be hard but the spot on the roof was without a doubt the safest one. With great difficulty I succeeded in climbing up, using the broken parts of the wall as rungs; while doing so my handkerchief dropped to the ground. I was about to go down to retrieve it when I heard a horse's gallop. I lay down on the roof.

Through a hole in the thatch I could see everything without being seen. Armando Heredia appeared; he dismounted, then released his horse. Had he forgotten about the precautions he had planned the day before? With the same absent attitude he had possessed when he leaned against the living-room chair in the ranch house, he now leaned on a log. Spying on someone who is alone is uncomfortable. I felt like climbing down and telling him in jest, "I was spying on you." If it had been some other friend I would have done it; with Heredia, any spontaneous gesture was out of the question.

María Gismondi tarried. A heavy awful silence spread over everything. Not even the birds sang; the only sound, from time to time, was that of a hard eucalyptus seed falling to the earth. Heredia didn't move. I was amazed by his absolute lack of uneasiness. To wait with such calm for a woman who didn't come—that's a sign of utmost indifference. Or did Heredia feign and dissimulate when he was alone, too?

A ray of sunlight fell on the place where I was hiding: the violent sun of three in the afternoon. I began to burn alive. I tried to protect my head with my hands, with some straw, with my arms, adopting bizarre positions. No doubt I made some noise. Heredia raised his head and looked for a moment in my direction. My heart beat violently; it seemed to me that it was beating so hard that the walls of the shack were shaking, falling down; it seemed to me as if it was not the wind but my heart that was moving the dark, broken rocking chair. Instant death seemed to me like the sweetest of destinies. But the movement of the sun behind the foliage put an end to my torture. The coolness of the shade revived me.

Why did Heredia continue in the same pose? Did I see his lips move slightly; did I hear his voice? I couldn't be sure.

Time passed slowly. The sun gradually descended, shifting the shadows. My watch said that it was six in the afternoon. That was when Heredia mounted his horse and galloped off.

I suspected that Heredia was mad. I saw the first symptoms of this in his attitude, his lies, in the fact that María Gismondi never came to the dates he arranged.

"Why do you waste your time," I dared to ask, "with such a silly girl? It's almost as if you had fallen in love with an image."

He looked at me indignantly. We were eating. He thrust his plate aside, banged his fist on the table, and answered, "Who is asking for your advice?"

"It's not advice, it's a reflection."

"Your reflections don't interest me."

He rose from his seat and left the dining room.

I dreamt about Esquivel's revolver. Later, with perplexity, I saw that the revolver was in Heredia's room. If he didn't shoot at targets, why had he taken the revolver? To kill me, or to kill the man who was coming to the ranch?

In the morning I went to the store in Cacharí. I bought a pack of cigarettes. The man who helped me was kind, slow, talkative. We talked about the weather: about the chances of rain, about the heat.

"Could you tell me where María Gismondi lives?" I asked him, intending to go by her house.

The man didn't answer right away.

"María Gismondi? What? Don't you know? She died some time ago—four years at least."

Terror spread through my body when I heard those words; terror and at the same time relief: María Gismondi wasn't the girl I had fallen in love with.

Persuading myself that Heredia was mad turned out to be nearly impossible for me. Events had made our friendship all the more precious. What should I do? Try to save him. How? By writing to his father; maybe a doctor could come to his aid. Leaving for the city, abandoning him in that state—wouldn't that be an act of cowardice? While thinking about these things I dreamt that I was carrying a letter to Cacharí, a letter that I had written to Mr. Heredia, telling him about his son's state. I wanted to take the letter to the post office myself. When I dismounted across from the post office I ran into Heredia. He said to me brusquely, "Who is that letter for?"

"For my parents."

I had taken the precaution of addressing the envelope to my father, with another envelope inside to be given to Mr. Heredia.

"Give it to me; I'll take it to the post office; I have stamps with me."

When I gave it to him I felt threatened by something that couldn't be undone.

"This envelope has another envelope inside."

"How do you know?"

"Its weight, its shape, everything suggests that. Open it immediately," pointing the revolver at me. "I will kill you more easily than I would kill a dove."

I opened the envelope, just as he said, and gave him the letter. As he read it, hatred darkened his face.

"I don't want to soil the entryway to this house. Let's go. We shouldn't stay here."

We returned to the ranch house. Heredia went in his room and I in mine. Immediately, I felt I must flee—but how? With what? No one was there. I looked for the horses and carriage; they weren't in the corral. Running, I went into the woods and followed one of the paths at random. My intention was to find something that could take me away. Something bothered me as I ran; I felt my waist; I noticed that I had a knife with me. I had gotten pretty far from the house so I slowed down to a walk. I heard the gallop of a horse. I lay down on the ground, hiding in deep grass in hopes of not being seen.

Heredia drew near, got down from his horse. I heard him talking to me in the familiar tone he used with his dogs, "Coward, I'll teach you how to play dead."

Then I heard the sound of a shot in the silence. I woke up with a start. But my dream continued with the post office in Cacharí. In the middle of the street was a dead dog covered with flies.

I couldn't make up my mind; all possible courses of action seemed rash, uncertain. I was afraid of unconsciously plagiarizing my own dream. At times, I was inclined to go to Buenos Aires and would start to pack; other times, I pulled out pen and paper to write to Mr. Heredia. Every course of action seemed repellent to me, since Armando Heredia, despite his madness, had never ceased being my friend: one of my closest friends.

I was in my room, meditating on all of these things, when Eladio came in with a piece of paper in his hand. I carefully opened the folded paper. I read these words: *I will be away for two days. Armando.* What should I do? Take advantage of his absence to communicate with his father? Wait for his return?

I thought: Maybe he isn't crazy. Maybe he wants to trick me. Maybe his girlfriend, to avoid getting caught and wanting to conceal her true name, had casually given the name of a dead girl. I imagined the awful letter I was about to write announcing Heredia's madness; I imagined his father's suffering, his arrival at the ranch house with a doctor, maybe with a nurse; my eternal shame before the world if Heredia didn't turn out to be crazy; my sorrow if they were to strap a straitjacket on him to take him back to Buenos Aires, strangers staring at him in the station; the awful prison of the madhouse. I would be guilty of everything; my conscience would dictate a string of effects.

Heredia returned at sunset. He brought me a silver dagger as a gift. I thanked him: it was the object I most craved. The handle had my initials surrounded by golden flowers and a pattern of lines. I felt unworthy of the gift. I took the knife out of its sheath. Feeling as if the cold blade was pointing at my heart, I caressed it sadly and said, "In Buenos Aires I will use it to cut the pages of my books."

"And here you will use it to kill someone?" Heredia asked.

"I don't think so," I answered. "I'm not attracted to María."

I put the knife back in its sheath, fastened it to my belt, and touched it with joy. I had forgotten the terrible problem I needed to resolve.

We lit a bonfire on the patio. That night, lit up by the fire, our faces seemed like masks. I took advantage of a moment of conciliation and emotion: "Heredia, for several days I have been meaning to tell you something: the girl you are interested in isn't named María Gismondi. María Gismondi died four years ago. No doubt from shyness or fear, so as not to give herself away, the girl told you that was her name."

I spoke to him while looking at the fire, as if the flames could purify the meaning of my words. When I raised my eyes Heredia wasn't there. Had he heard me? We end up thinking we are crazy when we suspect someone else of being crazy. I called Heredia. The door of his room was closed. He didn't answer. I saw a rainbow at the end of the hallway. I thought, "And if I accepted her, if I became an accomplice to his madness, how would I be able to relate to him again? How could I save him?" I counted the number of flagstones in the hallway, pondering what to do. Write to Buenos Aires, leave, stay (accepting his madness as something normal); write, go, stay, write, go, stay; I paced the flagstones; the last one, which was broken, gave me the worst advice: Just wait.

I remembered a phrase I had read in a book: "What is true is like God, not revealing itself immediately but construed through its many manifestations."

I tried to have another conversation with Heredia. The night was comfortable, quiet; we were smoking and the rings of smoke seemed to soften my uneasiness. "I've often asked myself, What was the name of that girl who rode the train with me from Buenos Aires? Her companion called her Claudia, but she had a broach made of fake rubies that spelled 'María.'"

"It's such a common name. What could it mean?"

"That the first name a girl assumes when she doesn't want to give her real one is María."

"So what?"

"So I think the girl on the train called Claudia pretended her name was María to whomever gave her the broach."

A blaze of madness illuminated Heredia's eyes.

"And so I'm the person who gave the girl that broach?"

"No, that's not what I mean. Don't be absurd! I've seen María Gismondi's portrait and the two don't look at all alike. Perhaps they each pretend to be María because they don't want to use their real names."

I spoke persuasively, without looking at the change taking over Heredia's face, though I could imagine it anyway. The madness beginning in the backs of his eyes, making his mouth contract, his cheeks sink, his forehead shrivel, his hands twist. I had to continue talking because words protected me from a terrifying silence. I went on, "People in the countryside are full of prejudices. That's why girls who live in such towns feel obligated to do strange things. When they have a boyfriend they assume the names of dead people without a second thought."

When I looked at Heredia, I saw the expression of terror in his eyes for the first time. Like a wounded animal, he fled from my side. His fear intensified mine.

Beyond the darkness, among the leaves of the trees, a shadow could barely be seen, an eye, a lock of hair. He was hiding, hunting for me in the plants, in the hallways, in the rooms of the house.

I couldn't lock myself in: all the keys to the house had been lost. I finally decided to write to Mr. Heredia. In a corner of my room, in almost total darkness, I began my letter:

Dear Mr. Heredia:

Your ranch house is very beautiful and large; in it I have spent some of the happiest days of my life, along with some of the most terrible, but I am of no importance right now. I want to express both my gratitude to you for having given me the chance to stay in such a place, and my sorrow in having to tell you about your son's condition. I am too disturbed to write a considered, clear letter, but trust that you will understand my words.

After having lived here for a month (which seems like years) with your son, without discovering in him any abnormality of character, save occasional violent outbursts like those of any young man; after having confirmed that he doesn't drink, nor frequent prostitutes, I have discovered evidence of madness in his behavior, in his actions, in his speech. I can scarcely believe it: Armando is in love with a woman who died four years ago; he has dates with her, speaks to her, imagines that he sees her, and yet he is always alone. He knows that I have found out and he hates me for it. If I don't communicate all this to you now, I would be afraid of never having sufficient strength of will to do so later—I would fear madness myself.

In a few days a friend of yours is coming to the ranch. Perhaps he can help us.

Sincerely yours,
Luis Maidana

I carefully tucked the letter in my pocket.

The heat of the day slowly declined. Night fell with its countless stars. I went into town to post my letter. The post office was closed and I didn't have any stamps. I remembered that it was Sunday. Four or five boys next door were building a house. They were trying to carry a huge sack full of stones onto the steps of the entryway. I stopped to watch them. It seemed like a task that exceeded their strength. I felt indignant at the people who had ordered them to do it. I sat down on a pile of sand to smoke a cigarette. I was tired. A few moments later a woman appeared, disheveled and furious, who dispersed the boys with her screams. Then I realized that the job which had made such a deep impression on me was actually a game, a game that deserved to be punished.

When I heard the hoarse voice of the woman, I recalled some memories from my childhood. I had played with that same seriousness. My games could be confused with the heaviest labors that men perform out of a feeling of obligation—nobody had respected me. I thought: Children have their own hell. Punishing and threatening the youngest child severely, she used the wonderful name: "I will send María to your houses to tell your mothers what you have done."

Ashamed, I slunk like a shadow through the streets of the town following that horrid woman. The streets seemed more twisting and ominous to me, infinite and at every step filthier, as if winding through a swamp. I crossed the railroad tracks, passed two shops, stopped in front of a drugstore; the streets capriciously became narrower then wider; I came to the avenue of the phoenix palms, when all of a sudden the woman disappeared around a corner.

On a balcony of a whitewashed brick house, there was a half-open window behind a cast-iron railing. Protected by the darkness of the night, I peeked through the window into the interior of the room. In the dizzying light of a mirror I saw the reflection of a girl whose face I could barely make out in the shadows. Her image became clearer, but her hair, like a river as shiny as silver, obscured her. I thought that María, suspecting that I was looking at her while crouching in the darkness, was hiding her body with her hair.

The light in the room went out. I heard the footfalls of bare feet on the wood floor and then total silence in the street.

With a leap I entered the room. I thought about dying. Love and death are alike: when we are lost we rely on others. Motionless, I waited, adjusting to the sudden darkness of the room. After a duration that seemed to connect me with eternity, the mirror began to light up. I saw a chair, then a bedside table, a sewing basket with spools of thread, the painted metal alarm clock, the vase with paper flowers, the narrow bed where the girl lay with her eyes open. "There are people who sleep with their eyes open," I thought, drawing near. "She doesn't see me. I can lean over her to see her better. I could kiss her without her feeling it." I leaned over. I felt her delicate breathing. I saw her hands on the white bedspread, her hair loose on a pillow-case embroidered with large daisies. "She no doubt embroidered this herself," I thought, seeing the blue pencil line beneath the wreaths. Kneeling by the bed I examined her eyes: she seemed to look at me without seeing me.

"María, now, for the first time, I can embrace you the way I've often dreamed of doing," I told her in a low voice, feeling as if I was shouting. I tried to keep my body away from mirror's light that shone in the room. I drew several steps back and banged into the bedside table; the alarm clock fell off. I crouched down expecting terrible things to happen but silence once more spread like a veil over the house. I stayed for a time holding still, not daring to move. I knelt once more by the edge of the bed. In the soft light of the mirror the girl's face shone with extraordinary clarity. Suddenly, as if my insistent gaze had woken her, she sat up. She looked at me with horror. She wanted to scream but I covered her mouth. She wanted to flee but I held her down.

Dawn was breaking when I left the house.

It was very early when I stepped out of my room. The dew shone on the leaves of the plants. Heredia appeared. He beat the stones, the branches, the thistles, the tree trunks—everything we encountered—with his whip.

"I have to speak to you," he said. "I have to explain some things to you."

Astonished, I listened without uttering a word.

"For me," he continued, "María Gismondi didn't die four years ago. Do you how she died, and for whom? Four years ago, in February, I wanted to deliver a letter to her. Her parents weren't supposed to know about it. The task was nearly impossible. One night (I remember it was a Sunday), overwhelmed, I wandered through the town and decided to enter her room like a thief. I intended to leave the letter under the mattress or in a drawer of the bedside table and then flee without being seen. I crept through the window. I hid in a space between the armoire and the wall. I heard some steps in the next room; someone opened the door and lit the lamp. I couldn't leave. (To this day I still feel my heart beat against the cold of the whitewashed wall.) I heard bare feet slowly walk across the floorboards. María Gismondi entered the room; she closed the window, lay down, and turned off the light. I waited for her to fall asleep. Never in my whole life have I waited so long. When I thought she was asleep, I left the letter on the bedside table and fearfully approached the window. I tripped on something. In the total silence of night, the noise echoed violently. I stood still. In the darkness, María Gismondi hunted for matches and lit the lamp. When she saw me she wanted to cry out; I put my hand over her mouth. I held her in my arms for the first time. When two people fight it seems as if they are embracing. I struggled with María Gismondi until daybreak. Afterwards I fled her house, as she was about to fall asleep. The next day they announced her death. For a few days I thought that I had killed her; then I thought that anyone who thought she was dead had killed her. I understood that our lives depend on a certain number of people who see us as living beings. If those people imagine that we are dead, we die. That's why I can't forgive you for saying María Gismondi is dead."

I searched for a calendar. I found one in the kitchen. Feverishly I consulted it. The twenty-eighth was only one day away. It was important to wait without fear. I thought, trying to calm myself down: Fear attracts misfortune. I went out to the patio; I gathered some stones and, with astonishing precision, tried out my marksmanship on a tree trunk.

Atop the kitchen roof, a white cat looked at me with green eyes. I threw the last stone at the cat. I heard the dry thud on the tiles and a sharp cry of distress.

The poor animal fled the roof, bleeding. I found a trail of blood around the house. I thought about how cruel people can be when they are afraid. Why had I thrown the rock? To deserve being punished? To prove that I could kill too? To prove something to someone? To myself. Nobody had seen me.

A cloudy sky brought the night on quickly. So as not to imitate my dream I decided to go to the post office in the carriage. Trembling, with the letter in my pocket, I crossed the hallway, the patio, and into the kitchen. The housekeeper told me that her husband had taken out the carriage. With a horribly ominous feeling I found the horse and saddled it.

"Are you cold?" Eladio asked.

I realized that I was still trembling.

I felt as if I wasn't moving forward, that I was riding a horse made of lead. Overwhelmed by a dreadful exhaustion, I reached the town. I felt calmer facing the low, yellow post office. Nobody was there. I dismounted. I only had to take a few steps to slip the letter into the mailbox and be free, but suddenly, as I held it out in my hand, Heredia appeared. I thought, "I am dreaming...I should be upset... soon I will wake up."

Heredia said very slowly to me, "Give me that letter; I'll put it in the mailbox." When he held the letter in his hand he added, "This envelope has another one of the same size inside it."

"You are a sorcerer," I answered, trying to keep reality from resembling the dream. "I put a letter to a classmate inside. I don't have his address."

A few yards away, Claudia or María came walking along a dirt path. (I still didn't know her name. I wouldn't ever find out what it was!) I felt calm: reality was diverging ever more from the dream; besides, that circumstance would allow me to speak about something else, to distract Heredia's attention. I told him in a low voice, gesturing with my eyes to where he should look, "That's the girl who traveled with me. You will see how she blushes. She pretends not to know me!"

Heredia looked at me scornfully. Did he suspect how much I had suffered thinking that we were in love with the same girl? I waited for her to draw near and then, removing my hat, asked her, as if I didn't know her, "Miss, could you tell me if the train schedule has changed?" I looked at my watch. "It's twelve and I still haven't heard a whistle."

She looked at me with surprise.

"The station is two blocks from here, ask the station chief."

"And the social club, miss, do you know where it is?"

"The social club is five blocks away, to the right."

"Will there be a dance soon?"

"Saturday night."

"Are you going, my beauty?"

When she heard the last word, which was not exactly what I intended to say, the girl blushed.

"I don't go to dances. I'm in mourning," she responded, with a proud twitch of her lips. She walked off with a quick grace, without saying goodbye.

We stood there watching her. We spoke about her legs, her age, her waist. But what had Heredia done with my letter? I saw that he had tucked it in his pocket, perhaps absentmindedly. I told him, in a trembling voice, "You've forgotten about my letter."

"Quite the opposite: I haven't forgotten it."

"Then why do you have it in your pocket?"

"So that you can read it to me aloud when we get back to the ranch."

I tried to grab it from him but he threatened me with the revolver—the revolver from the dream! We mounted the horses. As we rode, I thought about forcing the letter and the revolver from him. I looked at him out of the corner of my eye, waiting for a moment of distraction to flee, to ask for help, to hit him on the head. But he was much stronger than I was, and very fit, so I abandoned my plans. If I asked for help, they would think I was crazy anyway; if I fled, Heredia would shoot me in the back; if I attacked him, he would kill me like a dog.

Dying didn't matter to me. I looked at him with indulgence.

"And how do you think you can make me read you my letter?"

"With this," he said, putting the revolver on the table, "because you are incapable of defending yourself, even with this revolver, even with the knife strapped to your belt."

"I disdain violent means to reach an agreement."

"What means do you approve of, then?"

"Those of mutual understanding."

"Okay," he said, sitting down. "Now read me your letter."

"I won't."

"By violence, then," he said, picking up the revolver again.

Trembling, I took the letter that Heredia handed me. Once again I thought I was dreaming and that I would soon wake up. Perhaps the letter would turn into a completely different one.

Slowly I began to read. I read as they had taught me to read aloud in school, my body held straight, raising my head at the end of each paragraph, indicating the punctuation in an exaggerated way. When I finished, a century later, Heredia, without a word, stood up and left the room. I heard his steps stop on the flagstones in the hallway. As in my dream, I needed to flee. I shut Carbón in my room so that he wouldn't follow me. I looked for the carriage, the horses: they weren't there. With the heaviness produced by shameful fear, I ran. I entered my room again; I had forgotten the keys. I tucked them in my pocket. I put my notebook and books in the drawer of the table and departed once again. I left everything behind; anything I took with me could give me away or make my flight more difficult.

FINAL CONSIDERATIONS BY RÓMULO SAGASTA

Here the pages of this extravagant notebook come to an end. After having meditated upon the notebook's contents, I feel the need and duty to add the true conclusion.

Every life, with its experiences and illusions, is incomplete, fragmentary, and terrible: the life revealed in the preceding pages is an especially moving symbol in my view. Having corrected some grammatical errors, without modifying the simple, childish style of the sentences, I will now add the following:

On February 28, 1930, I left Constitution Station on the morning train for Cacharí. I did so unwillingly, not thinking that I would find myself facing the awful spectacle fate had in store for me.

The Swans, the ranch that I had visited so many times with my friend Raúl Heredia for weekends during the May holidays or during Carnival, evoked the warmest, sweetest memories in my heart.

The delicious lunches outside, the long siestas, the calm silence of the countryside are pleasures that no native of these parts can disdain. It is true that I am fond of hunting and that this entertainment is an additional attraction for me to country life. The first thing I did whenever I visited was to rent the shopkeeper's hunting dog for two pesos. A pointer, even one that's in bad shape, is of some use when the hunter is skillful. Without fail, at the end of the afternoon, I would return from the fields with eight or nine partridges.

I reached the Swans, I repeat, on February 28, 1930. I carried my shotgun with me to conceal the real motive for my journey.

It was a dazzlingly beautiful sunny day. Nobody was waiting for me at the station. I wandered around the platform for half an hour, and was beginning to regret my trip when the carriage appeared. Eladio Esquivel slowly climbed down like an old man and greeted me. I received him coldly, at once suspecting the tragic eloquence that was hidden in his slowness. Something grave had happened. With serious words, spoken with hesitation, he told me, "There has been an accident."

With my shotgun and suitcase, I hastened into the carriage and, as we rode to the ranch, I listened, confused, to the boy's story. The sun, the brightness of the day, Eladio's sleepy voice—everything seemed to call his words into question.

Then I saw the dead body. I spoke to the caretakers, the doctor, the police, and after dealing with the coffin, I went to examine the place where the accident had occurred. Along a road lined with eucalyptus trees and Australian pines, Eladio took me to a place surrounded by high grass where it was still possible to see bloodstains and traces, possibly, of a struggle. Later I learned that the black dog from the ranch had howled and, in wild desperation, dug up the earth where it saw the blood.

We never foresee the worst possibility. I had foreseen everything except what had actually happened. I again lamented my acceptance of such an unpleasant mission. My friendship with Raúl Heredia, my sympathy for his family, had impelled me to relent out a sense of duty. To visit a lonely ranch under the pretext of hunting partridges, to spy on and give counsel to a boy of eighteen, even if he was the son of my friend, struck me as intriguing but embarrassing. Now, finding myself in the face of such an unexpected and horrible event, it seemed as if my fears matched my forebodings in a natural way.

Since childhood, Armando Heredia had shown signs of madness. It is true that young boys always struck me as crazy; their conversations, the games they play, the words they utter, are often sure signs of madness to me. Surviving childhood is a severe test on the faculty of reasoning. Among children I have known, Armando Heredia was without a doubt the oddest. I see him as he was at fourteen, his eyes blazing, a whip in his hand, punishing a fictitious character (whose features he had drawn himself on the ground, in red ink) and then crying because of the character's death.

The Heredia family arrived on the afternoon train. I had never witnessed such a dramatic scene, watching a mother embrace her dead son. I am not particularly self-conscious, and yet I worried about acting with proper respect toward a mourning family I hold in such high esteem.

It was hard for me to recognize the happy ranch house, with its pleasant hallways and thick vines. In an instant, the atmosphere of a place can change forever. When I saw Raúl Heredia, I understood that we would never be able to return to the ranch as it was before. Certain events mark a point of no return in time, like those lines of white chalk in a game that signal the beginning and end of different periods.

They placed the coffin in the living room of the house, where we held the wake. In the flickering candlelight, the face of the young man wasn't disfigured. His dark skin, his narrow forehead, the purity of his profile were unchanged. The bullet had pierced the center of his heart. I was moved by the flowers that the mother had tried in vain to insert into the dead man's hands, by the resentment with which she spoke to him, the bitter, severe phrases.

At dawn, after several cups of coffee, Raúl Heredia led me to his son's room (a dark damp room). He opened the armoire and the drawers of the bedside table.

"My wife wouldn't be able to bear doing this. I know her well. Before leaving, I want to look at everything."

The light of dawn hit the blinds and the first birds sang weakly. Raúl Heredia stopped for a moment and said, "At this hour one suddenly understands what is definitive." Through the doorframe he pointed to the white sky. "Only when I've been drunk or sad have I seen the dawn; only after parties, births, or deaths, and this is the most bitter, the most hellish, the most unfair..."

We found a notebook with a blue cover in the drawer of the bedside table. The first page was titled "My Dreams." Raúl Heredia sadly turned over all the pages and gave the notebook to me.

"I don't have the courage to read these pages. But it would be a crime to destroy them. Armando was intelligent. I barely knew him! I give this notebook to you because you are my best friend. You can read it and perhaps discover within what motives impelled my son to commit this mad act—now no explanation can change anything."

I took the notebook and we returned to the living room where the candle flames flickered.

Many neighbors had come to the wake. The women cried with the force of poetry and spoke eloquently on death.

It would be futile to recall all the details of the sad conversations that night, the painful train journey, the arrival in Constitution Station.

After the burial in Buenos Aires, I began to read the notebook, with much astonishment. For several days I was terrified. I thought about destroying the pages. I still haven't found a solution to the problem. In vain I searched the phone book for the name of Luis Maidana. At the same time, I tried to avoid encounters with my friend Heredia. What if he spoke to me about the notebook? What if he asked me for it? I tried spending time with other family members, hoping to discover details of the boy's life, but it was fruitless.

Six months passed. Heredia came to visit me one day. With a jovial voice, he announced that they were going to Europe shortly. He spoke to me about his children and when he mentioned Armando, he said, "It was just as well that God took him away; boys like that never thrive. He caused his mother a lot of suffering."

Taking advantage of the opportunity, I gathered my confidence to speak to him about the notebook he had given me six months before, that it didn't contain descriptions of dreams and hadn't been written by his son but by someone named Luis Maidana. My news didn't surprise Heredia, or even interest him very much. He looked at me incredulously. He assured me that his son didn't have any friend with that name.

We studied the handwriting of the notebook; we compared school binders and letters that we assumed were written by him during the same period: the handwriting was the same. We asked Armando's friends if they had ever met a Luis Maidana. Nobody had ever heard of him. The caretakers at the Swans affirmed that nobody had visited Armando at the ranch house. I finally had to accept the incredible: the tales contained in the notebook with the title "My Dreams" had been written by Armando Heredia, not by Luis Maidana.

Even if those tales really were dreams, why had Armando pretended to be someone else? Was he pretending or was he really dreaming that he was someone else, seeing himself from the outside? Was he obsessed by the idea that he didn't dream, as he writes on one page of the notebook? Did he feel like a ghost, like a blank page? Was the obsession so strong that Armando had ended up inventing his dreams?

When he was thinking, perhaps Heredia believed he was dreaming. That was how the strange, hallucinatory links came to figure in his dreams: Armando Heredia suffered from doubling. He saw himself from the outside as Luis Maidana would see him, someone at once his friend and his enemy. "When we are awake, we live in a shared world, but when we sleep, each of us is hurled into a world of our own." I've been able to show that certain people, certain objects and events in these tales actually existed; others, like Luis Maidana or Dr. Tarcisio Fernández, do not exist and never have.

By committing suicide, did Armando Heredia think he was killing Luis Maidana? As during his childhood when he thought he had killed an imaginary person? Instead of red ink, had he used his own blood to play with his enemy? Did he love, hate, and kill an imaginary being?

Heredia asked me to manage the sale of the ranch. I returned to the Swans for one last time. I saw some objects mentioned in the notebook; I recognized them with unpleasant surprise. I saw the porcelain basket, the dizzying rocking chair, the landscape painting hanging above the bed, the tiger and jaguar painting attributed to Delacroix. In Cacharí, I met María Gismondi (whom I questioned in vain). Nobody had ever heard of Luis Maidana.

I still feel a deep unease when I think about the notebook. The secret contained in its pages will never be solved, since death forever sealed the lips of the author and actor, of the victim and the murderer, in this inconceivable story.

If I had arrived at the Swans on February 26th or 27th instead of the 28th, as I had originally intended, I—through the ghost of Maidana—could have saved Armando Heredia. But I may have ended up losing my own life. And if this were a mystery story, I most likely would have had an argument with Armando, and he (as it happened in reality) would have committed suicide, accusing me of being criminally responsible for his death. The consequences of any act are, in some sense, infinite.

Sometimes I think that only in dreams have I read the notebook, reflecting on its pages. Sometimes I think that Heredia's madness isn't alien to me.

On the surface, there is no distinction between our experiences— some are vivid, others opaque; some are pleasant, others cause agony upon recollection—but there is no way of knowing which are dreams and which are reality.

THE HOUSE MADE OF SUGAR

SUPERSTITIONS kept Cristina from living. A coin with a blurry face, a spot of ink, the moon seen through two panes of glass, the initials of her name carved by chance on the trunk of a cedar: all these would make her mad with fear. The day we met she was wearing a green dress; she kept wearing it until it fell apart, since she said it brought her good luck and that as soon as she wore another, a blue one that fit her better, we would no longer see each other. I tried to combat these absurd manias. I made her see that she had a broken mirror in her room, yet she insisted on keeping it, no matter how I insisted that it was better to throw broken mirrors into water on a moonlit night to get rid of bad luck. She was never afraid if the lamps in the house went out all of a sudden; despite the fact that it was definitely an omen of death, she would light any number of candles without thinking twice. She always left her hat on the bed, a mistake nobody else made. Her fears were more personal. She inflicted real privations on herself; for instance, she could not eat strawberries in the summer, or hear certain pieces of music, or adorn her house with goldfish, although she liked them a lot. There were certain streets we couldn't cross, certain people we couldn't see, certain movie theaters we couldn't go to. Early in our relationship, these superstitions seemed charming to me, but later they began to annoy and even seriously worry me. When we got engaged we had to look for a brand-new apartment because, according to her, the fate of the previous occupants would influence her life. (She at no point mentioned my life, as if the danger threatened only hers and our lives were not joined by love.) We visited all of the neighborhoods in the city; we went to even the most distant suburbs in search of an apartment where no one had ever lived, but they had all been rented or sold. Finally I found a little house on Montes de Oca Street that looked as if it were made of sugar. Its whiteness gleamed with extraordinary brilliance. It had a phone inside and a tiny garden in front. I thought the house was newly built, but discovered that a family had occupied it in 1930 and that later, to rent it out, the owner had remodeled it. I had to make Cristina believe no one had lived in the house and that it was the ideal place, the house of our dreams. When Cristina saw it, she cried out, "How different it is from the apartments we have seen! Here it smells clean. Nobody will be able to influence our lives or soil them with thoughts that corrupt the air."

A few days later we got married and moved in. My in-laws gave us a bedroom set, and my parents a dining-room table and chairs. We would furnish the rest of the house little by little. I was afraid Cristina would find out about my lie from the neighbors, but luckily she did her shopping away from the neighborhood and never talked to them. We were happy, so happy that it sometimes frightened me. It seemed our tranquillity would never be broken in that house of sugar, until a phone call destroyed my illusion. Luckily Cristina didn't answer it, but she might have on some other occasion. The person who called asked for Mrs. Violeta: she was no doubt the previous tenant. If Cristina found out that I had deceived her, our happiness would surely come to an end. She wouldn't ever speak to me again, would ask for a divorce, and even in the best possible case we would have to leave the house and go live, perhaps, in Villa Urquiza, or in Quilmes, as tenants in one of the houses where they promised to give us some space to build a bedroom and a kitchen. But with what? (Impossible: we didn't have enough money for good building materials.) At night I was careful to take the phone off the hook, so that no inopportune call would wake us up. I put a mailbox by the gate on the street; I was the only possessor of the key, the distributor of the letters.

Early one morning there was a knock on the door and someone left a package. From my room I heard my wife protesting; then I heard the sound of paper being ripped open. I went downstairs and found Cristina with a velvet dress in her arms.

"They just brought me this dress," she said with enthusiasm.

She ran upstairs and put on the dress, which fit her very tight.

"When did you order it?"

"Some time ago. Does it fit well? I could wear it when we go to the theater, don't you think?"

"How did you pay for it?"

"Mother gave me a few pesos."

That seemed strange to me, but I didn't say anything so as not to offend her.

We loved each other madly. But my uneasiness began to bother me, even when I embraced Cristina at night. I noticed that her character had changed: her happiness turned to sadness, her communicativeness to reserve, her calm to nervousness. She lost her appetite. She no longer made those rich, rather heavy desserts out of whipped cream and chocolate that I so enjoyed, nor did she adorn the house from time to time with nylon ruffles, covering the toilet seat or the shelves in the dining room or the chests of drawers or other places in the house, as had been her custom. She would no longer surprise me at teatime with vanilla wafers, and never felt like going to the theater or the movies at night, not even when we could get free tickets. One afternoon a dog entered the garden and lay down, howling, on the front doorstep. Cristina gave him some meat and something to drink; after a bath that changed the color of its hair, she announced that she would keep it and name it Love, because it had come to our house at a moment of real love. The dog had a black mouth, a sign of good pedigree.

Another afternoon I arrived home unexpectedly. I stopped at the gate because I saw a bicycle lying in the yard. I entered quietly, then hid behind a door and heard Cristina's voice.

"What do you want?" she repeated twice

"I've come to get my dog," a young woman's voice said. "He's passed by this house so many times that he's become fond of it. This house looks as if it's made of sugar. Since they painted it, everyone has noticed it. But I liked it better before, when it was the romantic pink color of old houses. This house has always been very mysterious to me. I like everything about it: the birdbath where the little birds came to drink, the vines with flowers like yellow trumpets, the orange tree. Ever since I was eight I've wanted to meet you, ever since that day we talked on the phone, do you remember? You promised you would give me a kite."

"Kites are for boys."

"Toys are sexless. I like kites because they resemble huge birds; I imagine flying on their wings. For you it was just an idle game promising me that kite; I didn't sleep all night. We met in the bakery, but you were facing in the other direction and I didn't see your face. Ever since that day I've thought of nothing but you, of what your face looked like, your soul, your lying gestures. You never gave me the kite. The trees spoke to me of your lies. Then we went to live in Morón with my parents. Now I've only been back here a week."

"I've lived in this house for just three months, and before that I never visited this neighborhood. You must be mistaken."

"I imagined you exactly the way you are. I imagined you so many times! By some strange coincidence, my husband used to be engaged to you."

"I was never engaged to anyone except my husband. What's this dog's name?"

"Bruto."

"Take him away, please, before I grow fond of him."

"Violeta, listen. If I take the dog to my house, he'll die. I can't take care of him. We live in a very tiny apartment. My husband and I both work and there isn't anyone to take him out for a walk."

"My name isn't Violeta. How old is he?"

"Bruto? Two years old. Do you want to keep him? I'll visit him from time to time, because I'm very fond of him."

"My husband doesn't like strangers in our house and wouldn't want me to accept a dog as a present."

"Don't tell him, then. I'll wait for you every Monday at seven in the evening in Colombia Square. Do you know where it is? In front of Santa Felicitas Church, or if you prefer I can wait for you wherever and whenever you like: for instance, on the bridge behind Constitution Station or in Lezama Park. I'll be happy just to see Bruto's eyes. Will you do me the favor of keeping him?"

"All right. I'll keep him."

"Thank you, Violeta."

"My name isn't Violeta."

"Did you change your name? For us you'll always be Violeta. Always the same mysterious Violeta."

I heard the dull sound of the door and Cristina's steps as she went upstairs. I waited a little before coming out of my hiding place and pretending I had just come in. Though I had witnessed the innocence of the dialogue, some muffled suspicion began gnawing at me. It seemed to me that I had watched a theatrical rehearsal and that the reality of the situation was something else. I didn't confess to Cristina that I had witnessed the young woman's visit. I awaited further developments, always afraid that Cristina would discover my lie and lament that we had moved to this neighborhood.

Every afternoon I passed the square in front of Santa Felicitas Church to see whether Cristina would keep the appointment. Cristina seemed not to notice my uneasiness. Sometimes I even came to believe that I had dreamed it all. Hugging the dog one day, Cristina asked me, "Would you like my name to be Violeta?"

"I don't like names based on flowers."

"But Violeta is pretty. It's a color."

"I like your name better."

One Saturday, at sunset, I ran into her on the bridge behind Constitution Station, leaning over the iron railing. I approached her and she showed no sign of surprise.

"What are you doing here?"

"Just looking around. I like looking down at the tracks."

"It's a very gloomy place and I don't like you wandering around here by yourself."

"It doesn't seem so gloomy to me. And why shouldn't I wander around by myself?"

"Do you like the black smoke of the locomotives?"

"I like transportation. Dreaming about trips. Leaving without ever leaving. *Leaving and staying and by staying leaving.*"

We returned home. Mad with jealousy (jealousy of what? of everything), I hardly spoke to her on the way.

"Perhaps we could buy a little house in San Isidro or Olivos; this neighborhood is so unpleasant," I said, pretending that I had the means to buy a house in one of those places.

"You're mistaken. We have Lezama Park very nearby here."

"It's desolate. The statues are broken, the fountains empty, the trees diseased. Beggars, old men, and cripples go there with sacks to throw out garbage or to pick it up."

"I don't notice such things."

"Before, you didn't even like sitting on a bench where someone had eaten tangerines or bread."

"I've changed a lot."

"No matter how much you've changed, you can't like a park like that one. Yes, I know it has a museum with marble lions guarding the entrance and that you played there when you were a girl, but all of that doesn't mean anything."

"I don't understand you," Cristina answered. And I felt she disliked me, with a dislike that could easily turn to hatred.

For days that seemed like years I watched her, trying to hide my anxiety. Every afternoon I passed the square by the church and on Saturdays went to the horrible black bridge at Constitution Station. One day I ventured to say to Cristina, "If we were to discover that this house was once inhabited by other people, what would you do, Cristina? Would you move away?"

"If other people lived in this house, they must have been like those sugar figurines on desserts, or birthday cakes: sweet as sugar. This house makes me feel secure. Is it the little garden by the entrance that makes me feel so calm? I don't know! I wouldn't move for all the money in the world. Besides, we don't have anywhere to go. You yourself said that some time ago."

I didn't insist, because it was so hopeless. To reconcile myself to the idea, I thought about how time would put things back as they had been.

One morning the doorbell rang. I was shaving and could hear Cristina's voice. When I finished shaving my wife was talking to the intruder. I spied on them through the crack in the door. The stranger had a deep voice and such enormous feet that I burst out laughing. "If you see Daniel again you'll pay dearly, Violeta."

"I don't know who Daniel is and my name isn't Violeta," my wife answered.

"You're lying."

"I don't lie. I have nothing to do with Daniel."

"I want you to know how things are."

"I don't want to listen to you."

Cristina covered her ears with her hands. I rushed to the door and told the intruder to get out. I could now closely see her feet, hands, and neck. I realized that it was a man dressed as a woman. I didn't have time to think what I should do; like a flash of lightning, he disappeared, leaving the door half open behind him.

Cristina and I never commented on the episode, though why I'll never know; it was as if our lips were sealed except for nervous, frustrated kisses, or useless words.

It was around that time, which was such an unhappy time for me, that Cristina suddenly started to sing spontaneously . Her voice was pleasant, but it exasperated me, being part of that secret world which drew her away from me. She had never sung before, so why did she sing now, day and night, as she dressed, bathed, cooked, or closed the blinds?

One day I heard Cristina say the enigmatic words, "I suspect I am inheriting someone's life, her joys and sorrows, mistakes and successes. I'm bewitched." I pretended not to have heard her tormented words. Nevertheless, I started, God knows why, to learn what I could in the neighborhood about who Violeta was, where she was, and all the details of her life.

Half a block from our house there was a shop where they sold postcards, paper, notebooks, pencils, erasers, and toys. For my purposes the shop clerk seemed like the best person: she was talkative, curious, and susceptible to flattery. Under the pretext of buying a notebook and pencils, I went to talk to her one afternoon. I complimented her eyes, hands, hair. I didn't venture to pronounce the word Violeta. I explained that we were neighbors. I finally asked her who had lived in our house. I said shyly, "Didn't someone named Violeta live there?"

She answered vaguely, which made me feel ever more uneasy. The next day I tried to find out some other details at the grocery store. They told me that Violeta was in a mental hospital and gave me the address.

"I sing with a voice that is not my own," Cristina told me, mysteriously once again. "Before, it would have upset me, but now I enjoy it. I'm someone else, perhaps someone happier than I."

Once more I pretended not to have heard her. I was reading the newspaper.

I confess I didn't pay much attention to Cristina, since I spent so much time and energy finding out details about Violeta's life. I went to the mental hospital, which was located in Flores. There I asked after Violeta and they gave me the address of Arsenia López, her voice teacher.

I had to take the train from Retiro Station to Olivos. On the way some dirt flew into my eyes, so that when I arrived at Arsenia López's house, tears were pouring out as if I were crying. From the front door I could hear women's voices singing scales, accompanied by a piano that sounded more like an organ.

Tall, thin, terrifying, Arsenia appeared at the end of a hallway, pencil in hand. I told her timidly that I had come for news of Violeta.

"You're her husband?"

"No, a relative," I answered, wiping my tears with a handkerchief.

"You must be one of her countless admirers," she told me, half closing her eyes and taking my hand. "You must have come for what they all want to know: What were Violeta's last days like? Please sit down. There's no reason to imagine that a dead person was necessarily pure, faithful, and good."

"You want to console me," I told her.

She pressed my hand with her moist hand and replied, "Yes, I want to console you. Violeta was not just my student; she was also my best friend. If she got angry with me, it was perhaps because she had confided too much in me and because she could no longer deceive me. The last days I saw her she complained bitterly about her fate. She died of envy. She repeated constantly, 'Somebody has stolen my life from me, but she'll pay for it. I will no longer have my velvet dress; she'll have it. Bruto will be hers; men will no longer disguise themselves as women to enter my house; I'll lose my voice, and it will pass to that unworthy throat; Daniel and I will no longer embrace on the bridge behind Constitution Station, imagining an impossible love, leaning over the iron railing as we used to, watching the trains go away.'"

Arsenia López looked me in the eyes and said, "Don't worry. You'll meet many other women who are more loyal. We both know she was beautiful, but is beauty the only good in the world?"

Speechless, horrified, I left that house without revealing my name to Arsenia López; when she said goodbye, she tried to hug me, to show her sympathy for me.

From then on, Cristina had become Violeta, at least as far as I was concerned. I tried following her day and night to find her in the arms of her lovers. I became so estranged from her that I viewed her as a complete stranger. One winter night she fled. I searched for her until dawn. I don't know who was the victim of whom in that house made of sugar, which now stands empty.

FORGOTTEN JOURNEY

SHE WAS trying to remember the day she was born. She furrowed her brows so much that the adults interrupted her telling her repeatedly to unwrinkle her forehead. That was why she couldn't reach the memory of her birth.

Before they were born, children were held at a large department store in Paris; their mothers ordered them, and sometimes went in person to pick them up. She would have liked to watch the package being unwrapped, the box in which the babies were shipped, but she never reached the houses of newborns quickly enough. They arrived quite hot from the trip because they couldn't breathe very well inside the box, and that was why they were so red and cried incessantly, their toes curled up.

But she had been born one morning in Palermo Park making nests for birds. She couldn't remember having gone out of her house that day; she had the feeling that she had made the trip without a car or a carriage, a trip full of mysterious shadows, and that she had woken up on a road lined with trees that smelled like Australian pines where she had suddenly found herself making nests for birds. The eyes of Micaela, her nursemaid, followed her like two guards. The making of the birds' nests wasn't easy; they had several rooms each: they even needed a bedroom and a kitchen.

The next day, when she returned to Palermo, she looked for the nests along the road lined with Australian pines. There weren't any left. She was about to cry when her nursemaid said, "The little birds have taken the nests up into the trees, which is why they are so happy this morning." But her cruel sister, who was three years older than she was, laughed, pointing with her linen glove at the Palermo gardener, a one-eyed man who was sweeping with a broom made of gray branches. In addition to the dead leaves he was sweeping up the last nest. At that moment, she felt like throwing up, as if she had heard the sound of hammocks in the backyard of her house.

Then time had passed, making the date of her birth seem desperately far away. Each memory was of a different baby girl, but all of them had her face. Each year she grew older the group of girls that surrounded her expanded.

Until one day, when she was playing in the study room, the daughter of the French chauffeur said, with atrocious bloodthirsty words, "Babies don't come from Paris," slowly adding, while looking around to see if the doors were listening, with unsuspected strength, "Babies come from the tummies of their mothers, and when they are born they come out through the belly button." Who knows what other words dark as sin emerged from Germaine's mouth, though she didn't even pale upon saying them.

That was when babies started to appear all over the place. Never before had so many children been born in her family. The women wore huge balloons on their stomachs; each time an adult spoke about a newborn an intense fire burned across her face and she bent down to the ground looking for a ring or a handkerchief that hadn't fallen. All eyes turned toward her like beacons lighting up her shame.

One morning, just out of her bath, watching the water swirling into the drain while her nursemaid wrapped her in a towel to dry her, she laughed and confided her horrible secret to Micaela. The nursemaid got very angry and assured her once again that babies came from Paris. She felt slightly relieved.

But when night returned, anguish mixed with the sounds of the street took hold of her whole body. She couldn't sleep even though her mother kissed her over and over before going to the theater. The kisses had lost their power.

And it was only after many days and many long dark nights—the enormous clock in the kitchen, the empty hallways of the house, the many grown-ups hiding behind doors—that she was lifted onto her mother's lap in the dressing room and her mother said that babies didn't come from Paris. Her mother spoke about flowers and birds, and everything mixed up with Germaine's horrible secrets. Still, she desperately believed that babies came from Paris.

A moment later, her mother said she was going to open the window, and after opening it, immediately her mother's face completely transformed: she was a lady in a feather-covered hat who just happened to be visiting the house. The window was almost shut, and when her mother told her that the sun was glorious, she saw the dark sky of night where no bird sang.

STRANGE VISIT

Before she would have lunch at a little table in the pantry and now she was allowed to have lunch at the big table. In the middle of the chatter, Leonor's eyes looked up through the windows searching for a bit of blue sky, but for the moment it was entirely covered with clouds. It was going to rain; she had been waiting for that day for a long time, because they had promised to take her to a house on the outskirts where she had only been once before. That was where a very tall man lived, isolated from the world perhaps by his height. He was a friend of Leonor's father and he had a daughter, two maids, and a gardener who lived in a tiny house with a spiral staircase. In the garden there was a tiny fountain with two conjoined tritons, with water coming out of their mouths, and a squat palm tree next to the wall of the house, and four rosebushes in double rows on either side of the path. Elena had incredibly black hair, and her face was so transparent that it was as if it had been erased; but all that was left of her hair was a very careful white knot, and her dress had five pleats in which Leonor's eyes got lost.

They had explored the house and the only thing that there was a lot of were hidden corners. They had gone up to the flat roof, from which it was possible to see the life of the neighboring houses, with retinues of clothes drying in the sun. They had hidden under the staircase and had grown weary when nobody came looking for them. They had peeked in the window of the study on the first floor where two men were talking, two men with faces as severe as their fathers', two men drowning in the seriousness of stiff collars and cigar smoke. Leonor, containing her laughter, squeezed her nose against the cold glass; her eyes had to travel across the expanse of a white curtain and a Diana the Huntress to reach her father who was sitting on a brown leather sofa. He hadn't taken off his overcoat, and yet, with the same gesture of drying his forehead on very hot days, he rubbed his face with his handkerchief up as far as his eyes, stopping as if he were about to cry. The noise of a sewing machine wrapped the house as if in a hem of silence and the only sound was the moaning that tears must make in order to squeeze out of closed eyes. Elena's father got up and came running over to the windowsill. After a while they heard the voices rise to the level where they were. Elena took the hand of Leonor, who was afraid, and they walked toward the playroom as if ordered to play, though they didn't play. Elena gave her a little medal that she lost three times on the floor while taking it out of a drawer. They said goodbye without looking at each other, with a kiss that brought their cheeks close together in the air.

In the car, on the way back, her father scolded her twice, and Leonor no longer believed that he had cried. Along the edges of his eyes she had seen the hardness of his wrinkled forehead and she couldn't reconcile the two images—one seen through the distant scene of the curtain, the other so near and in a remote region thanks to his ill humor sitting there in the car.

Leonor thought about Elena. The table was full of laughter during dessert. The sky turned darker and darker, and rain as fine as powdered sugar was falling. Leonor saw her father shaking his head and thinking that they wouldn't be going to Elena's house that day, and she felt a great ocean like the ones they showed her on maps that held her distant from the face she wanted to reach, and which they had erased from her memory, the face of Elena.

AUTOBIOGRAPHY OF IRENE

I NEVER felt so passionately eager to see Buenos Aires lit up on Independence Day, for sales at department stores festooned with green streamers, or for my birthday, as I was to arrive at this moment of supernatural joy.

Ever since I was a girl I've been as pale as I am now, "perhaps a little anemic," the doctor would say, "but healthy, like the whole Andrade family." On several occasions I imagined my death, while sitting before mirrors and holding a paper rose. Now that rose is in my hand (it was in a vase by my bed). A rose, a vain ornament smelling like a rag, with a name written on one of its petals. I don't need to smell it, to look at it: I know it's the very same one. Today I am dying, and my face is the very one I saw in the mirrors of my childhood. (I have hardly changed. Accumulated weariness, crying, and laughter have made my face more mature, forming and deforming it.) Every dwelling place seems old and familiar to me.

The unlikely reader of these pages will ask for whom I am telling this story. Perhaps the fear of not dying forces me to do so. Perhaps I write for myself: to read it over if by some curse I should keep on living. I need evidence that I am distressed only by the fear of not dying. I truly think that the only sad part about death, about the idea of death, is knowing that it cannot be remembered by the person who has died but solely, and sadly, by those who watched that person die.

My name is Irene Andrade. I was born twenty-five years ago in this yellow house, with balconies of black wrought iron and bronze plates bright as gold, six blocks from the church and square of Las

Flores. I am the oldest of four rambunctious children in whose childhood games I took a passionate part. My maternal grandfather was French; he died in a shipwreck that rendered the eyes of his portrait, venerated by guests in the shadows of the living room, misty and mysterious. My maternal grandmother was born in this town, a few hours after the first church burned down. Her mother, my great-grandmother, told her all the details of the fire that had hastened her birth. She passed those stories on to us. No one was better acquainted with that fire, with her own birth, with the main square sowed with alfalfa, with the death of Serapio Rosas, with the execution of two prisoners in 1860 near the atrium of the old church. I know my paternal grandparents only through two yellowing photographs, obscured in a kind of respectful haze. They look more like brother and sister than husband and wife; more like twins than mere siblings. They had the same thin lips, the same curly hair, the same detached hands resting idly on their laps, the same doting reserve. My father, who revered the education he had received from them, raised plants: he was as gentle with them as he was with his children, giving them remedies and water, covering them with canvas on cold nights, giving them the names of angels, and finally, "when they had grown," selling them with the utmost regret. He would caress the leaves as if caressing the hair of a child; I think that in his later years he talked to them, or at least that was my impression. All of this secretly annoyed my mother. She never told me as much, but in the tone of her voice, when she told her friends—"Leonardo is in there with his plants! He loves them more than his children!"—I guessed a perpetual mute impatience, the impatience of a jealous woman. My father was a man of average height, with beautiful, regular features, dark complexion and chestnut hair, and an almost blond beard. No doubt it is from him that I have inherited my seriousness, the admirable suppleness of my hair, the natural goodness of my heart, and my patience, a patience that might almost seem a fault, a sort of deafness, a bad habit. My mother, when she was younger, embroidered for a living: that sedentary life had filled her as if with still water, somewhat cloudy yet at the same time tranquil. No one rocked so elegantly in the rocking chair, no one handled fabric so eagerly. Now, she has that perfect kind of affectation that old age provides. In her I see only maternal whiteness, the severity of her gestures and voice: there are voices that you can see, that keep on revealing the expression of a face even after its beauty is gone. Thanks to that voice I can still recall her blue eyes and her high forehead. From her I must have inherited the whiteness of my skin, my fondness for reading or needlework, and a certain proud, disdainful shyness toward those who, even when they are shy, might be or at least seem to be modest.

Without bragging I can say that until I was fifteen, at the very least, I was the favorite at home because I was older and was a girl: circumstances most parents, who prefer boys and the younger siblings, would not have found so appealing.

Among the most vivid memories of my childhood I shall mention: a shaggy white dog named Jasmine; a Virgin four inches tall; the oil painting of my maternal grandfather which I have already mentioned; and a vine with trumpet-shaped orange flowers, called bignonia or war trumpet.

I saw the white dog in a kind of dream and later, more insistently, in my waking hours. I would tie him to the chairs with a rope, would give him food and water, would pet and punish him, would make him bark and bite. My loyalty to an imaginary dog, at the very time I scorned other more modest but more real toys, made my parents happy. I remember they would point at me proudly, telling the guests, "Look how she can entertain herself with nothing." They would frequently ask me about the dog, asking me to bring him into the living room or, at mealtimes, into the dining room; I obeyed enthusiastically. They pretended to see a dog that only I could see; they praised or teased him, to please or distress me.

The day my parents received a shaggy white dog from my uncle in Neuquén, nobody doubted that the dog's name was Jasmine or that my uncle had been a partner in my games. However, my uncle had been away for more than five years. I didn't write to him (I barely knew how to write). "Your uncle is a seer," I remember my parents saying at the moment they showed me the dog, "Here is Jasmine!" Jasmine recognized me without surprise; I kissed him.

Like a sky-blue triangle with golden borders, the Virgin began taking shape, acquiring density in the remoteness of a June sky. It was cold that year and the windows were dirty. I wiped them with my handkerchief, opening up little rectangles on the windowpanes. In one of those rectangles the sun lit up a cloak and a formless tiny, round red face that seemed sacrilegious to me at first. Beauty and saintliness were for me two inseparable virtues. I lamented the fact that her face wasn't beautiful. I cried for many nights, trying to alter it. I remember that this apparition impressed me more than the dog itself, because at the time I had a tendency toward mysticism. Churches and saints exerted a fascination on my spirit. I prayed secretly to the Virgin, offering her flowers and gleaming candies in little liqueur glasses, tiny mirrors, perfumes. I found a cardboard box about her size, and with ribbons and curtains I turned it into an altar. At first, when she watched me pray, my mother smiled with satisfaction; later, she was disturbed by the intensity of my fervor. One night by my bed, I heard her tell my father when they thought I was asleep, "Let's hope she doesn't turn into a saint! Poor thing, she doesn't bother anyone! She's so good!" She was also disturbed to see the empty box in front of a pile of wildflowers and votive candles, thinking that my fervor was leading to some sort of sacrilege. She tried to give me a Saint Anthony and a Saint Rose of Lima, relics that had belonged to her mother. I did not accept them; I told her that my Virgin was dressed in blue and gold. I showed her the size of the Virgin with my hands, explaining timidly that her face was small and red, sunburned, without any sweetness of expression, like the face of a doll, but shining like an angel's.

That same summer, at the market where my mother did her shopping, the Virgin appeared in a shopwindow: it was the Virgin of Luján. I didn't doubt that my mother had ordered it for me, nor was

I surprised that she had guessed the shape and color of the Virgin exactly, even the form of her mouth. I remember she complained of the price because it was damaged. She brought it home wrapped in newspaper.

My grandfather's painting, that majestic ornament of the living room, caught my attention when I was nine years old. Behind a red curtain, which made the image stand out even more, I discovered a frightening, dark world. Children sometimes find pleasure in such worlds. Deep, dark, vast expanses like green marble were trembling there, broken, icy, furious, tall, with scattered forms like mountains. Next to that painting I felt cold and tasted tears on my lips. Along wooden hallways, women with long hair and men in distress were fleeing, standing motionless. There was a woman covered with an enormous cape and a man whose face I never saw who walked, holding hands with a child carrying a rocking horse. It was raining somewhere; a tall flag was waving in the wind. That treeless landscape, so similar to the one I could see at dusk from the streets at the edge of town—so similar and at the same time so different—disturbed me. One summer day, sitting in an armchair, alone in front of the painting, I fainted. My mother said that when she woke me up I asked for water with my eyes closed. Thanks to the water she gave me, which she also used to cool my brow, I was saved from an unexpected, premature death.

One day at the end of spring, in the courtyard of our house, I saw the vine with orange flowers for the first time. When my mother sat knitting or embroidering, I would push off the boughs (which only I could see) so that they would not get in her way. I loved the orange color of the petals, the warlike name (confused with the history lessons I was studying at that time), and the light scent, like rain, given off by the leaves. One day, my brothers heard me utter its name and began speaking of San Martín and his grenadiers. In the endless afternoons, the gestures I made to pull the boughs from my mother's face, so they would not bother her, seemed intended to scare off the flies that sit aggressively still in certain points in space. Nobody foresaw the future vine. An inexplicable apprehensiveness prevented me from speaking of it before it arrived.

My father planted the vine in the very spot in the courtyard where I had anticipated its opulent form and color. It was in the very place where my mother would sit. (For some reason, perhaps because of the sun, my mother could not sit in any other corner of the courtyard; for some reason, perhaps for the very same reason, the vine could not be planted anywhere else.)

I was judicious and reserved. I'm not praising myself: these secondary virtues sometimes give rise to grave faults. Because of vanity or a lack of physical strength, I was more studious than my brothers. No lesson seemed new to me. I enjoyed the quiet that books afford. I enjoyed, above all else, the astonishment caused by my extraordinary facility for all kinds of study. Not all of my girlfriends liked me, and my favorite companion was solitude, which smiled on me during recess. I read at night, by candlelight. (My mother had forbidden me to read "because it was bad, not only for the eyes but also for the brain.") For a time I took piano lessons. The teacher called me "Irene the euphonious," and this nickname, which I did not understand and which other students repeated with sarcasm, offended me. I thought that my stillness, my seeming melancholy, and my pale face had inspired the cruel nickname "the cadaverous." For a teacher to make jokes about death seemed to me to be in poor taste; and one day, crying because I already knew how mistaken and how unfair I could be, I made up a slander against that young lady, who had only wanted to praise me. Nobody believed me, but one afternoon when we were alone in her living room, she took me by the hand and said, "How can you repeat such intimate, such awful things?" It was not a reproach: it was the beginning of a friendship.

I may have been happy, at least until I was fifteen. The sudden death of my father brought about a change in my life. My childhood was ending. I tried using lipstick and high heels. Men looked at me at the train station, and I had a boyfriend who waited for me on Sundays at the door of the church. I was happy, if happiness exists. I enjoyed being an adult, being beautiful, with a beauty criticized by some of my relatives.

I was happy, but the sudden death of my father, as I said before, brought about a change in my life. Three months before he died, I had already prepared my mourning dress and the black crepe; I had already cried for him, leaning majestically on the balcony railing. I had already written the date of his death on an etching; I had already visited the cemetery. All of that was made worse by the indifference I showed after the funeral. To tell the truth, after his death I never remembered him at all. My mother, a good soul, couldn't forgive me. Even now she looks at me with the same expression of rancor that, for the first time, had awoken in me the desire for death. Even now, after so many years, she cannot forget the mourning dress worn in advance, the date and name written on the etching, the unexpected visit to the cemetery, my indifference to his death at the very moment of our large family's greatest sorrow. Some people looked at me with suspicion. I couldn't hold back my tears when I heard certain bitter, ironic phrases, usually accompanied by a wink. (Only then did oblivion seem like bliss to me.) They said I was possessed by the devil; that I had wished for my father's death so that I could wear mourning and a jet-black clasp; that I had poisoned him so as to be able to spend my time at dances and at the train station without worrying about his prohibitions. I felt guilty at having unleashed such hatred around me. I spent long sleepless nights. I managed to get sick but was unable to die, as I had desired.

It had not occurred to me that I might have a supernatural gift, but when beings stopped seeming miraculous for me, I felt miraculous toward them. Neither Jasmine nor the Virgin (now broken and forgotten) existed. An austere future awaited me; my childhood grew more distant.

I felt guilty for the death of my father. I had killed him when I imagined him dead. Other people did not have this power.

Guilty and unlucky, I felt capable of infinite future joys, which only I could invent. I had projects for my happiness: my visions should be pleasant, I should be careful with my thoughts and try avoiding sad ideas, try inventing a happy world. I was responsible for everything that happened. I tried avoiding images of drought, floods, poverty, and illness when thinking about my family or acquaintances.

For a time this method seemed effective. But very soon I understood that my intentions were as vain as they were childish. At the entrance to a store I was forced to watch two men fight. I refused to see the concealed knife; I refused to see the blood. The struggle looked like a desperate embrace. It occurred to me that the death agony of one of them and the gasping terror of the other were a final sign of reconciliation. Without being able to erase the horrible image even for a moment, I was forced to witness the death in all its sharpness, the blood mixed with the dirt of the street, a few days later.

I tried to analyze the process, the form in which my thoughts developed. My visions were involuntary. It was not hard to recognize them; they always appeared in the company of certain unmistakable signs, which were always the same: a slight breeze, a curtain of mist, a tune I cannot sing, a door of carved wood, a clammy feeling in my palms, a little bronze statue in a distant garden. It was useless to try to avoid these images: in the icy regions of the future reality rules.

I then understood that to lose the ability to remember is one of the greatest misfortunes, since events, though infinite in the memory of normal beings, are extremely brief, indeed almost nonexistent, for one who foresees them and then merely experiences them. Those who do not know their destinies invent and enrich their lives with hopes of a future that will never turn out the way they imagine.

That imagined destiny, prior to the real one, exists in a sense, and is as necessary as the other. The lies my girlfriends spoke sometimes seemed truer than the truth. I have seen expressions of bliss on the faces of people who live on always frustrated hopes. I think that the essential lack of memories, in my case, did not proceed from a lack of memory: I think that my thoughts, so busy with seeing the future, so full of images, didn't have time to dwell on the past.

Leaning out on the balcony, I would see the children, on their way to school, passing by with the faces of grown-ups. That made me shy of children. I could see the future afternoons full of conversations, rosy or lilac clouds, births, terrible suffering, ambition, unavoidable cruelty against human beings and animals.

Now I understand the extent to which I viewed events as final memories. They replaced memories so inadequately. For instance: if I were not about to die, then this rose, right now here in my hand, would not live in my memory; I would lose it forever in a tumult of visions of a future destiny.

Hidden in the shadow of courtyards, of hallways, in the icy atrium of the church, I meditated constantly. I tried to take charge of my memories of my girlfriends, of my brothers, of my mother (always the most significant ones). It was then that the touching vision of a forehead, of certain eyes, of a face began to haunt and pursue me, forming my desires. That face lingered for many days and many nights before taking shape. The truth is: I had the burning desire to be a saint. I vehemently wished for the face to be God's or that of the infant Jesus. In church, in etchings, in books, and in medallions I searched for that adorable face: I didn't want to find it anywhere else, didn't want it to be human, or contemporary, or true. I don't think anyone has ever had so much trouble recognizing the danger signs of love. How I gave in to my adolescent tears! Only now can I remember the light yet penetrating aroma of the roses Gabriel gave me, while gazing into my eyes, as we left school. That prescience would have lasted a whole lifetime. In vain I tried to delay meeting him. I could foresee separation, absence, forgetting. In vain I tried to avoid the hours, paths, and places that favored a meeting. My prescient caution should have lasted a whole lifetime. But destiny put the roses in my hands and put the real Gabriel before me without my feeling surprise. My tears were useless. Uselessly I copied the roses on paper, writing names and dates on the petals: a rose can be invisible forever in a rose garden, before our window, or in the hands of the lover who offers it to us; only memory will preserve it intact, with its perfume, its color, and the devotion of the hands offering it.

Gabriel would be playing with my brothers, but when I appeared with a book or with my sewing basket, and sat down on a chair in the courtyard, he would leave his games to offer me the homage of his silence. Few children were as astute. He made little airplanes of flower petals, of leaves. He caught fireflies and bats; then he tamed them. From closely watching the movements of my hands, he learned to embroider. He embroidered without blushing: architects made house plans; he, when he embroidered, made plans of gardens. He loved me: at night, in the dark courtyard of my house, I could feel his involuntary love growing with all the naturalness of a plant.

Without knowing it, how I hoped to penetrate the chaste memory of those moments! Without knowing it, how I yearned for death, the only keeper of my memories! A hypnotic fragrance, the rustling of eternal leaves on the trees, comes to guide me along the paths, now so long forgotten, of that love. Sometimes an event that seemed labyrinthine to me, so slow to develop, so practically infinite can be expressed in two words. My name, written in green ink or with a pin, on his arm, on him who filled six months of my life, now fills only a single sentence. What is it to be in love? For years I asked the piano teacher and my girlfriends. What is it to be in love? Remembering a word, a look within the complexity of other spaces; multiplying and dividing and transforming these things (as if they were displeasing to us), comparing them unceasingly. What is a beloved face? A face that is never the same, a face that is ceaselessly transformed, a face that disappoints us...

A silence of cloisters and roses was in our hearts. No one could guess the mystery that linked us. Not even those colored pencils or the jujube candies or the flowers he bestowed on me gave us away. He would write my name on the trunks of trees with his penknife, and when he was being punished he would write it with chalk on the wall.

"When I die I will give you candies every day and write your name on all the tree trunks in heaven," he once told me.

"How do you know we'll go to heaven?" I answered. "How do you know there are trees and penknives in heaven? Are you sure that God will let you remember me? Are you sure that in heaven your name will be Gabriel and mine Irene? Will we have the same faces, and will we recognize each other?"

"We'll have the same faces. And even if we didn't, we would recognize each other. That day during Carnival celebrations, when you dressed up as a star and spoke with an icy voice, I recognized you. With my eyes closed, I've seen you so many times since then."

"You've seen me when I wasn't there. You've seen me in your imagination."

"I saw you when we were playing nurse and patient. When I was the one who was wounded and they were blindfolding my eyes, I guessed when you were coming."

"Because I was the nurse, and I had to come. You could see me under the blindfold: You were cheating. You always cheated."

"In heaven I'll recognize you without cheating. I'd recognize you even in disguise, I'd see you coming even with my eyes blindfolded."

"Then you believe there'll be no difference between this world and heaven?"

"Only what bothers us now will be lacking: some family members, bedtime hours, punishments, and the moments when I don't see you."

"Perhaps it's better in hell than in heaven," he said to me another day, "because hell is more dangerous and I like suffering for you. To live in flames because of your guilt, to save you continually from the demons and fire, would be a source of joy for me."

"But do you want to die in mortal sin?"

"Why mortal and not immortal? Nobody forgets my uncle: he committed a mortal sin and they didn't give him the last rites. My mother told me, 'He's a hero—don't listen to what people say.'"

"Why do you think about death? Usually young people avoid such dark, depressing topics of conversation," I protested one day. "Right now you look like an old man. Look at yourself in the mirror."

There was no mirror nearby. He looked at himself in my eyes.

"I don't look like an old man. Old men comb their hair in a different way. But I'm already grown up, and familiar with death," he answered. "Death is like an absence. Last month, when my mother took me to Azul for two weeks, my heart stopped and, with deep sorrow, I felt not blood coursing through my veins but cold water. Soon I will have to go far away, indefinitely. I console myself imagining something simpler: death or war."

Sometimes he lied to move me to pity: "I'm sick. Last night I fainted in the street."

If I criticized him for lying, he'd answer, "One only lies to people one loves: truth leads us to make many errors."

"I'll never forget you, Gabriel." The day I said that I had already forgotten him.

Without anxiety, without weeping, already accustomed to his absence, I withdrew from him before he left. A train pulled him from my side. Other visions already separated me from his face, other loves, less touching farewells. I last saw his face through the pane of the train window, sad and in love, erased by the superimposed images of my future life.

My life turned sad, but not for lack of amusements. Once I confused my own destiny with that of a character in a novel. I should confess:

I confused the face of an illustration I foresaw with a real face. I waited for a conversation between two characters that I later read in a book which was set in an unknown city in 1890. The antiquated clothing of the characters didn't surprise me. "How fashions are going to change," I thought with indifference. The figure of a king, who didn't look like a king because he only appeared in the plate of a history book, devoted his fond glances to me in the autumn twilight. Up until then, the texts and characters of books had not appeared to me as future realities; it's true that before I never had the chance to read many books. The books belonging to one of my grandfathers were stored in a room at the back of the house; bound with twine and wrapped in spiderwebs, I first saw them when my mother decided to sell them all. For several days we inspected the books, dusting the volumes with rags and feather dusters, gluing back the loose pages. I read during the moments I was alone.

Far from Gabriel, I understood by some miracle that only death would let me recover his memory. The afternoon when no other visions, no other images, when no other future disturbed me would be the afternoon of my death, and I knew I would wait for it holding this rose. I knew that the tablecloth I would embroider for months on end, with yellow daisies and pink forget-me-nots, with garlands of yellow wisteria and a gazebo surrounded by palm trees, would be used for the first time the night of my wake. I knew that this tablecloth would be praised by the guests who had made me weep ten years earlier, when I heard the voices, a chorus of female voices, repeating my name, disfiguring it with sad adjectives: "Poor Irene," "Unfortunate Irene!" Then I heard other names, not people's names but those of little cakes and plants, uttered with pained admiration: "What delightful palm trees," "What madeleines!" But then with the same sadness, and with the insistence of a psalm, the chorus repeated, "Poor Irene!"

The false splendor of death! The sun shines on the same world. Nothing has changed when everything has changed for only one being. Moses foresaw his own death. Who was Moses? I thought that no one had ever foreseen his own death. I thought that Irene Andrade, this modest Argentine woman, had been the only one in the world capable of describing her death before it happened.

I lived, waiting for life's limit that would draw me closer to memory. I had to put up with infinite moments. I had to love the mornings as if they were the last ones; I had to love certain shadows in the main square and Armindo's eyes; I had to get sick from typhus fever and cut my hair. I met Teresa, Benigno; I visited the Fountain of Love and the Sentinel in Tandil for the first time. In Monte, in the railroad station, with my mother I drank tea with milk after visiting a lady who taught needlework and knitting. In front of the Garden Hotel I saw the death agony of a horse that looked as if it was made of clay. (It was tormented by flies and by a man with a whip.) I never went to Buenos Aires: some calamity always prevented the trip I planned. I never saw the dark outline of the train in Constitution Station. Now I never will. I will die without seeing Palermo Park, the Plaza de Mayo all lit up, and the Colón Theater with its boxes and its desperate artists singing, their hands on their breasts.

I agreed to being photographed against a sad backdrop of trees with beautiful, tall hair, wearing gloves and a straw hat decorated with red cherries, so battered they looked real.

Slowly, I carried out the last episodes of my destiny. I will confess that I was oddly mistaken when I foresaw the photograph of myself: although I found it similar, I didn't recognize my own image. I felt indignant with that woman who, without neglecting my imperfections, had usurped my eyes, the position of my hands, the careful oval of my face.

For those who remember, time is not too long. For those who wait it is inexorable.

"In a small town everything is quickly over. There won't be any new houses or new people to meet," I thought, trying to console myself. "Here death arrives more quickly. If I had been born in Buenos

Aires, my life would have been interminable, my sorrows would never end."

I remember the solitude of the afternoons when I sat in the square. Would the light hurt my eyes so I would weep of something other than sorrow? "She's thirty years old and still has not married," some glances told me. "What is she waiting for," others said, "sitting here in the square? Why doesn't she bring her sewing? Nobody loves her, not even her brothers. When she was fifteen she killed her father. The devil possessed her—God knows in what form."

These dreary, monotonous visions of the future depressed me, but I knew that in the rarefied space of my life, where there was no love, no faces, no new objects, where nothing happened anymore, my torment was coming to its end, my happiness was beginning. Trembling, I was coming closer to the past.

The coldness of a statue took possession of my hands. A veil separated me from the houses, drew me away from the plants and people: nonetheless I saw them clearly outlined for the first time, minutely present in every detail.

One January afternoon, I was sitting on a bench by the fountain in the square. I remember the stifling heat of the day and the unusual coolness brought on by the sunset. Surely somewhere it had rained. My head rested on my hand; in my hand was a handkerchief: a sad pose, at times inspired by the heat, yet at that moment inspired by sorrow. Someone sat down next to me. She spoke to me with a woman's soft voice. This was our exchange:

"Excuse my impertinence. There isn't time for formal introductions. I don't live in this town; chance brings me here from time to time. Even if someday I will sit in this square again, it's unlikely that our conversation will be repeated. Perhaps I'll never see you again, not even in a store, or on a railway platform, or in the street."

"My name is Irene," I replied. "Irene Andrade."

"Were you born here?"

"Yes, I was born and will die in this town."

"I never thought about dying in a particular place, no matter how sad or enchanting it might be. I never thought of my death as a possibility."

"I didn't choose this town to die in. Destiny assigns places and dates without consulting us."

"Destiny decides things but doesn't participate in them. How do you know you'll die in this town? You're young and you don't look sick. One thinks of death when one is sad. Why are you sad?"

"I'm not sad. I've no fear of dying and destiny has never disappointed me. These are my final afternoons. These pink clouds will be the last ones, shaped like saints, like houses, like lions. Your face will be the last new face; your voice will be the last one I hear."

"What has happened to you?"

"Nothing has happened to me and, happily enough, few things are left that will happen to me. I feel no curiosity. I don't want to know your name, I don't want to look at you: new things disturb me and only delay my death."

"Haven't you ever been happy? Don't certain memories fill you with hope?"

"I have no memories. The angels will bring back all my memories on the day of my death. The cherubim will bring back the forms of all the faces. They will bring back all the hairstyles and ribbons, the positions of arms, past shapes of hands. The seraphim will bring me taste, sound, and fragrances, the flowers I received as gifts, landscapes. The archangels will bring back conversations and farewells, light, the silence of reconciliation."

"Irene, it seems to me as if I've known you for a long time! I've seen your face somewhere, perhaps in a photograph, with tall hair, ribbons of velvet, and a hat decorated with cherries. Isn't there such a picture of you, with a sad backdrop of trees? Didn't your father sell plants a long time ago? Why do you want to die? Don't lower your eyes. Don't you admit the world is beautiful? You want to die because everything becomes more definitive and more beautiful at times of parting."

"For me death will be a time of arrival, not of parting."

"Arrival is never pleasant. Some people couldn't even arrive in heaven and feel happy. One must get used to faces, to the places one has most loved. One must get used to voices, to dreams, to the sweetness of the country."

"I'll never arrive anywhere for the first time. I recognize everything. Even heaven sometimes scares me. The fear of its images, the fear of recognizing it all!"

"Irene Andrade, I'd like to write your biography."

"Ah! What a favor you would do me if you could help me cheat my destiny by not writing my biography. But you will write it. I can already see the pages, the clear script, and my sad destiny. It will begin like this:

I never felt so passionately eager to see Buenos Aires lit up on Independence Day, for sales at department stores festooned with green streamers, or for my birthday, as I was to arrive at this moment of supernatural joy.

Ever since I was a girl I've been as pale as I am now...

THE CLOCK HOUSE

Dear miss x,

Since I have always excelled in your classes with my compositions, I will keep my word: I will practice by writing letters to you. You ask what I did during the last few days of my vacation.

As I write to you, Joaquina is snoring. It's siesta time and as you know, now and at night Joaquina snores more than usual because she has a fleshy nose. It's too bad because she doesn't let anybody sleep. I am writing to you in my notebook from school because the letter paper I got from Pituco doesn't have any lines and my writing goes all over the place. Julia, the puppy, is asleep under my bed; she cries when moonlight comes in the window, but that doesn't matter to me because even Joaquina's snoring doesn't wake me up.

We took a trip to Laguna Salada. Swimming is wonderful. I sank up to my knees in the mud. I gathered herbs for the herbarium and also, among the trees some ways off, I gathered eggs for my collection: ringdove, magpie, and partridge eggs. The partridges don't lay their eggs in the trees but on the ground, poor things. I had a great time at the lagoon—we made mud castles—but I had even more fun last night at the party Ana María Sausa gave for little Rusito's baptism. The whole patio was decorated with paper lanterns and streamers. They set four tables, made out of boards and sawhorses, with all kinds of food and drink; it made you hungry just looking at it. They didn't have hot chocolate because of the milk strike and because my father gets overexcited just at the sight of it and it's bad for his liver.

That day, Estanislao Romagán put aside the pile of clocks he was working on to see how the preparations for the party were coming along and to help out a little (he who even on Sundays and holidays never stops working). I was very fond of Estanislao Romagán. Do you remember that hunchbacked watchmaker who fixed your clock? The one who lived on the flat roof of this building in the little hut he built himself that looked like a doghouse? I called it the Clock House. The one who specialized in alarm clocks? Who knows, maybe you've forgotten him, though I can hardly believe that! Watches and hunchbacks can't be forgotten just like that. Well, that was Estanislao Romagán. He would show me pictures of a sundial that triggered cannons at noon; of another clock that wasn't a sundial, that looked like a fountain on the outside; and of another, the Edinburgh clock, with a stairway, cars, horses, figures of women in tunics, and strange little men. You'll scarcely believe me, but it was wonderful to hear the different noises of all the alarm clocks going off, and the clocks striking the hour a thousand times a day. My father didn't agree. For the party, Estanislao pulled out a suit he had stored in a little trunk between two ponchos, a blanket, and three pairs of shoes that belonged to someone else. The suit was wrinkled, but Estanislao, after washing his face and combing his hair, which is very shiny and black and reaches almost to his eyebrows like a Spanish beret, looked quite elegant.

"Sitting down, with your head resting on the pillow, you will look very good. You have good posture, better than that of most of the guests," my mother commented.

"Let me touch your back," said Joaquina, running around the house after him.

He let her touch his back because he was very kind.

"And who will bring me good luck?" he said.

"You're a lucky man," responded Joaquina, "you have all the luck in the world."

But to me it seemed unfair to say that to him. What do you think, Miss X?

The party was wonderful. Whoever says otherwise is a liar. Pirucha danced rock and roll and Rosita did Spanish dances, which she does well even though she is blond.

We ate club sandwiches that were already rather dry, pink meringues, the little tiny ones that taste like perfume, and cake and candies. The drinks were delicious. Pituco mixed them, shook them, and served them like a real waiter in a restaurant. Everybody gave me a little of this, a little of that, and that way I was able to come up with at least three glassfuls altogether.

Iriberto asked me, "Hey, kid, how old are you?"

"Nine."

"Did you have anything to drink?"

"No, not even a sip," I answered, because I was ashamed.

"Well, then, have this glass."

And he made me drink something that burned my throat all the way down. He laughed and said, "That way you will be a man."

It's not right to do these things to a child, don't you think, Miss X?

People were very jolly. My mother, who hardly ever talks, was chattering away with some woman, and Joaquina, who is shy, danced by herself, singing a Mexican song she didn't know by heart. I, who am so unsociable, even talked with the mean old man who always tells me to go to hell. It had gotten late by the time Estanislao finally came down from his hut all dressed and brushed, apologizing for his wrinkled suit. They gave him a round of applause and something to drink. He got lots of attention; they offered him the best sandwiches, the best sweets, the tastiest drinks. One girl, the prettiest one, I think, in the whole group, picked a flower from a vine and stuck it in his buttonhole. You could say that he was king of the party; he grew happier and happier with each drink. The ladies showed him watches that were broken or didn't work right, though they all wore them on their wrists nevertheless. He looked at them smiling, promising to fix them at no charge. He apologized again for wearing such a wrinkled suit and said with a laugh that it was because he wasn't used to going to parties. Then Gervasio Palmo, who has a laundry around the corner, came up to him and said, "Let's iron it right away in my laundry. What are laundries for if not to press the suits of our friends?"

Everyone welcomed the idea enthusiastically. Even Estanislao, who is a very moderate man, cried with joy and danced a few steps in time to the music from a radio that was in the middle of the patio. That's how the pilgrimage to the laundry started. My mother, who was sad because they had broken the prettiest knickknack in the house and had messed up a macramé rug, held my arm. "Don't go, sweetheart. Help me clean things up."

Paying about as much attention as if the cat had spoken to me (please believe me), I went running after Estanislao, Gervasio, and the rest of the group. Except for Estanislao's clock house my favorite place in the whole neighborhood is the La Mancha Laundry. Inside there are hat blocks, huge irons, things with steam coming out of them, gigantic bottles, and a fish tank in the window with goldfish in it. Gervasio Palmo's partner, whose name is Nakoto, is Japanese, and the fish tank belongs to him. Once he gave me a little plant but it died a couple of days later. How could he expect a kid to take care of a plant? Those things are for grown-ups to care for, don't you think, Miss X? But Nakoto wears glasses, and he has very sharp teeth and enormous eyes; I didn't dare tell him that what I really wanted him to give me was one of the fish. Anyone who knew me would understand.

By then it had gotten dark. We walked for half a block, singing a song off-key that we made up. Gervasio Palmo, at the door to the laundry, looked for the keys in his pocket; it took him a while to find them because he had so many. When he opened the door, we all crowded together and nobody would go in, until Gervasio Palmo called us to order with his thunderous voice. Nakoto made us move to one side, and turned on the lights in the shop, taking off his glasses. We went into an enormous room I had never seen before. I stopped for a moment in front of something that looked like a horse's saddle, to look at where they would press Estanislao's suit.

"Shall I take it off?" asked Estanislao.

"No," responded Gervasio, "don't bother. We'll iron it with you in it."

"And the hump?" asked Estanislao, timidly.

It was the first time that I had ever heard that word, but I figured out what it meant by the context. (You can see I'm working on improving my vocabulary.)

"We'll iron it for you too," answered Gervasio, patting him on the shoulder.

Estanislao lay down on a long table, following Nakoto's instructions. Nakoto was getting the irons ready. A smell of ammonia and different chemicals made me sneeze: I covered my mouth with a handkerchief, as you taught me to, Miss X, but in spite of that someone called me a pig, which seemed to me like bad manners. What sort of example was that for a child? Nobody was laughing except for Estanislao. All of the men were bumping into things: into the furniture, the doors, the tools, one another. They brought wet rags, bottles, irons. Though you may not believe me, the whole thing resembled a surgical operation. A man fell down on the ground, tripping me so badly that I almost killed myself. Then, at least for me, the fun part was over. I started throwing up. You know I have a healthy stomach and that my classmates at school call me an ostrich because I can swallow anything. I don't know what happened to me. Someone grabbed me, pulled me out of there, and took me home.

I didn't see Estanislao Romagán again. Lots of people came to look at the watches and a van from Parcae Watch Repair Shop came and took away the last ones, among them my favorite, the one that looked like a wooden house. When I asked my mother where Estanislao was, she didn't feel like answering me properly. As if she were talking to the dog, she told me, "He went away," but her eyes were red from weeping over the macramé rug and the knickknack, and she made me shut up when I mentioned the laundry.

You can't imagine what I'd do to have news of Estanislao. When I find out I'll write to you again.

With warmest regards, your favorite student,

N. N.

MIMOSO

MIMOSO had been on his deathbed for five days. Mercedes fed him milk, juice, and tea with a little spoon. Mercedes called the taxidermist on the phone, giving him the height and length of the dog and inquiring about prices. Embalming him was going to cost a month's salary. She hung up and thought of taking him there right away so he wouldn't spoil. When she looked in the mirror she saw that her eyes were very swollen from crying; she decided to wait until Mimoso was dead. Sitting next to the kerosene stove, she filled a saucer and started giving the dog spoonfuls of milk again. He no longer opened his mouth and the milk spilled onto the floor. At eight o'clock her husband arrived; they cried together, consoling themselves with the thought of the embalming. They imagined the dog standing with glass eyes by the entrance to the room, symbolically guarding the house.

The next morning Mercedes put the dog in a sack. Maybe he wasn't completely dead yet. She made a package with burlap and newspaper so as not to attract attention on the bus and took him to the taxidermist.

In a display case at the house she saw many embalmed birds, monkeys, and snakes. She had to wait. The man appeared in shirtsleeves, smoking an Italian cigar. He took the package, saying, "You've brought the dog. How do you want it?" Mercedes seemed not to understand. The man took out an album of drawings. "Do you want him to be sitting, lying down, or standing up? On a wood mount painted black or white?"

Mercedes looked without saying anything for a moment, before replying, "Sitting down, with his little paws crossed."

"With his paws crossed?" the man repeated, as if he didn't like the idea.

"However you want them," Mercedes said, blushing.

It was hot, stiflingly hot. Mercedes took off her coat.

"Let's look at the animal," the man said, opening the package. He took Mimoso by the back paws, and continued, "He's not as plump as his owner," laughing loudly. He looked her up and down; she lowered her eyes and saw her breasts through her tight sweater. "When you see him, he'll be good enough to eat."

Abruptly, Mercedes put on her coat. She squeezed her black kid gloves in her hands and said, keeping herself from slapping the man or taking the dog away from him, "I want him to have a wood stand like that one," pointing to one with a carrier pigeon on it.

"I can see that madam has good taste," the man mumbled. "And how do you want the eyes? Glass eyes are a little more expensive."

"Glass eyes," Mercedes answered, biting on her gloves.

"Green, blue, or yellow?"

"Yellow," said Mercedes vehemently. "He had yellow eyes like butterflies."

"Have you ever seen the eyes of a butterfly?"

"Like the wings," Mercedes protested, "like the wings of butterflies."

"That's more like it. You'll have to pay in advance," the man said.

"I know," Mercedes answered, "you told me that on the phone." She opened her wallet and took out the bills; she counted them and left them on the table. The man gave her a receipt. "When will he be ready to be picked up?" she asked, putting away the receipt in her wallet.

"There's no need for that. I'll bring him to your house on the twentieth of next month."

"I'll come pick him up with my husband," Mercedes answered, suddenly rushing out of the house.

Mercedes's friends found out that the dog had died and wanted to know what they had done with the body. Mercedes told them that they were having him embalmed, and nobody believed her. Many people laughed. She decided it was better to say they had dumped him somewhere. Holding her knitting, she sat like Penelope, awaiting the arrival of the embalmed dog. But the dog didn't come. Mercedes was still crying and drying her tears with a flowered handkerchief.

On the appointed day Mercedes got a phone call: the dog had been embalmed, and all they had to do was go and get him. They lived too far away for delivery. Mercedes and her husband went to fetch the dog in a taxi.

"We have spent so much on this dog," Mercedes's husband said in the cab, watching the numbers going up.

"A child wouldn't have cost more," said Mercedes, taking a handkerchief out of her pocket and drying her tears.

"Well, that's enough; you've already cried plenty."

At the taxidermist's they had to wait. Mercedes didn't talk, but her husband was looking at her attentively.

"Won't people say you're crazy?" her husband inquired with a smile.

"So much the worse for them," responded Mercedes, vehemently. "They are heartless, and life is very sad for the heartless. Nobody loves them."

"I think so too, sweetie."

The taxidermist brought the dog almost too promptly. There was Mimoso, mounted on a piece of dark, varnished wood, half sitting, with glass eyes and a varnished mouth. He had never looked in better health. He was fat, well groomed, and shiny; the only thing he couldn't do was talk. Mercedes caressed him with trembling hands; tears burst from her eyes and fell on the dog's head.

"Don't get him wet," said the taxidermist. "And wash your hands."

"He looks as if he could talk," said Mercedes's husband. "How do you accomplish such miracles?"

"With poison, sir. I do it all with poison, wearing gloves and glasses, otherwise I would poison myself. It's my own system. You don't have any children in your house?"

"No."

"Will he be a danger to us?" asked Mercedes.

"Only if you eat him."

"We have to wrap him up," said Mercedes, after wiping away her tears.

The taxidermist wrapped the embalmed animal in newspaper and gave Mercedes's husband the package. They went out joyfully. On the way they talked about where they would put Mimoso. They chose the foyer of the house, next to the telephone table, where Mimoso would wait for them when they went out.

At home, after examining the taxidermist's work, they placed the dog in the chosen spot. Mercedes sat next to him, admiringly: this dead dog would keep her company just as the same dog had kept her company when he was alive, would defend her from thieves and from society. She caressed his head with her fingertips and, at a moment when she believed that her husband was not watching, she gave him a furtive kiss.

"What will your friends say when they see this?" her husband inquired. "What will the bookseller at Merluchi's say?"

"When he comes to dinner I will put Mimoso away in the dresser or say he's a present from the lady on the third floor."

"You'll have to tell the lady that."

"Yes, I will," said Mercedes.

That night they drank a very special wine and went to bed later than usual.

The lady on the third floor smiled when Mercedes made her request. She understood the perversity of a world in which a woman couldn't have her dog embalmed without people thinking her crazy.

Mercedes was happier with the embalmed dog than she had been with the live one; she didn't have to feed him, didn't have to take him outside, didn't have to bathe him, and he didn't mess up the house or chew on the rug. But happiness never lasts. Evil talk arrived in the form of an anonymous letter. An obscene drawing illustrated the words. Mercedes's husband shook with indignation: the hot oven was cooler than his heart. He took the dog on his knee, broke him in various pieces as if he were a dry branch, and threw him in the open oven.

"Whether or not what they say is true doesn't matter, what matters is that they're saying it."

"You'll not keep me from dreaming about him," Mercedes cried, going to bed still dressed. "I know who the perverse man is who sends these anonymous letters. It's that vendor of pornography. He'll never set foot in this house again."

"You'll have to receive him. He's coming to dinner tonight."

"Tonight?" said Mercedes. She jumped out of bed and ran into the kitchen to make dinner, a smile on her lips. She put the steak next to the pieces of dog in the oven.

She made dinner earlier than usual.

"We're having meat cooked in the hide," Mercedes announced.

At the door, even before saying hello, the guest rubbed his hands when he smelled what was in the oven. Later, when he was being served, he said, "These animals look as if they were embalmed," looking with wonder at the dog's eyes.

"In China," Mercedes said, "I'm told they eat dogs. Is that true or is it a shaggy-dog story?"

"I don't know. In any case, I wouldn't eat them for anything in the world."

"You should never say 'dog eat dog,'" responded Mercedes with a charming smile.

The guest was amazed that Mercedes could talk so frankly about dogs.

"We'll have to call the barber," said the guest, seeing some hairs in his meat cooked in the hide, and, with a hearty, contagious laugh, he asked, "Do you eat meat cooked in the hide with sauce?"

"It's a new recipe," Mercedes answered.

The guest served his plate from the platter, sucked on a piece of meat covered with sauce, chewed on it, and fell over dead.

"Mimoso still defends me," said Mercedes, picking up the plates and drying her tears, for she was laughing and crying at the same time.

THE SIBYL

THE TOOLS of my trade are in the police station: gold wristwatch, gloves, piece of wire, wooden box with lock and key, flashlight, pliers, screwdriver, and briefcase (to look more serious I always carry a briefcase). Weapons? I never wanted them. What are my hands for? I say. They are iron claws; if they don't strangle, they punch hard, God willing.

Lately I've felt discouraged. There's so much competition, so much poverty. Everyone knows that! The life of a butcher is less tedious than ours. At night, I didn't feel like going out for a walk, to roam around certain blocks and acquaint myself with some particular neighborhood of Buenos Aires or a certain house; I felt utterly bored. In the northern part of the city, I liked Palermo because of its fountains and lakes, places where you can drink and wash the nails of your several fingers; in the southern part of the city, I liked Constitution, no doubt because there I met my comrades on the escalator while going up and down, down and up, pursuing our vocation. I sat in the squares, eating oranges or bread, or, when I was lucky, salami or cream cheese. Sometimes the passersby would look at me as if they noticed something strange about me. I don't wear a beard to my navel, or go around with my toenails showing, or have gold teeth or enormous birthmarks between my eyebrows. The other day I asked one of them, "Do I have two noses?" forgetting my responsibility, my age, my situation. Perhaps my blue flannel pants are loud, with a zipper instead of buttons in the crotch. Everything you do to avoid attracting attention to yourself ends up attracting it. What can you do? If I slide along like a worm, everybody notices how I walk. If I dress badly, the color of trees or walls or dirt, everyone looks at my clothing. If I try not to raise my voice, God help me, everybody strains to hear me. Eating ice cream is impossible for me. The girls stare and nudge one another with their elbows. Sometimes it's not pleasant to be nice to women; I have to hear silly things all day long. Luckily, I can no longer hear out of one ear. I turned deaf at sixteen. They punctured my eardrum with a splinter. I lived with my family in Punta Chica, in a house built on pilings. One night, when I had put catfish in their beds as a joke, my father, who is always in a foul mood, and my brothers, who are grouchy, plucked up their courage and held me down on the floor. While the others held me, one of them stuck the splinter in my ear. After that, of course, so that I wouldn't talk, they stuffed me in a sack and threw me into the river. The neighbors saved me. It seemed strange to me. Later I found out that they did it to make me talk. People are so curious! Everybody hates me, except for women; nevertheless, Miss Rómula, who lives by the store, summoned me one day because I had killed a cat with a blow to the head near the door of her room. "You scoundrel," she said, "can't you do such things somewhere else?"

How could a few drops of blood on the floor bother her? They can be wiped up in a couple of seconds. She never forgave me. She's lazy, that's what she is. When they hired me at the Firpo Pharmacy, people started staring at me like I was a guy who attracts attention. "Sluggard," they called me when I ran, "Express Train" when I walked slowly, "Pigpen" when I had bathed, "Palmolive" when I hadn't. But what most infuriated me was when they called me "Pizza," unfairly, because they saw me one day, while I was making deliveries on my bicycle, eating a piece of Easter cake that Susana Plombis put in my pocket for a snack.

It was then that I got familiar with the interiors of many houses. None of them made such an impression on me as Aníbal Celino's, probably because I entered through the front door. In the other houses I had to go in through the kitchen. I still have some spoons, some silver saltshakers, which I took from the drawers while the servants were looking for money to pay the bill, things that were of no use to me. Aníbal Celino's house was no less than a palace. The first time they sent me there with a package from the Firpo Pharmacy, the service entrance looked like the front door and I searched for the other one, thinking that it was the service entrance because it was so dirty. I'm well acquainted with today's houses. A very luxurious house is a dirty house. The door was closed but it opened when I banged the door knocker, a bronze lion's face biting a bronze ring. I stepped inside and couldn't see anyone. I stepped out again and there in the garden I noticed the unkempt wigs of some palm trees. What trees! Even a dog wouldn't like them. I went back in: the door opened by itself. There was still no one there. I bumped straight into a marble staircase with a balustrade as shiny as the lion on the door knocker. Then a few steps later I entered an enormous room full of glass cabinets; it looked like a store or a church. All around me I saw statues, candy dishes, miniatures, necklaces, fans, reliquaries, dolls. I saw a candy dish, gold colored with turquoise inlay, and absent-mindedly picked it up and put it in my pocket. Next I picked up a little figurine that was glittering on a table and dropped it into my other pocket. (My pockets have double bottoms, in case of need. Rosaura Pansi is in charge of lining them. I give her lots of presents and the poor thing is so grateful it's embarrassing.) As I left the living room I heard a little noise on the staircase, maybe a mouse. My heart stopped, for I saw a very young girl, sitting on the bottom step, watching me with a mischievous expression. She made me laugh.

"I have a package from the Firpo Pharmacy," I told her.

"What a shame!" she answered. "Then you are not the Lord."

"So I'm not a gentleman? What am I, then? I've brought a bottle of rubbing alcohol, milk of magnesia, and rice powder," I said, reading the bill.

"This isn't the service entrance. Go out"—she said, taking the bill from me and looking at it—"around the corner. There they will receive you."

I wanted to strangle the girl; she was as white and smooth as the porcelain angel I once saw in a display case in a store for religious artifacts.

"Aren't all the doors the same?"

"All of them," she replied, "except the door to heaven."

"So why don't you accept the package and pay for it?"

"Because I don't have money to pay any bills; I only have money to give away or to lose."

"To give to whom?"

"To give to anybody who's not a member of my family or one of my friends."

"And how do you lose it?"

"Lose it? In a thousand different ways."

She took a change purse full of silver coins out of the pocket of her smock and lined up the coins in a row along the step.

"You lose coins when you play with them to read a fortune," she said, "throw them into fountains, or wherever. What matters is that they disappear. What good are coins?"

She seemed a little less repulsive to me and I said to her, "Goodbye, Kitty."

"'My name is Aurora," she answered with a bossy tone.

"Is it my fault that you have the eyes of a cat? Are you angry?"

She didn't answer me and ran skipping up the staircase.

For some time I didn't see Aurora again, no matter how often I went to her house to make deliveries.

When they fired me from the Firpo Pharmacy, I met Penknife and Lathe. We understood one another, though I can't say we were brothers, given the fight I once had with my own brothers—we understood one another as if we were inseparable friends. That is to say, many times we couldn't look one another in the eye without bursting out laughing, even when surrounded by people. The truth is that everything was a game. One day, as we walked down Canning Street, I told them about Aníbal Celino's house and Aurora, and recounted all the objects I had seen there. It was a real inventory! None of the valuable things in that palace had escaped my notice. Penknife looked at me, discouraged. "What a lot of junk! What could we do with it?" he said.

But Lathe's eyes lit up. Sharper than Penknife, he whispered with that voice of his that sounded like a whistle in the dark, "We'll pay a visit this week."

We each had eight ice-cream cones and then went to the zoo to look at the monkeys. The sun was burning hot. We stopped to listen to the music of a merry-go-round, because Lathe likes all kinds of music. That's not surprising: his father played the concertina. Though it seemed as if his mind was wandering, he was really planning the break-in.

For several days, as was our custom, we walked around the neighborhood where the house was situated. One whole day I sat on what remained of an old wall in a vacant lot, watching people going in and out. Fortunately there wasn't a guard or anything at the corner. The only danger, perhaps, was the silence of that area. It was so hot that I had to take off my shirt, though no one said anything to me, maybe because sweating disgusts people.

The night we had been waiting for finally arrived. I entered the house first because I was familiar with it and am the least nervous. Penknife and Lathe stayed outside in the bushes holding an empty sack with which to carry the stolen objects. I was supposed to give them the all clear to come in by hissing like an owl. That night we ate like pigs, drinking red wine and then finishing with brandy. The party cost us a bundle.

After some arguments about what time would be best to infiltrate Aníbal Celino's house, consulting our watches every fifteen minutes, we finally walked down Canning Street and stopped in front of the garden of the house, as if we were lost. All of a sudden Penknife and Lathe jumped over the garden fence and hid behind the bushes. I took refuge in the darkness of the entrance to the house, with the picklock in my hand. The shiny face of the lion biting on the ring distracted me from my task for a moment; the door suddenly opened. I jumped back and hid in the plants, but the door remained open. For an endless moment a clock struck the hour with a variety of chimes: quarter past, then half past. I waited for something to happen, scratching my ankle on some damn branch. Nothing happened; silence succeeded silence, sealing my eyes with sleep, while ants climbed up my legs to my navel. I waited another fifteen minutes and then warily approached the door, which still stood open. I entered the house and turned on the flashlight. I spun the little circle of light around me and then pointed it toward the staircase: there sitting on one of the steps was Aurora. I think it was the first time in my life that I was frightened: she looked like a real dwarf, wearing a long nightgown, her hair gathered on top of her head. As if she were waiting for me, she came up to me and whispered in my ear. "You are the Lord. I have been waiting for you a long time."

I began trembling and whispered, "Who are you waiting for?"

As if she had not heard me, she waved one of her legs the way a cat does when cleaning its face, then replied, "Clotilde Ifrán is waiting for me."

"Who is Clotilde Ifrán? Where is she?"

"She's in heaven. She's a seer who read my palm. When she died she lay in a beautiful bed in her shop. She sold corsets. She made girdles and brassieres for ladies and her room had drawers full of pink and blue ribbons, elastic and snaps, buttons and lace. When I visited her house with Mommy and we had to wait, she let me play with everything. Sometimes, when I wasn't at school, and Mommy was off at the theater or God knows where, she would leave me at Clotilde Ifrán's house, for her to take care of me. That's when I really started having fun. She didn't just give me candies or let me play with her needles and scissors and ribbons; she also read my palm or my future in her cards. One day, lying on her bed, pale as a ghost, she said to me, 'The Lord will come get me, and then He will come for you: after that we'll be together in heaven.' 'And will we have as much fun there as we do here?' I asked her. 'Much more,' she answered, 'because the Lord is very good.' 'And when will He come to get me?' 'I don't know when or how, but I'll read the cards to find out,' she answered. The next day, huge black horses took her to Chacarita in a coach covered with black decorations and flowers. I never saw her again, not even in my dreams. You are the Lord she spoke to me about, one for whom there are no closed doors. You wanted to test my loyalty, didn't you, when you came here with that package from the Firpo Pharmacy? You are the Lord, because you have a beard."

"I must be, since you say so."

"A Lord, to whom we must give everything we have."

"We'll take beautiful, shiny things, right?"

"We'll put everything in a picnic basket. Wait for me."

Aurora returned with the basket. We went into the living room. Aurora climbed onto a chair and retrieved a little key from the top of a cabinet. She opened the glass cabinet and started taking out objects to show me. When the basket was full, she closed the cabinet with the key.

"That's it," Aurora said.

When Aurora raised her voice I told her, afraid, "Be careful. Don't make any noise."

"Mommy takes sleeping pills and not even thunder could wake up Daddy. Do you want me to read the cards? I'll do for you what Clotilde Ifrán did for me. Do you want me to?"

She hopped back up the stairs and retrieved a deck of cards, then sat down on a step.

"This is how Clotilde Ifrán read the cards."

Aurora shuffled the cards; then she dealt them in a row, one by one, on three of the stairs. The movement of her hands back and forth made me dizzy. (I was afraid of falling asleep: that's the danger of my calm nature.) I proposed going to the living room, thinking about the objects I had left there, but she didn't listen to me. With her bossy tone, she began to relate the meaning of the cards.

"This king of spades, with a very serious face, is your enemy. He's waiting for you outside; they're going to kill you. This jack of spades is also waiting for you. Can't you hear the noise in the street? Can't you hear the steps of someone approaching? It's hard to hide at night. At night every sound can be heard and the moonlight is like the light of your conscience. And the plants. Do you think plants can help you? They're our enemies, sometimes, when the police arrive with their weapons drawn. That's why Clotilde Ifrán wanted to take me with her. There are so many dangers."

I wanted to leave, but a strange weariness, as if I had just eaten a large meal, held me back. What would Lathe, the leader, think? Like a drunkard, I went to the door and half opened it. Someone fired; I fell to the floor like a corpse, losing consciousness.

THE BASEMENT

THIS BASEMENT, which is extremely cold in winter, is an Eden in the summer. Some people sit by the front door upstairs for some cool air on the hottest days in January, dirtying the floor below. No window lets in the light or the horrible heat of the day. I have a large mirror, a couch or cot given me by a client who was a millionaire, and four mattresses I have acquired over the years from other girls. In the morning I fill pails (lent to me by the doorman of the next building) with water to wash my face and hands. I'm very clean. I have a hanger for my clothes behind a drape, and a mantel for the candlesticks. There is no electricity or water. My bedside table is a chair, and my chair is a velvet pillow. One of my clients, the youngest one, brought bits of old curtains from his grandmother's house, and I use them to decorate the walls, along with pictures I cut from magazines. The lady upstairs feeds me lunch; for breakfast I have candy or whatever I can stuff in my pockets. I have to live with mice, and at first it seemed to me that was the only defect of this basement, where I don't have to pay rent. Now I have noticed that these animals are not so terrible; they are quite discreet. When all's said and done they're preferable to flies, so abundant in the fanciest houses in Buenos Aires, in the places where they used to give me leftovers when I was eleven. While the clients are here the mice keep out of sight: they know the difference between one kind of silence and another. As soon as I am alone they come out in a ruckus. They skitter by, stopping for a moment to look at me out of a corner of their eyes, as if they guessed what I think of them. Sometimes they eat a bit of cheese or bread from the floor. They're not afraid of me, nor I of them. The worst part is that I can't store any food because they eat everything before I have a chance to touch anything myself. There are evil-minded people who are pleased with this and call me Fermina, the Mouse Lady. I don't like humoring these name-callers, which is why I refuse to ask for any mousetraps. One mouse, the oldest, is named Charlie Chaplin, another is Gregory Peck, another Marlon Brando, another Duilio Marzio; the playful one is named Daniel Gélin, another is Yul Brynner; one female is Gina Lollobrigida and another is Sophia Loren. It is strange how these little animals have taken possession of a basement where they must have lived before I arrived. Even the damp spots on the wall have taken the form of mice; they are dark and rather long, with two little ears and a long pointed tail. When nobody is watching, I gather food for them in one of the saucers I was given by the man who lives in the house across the way. I don't want the mice to leave me. If some neighbor comes and wants to exterminate them, I'll make a fuss he'll never forget as long as he lives. They've announced that this house will be torn down, but I won't leave here until I die. Up above they're packing trunks and baskets and constantly taping up packages. There are moving vans by the front door, but I walk by them as if I don't see them. I never begged for a cent from those people. They spy on me all day long and believe I am with clients because I talk to myself to annoy them. Since they're angry with me, they lock me in; since I'm angry with them, I don't ask them to open the door. For the last two days the mice have been acting very strangely: one brought me a ring, another a bracelet, and a third, the smartest one, brought me a necklace. At first I couldn't believe it, and nobody else will believe it. I'm happy. What does it matter if it's all a dream? I'm thirsty: I drink my own sweat. I'm hungry: I chew on my fingers and hair. The police won't come looking for me. They won't ask me for a health certificate or a certificate of good conduct. The ceiling is falling apart, bits of straw are floating down: it must be the beginning of the demolition. I hear cries, none of them calling my name. The mice are afraid. Poor things! They don't know, don't understand how the world is. They don't know the joy of revenge. Since learning to look at myself in a little mirror, I have never looked so beautiful.

THE PHOTOGRAPHS

I ARRIVED with my presents. I greeted Adriana. She was sitting in the middle of the patio in a wicker chair, surrounded by the guests. She was wearing a very full, white organdy skirt over a starched petticoat (the lace hem peeking out slightly whenever she moved), and had a metal clasp with white flowers in her hair, leather orthopedic boots, and a pink fan in her hand. That vocation for misfortune that I had discovered in her long before the accident was not evident in her face.

Clara, Rossi, Cordero, Perfecto, and Juan were all there, along with Albina Renato, Maria (the one with the glasses), that nitwit Acevedo with his new teeth, the dead woman's three boys, a blond boy nobody introduced me to, and that tramp Humberta. Luqui was there, as was little Dwarf, and the kid who used to be Adriana's boyfriend but who didn't talk to her anymore. I was shown the presents: they were arranged on a shelf in the bedroom. The table, which was very long, had been moved to under a yellow tent in the courtyard; it was covered with two tablecloths. The ham and colorful vegetable sandwiches, and the beautifully decorated cakes, whetted my appetite. Half a dozen bottles of sparkling cider and many glasses glittered on the table. It all made my mouth water. A vase with orange gladioli and another with white carnations decorated either end of the table. We were awaiting the arrival of Spirito, the photographer: we were not to sit down at the table, open the bottles of cider, or taste the cakes until he arrived.

To make us laugh, Albina Renato danced "The Death of the Swan." She was studying classical ballet, but danced in a spirit of fun.

It was hot and there were lots of flies. The flowers of the catalpa trees stained the tiles of the patio. All the guests fanned themselves—the men with their newspapers, the women with fancy fans or other objects—or they fanned the cakes and sandwiches. That tramp Humberta fanned herself with a flower to attract attention. No matter how much you wave it back and forth, how much breeze can you make with a flower?

We waited around for an hour, asking ourselves each time the doorbell rang whether Spirito was coming or not, and entertaining ourselves with stories of more or less fatal accidents. Some of the victims had been left without arms, others without hands, others without ears. "The misfortune of the many is the consolation of the few," said a little old lady, referring to Rossi, who has a glass eye. Adriana smiled. The guests kept arriving. When Spirito came in, the first bottle of cider was opened. Of course nobody tried it yet. Various glasses were served and the extended prelude to the long-awaited toast began.

In the first photograph, Adriana, at the head of the table, tried to smile with her parents. It was very hard to arrange the group right, since it didn't come together naturally: Adriana's father was robust and very tall, and the parents knitted their brows quite noticeably while holding their glasses aloft. The second photograph wasn't any easier: the younger brothers and sisters, the aunts and the grandmother, clustered around Adriana in disorder, blocking her face. Poor Spirito had to wait patiently for a moment of calm once each individual assumed the position he had assigned. In the third photograph, Adriana brandished the knife to cut the cake, which was decorated with her name, the date of her birthday, and the word "Happiness," all written in pink icing, and covered with rainbow sprinkles.

"She should stand up," the guests said.

An aunt objected: "And if her feet come out wrong?"

"Don't worry," responded the friendly Spirito. "If her feet come out wrong, I'll cut them off later."

Adriana grimaced with pain, and once more poor Spirito had to take her picture sunken in her chair surrounded by the guests. In the fourth photograph, only the children accompanied Adriana; they were allowed to hold their glasses high in imitation of the adults. The children caused less trouble than the adults. The most difficult moment still remained. Adriana had to be carried off to her grandmother's bedroom for the last photographs to be taken. Two men carried her in her wicker chair and put her in the room, along with the gladioli and the carnations. They sat her down on a couch, between piles of pillows. There must have been about fifteen people in the bedroom, which measured fifteen by twenty feet; they all drove poor Spirito crazy, giving him directions and telling Adriana how she should pose. They fixed her hair, covered her feet, added pillows, arranged flowers and fans, raised her head, buttoned her collar, powdered her nose, painted her lips. You couldn't even breathe. Adriana sweated and grimaced. Poor Spirito waited for more than half an hour without saying a word; then, with a great deal of tact, he took away the flowers they had put around Adriana's feet, saying that the girl was dressed in white and that the orange gladioli did not go with the ensemble. Patiently, Spirito repeated the well-known command: "Watch the birdie."

He turned on the lamps and took the fifth photograph, which ended in a thunder of applause. From outside, people said, "She looks like a bride, like a real bride. What a shame about the boots."

Adriana's aunt asked that they take a picture of the girl holding the aunt's mother-in-law's fan. It was a fan of alençon lace and sequins, decorated with little pictures painted by hand on the mother-of-pearl ribs. Poor Spirito didn't think it in good taste to introduce a sad black fan, no matter how valuable it might be, into the portrait of a fourteen-year-old girl. But they insisted so strongly that he gave in. With a white carnation in one hand and the black fan in the other, Adriana appeared in the sixth photograph. The seventh photograph stirred up much debate: whether it should be taken inside the room or on the patio, next to Adriana's cranky grandfather who did not want to move from his corner. Clara said, "If this is the happiest day of her life, how can you fail to take her picture with her grandfather, who loves her so much!" Then she explained, "For a year this girl has been hovering between life and death, and is now paralyzed."

The aunt declared, "We've been killing ourselves to save her, sleeping by her side on the tile floors of the hospitals, giving our blood for transfusions. And now, on her birthday, are we to neglect the most solemn moment of the banquet, and forget to put her beside the most important individual of all, her grandfather who was always her favorite?"

Adriana was complaining. I think she was asking for a glass of water, but she was so upset she couldn't utter a word; besides, the racket people made when they moved around and talked would have drowned out her words even if she had uttered them. Two men carried her, once more, in the wicker chair to the patio, and set her down at the table. At this moment the traditional "Happy Birthday" song blared out of the loudspeaker. Adriana, sitting at the head of the table, next to her grandfather and the cake covered with candles, posed for the seventh photograph with great serenity. The tramp managed to slip into the front of the picture, her shoulders and breasts showing (as always). I accused her in public of butting in and advised the photographer to take the picture over, which he did willingly enough. Humberta resentfully slunk into a corner of the patio; the blond boy nobody had introduced me to followed her and, to make her feel better, whispered something in her ear. If it had not been for that tramp the catastrophe wouldn't have happened. Adriana was about to faint when they took her picture again. Everybody thanked me. They opened the bottles of cider; the glasses overflowed with foam. They cut the two cakes in big slices that were handed around on plates. These things took time and attention. Some glasses were spilled on the tablecloth; they say that brings good luck. With our fingertips we moistened our brows. Some people with no manners had already drunk their cider before the toast. The tramp Humberta set the example, handing her cup over to the blond boy. It wasn't until later, when we tasted the cake and toasted Adriana's health, that we noticed Adriana was asleep. Her head hung down from her neck like a melon. Since this was her first day out of the hospital, it was not odd that exhaustion and emotion should have overcome her. Some people laughed; others approached her and clapped her on the back to wake her up. That tramp Humberta, that killjoy, jostled her by the arm and cried out to her, "You're frozen."

Then that bird of ill omen said, "She's dead."

Some people farther from the head of the table thought it was a joke and said, "Who wouldn't burst with happiness on such a day!"

The nitwit Acevedo didn't let go of his glass. Everyone stopped eating except Luqui and Dwarf. Others, on the sly, slipped pieces of squashed cake without icing into their pockets.

How unfair life is! Instead of Adriana, who was an angel, that tramp Humberta should have died!

MAGUSH

A THESSALIAN witch read the future of Polycrates in the designs the surf made on its way down the beach; a Roman vestal virgin read Caesar's future in a little pile of sand next to a plant; Cornelius Agrippa of Germany used a mirror to read his own future. Some present-day sorcerers read one's destiny in tea leaves or in the dregs of coffee at the bottom of a cup; some read it in trees, in rain, in ink-blots or egg whites, others in the lines of the palm, others in crystal balls. Magush reads the future in a vacant building opposite the charcoal yard where he lives. The six huge picture windows and the twelve little windows of the adjacent building are like cards for him. Magush never thought of associating windows and cards: that was my idea. His methods are mysterious and can be explained only in part. He tells me that during the day he has trouble drawing conclusions, because the light disturbs the images. The most propitious moment to carry out his task is at sunset, when certain slanting rays of light filter through the side windows of the building and are reflected onto the glass of the windows in front. That is why he always makes appointments with his clients for that hour of the day. I know, having learned from careful research, that the upper part of the building has to do with matters of the heart, the lower part with money and work, and the middle with problems of family and health.

Magush, despite the fact that he's only fourteen, is my friend. I met him by chance one day when I went to buy a sack of charcoal. I wasn't slow to guess his gift of prophecy. After several conversations in the patio of the charcoal yard (surrounded by sacks of charcoal in the freezing cold), he asked me into the room where he works. The room is a sort of hallway, every bit as chilly as the patio; from there, through a combination of skylights of colored glass and a tall narrow window (shaped for a giraffe), the facing building can easily be seen, its yellowing façade marked by rain and sun. After a while, in the room I felt the chill lifting and a pleasant feeling of warmth replacing it. Magush told me that this phenomenon occurs during the moments of prophecy, and that it is not the room but the body that absorbs those beneficent rays.

Magush was extraordinarily kind to me. At the right moment, he let me look at the windows of the building myself, one by one. (Incomprehensible scenes were sometimes visible; in that respect, I was lucky at first.) In one of the windows I saw, for my sins, the woman who later became my fiancée embracing my rival. She was wearing the red dress I found dazzling, her hair loose in the front and wrapped in a little bun that rested on the back of her neck. To see that detail I must have had the eyes of a lynx, but the sharpness of the image was due to the magic that surrounded it and not to my eyesight. (At the same distance, I've been able to read letters or newspaper clippings.) Then I saw the painful scene I had to suffer later, in the flesh. I saw the bed covered with pink blankets and the horrible ladies going in and out with packages. There, in the window aglow at sunset, I saw the excursions to Tigre and to the Luján River. There I was about to strangle someone. Later, when I lived through these events, the reality seemed a little faded to me, and my fiancée perhaps less beautiful.

After those experiences, my interest in living what was destined for me diminished. I consulted with Magush. Was it possible to avoid your destiny? To refrain from living it, somehow—was that possible? Magush thought this over with his deep intelligence. For several days I didn't leave his side. I entertained myself watching images, refraining from seeking them out and living them. Finally, Magush said that because of our close friendship of many years, he would make an exception—he would never let anyone else experience my entertainment, watching my fate appear in those windows while he played tricks on his clients, giving them my fate as if it were theirs.

"It's more prudent to have someone live out your destiny right away, as soon as it appears in the windows. Otherwise it might come looking for you: destiny is like a man-eating tiger lying in ambush for its owner," Magush would say to me. He would add, to reassure me, "One day, perhaps, there'll be no more of you in those windows."

"Will I die?" I asked uneasily.

"Not necessarily," answered Magush. "You might live without a destiny."

"But even dogs have a destiny," I protested.

"Dogs can't avoid it: they're obedient."

What Magush had foretold happened in part, and I lived for a time bored and calm, devoted to my work. But life attracted me and I missed standing by Magush, watching the building. The figures intended to elucidate my fate had still not been extinguished. In each window, intricate new shapes sometimes surprised us. Somber lights, ghosts with the faces of dogs, criminals: everything indicated that it would be better if those pictures I saw didn't come true.

"Who would want to live out those misfortunes?" I asked Magush. He resolved one day, in order to distract me, to become an adviser and a magician at once. I began to see fireworks, puppets, Japanese lanterns, dwarfs, people dressed as bears and cats. I said to him hypocritically, "I envy you. I wish I were fourteen."

"I'll switch destinies with you," Magush said.

I accepted, although his proposal seemed impertinent to me. What would I do with those dwarfs? We talked for far too long about the difficulties that might be entailed in the difference in our ages. Perhaps we lost the faith we needed.

We didn't carry out our project. Both of us missed the chance to satisfy our curiosity. Sometimes we feel anew the temptation to switch destinies; I give it a try, but always come up against the same obstacle: if I think about the difficulties Magush has overcome, the idea seems absurd. Not long ago I was about to leave. I packed my bags. We said goodbye. The images in the windows were tempting.

Something stopped me at the last moment. The same thing happened to Magush: he didn't have the nerve to escape from the charcoal yard.

I'm always fascinated by Magush's destiny and he by mine (no matter how bad it is), but in reality the only thing that both of us want is to continue contemplating the windows of the building and giving others our own destinies, so long as they strike us as extraordinary.

THE OBJECTS

FOR HER twentieth birthday someone gave Camila Ersky a golden bracelet with a rose of rubies. It was a family heirloom. She liked the bracelet and wore it only on certain occasions, when she was going to some gathering or to the theater for opening night. Nevertheless, when she lost it she did not share the pain of her loss with the rest of the family. In her view, objects could not be replaced whatever their value—she only appreciated people, the canaries in her home, and her dogs. In the course of her life, I think she only wept over the loss of a silver chain with a medal of the Virgin of Luján set in gold, a present from one of her boyfriends. The idea of losing things, those things we lose as if by fate, didn't trouble her as much as it did the rest of the family or her friends, who were a vain lot. Without tears she had seen her childhood home stripped, once by fire, once by a poverty as ferocious as fire: stripped of its most beloved furnishings (paintings, tables, commodes, screens, vases, bronze statues, fans, marble cherubs, porcelain dancers, bottles of perfume in the shape of radishes, whole cases of miniatures with curls and beards), some horrible but valuable. I suspect that her complacency was not a sign of indifference, and that she had an anxious foreboding that these objects would someday rob her of something more precious than her childhood. Perhaps she cared for them more than those who wept over their loss. Sometimes she saw these objects. They came to visit her like people, in processions, especially at night, when she was about to fall asleep, when she was traveling by train or by car, or even when she was going through her daily routine, on her way to work. Often they bothered her like insects: she wanted to scare them off, to think of other things. Often, from a lack of imagination, she described the objects to her children, in the entertaining stories she told them when they were eating. She didn't add to the objects' glow or beauty or mystery: that wasn't necessary.

One afternoon, returning from some errands, she crossed a square and stopped to rest on a bench. Why imagine only Buenos Aires? There are other cities with squares. The light of the setting sun bathed the branches, streets, houses around her: the light that sometimes increases the wisdom of joy. She contemplated the sky for a long while, stroking her stained kid gloves; then, attracted by something shiny on the ground, she looked down and, a few moments later, realized it was the bracelet she had lost more than fifteen years ago. With the emotion that saints must feel when they work their first miracle, she picked the object up. Night fell before she decided to put the bracelet on her left wrist as she had long ago.

When she got home, after looking at her wrist to make sure that the bracelet had not vanished, she told the news to her children, who didn't stop playing, and to her husband, who looked at her skeptically, not interrupting his reading of the paper. For days, despite her children's indifference and her husband's suspicions, she woke with the joy of having found the bracelet. The only people who would have been truly surprised were all dead.

She began to remember with greater precision the objects that had peopled her life; she remembered them with nostalgia, with an unknown anxiety. Like an inventory, in reverse chronological order, her memory was filled with a crystal dove with broken wings and beak; a candy box in the shape of a piano; a bronze statue that held up a lantern with little lightbulbs; a bronze clock; a marble cushion with bluish streaks and tassels; opera glasses with a mother-of-pearl handle; an inscribed cup; and ivory monkeys with little baskets full of baby monkeys.

In ways completely normal to her and completely unbelievable to us, she slowly recovered the objects that had long dwelled only in her memory. At the same time she noticed that the happiness she had felt at first was turning into a feeling of discomfort, of fear, of worry.

She hardly looked at the things around her for fear of discovering a lost treasure.

While Camila was troubled and tried to think of other things, the objects appeared, in the market, at stores, in hotels, in all sorts of places, everything from the bronze statue with the torch that used to light up the entrance to the house to the jeweled heart pierced by an arrow. The gypsy doll and the kaleidoscope were the last ones. Where did she find those toys, belonging to her childhood? I am ashamed to say, because you, my readers, will think that I seek only to surprise you and not tell you the truth. You will think that the toys were different ones, similar to the old ones, not the very same, that of course there isn't only one gypsy doll in the whole world, not only one kaleidoscope. But fate dictated that the doll's arm was tattooed with a butterfly in India ink and that, engraved on the copper tube, the kaleidoscope bore Camila Ersky's name.

If it weren't so pathetic, this story would be tedious. If it doesn't seem pathetic to you, my readers, at least it's short, and telling it will give me practice. In the dressing rooms of the theaters that Camila often attended, she found toys that belonged, by a long series of coincidences, to the daughter of a dancer; the girl insisted on trading them for a mechanical bear and a plastic circus. She came home with the old toys wrapped in newspaper. Several times, on the way home, she wanted to put the package down at the bottom of a staircase or on the threshold of a door.

Nobody was home. She opened the windows wide, taking a deep breath of the evening air. Then she saw the objects lined up against the wall of her room, just as she had dreamed she would see them. She knelt down to caress them. She lost track of day and night. She saw that the objects had faces, the horrible faces they acquire when we have stared at them too long.

Through a long series of joys, Camila Ersky had finally entered hell.

THE FURY

SOMETIMES I think I can still hear that drum. How can I leave this place without being seen? And, imagining that I could leave, once free how would I be able to take the child home? I would hope someone is running ads on the radio or in the newspaper, searching for him. Make him disappear? Impossible. Kill myself? Only as a last resort. Besides, how would I do it? Escape? But in which direction? Right now the corridors are full of people. The windows are walled up.

I asked myself these questions a thousand times before I noticed the penknife the child was holding in his hand, then put back in his pocket. I calmed down, thinking that if all else failed I could kill him, slitting the veins of his wrists in the bathtub so as not to bloody the floor. Once he was dead, I would stuff him under the bed.

So as not to go crazy I took out the notebook I always carry in my pocket, and while the child played strange games with the fringe of the bedspread, with the rug, with the chair, I wrote down everything that had happened to me since I met Winifred.

I met her in Palermo Park. I now realize that her eyes glistened like a hyena's. She reminded me of one of the Furies. She was fragile and nervous, like all the women you don't like, Octavio. Her black hair was curly and fine, like armpit hair. I never found out what perfume she used, plus her natural odor mixed with the contents of that unlabeled bottle, decorated with cupids, which I had glimpsed in the disorder of her purse.

Our first dialogue was brief:

"Sweetheart, you don't look like you're from this country."

"Of course not. I'm Filipina."

"Do you speak English?"

"Of course."

"You could teach me."

"Why?"

"It would help me with my studies."

She was walking with a child; I, with a math or logic book under my arm. Winifred was not especially young—I could tell from the veins on her legs, which formed little blue trees behind her knees, and from her swollen eyelids. She told me she was twenty.

I saw her on Saturday afternoons. For a while, we would always take the same path we had taken the first day, walking from the bust of Dante by a terebinth tree up to the monkey house. We would stare at the tips of our shoes covered with dust, or feed raw meat to the cats; we would repeat nearly the same dialogue, with different emphases, or, one could say, with different meanings. The child banged constantly on his drum. We got tired of the cats the first day we held hands: we no longer had time to cut up so many tiny pieces of raw meat. One day I took bread for the pigeons and swans: this served as a pretext for a picture taken at the foot of the bridge that leads to the little walled island in the middle of the lake, where there's a gate covered with pornographic inscriptions. She wanted me to write her name and mine next to one of the most obscene messages. I obeyed her reluctantly.

I fell in love with her the day she spoke in verse (Octavio, you taught me everything about meter).

"I remember my angel wings as a child."

To steady myself, I looked at her reflection in the water. I thought she was crying.

"You had angel wings?" I asked in a sentimental voice.

"They were made of cotton and were very large," she answered. "They framed my face. They looked as if they were of ermine. For the Day of the Virgin Maria, the nuns at the school dressed me as an angel in a light blue dress: a tunic, not a dress. Underneath I wore light blue tights and shoes. They made curls and pasted them on." I put my arm around her waist, but she kept on talking.

"On my head they placed a crown of artificial lilies. A very fragrant kind of lily, tuberose I believe. Yes, tuberose. I threw up all night long. I'll never forget that day. My friend Lavinia, who was as well liked at the school as I was, received the same distinction: they dressed her as an angel, a pink one. (The pink angel was less important than the blue one.)"

(I remembered your advice, Octavio: there's no need to be shy when seducing a woman.)

"Don't you want to sit down?" I said to her, taking her in my arms toward a marble bench.

"Let's sit on the grass," she said to me.

She took a few steps and threw herself down on the ground.

"I'd like to find a four-leaf clover ... and to give you a kiss."

She went on, as if she hadn't heard me: "My friend Lavinia died that day; it was the happiest and the saddest day of my life. Happy, because the two of us were dressed as angels; sad, because it was when I lost happiness forever."

I put my hand on her cheek to touch her tears.

"Every time I remember her, I cry," she said, her voice cracking. "That special day ended in tragedy. One of Lavinia's wings caught fire in the flame of the tall candle I was holding. Lavinia's father rushed over to save his daughter: he picked up that living torch, rushed onto the chancel, crossed the patio, and into the bathroom. When he turned on the bathwater, it was already too late. My friend Lavinia lay there in cinders. All that was left of her body was this ring I treasure as if it were gold dust," she told me, showing me a little ruby ring on her third finger. "One day, when we were playing, she promised me the ring when she died. Of course there were those who accused me of having set Lavinia's wings on fire deliberately. The truth is that I can only take pride in having been good to one person in my life: to her. I took care of her as if she were my daughter, educating her, correcting her faults. We all have faults: Lavinia was proud and fearful. She had long blond hair and very white skin. One day, to correct her pride, I cut off a lock of her hair, stashing it away secretly in a drawer—they had to cut the rest of her hair to even it out. Another day I spilled a bottle of cologne on her neck and cheek, the fragrance seeping into her skin."

The child was playing the drum next to us. We told him to go somewhere farther off but he didn't listen.

"And if we were to take his drum away?" I asked impatiently.

"He would have a fit," Winifred answered me.

"Sometime, may I see you without the child or without the drum?"

"Not for the moment," answered Winifred.

She spoiled him so much that I came to believe he was her own child.

"And his mother, his mother can't ever be with him?" I asked her once, bitterly.

"That's why they pay me," she answered, as if I had insulted her.

After several kisses, exchanged in the foliage, she continued with her confidences, though the child continued to play the drum without pause.

"In the Philippines there are paradises."

"Here, too," I answered, thinking she was talking of a kind of tree.

"Paradises of happiness. In Manila, where I was born, the windows of the houses were decorated with mother-of-pearl."

"Can one be happy with windows decorated with mother-of-pearl?"

"Being in paradise is to be happy; but the serpent is always on its way, and one always awaits it. The earthquakes, the Japanese invasion, Lavinia's death, everything that happened later. Nevertheless, I had premonitions. My parents always left a bowl of milk for the snakes just outside our house by the front door, so they wouldn't come in. One night they forgot to put the milk outside. When my father went to bed, he felt something cold between the sheets. It was a snake. He had to wait till the next morning before shooting it. He didn't want to scare us with the noise. That was when I foresaw everything that was going to happen. It was a premonition. Kneeling in the chapel at school I tried to ask for God's protection, but every time I knelt down my feet bothered me. I would turn them in and out, put them to one side, then to the other, without being able to find a posture that would allow contemplation. Lavinia looked at me with astonishment; she was very intelligent, not able to understand that one could have these difficulties before God. She was sensible; I was romantic. One day, while reading in a field of irises, I fell asleep. It was late. They looked for me with flashlights; the group was led by Lavinia. There the irises make you sleepy; they're narcotic. If they hadn't found me, you'd certainly not be talking to me today."

The child sat down next to us, playing his drum.

"Why don't we take his drum away from him and throw it in the lake?" I dared to suggest. "The noise is driving me crazy."

Winifred folded her red raincoat, stroked it, and went on talking. "In the dormitories at school, Lavinia would cry at night because she was afraid of animals. To combat her baseless fear, I would put live spiders in her bed. Once I put a dead rat that I had found in the garden; another time I put a toad. Despite all my efforts I didn't succeed in correcting her; quite the contrary, her fear worsened. It reached a climax the day I invited her to my house. Around the little table where the tea set was arranged with the pastries, I placed the beasts my father had hunted in Africa and had gotten stuffed: two tigers and a lion. Lavinia didn't try the milk or the pastries that day. I pretended to give food to the animals. She kept crying until nightfall. Then I hid in the darkness, behind some plants. Fear dried her tears. She thought she was alone. The hammocks were some distance away from the house. She stood among them, next to a rough bench, nervously scratching her knees, until I appeared covered with banana leaves. In the darkness I could imagine the pallor of her face and the two thin trails of blood on her scratched knees. I cried out her name three times, "Lavinia! Lavinia! Lavinia!," trying to alter my voice. I touched her icy hand. I believe she fainted. That night they placed hot water bottles onto her feet and bags of ice on her head. Lavinia told her parents that she didn't want to see me ever again. We later reconciled, as was to be expected. To celebrate, I brought some gifts to her house: chocolate, a fishbowl with a goldfish in it, but the gift that Lavinia found most unpleasant was a little monkey, dressed in green, with four bells hanging from it. Lavinia's parents received me affectionately and thanked me for the presents, but Lavinia didn't say anything. I believe the fish and monkey starved to death. As for the chocolate, Lavinia never touched it. She disliked sweets, something they scolded her for; sometimes they would even force her to eat the candies I brought her as presents.

"Don't you want to go somewhere else?" I asked, interrupting her confidences. "It's raining."

"All right," she answered, putting on her raincoat.

We walked, crossed the avenue lined with palm trees, reached the Monument to the Spaniards. We looked for a taxi. I gave directions to the driver. On the way we bought chocolate and bread for the child. The house was like others of the same kind, perhaps a bit larger. The room had a mirror with a gold frame and a clothes rack; the hangers were each painted like the neck of a swan. We hid the drum under the bed.

"What shall we do with the child?" I asked. The only answer I received was the embrace that led us into a labyrinth of other embraces. We made our way inside, pausing in the darkness as if it were a tunnel, still blinded by the light of the garden we had just left.

"And the child?" I asked again, seeing her straw hat and white gloves in the twilight, but not him. "Could he be hiding under the bed?"

"That miscreant must be wandering the hallways."

"And if someone sees him?"

"They'll think he's the manager's kid."

"How come they let him in?"

"They didn't see him under your raincoat."

I closed my eyes and smelled Winifred's perfume.

"How cruel you were to Lavinia," I told her.

"Cruel? Cruel?" she said emphatically. "I'm cruel to everyone. I'll be cruel to you," she said, biting my lips.

"You can't."

"Are you sure?"

"I'm sure."

Now I understand that she wanted to redeem herself for what she had done to Lavinia by committing still greater cruelties with everyone else. Redemption through evil.

I went to look for the child, as she had asked me to. I wandered around the hallways. No one. I stood by the veranda where the taxis arrived with couples who tried to hide their laughter, their joy, their shame. A white cat climbed up a vine. The child was peeing by a wall. I picked him up and carried him back with me, hiding him as best as I could. When I entered the room, I couldn't see anything at first; it was pitch-dark. Then I saw that Winifred wasn't there anymore. Nor were her things; not her purse, her gloves, nor her scarf with light blue initials. I ran to open the door and see if I could spot her down the hall, but I couldn't even smell her perfume. I closed the door again, and while the child played dangerously with the fringes of the bedspread, I found the drum. I searched everywhere for some clue Winifred might have absentmindedly left behind that could lead me to her: a scrap with her address on it, or a friend's address, or her last name.

I tried several times to talk to the child, but it was hopeless.

"Don't play the drum. What's your name?"

"Cintito."

"That's your nickname. What's your real name?"

"Cintito."

"And your nanny?"

"Nana."

"Where does she live?"

"In a little house."

"Where?"

"In a little house."

"Where's the little house?"

"I don't know."

"I'll give you some candy if you tell me your nanny's name."

"Give me some candy."

"Later. What's her name?"

Cintito kept playing with the bedspread, the rug, the chair, the drumsticks.

What should I do? I thought, as I talked to the child.

"Don't play the drum. It's more fun to roll it."

"Why?"

"Because it's better not to make noise."

"But I want to."

"I told you not to."

"Then give me my penknife back."

"It's not a toy for children. You could hurt yourself."

"I'm going to play the drum."

"If you play the drum I'll kill you."

He started screaming. I took him by the neck. I asked him to be quiet. He refused to listen to me. I covered his mouth with the pillow. He struggled for a few minutes; then he lay still, his eyes closed.

Indecisiveness is one of my faults. For several minutes, I experienced eternity for the first time as I repeated over and over: What will I do?

Now I can only wait for the door of this cell to open. That's the way I was: to avoid a scandal, I managed to commit a crime.

AZABACHE

I AM ARGENTINE. I joined the crew of a ship. In Marseille I found a doctor to sign a document certifying that I was crazy. It was easy for him to do because he must have been crazy himself. That way I was able to leave the ship but then they locked me in a madhouse and now I have no hope that anyone will ever get me out.

This is my story: to escape from my country I joined a ship's crew, and escaping the ship I was locked in a madhouse. When I fled from my country and when I fled from the ship I thought I was fleeing from my memories, but every day I relive the story of my love, which is my prison. They say that I fell in love with Aurelia because of my hatred for elegant women but that's not true. I loved her as I had never loved another woman in my life. Aurelia was a servant; she barely knew how to read or write. Her eyes were black, her hair black and straight like a horse's mane. As soon as she finished washing the dishes or the floors she would take a pencil and paper and go to a corner to draw horses. That was all she knew how to draw: horses galloping, jumping, sitting, lying down. Some were roan, others chestnut, red, bay, black, bluish, white. Sometimes she drew them with chalk, when she could find chalk; other times with colored pencils, when available; other times with ink or paint. They all had names: her favorite was Azabache because he was jet-black and skittish.

When she brought me my breakfast in the morning, I would hear her neighing laughter moments before she entered my bedroom, nervously kicking open the door. I was unable to educate her, in fact refused to educate her. I fell in love with her.

I left my parents' house and went to live with her in Chascomús, on the outskirts of the town. I didn't like big cities, thinking that their growth causes our unhappiness. Filled with joy I sold all of my belongings—my car, my furniture—to be able to rent a tiny farm where I could live simply, enchanted by our impossible love. At an auction I bought some cows and the horses I would need to work the land.

At first I was happy. What did I care that I didn't have indoor plumbing or electric light or a refrigerator or clean sheets! Love replaced all of that. Aurelia had bewitched me. What did I care that the soles of her feet were rough, that her hands were always red, and that her manners were not the finest: I was her slave!

She liked eating sugar. I would put sugar cubes in the palm of my hand, and she would eat them. She liked me to stroke her on the head, and so I would caress her for hours on end.

Sometimes I would look for her all day long without finding her anywhere. How could she find a hiding place on that tract of land, completely flat and treeless? She would come back barefoot, her hair so tangled that no comb could smooth it. I warned her that along the coast, not too far away, there were swamps full of crabs.

Sometimes I'd find her talking to the horses. She, who was so quiet, would speak incessantly with them. They loved her and would gather around her. Her favorite was named Azabache.

Some people called me a degenerate; others, but they are few, felt sorry for me. They sold me bad meat, and at the store tried to charge me twice for the same things, thinking me absentminded. Living in that hostile solitude was bad for me.

I married Aurelia so that they would sell me better-quality meat at the butcher shop; that is what my enemies said, but I can assure them that I did it to live respectably. Aurelia amused herself kissing the noses of the horses; she would braid her hair with the horses' manes. These games expressed her youth and the tenderness of her heart. She was mine, in a way that the horrible, elegant woman with painted nails I had fallen in love with years before had never been.

One afternoon I found Aurelia speaking to a beggar about horses.

I didn't understand anything they were saying. I took Aurelia by the arm and dragged her home, not saying a word. That day she cooked unwillingly and broke the kitchen door by kicking it too hard. I locked her inside a room and told her I was punishing her for speaking to strangers. She didn't seem to understand me, and slept until I let her out.

To keep her from straying too far from the house again I told her how people and animals had died by falling into the swamps and being devoured by the crabs. She didn't listen to me. I took her by the arm and shouted in her ear. She stood up and left the house, head high, walking toward the coast.

"Where are you going?" I asked her.

She kept walking, not saying a word. I grabbed her dress, struggling with her until it tore. I knocked her down in my desperation. She stood up and resumed walking. I followed her. When we neared the river, I asked her not to go on because of the foul-smelling, muddy swamps. She kept walking. She followed a narrow path through the swamps. I went after her. Our feet sank into the mud and we heard the cries of countless birds. No trees could be seen, and reeds filled the horizon. We reached a place where the trail turned a corner; there we saw Azabache, the black horse, sunk in the swamp up to his belly. Aurelia stopped for a moment without showing surprise. Quickly, in a single leap, she jumped into the swamp and began to sink. While she struggled toward the horse I tried to reach her and save her. I lay down in the swamp, slithering along like a reptile. I took her by the arm and began to sink with her. I thought we were going to die. I looked into her eyes and saw that strange light that appears in the eyes of the dying; I saw the horse reflected in them. I let her arm go. Inching like a worm along the disgusting surface of the swamp, I waited until dawn (though it seemed endless to me) for Aurelia and Azabache to sink into the swamp.

THE VELVET DRESS

Sweating, mopping our brows with handkerchiefs that we had moistened in the Recoleta fountain, we finally arrived at the house on Ayacucho Street, the one with a garden. How amusing!

We took the elevator to the fifth floor. I was in a foul mood because my dress was dirty and I hadn't really wanted to go out. I had planned to spend the afternoon washing and ironing my bedspread. We rang the bell: the door opened and we—Casilda and I—stepped into the house with the package. Casilda is a dressmaker. We live in Burzaco and our trips to the capital make her ill, especially when we have to travel to the northern part of the city, so far away. Right away, Casilda asked the servant for a glass of water to take the aspirin she had brought in her purse. The aspirin fell to the floor, along with the glass and the purse. How amusing!

We went up a carpeted staircase (which smelled of mothballs), preceded by the servant, who showed us into the bedroom of Mrs. Cornelia Catalpina, whose very name was torture for me to remember. The bedroom was completely red, with white drapes and mirrors in golden frames. We waited for a century or two for a lady to come from the next room, where we could hear her singing scales and arguing with various voices. Her perfume entered; then, a few moments later, she herself entered with a different scent. She greeted us with a complaint: "How lucky you are to live outside Buenos Aires! At least there's no soot there. There may be rabid dogs and garbage dumps... Look at my bedspread. Do you think it's supposed to be gray? No. It's white. Like a snowflake." She took me by the chin and added, "You don't have to worry about things like that. What a joy to be young! You're eight, right?" Then, addressing Casilda, she added, "Why don't you put a stone on her head so she won't grow up? We're young only as long as our children are."

Everyone thought my friend Casilda was my mother. How amusing!

"Ma'am, do you want to try it on?" Casilda asked, opening the package, which was all pinned together. Then she said to me, "Get the pins from my purse."

"Trying things on! It's torture for me! If only someone could try on my dresses for me, how happy I would be! It's so tiring."

The lady undressed and Casilda tried to help her into the velvet dress.

"When are you supposed to leave on your trip, ma'am? " she asked to distract her.

The lady couldn't answer. The dress was stuck to her shoulders: something kept it from going past her neck. How amusing!

"Velvet is very sticky, ma'am, and it's hot today. Let's put on a little talcum powder."

"Take it off, I'm suffocating," the lady cried out. Casilda held the dress and the lady sat down in an armchair, about to faint.

"When is the trip supposed to be, ma'am?" Casilda asked again to distract her.

"I'm leaving any day now. Today, thanks to airplanes, you can leave whenever you feel like it. The dress will have to be ready. To think that it's snowing there. Everything is white, clean, and shiny."

"You're going to Paris?"

"I'm also going to Italy."

"Won't you try on the dress again, ma'am? We'll be finished in a moment."

The lady nodded with a sigh.

"Raise both of your arms so we can first put on the two sleeves," Casilda said, taking the dress and helping her put it on once again. For a few seconds Casilda tried unsuccessfully to pull the skirt of the dress down over the lady's hips. I helped as best I could. She finally managed to put on the dress. For a few moments the lady rested in the armchair, exhausted; then she stood up to look at herself in the mirror. The dress was beautiful and complex! A dragon embroidered with black sequins was shining on the left side of the gown. Casilda knelt down, looking in the mirror, and adjusted the hem. Then she stood up and began putting pins in the folds of the gown, on the neck and sleeves. I touched the velvet: it was rough when you rubbed it one way and smooth when you rubbed it the other. The plush set my teeth on edge. The pins fell on the wood floor, and I picked them up religiously, one by one. How amusing!

"What a dress! I don't think there's such a beautiful pattern in all of Buenos Aires," said Casilda, letting a pin drop from her lips. "Don't you like it, ma'am?"

"Very much. Velvet is my favorite material. Fabric is like flowers: one has one's favorites. I think that velvet is like spikenard."

"Do you like spikenard? It's so sad," Casilda protested.

"Spikenard is my favorite flower, yet it's harmful to me. When I smell it I get sick. Velvet sets my teeth on edge, gives me goose bumps, the same as linen gloves used to when I was a girl, and yet for me there's no other fabric like it in the whole world. Feeling its softness with my hand attracts me even if it sometimes repels me. How can a woman be better dressed than in black velvet? She doesn't need a lace collar, or a string of pearls; everything else is unnecessary. Velvet is sufficient by itself. It's sumptuous and sober."

When she had finished talking the lady was breathing with difficulty. The dragon also. Casilda took a newspaper from the table and fanned her, but the lady made her stop, saying that fresh air did her no good. How amusing!

I heard the cries of some street vendors outside. What were they selling? Fruit, maybe ice cream? The whistle of the knife sharpener and the ringing bell of the ice-cream vendor also went up and down the street. I didn't run to the window to see them, as I had on other occasions. I couldn't tear myself away from watching the fittings of the dress with the sequin dragon. The lady stood up again and, staggering slightly, walked over to the mirror. The sequin dragon also staggered. The dress was now nearly perfect, except for an almost imperceptible tuck under the arms. Casilda took up the pins once more, plunging them perilously into the wrinkles that bulged out of the unearthly fabric.

"When you grow up," the lady told me, "you'd like to have a velvet dress, wouldn't you?"

"Yes," I answered, feeling the velvet of the dress strangling my neck with its gloved hands. How amusing!

"Now help me take it off," the lady said.

Casilda tried to help her to take it off, holding the hem in both hands. She pulled on it unsuccessfully for a few seconds, then put it back on the way it was before.

"I'll have to sleep in it," the lady said, standing before the mirror, looking at her pale face, the dragon trembling with each beat of her heart. "Velvet is wonderful but it's very heavy," she said, wiping her brow. "It's a prison. How to escape it? They should make dresses of fabric as immaterial as air, light, or water."

"I recommended raw silk to you," Casilda protested.

The lady fell to the floor, the dragon writhing. Casilda leaned over the body until the dragon lay still. I again caressed the velvet, which seemed like a live animal. Casilda said sadly, "She's dead. And I had so much trouble making this dress! It cost me so very much!"

How amusing!

LEOPOLDINA'S DREAMS

EVER SINCE Leopoldina was born, all the women in the Yapurra family have been given names that start with L, and I, since I am so tiny, am called Changuito.

Ludovica and Leonor, who are the youngest ones, waited by the stream for a miracle every evening at dusk. We would go to the spring called Agua de la Salvia. We would leave the water jars by the spring, sitting down on a rock and waiting for nightfall, our eyes wide open. Our conversations were always about the same topic.

"Juan Mamanis must be in Catamarca," Ludovica would say.

"Oh, what a pretty bicycle he had! Every year he visits the Virgin of the Valley."

"Would you vow to go on foot, like Javiera?"

"I have tender feet."

"If only we had a Virgin like that one!"

"Then Juan Mamanis wouldn't go to Catamarca."

"I'm not concerned about that. The Virgin is what worries me."

I could never sit still; they knew my habits. "Changuito, leave that alone," Ludovica would say to me, "spiders are poisonous," or "Changuito, don't do that. Don't pee in the spring."

Someone, perhaps the witch doctor, had told them that at a certain hour a light shone on the hollow amidst the stones and that a shadow appeared by the bank of the stream.

"One day we'll find her," Leonor would say. "She must look like the Virgin of the Valley."

"It might be a ghost," Ludovica would answer. "I don't have any illusions," she would say, sinking her feet in the stream and in the process sprinkling water on my eyes and ears. I was trembling. "What will you do, Changuito, when snow falls, when all the trees and the ground are white? You won't go away from the edge of the fireplace, will you? Even warm water makes you shiver like a star."

"If we discover a new Virgin we'll be in the papers. This is what they'll say, 'Two girls in Chaquibil witnessed the apparition of a new Virgin. The highest authorities will be present at the tribute to them.' They'll build an illuminated grotto for the statue and later on there'll be a basilica. I can imagine the Virgin of Chaquibil very clearly: dark, with a scarlet gown, glasses, and a blue mantle hemmed in gold."

"I would be happy if she had a skirt like ours on and a kerchief in her hair, as long as she gave us presents."

"Virgins don't give presents or dress the way we do."

"You think you're always right."

"When I'm right, I do."

"When agreeing with you, one can't even say 'This is what I think,'" Leonor commented, stroking me on the head.

Suddenly night fell, smelling of mint and rain.

Ludovica and Leonor filled the water jars, drank some water, and went home. On the way they stopped to speak with an old man who was carrying a sack. They spoke about the long-awaited miracle. They said that at night they heard the apparition calling them. The old man replied, "It must be the fox singing. Why look for miracles away from home, when you have Leopoldina, who works miracles in her dreams?"

Ludovica and Leonor asked themselves if that was true.

In the kitchen, sitting on a high-backed wicker chair, Leopoldina was smoking. She was so old that she looked like a scribble; you couldn't see her eyes or her mouth. She smelled like earth, grass, dry leaves: not like a person. She announced storms and good weather like a barometer; even before I did, she could smell the mountain lion coming down from the hills to eat the young goats or twist the necks of the colts. Despite not having left the house for thirty years she knew, as birds know, where there were ripe nuts, figs, and peaches, in what valley, beside which stream. Even the crispin bird, with its sad song, shy as a fox, came down one day to eat bread crumbs dipped in milk out of her hands, surely believing that she was a bush.

Leopoldina dreamed, sitting in the wicker chair. Sometimes, when she awoke, she would find the objects that had appeared in her dreams on her lap or next to the leg of the chair. However, her dreams were so modest, so poor—dreams of thorns, of stones, of branches, of feathers—that no one was surprised by the miracle.

"What did you dream about, Leopoldina?" Leonor asked, that night, when she came in.

"I dreamed that I was walking along a dry stream bed, picking up round pebbles. Here's one of them," Leopoldina said, with her flute-like voice.

"And how did you get the pebble?"

"Just by looking at it," she answered.

Leonor and Ludovica no longer waited for night to come beside the spring, as they had on other afternoons, in hopes of witnessing a miracle. They went home, with hurried steps.

"What did you dream about, Leopoldina?" asked Ludovica.

"About the feathers of a ringdove, falling to earth. Here's one of them," Leopoldina added, showing her a little feather.

"Tell me, Leopoldina, why don't you dream of other things?" asked Ludovica, impatiently.

"Honey, what do you want me to dream of?"

"Of precious stones, of rings, of necklaces, of bracelets. Of something that's good for something. Of automobiles."

"Honey, I don't know."

"What don't you know?"

"What those things are. I'm about a hundred and twenty and I've always been very poor."

"It's time to get rich. You can bring wealth to this household."

The next several days Leonor and Ludovica sat next to Leopoldina, watching her sleep. Every little while they would wake her up.

"What were you dreaming?" they would ask. "What were you dreaming?"

Sometimes she answered that she had dreamt of feathers, sometimes of pebbles, and sometimes of grass, branches, or frogs. Ludovica and Leonor protested, sometimes bitterly, other times tenderly, trying to move her, but Leopoldina didn't own her dreams: the two of them disturbed her so much that she couldn't sleep. They decided to give her a stew that would be hard to digest.

"A heavy stomach makes you sleepy," said Ludovica, preparing a dark fritter that smelled wonderful.

Leopoldina ate, but wasn't sleepy.

"We'll give you some wine," said Ludovica. "Warm wine."

Leopoldina drank it, but didn't fall asleep.

Leonor, who was clever, went to the folk healer for some soporific herbs. The healer lived in a very remote place. We had to cross the swamp, and one of the mules sank in. The herbs Leonor got from her were just as useless as everything else. For several days Ludovica and Leonor discussed where they should go looking for a doctor: whether to Tafí del Valle or Amaicha.

"If we go to Amaicha we can bring home grapes," Leonor said to Leopoldina, to console her. "But it's not grape season."

"And if we go to Tafí del Valle, we can buy cheese at the cheese factory at Churqui," said Ludovica.

"Why don't you take Changuito, to get him out of the house?" Leopoldina answered, as if she didn't like cheese or grapes.

We went to Tafí del Valle. We rode slowly on horseback across the swamp where the mule had died. In town we came to the hospital and Leonor went to find the doctor. We waited for her on the terrace. While Leonor was speaking with the doctor, we had time to take a walk around town. When we returned, Leonor was waiting for us at the hospital entrance, a package in her hand. The package contained some medicine and a syringe set for giving shots. Leonor knew how to give shots: a nurse she had known had taught her the art of sticking the needle in an orange or an apple. We spent the night at Tafí del Valle and the next morning very early set out on our way home.

When Leopoldina saw us come back, she said she was very tired, as if she had made the trip, and slept for the first time after twenty days of insomnia.

"What a rogue," Ludovica said. "She sleeps to show us her scorn." As soon as they saw her waking up they asked her, "What did you dream about? You must tell us what you dreamed."

Leopoldina stammered a few words. Ludovica shook her by the arm.

"If you don't tell us your dream, Leonor will give you a shot," she added, showing her the syringe.

"I dreamt that a dog was writing my story: here it is," Leopoldina said, showing several sheets of wrinkled, dirty paper. "Won't you read them out loud, my dears, so that I can listen to them?"

"Can't you dream about more important things?" said Leonor indignantly, throwing the sheets on the ground. Then she brought a huge book that smelled of cat urine, with color plates, that the teacher had lent her. After carefully looking through it, she paused over several of the plates, which she showed Leopoldina, rubbing them with her index finger. "Automobiles," she said, then, turning the page, "necklaces," another page, "bracelets," blowing on the pages, "jewels," wetting her finger with a drop of spit, "clocks," turning the pages with their fingers. "These are the things you have to dream about, not all that trash."

It was at that moment, Leopoldina, that I spoke to you, but you didn't hear me, because you were sleeping again and something had changed from the time of your last dream to this one.

"Do you remember my ancestors? If you see them in me—big-bellied, rude, hot-blooded, and trembling—you will remember the most sumptuous objects you ever saw: the medallion, gold-plated with a lock of hair inside, that you received as a wedding gift; the stones of your mother's necklace, which your daughter-in-law stole; the box full of aquamarine pendants, the sewing machine, the clock, the carriage drawn by horses so old they were docile. It seems incredible, but all that existed once. Do you remember the dazzling shop in Tafí del Valle where you bought a clasp with a picture of a dog that resembled me, carved in a stone? I am the only one who can remind you of those, I who wrapped your breast to cure you of asthma."

"If you don't sleep we'll give you a shot," threatened Ludovica.

Terrified, Leopoldina went back to sleep. Rocking back and forth, the wicker chair made a strange noise.

"I wonder if there are thieves," said Leonor.

"There's no moon."

"It must be the spirits," answered Leonor.

"Did you know why I was crying? Because I felt the hot wind blowing from the Andes."

Neither Leonor nor Ludovica could hear it, because their voices echoed so. Desperate, or perhaps hopeful, they asked, "What did you dream? What did you dream?"

But Leopoldina left without answering. She said to me, "Let's go, Changuito—it's time."

At that very moment a hot wind started blowing. In former days it had always made itself known to Christians in advance, with a very clear sky, a pale sun, its outline distinct, and a threatening noise like the sea (which I have never seen) in the distance. But this time it arrived like lightning, sweeping the patio, piling up leaves and branches in the hollows of the hills, beheading the animals against the rocks, destroying the harvest. A whirlwind swept Leopoldina and me into the air: I, her little dog Changuito, who wrote this story during my mistress's next-to-last dream.

THE WEDDING

FOR A YOUNG woman of Roberta's age to pay attention to me, to go out for walks with me, to confide in me, was a joy that none of my friends could share. She had control of me, and I loved her, not because she gave me candy or marbles or colored pencils but because she sometimes spoke to me as if I were big, sometimes as if both of us were six years old.

The control Roberta had over me was mysterious: she said I guessed her every thought and desire. She was thirsty: I would bring her a glass of water she hadn't asked for. She was hot: I fanned her or brought her a handkerchief moistened in cologne. She had a headache: I offered her an aspirin or a cup of coffee. She wanted a flower: I gave it to her. If she had given me an order—"Gabriela, jump out of the window," or "Put your hand in the coals," or "Run on the railroad tracks so the train will hit you"—I would have obeyed instantly.

We all lived on the outskirts of the city of Córdoba. Arminda López was my next-door neighbor and Roberta Carma lived across the street. Arminda López and Roberta Carma loved each other like cousins, which they were, but at times they addressed each other rather harshly: that happened especially when they were talking about clothes, underwear, hairstyles, or boyfriends. They never thought about their jobs. Half a block from our houses was the Lovely Waves beauty salon. Once a month Roberta took me there. While they bleached her hair with peroxide and ammonia, I played with the stylist's gloves, spray bottle, combs, hairpins, a hair dryer that looked like a warrior's helmet, and an old wig the hairdresser was especially kind to let me play with. That wig pleased me more than anything in the world, more than the walks to Ongamira or the Sugarloaf, more than fruit pastries or the bluish horse that crossed the vacant lot when it was wandering around the block, without reins or saddle, distracting me from my school studies.

Arminda Lopez's engagement distracted me more than the beauty parlor or the strolls. During those days I got bad grades, the worst of my whole life.

Roberta took me by trolley to the Oriental Café. There we had hot chocolate with vanilla wafers and a young man came up to talk to her. On the way back in the trolley Roberta told me that Arminda was luckier than she was because at twenty women either had to fall in love or throw themselves in the river.

"Which river?" I asked, disturbed by these confidences.

"You don't understand. How could you? You're still very young."

"When I marry, I'm going to have a beautiful hairpiece," Arminda said. "My hair will catch every eye."

Roberta laughed and protested, "How old-fashioned. Nobody wears hairpieces anymore."

"You're wrong. They're in fashion again," Arminda answered. "You'll see: everybody will look at me."

The preparations for the wedding were long and painstaking. The gown was sumptuous. A piece of fine lace from her maternal grandmother adorned her dress, while a piece of lace from the paternal grandmother (so as not to make her jealous) adorned her veil. The dressmaker had Arminda try on the dress five times. Kneeling, her mouth full of pins, the dressmaker adjusted the hem or added pleats to the dress. Holding her father's arm, Arminda crossed the patio of her house five times, entering her bedroom and stopping in front of a mirror to see how the pleated dress looked when she moved. Her hair was perhaps what most worried Arminda. She had dreamed about it all her life. She had an enormous hairpiece made with a lock of hair she had had cut off when she was fifteen. A delicate golden net with little pearls held it together; the hairdresser showed it off in his shop. According to her father, her hairpiece looked like a wig.

On the morning of her wedding, the second of January, the thermometer reached 105. It was so hot that we didn't have to wet our hair before combing it or rinse our faces with water to remove the dirt. Exhausted, Roberta and I were on the patio. It was getting dark. The sky, a leaden gray color, frightened us. The storm turned out to be only a lot of lightning and millions of bugs. A huge spider was sitting in the vine on the patio: to me, it seemed to be looking at us. I fetched a broomstick to kill it, but something stopped me. Roberta cried out, "It represents hope! A French lady once told me that a spider in the evening means hope."

"If it means hope, let's keep it in a little box," I said.

Moving like a sleepwalker because she was tired (and virtuous), Roberta went to her room to look for a box.

"Be careful. They're poisonous," she said.

"And if it bites me?"

"Spiders are like people: they bite to defend themselves. If you don't do anything to them, they won't do anything to you."

I opened a little box in front of the spider, and with a single hop it jumped inside. Afterwards I closed the top, making air holes in it with a pin.

"What are you going to do with it?" Roberta asked.

"Keep it."

"Don't lose it," Roberta answered.

From then on, I walked around with the box in my pocket. The next morning we went to the beauty salon. It was Sunday. They were selling tablecloths and flowers on the street. Those joyful colors seemed to celebrate the nearness of the wedding. We had to wait for the hairdresser, who was at mass, while Roberta sat under the dryer.

"You look like a warrior," I shouted.

She didn't hear me and kept on reading her missal. Suddenly, I felt like playing with Arminda's hairpiece, sitting there beside me. I took off the hairpins that held the locks together beneath the beautiful hairnet. Roberta seemed to be looking at me, but she must have been distracted and was just staring fixedly into space.

"Shall I put the spider inside?" I asked, showing her the hairpiece.

No doubt the noise of the hair dryer prevented her from hearing my voice. She didn't answer me, but nodded as if in agreement. I opened the box, turning it upside down onto the hairpiece, and the spider fell inside. Then I rearranged the hair, quickly putting back the fine netting and the pins so no one would catch me by surprise. I must have done it with skill, because the hairdresser didn't notice anything unusual in his work of art, as he himself termed the bridal adornment.

"All of this will be a secret between us," Roberta said, as we left the beauty shop, twisting my arm till I cried out. I couldn't recall what secret she had told me that day. So I answered the way adults talk, "I'll be silent as the grave."

Roberta wore a fringed yellow dress, and I wore a white starched dress with plumes and a lace insert. In the church, I didn't stare at the bride because Roberta told me you didn't have to stare at her. The bride was very pretty with a white veil full of orange blossoms. She was so pale she looked like an angel. Then she fell down, senseless. From afar, she looked like a curtain that had dropped. Many people rushed up to help her, fanning her, going to the chancel for water, patting her face. For a moment they thought she had died; the next moment they thought she was alive. They carried her to her house, cold as marble. They didn't want to undress her or take off her hairpiece before putting her in the coffin. Shy, uncomfortable, ashamed, during the two days of the wake I accused myself of killing her.

"How did you kill her, you nasty kid?" asked a distant relative of Arminda's, who drank coffee incessantly.

"With a spider," I answered.

My parents conferred, worried that they needed to call a doctor. Nobody ever believed me. Roberta hated me. I think I disgusted her and she never went out with me again.

VOICE ON THE TELEPHONE

No, DON'T invite me to your nephews' house. Children's parties depress me. That probably seems silly to you. Yesterday you got mad because I didn't want to light your cigarette. Everything is connected. So I'm crazy? Maybe. Since I can't ever see you, I'm going to have to explain things on the phone. What things? The story of the matches. I hate the phone. Yes. I know you love it, but I would have preferred to tell you everything in the car, or on the way out of the movie theater, or in a coffee shop. I have to return to my childhood.

"Fernando, if you play with matches, you'll burn the house down," my mother would tell me, or something like, "The whole house is going to be reduced to a little pile of ashes," or maybe, "We will all fly away like fireworks."

Does that seem normal to you? That's what I think too, but it made me want to touch matches even more, to caress them, to try lighting them, to live for them. The same thing happened with you and erasers? But they didn't forbid you to touch them. Erasers don't burn. You ate them? That's different. The memories of when I was four tremble as if lit by fire. As I told you already, the house where I spent my childhood was huge: it had five bedrooms, two entrance halls, two living rooms with ceilings painted with clouds and little angels. You think I lived like a king? No, you're wrong. There were always fights among the servants. They were divided into two groups: the supporters of my mother and the followers of Nicolás Simonetti. Who was he? Nicolás Simonetti was the cook: I was crazy about him. He threatened me, in jest, with a huge shiny knife, and gave me little slices of meat and lettuce to play with, and caramels I spilled on the marble floor. He contributed as much as my mother did to awakening my passion for matches, lighting them so I could blow them out. Due to my mother's supporters, who were tireless, the food was never ready, or tasty, or cooked properly. There was always a hand that intercepted the plates and let them cool, that added talcum powder to the noodles, that dusted the eggs with ashes. All of this culminated in the appearance of a tremendously long hair in the rice pudding.

"That is Juanita's hair," my father said.

"No," said my aunt, "I don't want to 'get her hair in my milk'—to me it tastes like Luisa's."

My mother, who was very proud, stood up from the table in the middle of the meal and, grasping the hair between her fingertips, carried it to the kitchen. My mother was annoyed by the face of the cook, who was entranced, seeing it not as a hair but as a strand of black thread. I don't know what sarcastic or wounding phrase made Nicolás Simonetti take off his apron, wrap it up in the shape of a ball as if to throw it away, and announce that he was leaving the household. I followed him to the bathroom where he got dressed and undressed each day. This time, he who paid me so much attention dressed without even looking at me. He combed his hair with a bit of grease he had left on his hands. I never saw hands that so resembled combs. Then, with dignity, he gathered up the molds, enormous knives, and spatulas in the kitchen, put them in the briefcase he always carried, and went toward the door with his hat on. To make him look at me I gave him a kick in the shins; he put his hand, smelling of lard, on my head, saying, "Goodbye, kid. Now many people will be able to appreciate Nicolás's food. They'll lick their lips."

You think that's funny? I'll keep on with my list: there were two studies. Why so many? I ask myself the same thing—nobody wrote. Eight hallways, three bathrooms (one with two sinks). Why two? Perhaps they washed with four hands. Two stoves (one inexpensive, the other electric), two rooms for washing and ironing (my father said one was so the clothes could get wrinkled), a pantry, a vestibule by the dining room, five servants' bedrooms, a room for the trunks.

Did we travel a lot? No. Those trunks were used for many different things. Another room was for chests of drawers; another, for odds and ends, was where the dog slept and where my hobbyhorse sat on a tricycle. Does that house still exist? It exists in my memory. The objects are like milestones showing you how far you've gone: the house had so many of them that my memory is full of numbers. I could say what year I ate my first apple or bit the dog's ear, or when I peed in the candy dish. You think I'm a pig! I preferred the rugs, chandeliers, and glass cabinets in that house to my toys. For my birthday my mother organized a party. She invited twenty boys and twenty girls so they would bring me presents. My mother had foresight. You're right, she was a sweetheart! For the party, the servants took out the rugs, and my mother replaced the objects in the glass cabinets with little cardboard horses filled with surprises, and little plastic cars, rattles, cornets, and piccolos for the boys, and bracelets, rings, change purses, and little hearts for the girls. In the middle of the dining table they put a cake with four candles, sandwiches, and chocolate milk. Some children (not all of them with presents) arrived with their nursemaids, others with their mothers, others with an aunt or a grandmother. The mothers, aunts, or grandmothers sat down to chat. Standing in the corner, blowing on a cornet that made no sound, I listened to them.

"How pretty you are today, Boquita," my mother said to the mother of one of my girlfriends. "Did you come from the country?"

"It's the season of the year when you want to get a little tan and end up looking like a monster," Boquita answered.

I thought she was referring to fire rather than to the sun. Did I like her? Who? Boquita? No. She was horrible, with a tiny mouth, no lips, but my mother said that you should never compliment the pretty ones for their beauty, but instead the ugly ones because that was good manners; she said beauty was of the soul and not of the face; that Boquita was a fright, but "had a certain something." Besides, my mother didn't lie: she always managed to utter the words in an equivocal way, as if her tongue were stuck, and that's how she said, "How pretty you are, Boquita," which could also be taken as a compliment due to her friend's strong personality. They spoke of politics, of hats and clothes, of economic problems, of people who hadn't come to the party: I assure you I'm repeating the exact words I heard them say. After the balloons were passed out, after the puppet show (in which Little Red Riding Hood terrified me as much as the wolf did the grandmother, in which the Beauty seemed as horrible as the Beast), after blowing out the candles on my birthday cake, I followed my mother into the most private room in the house, where she shut herself in with her friends, surrounded by embroidered pillows. I managed to hide behind an armchair, trampling on a lady's hat, squatting down, leaning against a wall so as not to lose balance. I'm clumsy, you know. The ladies were laughing so hard that I could hardly understand what they were saying. They spoke of bodices, and one of them unbuttoned her blouse to the waist to show the one she wore. It was as translucent as a Christmas stocking; I thought it must have some toy inside and yearned to stick my hand in. They spoke of sizes: it turned out to be a game. They took turns standing up. Elvira, who looked like a huge baby, mysteriously took a tape measure out of her purse.

"I always carry a nail file and a tape measure in my pocketbook, just in case," she said.

"What a madwoman," Boquita shouted boisterously, "you look like a dressmaker."

They measured their waists, busts, and hips.

"I bet you my waist is a twenty-two."

"I bet you mine is less."

Their voices echoed as in a theater.

"I would like to win for my hips," one said.

"I would be happy to win for my bust," another one said. "Men are more interested in breasts, haven't you seen them staring?"

"If they don't look me in the eye I don't feel anything," said another, who was wearing a sumptuous pearl necklace.

"It's not a matter of what you feel, it's what they feel," said the aggressive voice of one woman who wasn't anyone's mother.

"I couldn't care less," the other answered, shrugging her shoulders.

"Not me," said Rosca Pérez, who was beautiful, when it was her turn to be measured; she bumped against the armchair where I was hiding.

"I won," said Chinche, who was as pointed as a small-headed pin, shaking the nine silver bangles she wore on one arm.

"Twenty," Elvira exclaimed, examining the tape measure that was wrapped around Chinche's tiny waist.

Who had a twenty-inch waist, except maybe a wasp? She must have been a wasp. Could she make her stomach go down like a yogi? She was no yogi, but she was a snake charmer. She fascinated perverted women. Not my mother. My mother was a saint. She felt sorry for her. When people gossiped about Chinche she would comment, "Such nonsense."

Not on your life. I had never heard a scoundrel say "such nonsense." It would have been out of character. That was very typical of her. I'll go on with my story. At that moment the phone rang beside one of the armchairs. Chinche and Elvira answered it together. Then, covering the receiver with a pillow, they told my mother, "It's for you, dear."

The others jostled one another, and Rosca took the phone to listen to the voice.

"I bet it's the one with the beard," one of the ladies said.

"I bet it's the elf," said another, chewing on her necklace.

Then a phone conversation began in which they all took part, passing the phone along from one to the next. I forgot I was supposed to be hiding and stood up to watch the ladies' enthusiasm, marked by the ringing sounds of bracelets and necklaces. When my mother saw me, her voice and expression changed. As if she were in front of the mirror she smoothed her hair and pulled up her stockings; she then carefully put out her cigarette in the ashtray, twisting it two or three times. She took me by the hand and I, taking advantage of her confusion, stole the fancy long matches that were on the table next to the whiskey glasses. We left the room.

"You have to attend to your guests," my mother said severely. "I'll attend to mine."

She left me in the dismantled living room, without a carpet, without the usual objects in the glass cabinet, without the most valuable furniture, filled instead with hollow horses made of cardboard, with cornets and piccolos on the floor, with little cars whose owners seemed like impostors to me. Each of the children was hugging and pulling on a balloon in an alarming way. Atop the piano, covered with cloth, someone had put all of the presents my friends had brought me. Poor piano? Why don't you say poor Fernando instead! I noticed that some presents were missing: I had carefully counted and examined them as soon as I received them. I thought they must be somewhere else in the house and began wandering through the hallway that led to the garbage can, where I dug out some cardboard boxes and pieces of newspaper. These I triumphantly took back to the dismantled living room. I discovered that some of the children had taken advantage of my absence to take possession once more of the presents they had brought me. Smart? Shameless. After much hesitation and much trouble dealing with the children, we sat down on the floor to play with some matches. A nursemaid came in and told her companion, "There are very fine decorations in this house: there are flower vases that would crush your foot if they fell on it." Looking at us as if she were speaking of the same vases, she added, "Each one alone is a devil, but together they're like the baby Jesus."

We made buildings, plans, houses, bridges out of matches; for a long while we twisted their heads. It was not until later, when Cacho arrived with his glasses on and a wallet in his pocket, that we tried lighting the matches. First we tried to light them on the soles of our shoes, then later on the stones of the fireplace. The first spark burnt our fingers. Cacho was very wise and told us that he knew not only how to prepare but how to light a bonfire. He had the idea of surrounding the vestibule next to the dining room, where his nursemaid was, with fire. I protested. We should not waste matches on nursemaids.

Those fancy matches were destined for the private room where I had found them. They were the matches belonging to our mothers. On tiptoe we approached the door to the room where we could hear voices and laughter. I was the one who locked the door with the key; I was the one who took the key out and put it in my pocket. We piled up the paper the presents had been wrapped in, and the cardboard boxes full of straw; also some newspaper that had been left on a table, the bits of trash I had collected, and some pieces of firewood from the fireplace, where we sat for a moment to watch the future bonfire. We heard Margarita's voice, saying, "They've locked us in." I haven't forgotten her laughter.

One of them answered, "That's better, that way they'll leave us alone."

At first the fire threw off only a few sparks, then it exploded, growing like a giant, with a giant's tongue. It licked the most expensive piece of furniture in the house, a Chinese chest with lots of little drawers, decorated with millions of figures that were crossing bridges, looking out of doorways, walking along the banks of a river. Millions and millions of pesos had been offered to my mother for that piece, and she had never wanted to sell it at any price. You think that's a shame? It would have been better to sell it. We drew back to the front door where the nursemaids had gathered. The voices calling for help echoed down the long service staircase. The doorman, who was chatting at the street corner, didn't arrive in time to use the fire extinguisher. They made us go down to the courtyard. Bunched together under a tree, we saw the house in flames, and the useless arrival of the firemen. Now do you understand why I refused to light your cigarette? Why matches make such an impression on me? Didn't you know I was sensitive? Naturally, the ladies gathered by the window, but we were so interested in the fire that we barely noticed them. The last vision I have of my mother is of her face pointed downward, leaning against the balcony railing. And the Chinese chest of drawers? The Chinese chest was saved from the fire, luckily. Some little figures were ruined: one was of a lady who was carrying a child in her arms, slightly resembling my mother and me.

THE PUNISHMENT

WE WERE facing a mirror that reflected our faces and the flowers in the room.

"What's the matter?" I asked her. She was pale. "Are you hiding something from me?"

"I don't hide anything from you. That mirror reminds me of my misfortune: that we are two, not one," she said, covering her face. "When I see you looking so stern I feel guilty. Everything feels like infidelity to me. I'm twenty years old. What good is that? For fear of losing me, you don't want me to look at anything, to try anything; you don't want me to live. You want me to be yours once and for all, like a thing. If I went along with you, I'd end up retreating to the first moments of my life or would be driven to my death or, perhaps, to madness," she told me. "Aren't you scared of that?"

"You're hiding something from me," I insisted. "Don't try distracting my attention with your complaints."

"If you really think I'm hiding something from you, I'll recount everything that has happened to me during the last twenty years, my whole life up till now—I'll sum it all up."

"As if I didn't know the story of your life!" I answered.

"You don't. Let me rest my head on your knees, because I feel sleepy."

I settled into the sofa and let her rest comfortably on me, rocking her as if she were an infant.

"The only sin that existed for me was infidelity. But—how to be faithful without being dead to the rest of the world and to yourself? In a room with flowers painted on the wall, Sergio held me naked in his arms. He suspected I had deceived him and he wanted to kill me. I hadn't deceived him, because in my acts of unfaithfulness, if there were any, I had been searching for him."

"Why do you name me as if you were speaking of someone else?"

"Because Sergio was someone else. For three years I knew perfect love. Everything united us: we had the same tastes, the same character, the same sensibility. He controlled me: he devoured me the way a tiger devours a lamb. He loved me as if he had me inside him, and I loved him as if I had emerged from him. After three years of joy and of torture, we learned, little by little, in ways ever more romantic and modest, to know not how to even kiss each other. Shame covered my body, like a dress that's too tight, with too many snaps and ties. I refused to see him anymore. I felt repelled by his kisses. He wrote me a letter suggesting obscene things to me. I threw the letter in the fire. 'What will be inside this letter?' I thought when I saw the envelope; I was full of hope. I held it in my hands for a while before opening it.

"We arranged to meet in a church; we scarcely looked at each other. Later, furtively, in a square. For a time I lived enveloped in a sort of fog, troubled yet fortunate.

"Some months later I met Sergio in a theater."

"Don't name me as if you didn't know me. I feel like I could strangle you," I told her. She continued as if she hadn't heard me:

"How handsome a stranger is! I was moved to see those eyes looking at me for the first time. I trembled with emotion, like someone who sees the beginning of spring in a single tiny leaf while the rest of the garden is still deep in winter, or like someone who sees a cliff amidst blue mountains and bushes with dazzling, distant flowers. Vertigo, I felt only vertigo. Surely we'd met in some previous incarnation: we didn't greet each other, and yet it seemed natural to me. 'I would like to know him in this life,' I thought with some vehemence. Swiftly I forgot Sergio."

"I forbid you to play with our love," I told her, trying to disrupt her thoughts. She didn't listen to me.

"I was happy, with that happiness produced by anticipation. I danced before the mirror. I played the piano incredibly well, or at least that's what I thought. I was waiting for—what? I didn't know. For a boyfriend, no doubt. I was already tired of studying. Not even bashfulness saved me from boredom, from nervousness during exams. My philosophy teacher was my best friend. I brought her bouquets of roses, or of flowers that I had picked in the countryside. She invited me to have tea at her house. She stopped being my friend. She treated me with scorn or indifference.

"'Take a bouquet of flowers to your teacher; if you don't pay attention to her, she'll never show you any kindness,' my mother told me one day.

"'Does kindness have to be bought?'

"'Who taught you that ugly word?' she said to me.

"'Which one?' I asked, with obvious prevarication.

"'Bought. You can buy fruit, food, clothing, God knows what, but not human feelings,' she answered proudly.

"'Everything can be bought, with or without money,' I told her.

"I don't know why I remember that conversation so clearly. The days were growing longer, wider, deeper. There was time for everything, mostly for forgetting. It took me a long time to forget how to dance and play the piano. My body lost its balance; when I tried to stand on tiptoe I wobbled; my fingers lost their agility, sticking to the keys as they stumbled over scales. I felt humiliated. I tried to kill myself one winter night, sitting naked by an open window, motionless, shivering with cold until dawn; and later, with sleeping pills I secretly bought at a drugstore; and again, with a revolver I found in my father's room. I always failed because of my indecisiveness, my nervousness, my good health, but not because of any love for life. Alicia disappointed me with her betrayals and lies. I resolved not to see her anymore and, before parting forever, to recount her sins to her whole family, some day when they would all be gathered before those mystical paintings so carefully illuminated in their living room. Alicia and I confided in each other. She was my best friend. We slept together in the summer with mosquito nets over our faces. We always fell in love with the same boy, but he would always be in love with me. Alicia thought they were in love with her. We got annoyed with each other for no reason. We laughed at everything, without cause: at death, at love, at misfortune and happiness. We didn't know what we wanted, and what we most enjoyed sometimes turned out to be tedious and boring.

"'These kids think they're grown-ups,' my mother would say, or my aunt, or one of the servants, 'they need a good beating.'

"We read pornographic books that we hid under the mattress; we smoked, we went to the movies instead of studying.

"We swam every morning at the municipal pool, and won prizes in four or five races. We swam in the river too, when we were invited to spend the day in some resort at Tigre; or in the sea, that summer we spent in a house my aunt rented at Los Acantilados. I saw the sea for the first time! There we learned to float, learning with some difficulty because we were afraid. We were forgetting how to swim. Oh, how we sank in the water! One day we almost drowned, hanging on to each other, trying to save ourselves or pull each other under.

"'You're going to drown,' my mother warned me. 'When you learn to swim, you'll lose your fear, and soon you'll be winning races.' In my chest of drawers I collected postcards I received from Claudina. I couldn't sleep for the thought of going to school: shame before the other children, fear of the older ones, curiosity about sexual pangs. Everything tormented me.

"We spent days and days of happiness in a huge garden with two stone sphinxes that guarded the entrance by the gate. In the afternoon we went down to the river for a walk. From the road to the Yacht Club you could see the church of San Isidro, where they took me to hear Sunday mass. I was a mystic, devoted to the Virgin of Luján. Instead of wearing a bracelet on my wrist I wore a rosary. Claudina went to Europe. We bought fresh eggs in a little house hidden behind a gigantic vine. Sometimes they let me go on a bicycle, with Claudina or by myself. During one of my outings a man looked at my tiny breasts and said obscene things to me. I was frightened and told Claudina about it. I wasn't used to having breasts. Time passed and the bicycle became extremely tall for me. I lacked the balance necessary to ride it.

"*'Fraidy cat,' the gardener would say to me, looking at my knees and stroking his mustache.*

"The scar I have on my forehead is from a blow when I hit a post while going downhill.

"I took my first communion. I dreamed about my white dress. I had a straight body—no hips, no breasts, no waist—like a boy's. They took us, Claudina and me, to the photographer's house, dressed in white tulle, bearing missals and evil thoughts. I still have the pictures.

"I remember the day the new bicycle arrived at our house, still in its crate. And later, my mother promising it to me if I got good grades in school. 'Riding on a tricycle is boring! When do I get a bicycle?' my voice said.

"I rode around and around the furniture in the house on my tricycle, thinking about that bicycle. We were in the city.

"With a crew cut, like a boy, I climbed trees. I was convalescing only slowly, for my mother couldn't get me to keep still. Three doctors surrounded my bed. I heard them talking about typhus. I was shaking in bed, constantly drinking water and orange juice. My mother was frightened: her eyes shone like precious stones. A doctor must be called.

"That same morning she said, *'My daughter doesn't have anything. She has an iron constitution,'* and she sent me to school with the nursemaid.

"I was drinking water from a swamp full of garbage the day I met Claudina. Nobody ever spoke of my prank.

"I didn't yet know how to ride a tricycle. The pedals hurt my legs.

"We took a trip to France: the sea, which I saw for the last time, fascinated me. And later, for a long time, I asked my mother, *'What will France be like? What's the sea like?'*

"I pretended to read the newspaper, like the adults did, sitting in a chair. Rosa, Magdalena, and Ercilia were my friends. We were all the same age, but I was the most precocious. I could recognize any tune. On the swings at Palermo Park, I swung without any fear, and would climb the tallest slide without a moment's hesitation. Then, little by little, they no longer allowed me to climb any but the lowest slide, because the other one was dangerous. Danger, danger: What was danger? They tried to teach me what it was: with knives, with pins, with broken glass, with electric outlets, with heights. They didn't allow me to eat chocolate or ice cream, or ride on the merry-go-round by myself.

"Why can't I eat chocolate?' I would ask. 'Because it will give you indigestion,' they would answer. I adored my mother: I cried when she didn't come back home early. My friends stole my toys.

"Someone scared me one night with a stuffed monkey, and the next day gave me the same monkey, which I didn't like. People made me afraid or happy. I didn't know how to write except with rubber blocks: rose, house, mommy. The days grew longer and longer. Each day included little dawns, little afternoons, little evenings, repeated over and over. I cried when I saw a dog or a cat that wasn't a toy. I couldn't recognize letters, not even the easy ones like *O* or *A*. I couldn't recognize the numbers, not even zero that looked like an egg, or the one that looked like a little soldier. I started tasting certain fruits and soups for the first time, then the sweet taste of milk. This is my life," she told me, closing her eyes. "Remembering the past is killing me."

"Are you making fun of me?" I asked her.

She didn't answer. Her lips closed: she never opened them again to say she loved me. I couldn't cry. As if I were seeing her from the top of a mountain, I watched her, distant, defenseless, unassailable. Her madness was my only rival. I embraced her for the last time and it was like I was being raped. During her story, time had run backwards for me: twenty years less for her had meant twenty more for me. I gazed into the mirror, hoping that it would reflect creatures less afflicted, less demented than ourselves. I saw that my hair had turned white.

THE PRAYER

LAURA was in church, praying:

Oh, my God, won't You reward the good deeds of Your servant? I know that sometimes I wasn't good. I'm impatient and deceitful. I lack charity, but I always try to merit Your forgiveness. Haven't I spent hours kneeling on the floor of my room before the image of one of Your Virgins? This horrible child I've hidden in my house, to save him from those who wanted to lynch him, won't he bring me any satisfaction? I have no children, I'm an orphan, I'm not in love with my husband: all this You know well. I don't hide anything from You. My parents led me to marriage as one leads a girl to school or to the doctor. I obeyed them because I thought everything would turn out all right. I can't hide it from You: love can't be forced, and even if You Yourself had given me the command to love my husband, I wouldn't be able to obey You unless You inspired the love in me that I need. When he embraces me I want to run away, to hide in a forest (ever since childhood I've imagined an enormous forest where even in distress I can't hide because it's covered with snow). He tells me, "You're so cold . . . it's like you were made of marble."

I much prefer the ugly box-office attendant who sometimes gives me tickets so I can see movies with my little sister, or the rather repulsive salesman in the shoe store who caresses my foot between his legs when I'm trying shoes on, or the blond bricklayer at the corner of Corrientes and 9 de Julio, next to the house where my favorite student lives, the one I like, the one with dark eyes who sits on the ground eating a steak sandwich, onions, and grapes, the one who asks me, "Are you married?" and then says, without waiting for an answer, "What a shame."

The one who made me navigate scaffolding to see the apartment soon to be occupied by newlyweds.

Four times I visited the apartment under construction. The first time was in the morning—they were laying bricks for a partition. I sat on the pile of lumber. It was the house of my dreams. The brick-layer (whose name is Anselmo) took me to the highest part of the house so I could see the view. You know that Your servant had no desire to stay so long at the construction site and that it was only because she twisted her ankle that, without wanting to, she had to stay with the men for a long time, waiting for the pain to subside. The second time I arrived in the afternoon. They were installing the windows and I went to look for a change purse I had forgotten. Anselmo wanted me to see the terrace. It was six o'clock in the afternoon when we came down and all the other workers had left. While passing a wall I got whitewash on my arm and cheek. Anselmo, with his handkerchief, without asking my permission, rubbed off the spots. I saw that his eyes were blue and his mouth bright red. I looked at him, perhaps too hard, because he told me, "What eyes you have!"

We climbed down through the scaffold holding hands. He asked me to return at eight o'clock the next night because one of his fellow workers was going to play the accordion and the wife of another was going to bring some wine. You know, oh my God, that I went not for my own sake but in order not to offend him. Anselmo's co-worker was playing the accordion when I arrived. The others were gathered around some bottles by the light of a lantern. The woman had brought a basket full of bottles of wine, which we drank. I left before the party was over. Anselmo guided me with a lantern to the entrance. He wanted to accompany me for a few blocks. I didn't let him.

"Will you come back?" he said in parting. "You still haven't seen the tile work."

"What tile work?" I asked, laughing.

"In the bathroom," he answered, as if kissing me. "Come back, tomorrow they're coming."

"Who?"

"The newlyweds. We can spy on them."

"I'm not used to spying."

"I'll show you a neon sign, some shoes with wings. Have you ever seen them?"

"No."

"I'll show you them tomorrow."

"Okay."

"Will you come?"

"Yes," I answered, and then I left.

The third time there wasn't anyone in the building. Behind a wooden fence there was a fire burning; a pot rested on some stones.

"Tonight I'm replacing the night watchman," he told me when he saw me coming.

"And the couple?"

"They have already left. Shall we go up to see the neon sign?"

"Okay," I said, trying to hide my nervousness.

Oh my God, I had no idea what awaited me on the seventh floor. We ascended. I thought my heart was beating because of having to climb so many stairs and not because I was alone in that building with that man. When we got to the top, I was happy to see the neon sign from the terrace. I was afraid. There was no railing and I retreated to the bedroom. Anselmo took me by the waist.

"Don't fall," he said, adding, "Here's where they're going to put the bed. It must be beautiful to be married, to have a place."

As he said these words he sat down on the floor next to a little suitcase and a bundle of clothing.

"Do you want to see some pictures? Sit down."

He put a newspaper on the floor so I could sit. I sat down. He opened the suitcase and from inside it he took out an envelope, and, oh my God, from inside the envelope some pictures.

"This was my mother," he said, pressing close to me. "You can see how beautiful she was," addressing me now with the familiar form. "And this is my sister," he said, blowing lightly on my face.

He had me cornered and moved to embrace me, not even letting me breathe. Oh my God, You know I tried in vain to free myself from his arms. You know I pretended to be hurt in order to force him to come to his senses. You know I ran away crying. I hide nothing from You. I know I'm not virtuous, but do You know many virtuous women? I'm not one of those who wear tight pants and have half their breasts showing when they go to the riverside on Sunday. Of course my husband would be opposed to such things, but there are times I could take advantage of his distraction and let loose a little. I'm not to blame if men look at me: they look at me as if I were a little girl. I'm young, that's true, but what they like about me isn't that. They don't even look at Rosaura or Clara when they walk down the street: they don't get even one whistle during summer vacation, I'm sure of it. Not even indecent remarks, the kind which are so easy to get. I'm pretty: Is that really a sin? It's worse to be embittered. Since marrying Alberto, I've lived on a dark street in Avellaneda. You know very well that it's not paved and that at night I twist my ankles on the way home when I wear very high heels. Walking to work on rainy days, I wear rubber boots that are old now, and a raincoat that looks like a sack. Of course sacks are in fashion now. I'm a piano teacher and could have been a great pianist if it weren't for my husband, who is against it, as well as my lack of vanity. Sometimes, when we have people over, he insists I play tangos or jazz. Mortified, I sit down at the piano and obey unwillingly, because I know he likes it. My life is joyless. Every day, at the same hour, save on Saturdays and holidays, I walk down España Street to the home of one of my students. About three weeks ago (a period that has seemed like eternity to me), on a lonely stretch of unpaved road (deeply rutted), I saw five boys playing. Absentmindedly I saw them in the mud, by a ditch, as though they were not real children. Two of them were fighting: one had taken the other's blue and yellow kite and was grasping it firmly to his chest. The other took him by the neck (forcing him to fall into the ditch) and pushed his head under water. They struggled for a few moments: one trying to make the other's head stay under water, the other trying to pull it out. Some bubbles appeared in the muddy water, as when immersing an empty bottle in water and it goes glug glug glug. The boy didn't release his head but firmly gripped his victim, who no longer had the strength to defend himself. Their companions clapped their hands. Sometimes minutes seem very long or very short. I watched the scene, as if in a movie theater, without thinking of intervening. When the boy finally released the head of his adversary, it sank into the silent mud. Then they scattered. The boys ran away. I discovered that I had watched a crime, a crime in the midst of what at first seemed an innocent game. Running to their respective homes, the boys announced that Amancio Aráoz had been murdered by Claudio Herrera. I pulled Amancio out of the ditch. It was then that the women and men in the neighborhood, armed with clubs and tools, wanted to lynch Claudio Herrera. Claudio's mother, who was very fond of me, asked me while sobbing to hide him in my house, which I did willingly enough, after leaving the little corpse in the bed where they wrapped him in his shroud. My house was some distance from that of Amancio Aráoz's parents and that made things easier. During the funeral people didn't cry over Amancio but instead cursed Claudio. They carried the coffin around the block. They stopped by each doorway to yell insults about Claudio Herrera, so that people would know of the crime he had committed. They were so enraged they looked happy. On Amancio's white coffin they had put bright flowers, which were constantly praised by the women. Various children who were not related to the dead boy followed the procession to amuse themselves; they made a commotion, laughing, dragging sticks along the cobblestones. I don't think anyone cried— indignation requires no tears. Only one old lady, Miss Carmen, was sobbing, because she didn't understand what had happened. Oh my God, how miserable, how lacking in ceremony the funeral was! Claudio Herrera is eight years old. It's impossible to know to what extent he is conscious of the crime he has committed. I protect him like a mother. I can't explain why exactly! I feel so happy. I turned my living room into a bedroom for him. In the back of the house, where the chicken coop used to be, I made him a swing and a hammock; I bought him a bucket and a shovel so he could make a little garden and amuse himself with the plants. Claudio loves me or at least behaves as if he loves me. He obeys me more than he does his mother. I forbid him from going out on the balconies or the flat roof of the house. I don't allow him to answer the telephone. He never disobeys me. He helps me wash the dishes when we're done eating. He washes and peels the vegetables, and sweeps the courtyard in the morning. I don't have any reason to complain; nevertheless, perhaps under the influence of the neighbors' opinion, I've begun to view him as a criminal. I'm sure, oh my God, that he has tried to kill my dog Jasmine in various different ways. First I noticed that he had put cockroach poison in the plate where we put Jasmine's dinner; later, he tried to drown her under the faucet and in the pail we use to wash the courtyard. For the last few days I'm sure he didn't give her any water; if he did, it was mixed with ink, because Jasmine rejected it immediately, barking profusely. I attribute her diarrhea to some devilish mixture he put in the meat we feed her. I consulted the doctor who always gives me advice. She knows that I have many medicines in my medicine cabinet, among them barbiturates. The last time I went to see her she told me, "My dear, lock your medicine cabinet. Children's crimes are dangerous. Children use any means to reach their ends. They study dictionaries. Nothing gets by them. They know everything. He could poison your husband, whom he loathes, or so you've told me."

I replied, "For people to recover their goodness it's necessary to have faith in them. If Claudio suspects that I don't trust him, he'll be capable of horrible things. I already explained the contents of every bottle to him and showed him the ones with red labels that have the word 'Poison' on them."

Oh my God, I didn't lock the medicine cabinet, intentionally, so that Claudio can learn to repress his instincts, if it's true he's a criminal. The other night, during dinner, my husband sent him to the attic to get his toolbox. My husband enjoys carpentry. Since the boy didn't come back quickly enough, he went up to the attic to spy on him. Claudio, according to my husband, was sitting on the floor, playing with the tools, drilling a hole in the cover of the shiny wooden box my husband prized so much. Furious, he gave him a beating right then and there. He dragged him by the ear down to the table. My husband has no imagination. When dealing with a boy we suspect is abnormal, how dared he inflict a punishment on him that would have even infuriated me? We continued our dinner in silence. Claudio, as usual, bid us good night, and when we were alone, my husband told me, "If that monster doesn't leave this house soon, I'm going to die."

"How impatient you are," I answered. "I'm doing this as an act of charity. You must recognize that."

And to impress him still more, I invoked Your name. Before going to bed, as both of us suffer from insomnia, we always take a sleeping pill: he, because he can't sleep, rustles a book or a newspaper in bed, or lights a cigarette; and I, because I hear him and wait for him to fall asleep, and become more anxious about not falling asleep. He thought the same thing that the doctor recommended: that I should lock the medicine cabinet where we keep the sleeping pills. I didn't pay any attention to him, as I insist that trust is the means to improving the situation. My husband doesn't agree. For the past few days he has become apprehensive. He says that the coffee has a strange taste and that after he drinks it he feels dizzy, something that never happened to him before. To reassure him, I lock the medicine cabinet when he's home. Then I open it again. Many of my friends no longer come over—I can't let them visit, since I've told no one my secret, except for the doctor, and You, who know all. Nevertheless, I'm not sad. I know one day I'll have my reward and that day I will be happy again, as I was when I was single and lived next to Palermo Park, in a little house that no longer exists except in my memory. Everything is so strange, oh my God, what's happening to me now. I would prefer never to leave this church and I could almost say that I foresaw this is what I would feel, and so packed some candies in my purse in order not to faint from hunger. Lunchtime has already passed and I haven't had a bite to eat since seven this morning. You'll not be offended, oh my Lord, if I have one of the candies. I'm not gluttonous; You know I'm a bit anemic and that chocolate gives me courage. I don't know why I am afraid that something has happened in my house: I have premonitions. Those ragged ladies with black hats and feathers, and the priest who disappeared into the confessional, serve as omens for me. Has anyone ever hidden in one of Your confessionals? It's the ideal place for a child to hide. And don't I resemble a child at a moment like this? When the priest and the ladies covered with feathers come out, I'll open the little door of the confessional and hide inside. I will not confess to a priest but to You. And I will spend the whole night in Your company. Oh my God, I know You will reward the good deeds of Your servant.

FRIENDS

MANY MISFORTUNES happened in our village. A flood cut us off from the center of town. I remember that for two months we couldn't go to school or to the drugstore. The currents of the river, overflowing its banks, made some of the walls of the school fall down. The next year an epidemic of typhoid fever killed my aunt, who was a very devout but severe woman, as well as the teacher and the parish priest, who was deeply respected by my parents. In three weeks thirty people died. Nearly the whole town was in mourning; the cemetery looked like a flower show, and the streets sounded like a bell-ringing contest.

My friend Cornelio lived on the third floor of our house. We were seven years old. We were like brothers because our families were so close. We shared games, parents, aunts, meals. We went to school together. Cornelio learned any lesson easily, but he didn't like studying. I learned with difficulty, but I liked studying. Cornelio hated the teacher; I liked her.

"He'll be declared a saint," Aunt Fermina said sadly.

"It's just a phase he's going through," said Aunt Claudia, who looked like an ostrich. "Don't worry."

As an ostrich shakes its wings; she shook her shoulders when she spoke.

"What's wrong with being declared a saint?" my mother asked all of a sudden.

"If it were your son, you wouldn't like it much," Cornelio's mother answered.

"Why not? Isn't it beneficial to be on good terms with God?"

"The hair shirt, the fasting, the retreats," Cornelio's mother said slowly with terror and at the same time with a kind of pleasure.

"Would you prefer drinking, or women, or politics? Are you afraid that they'll steal your son from you? God or the world will take him from you."

"God? That's a more serious matter."

Our mothers smiled sadly, as if they had come to an agreement. I listened in silence. At odd hours, I had seen Cornelio in his white smock, a missal in hand, kneeling by the window in prayer. When I entered his room, he blushed and pretended to be studying a grammar or a history textbook, quickly hiding the missal under his chair or in a drawer so that I wouldn't see it. I asked myself, Why is he ashamed of his piety? Does he think prayer is something like playing with dolls? He never confided in me or spoke about religious matters. Despite our youth, we acted like men and spoke frankly of girlfriends, sex, and marriage. It contradicted Cornelio's withdrawn, mystical attitude.

"When I pray to be granted a favor, it is granted," he told me one day, singing to himself proudly.

I told my aunts what he had said, and they commented on it at length. They attributed Cornelio's devotion to the strong impressions made on him by the catastrophes that had afflicted our town. When a boy our age had seen so many deaths in such a short time, it had to make some impression on his soul. If these events had not affected my own character, it was because I was by nature insensitive and a bit perverse. Cornelio's mysticism had begun before the flood and the epidemic; hence, it was absurd to attribute it to those circumstances. I hinted broadly at the mistake all the adults were making but as usual kept quiet and accepted what they said. So I embraced my role as a perverse child, unlike Cornelio, who was the personification of sensitivity and goodness. I never failed to feel jealous, and was surprised by the guilt I felt due to my inferiority. I'd often shut myself up in my room and cry for my sins, asking God to grant me the favor of making me more like my friend once again.

The power Cornelio had over me was great: I never wanted to

disagree with him, or displease or hurt him, yet he forced me to disagree with him, displease him, and hurt him.

One day he became annoyed because I had taken his penknife. I had to play tricks like that on him so he would not despise me. Another day I took his toolbox; he hit and scratched me.

"If you ever touch any of my other things, I'll pray for your death," he said. I laughed. "You don't believe me? Wasn't there a flood and an epidemic a while ago? Do you think it was by chance?"

"The flood?" I asked.

"I caused it. It was my doing."

He may not have said these exact words, but he spoke like a man and his words were deliberate.

"Why?"

"So as not to have to go to school. Why else? What else could one pray for?"

"And the epidemic?" I murmured, holding my breath.

"That too. That was even easier."

"Why?"

"So the teacher and my aunt would die. I can make you die too, if I feel like it."

I laughed, because I knew he would despise me if I didn't. In the mirror of the wardrobe, across from us, I saw myself frowning. I froze with fear, and as soon as I could went running to my aunts to recount my conversation with my friend. My aunts laughed at my distress.

"It's just a joke," they said. "The boy's a saint."

But Rita, my cousin, who looked like an old woman and always listened in on other people's conversations, said, "He's not a saint. He doesn't even pray to God. He has a pact with the devil. Haven't you seen his missal? The cover is the same as every other missal but the inside is different. Nothing printed in those horrible pages makes sense. Do you want to see it? Bring the book," she ordered me. "It's in the drawer of the bureau, wrapped in a handkerchief."

I hesitated. How could I betray Cornelio? Secrets are sacred, but finally weakness won out. I snuck into Cornelio's room and, trembling, took out the missal, which was indeed wrapped in a handkerchief. My aunt Claudia untied the corners of the handkerchief and took out the book. Pages were pasted on top of the original pages. I saw the incomprehensible signs and devilish drawings that Rita had described.

"What are we to do?" my aunts wailed.

Cornelio's mother returned the book to me and demanded, "Put it back where you found it!" Then addressing Rita, she said, "You deserve to be sued for slander. Would that we were in England!"

My aunts hissed like owls that have been disturbed.

"The boy's a saint. He may have his own language to speak to God," my mother declared, staring severely at Rita, who was choking on a mint.

"And if he causes my death?"

All of the women laughed, even Rita, who a few moments before had asserted that there was a pact between Cornelio and the devil.

Were adults ever serious when they spoke? Who would believe me or take me seriously? Rita had made fun of me. So, to prove the veracity of my words, I went up to Cornelio's room and, instead of putting the missal back in the drawer, I put it in my pocket and took the object that he most treasured: a plastic watch with moving hands. I remember it was late and the whole family had gathered for dinner. As it was summer, after dinner I strolled into the garden with my aunt. No doubt Cornelio had not yet gone into his room or noticed that anything was missing.

What power could Cornelio possess for his prayers to be answered? What sort of death would he demand for me? Fire, water, blood? All of these words crossed my mind until I heard steps in the corridor and in his room. I couldn't distinguish the muffled sound of the steps from that of my heart. I was about to flee, to bury the watch and the missal in the garden, but I knew I couldn't fool Cornelio, since he was in league with some power greater than our own. I heard him call me: his cry was a roar, tearing my name apart. I went up the stairs to his room. I stopped for a moment on the landing, observing his movements through the half-open door; then I went up the creaky, broken ladder to the attic. Cornelio questioned me from the other landing and I, instead of answering him, threw the book and the watch at his head. He didn't say anything. He picked them up. He knelt down and eagerly read the pages. For the first time Cornelio was not ashamed to be seen praying. The step where I was standing creaked and then suddenly gave way: when I fell I banged my head against the iron bars of the balustrade.

When I came to, the whole family was gathered around me; Cornelio sat still in a corner of the room, his arms crossed.

I had no doubt I was going to die, as I could see the faces peering over my own as if looking down a well.

"Why don't you ask God to save your little friend? Didn't you say that God grants you everything you ask for?" my aunt Fermina dared to whisper.

Cornelio prostrated himself on the floor like a Muslim. He banged his head against the floor and answered, speaking with the voice of a spoiled child, "I can only bring sickness or death."

My mother looked at him with horror, kneeling down next to him, tugging on his hair as if he were a dog, and saying, "Try, my child. You won't lose anything if you pray. God will have to hear you."

For days I floated in a pink and blue limbo, between life and death. The voices were far away. I could not recognize any faces— they were floating at the bottom of the water. When I recovered, two months later, they gave Cornelio credit for my good luck: according to my aunts and our mothers, he had saved me. Once again I heard them singing the praises of Cornelio's saintliness. They no longer remembered the tears they had shed for me, nor the fondness that the gravity of my illness had inspired in them. Once again I found myself the insensitive and somewhat perverse child, wholly inferior to my friend.

Through my aunts, the seamstress, and some friends of the household, contradictory details about what had happened reached the people in town. There were comments on Cornelio's mystical tendencies. Some people thought that my friend was a saint, others that he was a sorcerer and that it was better not to come to our house due to his maledictions. When my aunt Claudia got married, no one came to the reception.

Was Cornelio a sorcerer or a saint? Night after night, flipping my pillow over, searching for a cool place to rest my feverish head, I thought of Cornelio's saintliness—or was it witchcraft? Had even Rita forgotten her suspicions?

One day we went fishing at the Arroyo del Sauce. We brought a picnic basket full of food, so as to spend the day there. Our neighbor Andrés, who loved fishing, was already standing on the bank with his rod. A dog ambled over and jumped around, playing cute tricks as lost dogs often do. Andrés said he would take the dog home, but then Cornelio said he wanted to, and the two of them started to argue. They eventually started to punch each other and Cornelio fell down, defeated. Andrés, conceited as could be, picked up his rod, took the dog in his arms, and left. Lying on the ground, Cornelio began reciting his curses: the noise his lips made was like that of a liquid about to come to a boil. Andrés had walked only about twenty paces when he fell down, foam pouring from his mouth. The dog, now free, ran toward us. We later found out that Andrés had suffered an epileptic seizure.

When Cornelio and I walked down the street, people whispered: they knew he was a sorcerer and not a saint as some of our family described him. One Good Friday the children wouldn't let us enter the church and threw stones at us.

What could I do to punish Cornelio? Would my death achieve something meaningful and serve as evidence of my truthfulness and his perversity? For a moment I imagined his life ruined forever, pursued by my memory, as Cain was by Abel. I sought out some means of infuriating him. I had to make his curses fall on me again. I lamented that death would prevent me from bearing witness to his remorse, after his will had been accomplished. Would remorse stop him from repeating those accursed prayers? We were on the banks of the Arroyo del Sauce. We watched a kingfisher plunge into the water over and over with dizzying speed. Each of us had a slingshot. We aimed: Cornelio at the kingfisher, I in the air, so that my shot would go astray. Cornelio, who was a good shot, hit the bird on the head, and it fell down, wounded. We jumped in the water to retrieve it. Then, near the shore, an argument broke out over who had killed the kingfisher. I firmly insisted that the catch was mine.

There was a very deep place in the stream, where we couldn't stand up. I knew where it was, because it looked like a sort of eddy. My father had pointed it out to me. I picked up the bird and ran along the bank until I reached the place where I could see the mysterious stirring of the water. Andrés was nearby, fishing as always. I stopped, throwing the kingfisher into the whirlpool. Cornelio, who was chasing after me, threw himself down on his knees. I heard the terrifying murmur on his lips—he was repeating my name. A cold sweat bathed the back of my neck, arms, hair. Fields, trees, ravines, the stream, Andrés, everything started shaking, spinning around. I saw Death with his scythe. Then I heard Cornelio utter his own name. Such was my surprise that I didn't hear him jump into the water. He didn't know how to swim, nor did he try to reach the bird, but flailed in the water and slowly sank. Andrés, calm as could be, shouted at him with a bitter voice, like a parrot, "Idiot! What good is your sorcery to you now?"

For some reason I didn't understand until many years later that at the last moment Cornelio changed the words of his last prayer: instead of continuing to pray for my death, which had perhaps already been granted, he asked for his own death and saved my life.

REPORT ON HEAVEN AND HELL

FOLLOWING the example of the great auction houses, Heaven and Hell have galleries full of objects that will surprise no one, since they are the same things that usually fill the houses of the earthly world. But it is not enough to speak only of objects: in those halls there are also cities, towns, gardens, mountains, valleys, suns, moons, winds, seas, stars, reflections, temperatures, flavors, perfumes, and sounds, for eternity gives us all sorts of spectacles and feelings.

If the wind roars like a tiger, or the angelic dove, and looks at you with the eyes of a hyena; if the rich man crossing the street is dressed in lascivious rags; if the prizewinning rose they give you is faded and ordinary, less interesting than a sparrow; if your wife's face is an angry bare stick, then your eyes, not God, made them that way.

When you die, the demons and the angels are equally eager, knowing that you are asleep, still in one world and partly in another, and will come in disguise to your bed, stroke your head, and ask you to choose the things you had preferred during your life. First, they will show you the simple things, as if opening a book of samples. If they show you the sun, the moon, or the stars, you will see them in a ball of painted crystal, and you will think the crystal ball is the world; if they show you the sea or the mountains, you will see them in a stone and will think the stone is the sea or the mountains; if they show you a horse, it will be a miniature figurine, but you will think the horse is a real horse. The angels and the demons will confuse your spirit with pictures of flowers, glazed fruit, and candies. Making you think you are still a child, they will seat you in a chair formed from their hands called the queen's chair, or the golden seat, and in this way they will carry you with their hands clasped through those hallways to the center of your life, where your favorite things are hidden. Be careful. If you choose more things from Hell than from Heaven, you may be sent to Heaven; on the other hand, if you choose more things from Heaven than from Hell, you risk going to Hell, because your love of celestial things could be a sign of greed.

The laws of Heaven and Hell are flexible. Whether you're sent to one place or the other depends on the slightest detail. I know people who because of a broken key or a wicker birdcage went to Hell, and others who for a sheet of newspaper or a glass of milk went to Heaven.

THUS WERE THEIR FACES

*Thus were their faces: and their wings were stretched upward; two
wings were joined one to another, and two covered their bodies.*

Ezekiel 1:11

HOW DID the younger children come to know it? That will never
be explained. Besides, one would need to clarify what it was that
they came to know, and whether the older ones already knew it. One
assumes, nevertheless, that it was a real event and not a fantasy; only
people who didn't know them, their school, or their teachers could
deny it without question.

At the hour when the bell was rung—uselessly, routinely, ritu-
ally—to announce the milk break, or later, during recess, when they
ran to the back courtyard, they surely came to know it, slowly, unconsciously, without distinction of age or sex (I say "came" because
various signs revealed that up to that moment they were waiting for
something that would allow them to wait again, and once and for
all, for something very important). We know for certain that from
then on (from that moment I am referring to, now the subject of
thousands of conjectures), when they lost the indifference (but not
innocence) so characteristic of childhood, the children could think
of nothing else.

After long reflection, one can only assume that the children discovered it simultaneously. In the dormitories, as they fell asleep; in
the dining hall, as they ate; in the chapel, as they prayed; in the
courtyards, as they played tag or hopscotch; at their desks, as they

studied or were being punished; on the playground, as they played on the swings; or in the bathroom, as they devoted themselves to keeping clean (important moments when worries are forgotten), with the same sullen, withdrawn look on their faces, their minds, like little machines, were spinning the web of a single thought, a single desire, a single expectation.

People who saw them walking by in their Sunday best, neat and well-groomed, on national or religious holidays, or on a Sunday, would say, "Those children all belong to the same family or to the same mysterious society. They're identical! Their poor parents! They must not be able to recognize their own children! These modern times, the same barber must cut all their hair (the little girls look like boys and the boys look like girls). Oh the cruel, unspiritual times."

In fact, their faces did resemble one another to a certain degree; they were as lacking in expression as the *escarapela** they wore on their lapels or the portraits of the Virgin of Luján they wore on their breasts.

But in the beginning each child felt alone, as if enveloped by an iron carapace, stiffening their bodies in isolation. Each child's pain was individual and terrible, as was their happiness, which made their happiness itself painful. Humiliated, they imagined themselves different from one another, like dogs of various breeds, or like prehistoric monsters in illustrations. They thought the secret, splitting at that very moment into forty secrets, wasn't shared and could never be shared. But an angel arrived, the angel who sometimes attends to multitudes; he came with his shining mirror held high, like the image of the candidate or hero or tyrant that is carried aloft in demonstrations, and showed the children that their faces were identical. Forty faces were exactly the same face, forty minds the same mind, despite differences in age and lineage.

---

*The *escarapela*, also known as the Roundel of Argentina, is a heraldic piece of circular cloth that bears the blue-and-white colors of the Argentine flag and has been worn on the lapel on national holidays since 1812.

No matter how horrible a secret may be, when it is shared it can stop being horrible because the horror of it gives pleasure: the pleasure of perpetual communication.

But those who suppose it was horrible are jumping to conclusions. In reality, we don't know whether it was horrible and then became beautiful, or whether it was beautiful and later became horrible.

When they felt surer of themselves, they wrote letters to one another on sheets of colored paper with lace borders and pasted pictures. At first the letters were laconic, then gradually grew longer and more confused. They chose strategic hiding places to serve as mailboxes, dropping off and picking up in secret.

Since they were now happy conspirators, the everyday difficulties of life no longer troubled them.

If one of them planned to do something, the others resolved immediately to do that very thing.

As if they wanted to become equal, the shorter ones walked on tiptoe so as to look taller; the taller ones stooped over to look shorter. The redheaded ones reduced the brilliance of their hair and others lightened the color of their warm bronze skin. Their eyes all shone with the same brownish-gray color characteristic of light-colored eyes. Now all at once none of them chewed nails or sucked thumbs.

They were also linked by the violence of their gestures, by their simultaneous laughter, by a boisterous and sudden feeling of sadness in solidarity hidden in their eyes, in their straight or slightly curly hair. So indissolubly united were they that they could defeat an army, a pack of hungry wolves, a plague, hunger, thirst, or the abrupt exhaustion that destroys civilizations.

At the top of a slide, out of excitement not wickedness, they almost killed a child who had slipped in among them. On the street, in the face of their admiring enthusiasm, a flower vendor almost perished, trampled with his merchandise.

In the dressing rooms at night, the navy-blue pleated skirts, the pants, the blouses, the rough white underwear, and the handkerchiefs were all crammed together in the darkness, along with the life their owners had given each item during the day. The shoes, gathered together, tightly together, forming a vigorous, organized army; the children walked as much barefoot during the night as they had wearing the shoes during the day. Unearthly dirt clung to their soles. Shoes seem lonely when they are not worn! The bar of soap passed from hand to hand, from face to face, chest to chest, acquiring the form of their souls. Bars of soap lost between the toothpaste and the hairbrushes and toothbrushes! All the same!

"One voice is dispersed among those who talk. Those who don't talk transmit the voice's force to the objects that surround them," said Fabia Hernández, one of the teachers; but neither she nor her colleagues Lelia Isnaga and Albina Romarín could penetrate the closed world that sometimes dwells in the heart of solitary people (who defend themselves, opening up only to grief or joy). The closed world that dwelled in the heart of forty children! The teachers, who loved their work with utmost dedication, wanted to catch the secret by surprise. They knew that secrets can poison the soul. Mothers fear the effects they may have on their children—no matter how beautiful a secret may be, who knows what monsters it may conceal!

They wanted to catch the children by surprise. They would suddenly turn on the lights in the bedroom, pretending to inspect the ceiling where a pipe had burst or to chase the mice that had invaded the main office. With the pretext of imposing silence, they would interrupt recess, saying that the noise bothered a sick neighbor or the celebration of a wake. Assuming the duty of supervising the religious conduct of the children, they would disrupt them in the chapel, where the heightened mysticism allowed for raptures of love, disjointed, interwoven words uttered before the flames of the candles lighting up the children's hermetic faces.

Fluttering like birds, the children would burst into movie theaters or concert halls, where they'd distract themselves with dazzling shows. Their heads turned at the same time right to left, left to right, revealing the fullness of their pretense.

Miss Fabia Hernández was the first to discover that the children not only dreamed the same dreams but made the same mistakes in their notebooks; when she scolded them for having no personality of their own, they smiled sweetly, a behavior they rarely practiced.

No child was troubled when punished for a classmate's mischief. None were troubled when others were given credit for their own work.

On various occasions the teachers accused one or two students of completing the assignments for the rest of the class; otherwise, it was too difficult to explain why their handwriting and sentence composition were so similar. But the teachers later realized that they had been mistaken.

In art class, the teacher wanted to stimulate the children's imaginations and asked them to draw any object they felt moved to draw. Each child, for an alarmingly long time, drew wings, of various forms and dimensions, though the differences did not reduce what she termed the monotony of the whole. When the children were scolded, they grumbled and finally one wrote on the blackboard, "We feel the wings, miss."

Is it wrong to think they were happy? To the extent that children can be happy—given life's limitations—there is no reason to think that they were sad, except in the summer. The heat of the city weighed down on the teachers. At the hour when the children liked to run, climb trees, roll around on the lawn, or somersault down a hill, all of these amusements were replaced by the siesta, the dreaded custom of the siesta. The cicadas sang but the children didn't hear that song which makes the heat even more intense. The radios blared, but the children didn't hear that racket which makes the summer, and its sticky asphalt, unbearable.

They wasted hours sitting behind the teachers, who held parasols as they waited for the sun to drop and the heat to subside. When they were alone they played seemingly innocent pranks, like calling a dog from a balcony, and when the dog saw so many possible owners at once, it would leap madly into the air to reach them. Or, a child would whistle at a lady walking along the street, and the lady would angrily ring the bell to complain of their insolence.

An unexpected donation provided a vacation by the sea. The little girls made themselves modest swimsuits; the boys bought theirs at a discount store, the material smelling of castor oil, but the style was modern, making the suit look good on anyone.

To heighten the significance of their first vacation, the teachers, using a pointer, showed them the blue dot on the map, by the Atlantic, where they would be staying.

They dreamed of the Atlantic and the sand: the same dream.

When the train left the station, the handkerchiefs waved back and forth out of the train windows like a flock of doves—this image captured in a photograph published in the newspaper.

When the children arrived at the sea they hardly looked at it; they only saw the sea that they had imagined instead of the real one. When they adapted to the new landscape, it was difficult to control them. They ran after the foam, which formed drifts similar to those formed by snow. But joy didn't let them forget their secret, and they would return gravely to their rooms, where communication was easier for them. If what they felt wasn't love, then something very similar to love linked and gladdened them. The older ones, influenced by the younger ones, blushed when the teachers asked them trick questions, and answered with a quick nod. The younger ones, all very serious, looked like adults whom nothing could disturb. The majority of them were named after flowers, like Jacinto, Dahlia, Daisy, Jasmine, Violet, Rose, Narcissus, Hortense, Camila—affectionate names chosen by their parents. They carved their names in the trunks of trees with their fingernails, which were as hard as a tiger's claws; they wrote their names on the walls with gnawed-on pencils, and in the sand with their fingers.

They set off on the trip back to the city, hearts bursting with joy, since they would travel by plane. A film festival was to begin that day, and they caught glimpses of furtive stars at the airport. Their throats hurt from so much laughing. Their eyes turned bright red from so much gazing.

The news in the papers appeared like this: *Forty children from a school for the deaf were flying back from their first vacation by the sea when their plane suffered a terrible accident. A door mysteriously opened during the flight and caused the disaster. Only the teachers, the pilot, and the crew were saved. When interviewed, Miss Fabia Hernández said, with conviction, that when the children threw themselves into the void they had wings. She tried to hold back the last child, who escaped from her arms to follow the others as if an angel. She said the intense beauty of the scene convinced her that it wasn't a disaster but rather some kind of celestial vision she will never forget. She still doesn't believe in the children's disappearance.*

"God would be playing a mean trick on us if he showed us heaven while casting us into hell," declares Miss Lelia Isnaga. "I don't believe in the disaster."

Albina Romarín says, "It was all a dream the children had, hoping to astonish us, just as they did on the swings in the yard. Nobody can convince me they have vanished."

Neither the red sign announcing that the school building is for rent nor the closed blinds dishearten Fabia Hernández. With her colleagues, to whom she is linked as the children were linked among themselves, she often visits the old building. There she contemplates the students' names written on the walls (inscriptions they were punished for), and some wings drawn with childish skill, bearing witness to the miracle.

REVELATION

WHETHER he opened his mouth or not, people inevitably guessed the truth from the way he looked: Valentín Brumana was an idiot. He would say, "I'm going to marry a star."

"Sure, he's going to marry a star," we would reply to make him suffer.

We enjoyed torturing him. We'd make him lie in a hammock, then we would tie the sides together so he couldn't escape, and rock him back and forth until he got so dizzy he would close his eyes. We would make him ride the swing, rolling up the ropes on either side, then letting them go all at once while pushing him dizzily off into space. We didn't let him taste the desserts we ate, but would rub candy or sticky sugar in his hair and make him cry. We put the toys he asked to borrow on top of a tall chest; to reach them he would climb unsteadily on a wobbly table with two chairs piled on each other, one of them a rocker.

When we discovered that Valentín Brumana, without making any show of it, was a sort of magician, we began to feel some respect for him, mixed with a little fear.

"Did you see your girlfriend tonight?" he would say to us. That evening we had met one of our girlfriends on the sly in a vacant lot. We were so precocious!

"Who are you hiding from?" he would ask us. It was the day we received our report cards, which were full of bad grades, and we were hiding because our father was looking for us to punish us, or, a thousand times worse, to give us a sermon.

"You're sad, with a mournful face," he would exclaim. He said it at the very moment we wanted to kill ourselves from sorrow, from a sorrow we concealed like our dates with our girlfriends.

Valentín Brumana's life was full of excitement, not just because of what we did to him but also because of his intense activity. He had a pocket watch his uncle had given him. It was a real watch, not one made of chocolate or tin or plastic, as he really deserved, according to us; I think it was made of silver, and attached to the chain was a little medal of the Virgin of Luján. The sound the watch made, banging against the medal each time he took it out of his pocket, demanded respect, as long as we didn't look at the watch's owner, who made you laugh. A thousand times a day he would take the watch out of his pocket and say, "I have to go to work." He would get up and abruptly leave the room; then he would come right back.

Nobody paid him any attention. They gave him old records, old magazines to amuse him.

When he worked as a scribe, he would use toilet paper, if that was all he could find, and pencils he carried in a broken briefcase; when he worked as an electrician, the same briefcase would be used as a toolbox to carry insulating tape and wire, which he would collect in the garbage; when he worked as a carpenter, his tools were a wash rack, a broken bench, and a hammer; when he worked as a photographer, I would lend him my camera, without film. Nevertheless, if anyone asked him, "Valentín, what are you going to be when you grow up?" he would answer, "A priest or a waiter." "Why?" we would ask. "Because I like to clean silver."

One day Valentín Brumana woke up with a fever. The doctors said, in their roundabout way, that he was going to die and that, considering what his life was like, perhaps that was for the best. He was there and heard those words without alarm, though they reverberated through the desolate house. The whole family, including us, his cousins, thought that Valentín Brumana made people happy because he was so different, and that when he was gone he would be irreplaceable.

Death didn't keep us waiting long. She arrived the next morning: I'm convinced that Valentín in his agony saw her coming through the door to his room. The joy of greeting a loved one lit up his face, which usually only expressed indifference. He stretched out his arm and pointed a finger at her.

"Come," he said. Then, looking at us out of the corner of his eye, he exclaimed, "How lovely she is!"

"Who? Who is lovely?" we asked him, with a daring that now strikes me as rude. We laughed, but our laughter could easily be confused with crying, tears pouring from our eyes.

"This lady," he said, blushing.

The door opened. My cousin assures me that the lock was broken and the door always opened by itself, but I don't believe her. Valentín sat up in bed and greeted an apparition we couldn't see. It's very clear that he saw her, that he touched the veil that hung over her shoulders, that she whispered some secret to him that we would never hear. Then something even more unusual happened: with great effort Valentín gave me the camera that had been on his bedside table, asking me to take a picture of them. He showed his companion how to pose.

"No, don't sit like that," he told her.

Or instead, in a whisper, almost inaudible, "The veil, the veil is hiding your face."

Or instead, in an authoritarian tone, "Don't look away."

The whole family, and some of the servants, laughed loudly and raised the velvet drapes, so tall and heavy, so that more light could rush in; someone paced out the number of meters that separated the camera from Valentín to help focus the picture. Trembling, I focused on Valentín, who pointed to the place, more important than him and a little to the left, that needed to be in the picture: an empty space. I obeyed.

Soon thereafter I had the film developed. Of the six photographs, I thought they had given me one by mistake, one taken by some other amateur. Nonetheless, Pygmy, my pony, came out clear enough; Tapioca, Facundo's puppy, did too; the baker bird's nest was visible, if a bit dark and blurry; as for the one of Gilberta, in a bathing suit, well, it could have been entered in any photo contest, even today; and then the picture of the façade of the school could have been used as a photogravure in *La Nación*. I had shot all those pictures the same week.

At first I didn't look too carefully at the blurry, unrecognizable photograph. Indignant, I went to the lab to protest, but they assured me they had not made a mistake and that it must have been some snapshot taken by one of my little brothers.

It was only later, after careful study, that I was able to make out the room, the furniture, and Valentín's blurry face in the famous photograph. The central figure—clear, terribly clear—was that of a woman covered with veils and scapulars, already rather old, with big hungry eyes, who turned out to be the actress Pola Negri.

VISIONS

DARKNESS. Nonbeing. Can anything more perfect exist? Different moments grow confused. Sound slips down my throat like a snake. The doctor is at once torturer and jeweler: he bends over and dazzles me with a flash of intense light. He gives me orders, pierces me, torments me. My body surrenders to him. I am docile. I do not suffer. One has to surrender. I return to the darkness. I return to nonbeing.

Half awake, the first thing I try to decipher is a painting. I think of the worst of the English painters, settling on Dante Gabriel Rossetti. The woman, her hair lit from behind, is Beata Beatrix. I remember the Latin inscription Rossetti wrote on the frame: *Quomodo Sedet Sola Civitas*. Why am I seeing that painting, and in a light that seems so false? I close my eyes, then open them again. It is not a painting. It is a person who is taking care of me, her hair lit up, her face in shadow. The room is dark. When the light is turned on, I look at the room and think it's my own. Unless I left my house I must be in it, in my room.

The door is on the left; in my room it's on the right. There is a small dark piece of furniture, topped by an oval mirror; in my room there is a large bureau, with a Virgin inside a glass bell jar. The blinds are of wood, and can be raised and lowered with cords; in my room the blinds are of iron and open sideways, in three sections. The electric light in the room is coming from a square glass fixture in the center of the ceiling; in my room there are only two silver standing lamps on the bedside tables. I am absentminded. I have lived in this house for many years without noticing that there are two kinds of blinds in my room: some modern ones that go up and down, made of slats of light wood, and other, old-fashioned ones of heavy iron that open sideways in three sections. I am so absentminded that I never noticed that light came not only from the silver standing lamps but also from the square glass fixture on the ceiling that I didn't turn on because I couldn't find the switch. Nevertheless, I'm surprised that I never noticed that ground-glass lamp on the ceiling until now; it's very obvious now that I look at it all the time. Besides, the Virgin in the bell jar isn't there, nor the bureau. The Virgin troubles me. If I turned my head back suddenly, like an owl, perhaps I would find it. To clean the objects in this room without breaking them, even those that are rarely cleaned (and hence always dirty), someone must take the objects from their usual places and put them somewhere else. The Virgin must be in a corner, under some piece of furniture, or underneath the bedstead. I wonder if a servant cleaned it. But I cannot turn around. Instead of the bureau, which was on a side wall, not across from the bed, I see an amorphous little chest with a small mirror. Am I in Córdoba? Could I be dreaming of Córdoba? I have been to a house there with the same piece of furniture. No, I'm not in Córdoba. It must be a present someone gave me for my birthday, someone who's fond of me but doesn't know the kinds of gifts I like. When were those objects brought to my room, and who brought them? They must be very light. Anyone could pick them up and carry them from one place to another. I don't need to worry. What does it matter who brought them! I could thank any of the people here for this gift I don't like. I smile just in case one of them gave it to me. And that little picture? It's hanging on the wall on the left above a sort of cot, no doubt a very comfortable one, which I can see from my bed as if I were up on a mountainside. I never saw that cot in my room, or in any other room in my house. Furniture has its own life; it's not strange for pieces to come and go, change places, and be replaced whenever possible. Isn't it better this way? What's wrong with this room? Is it worth saying something about it to someone? Perhaps I should speak to the first person who approaches: the nurse. Her apron crackles—it's crisp with starch, so much starch that it looks as if the shirt were made of plaster (if plaster could gleam). This woman enjoys being a nurse. What a shame that the others don't enjoy their work as much as she does. She's happy. Sometimes a quick little dog follows her, but I can't see it very well.

But before I can ask her, the nurse replies with a question: "Don't you know where you are, dear?"

"No."

"In a hospital, my dear."

"Oh, that's why."

"What?"

"Why I didn't recognize my room."

"Don't be frightened."

How short life would be if certain unpleasant moments didn't make it feel endless! In a room that's not my own, for hours and hours I've believed is mine, trying to figure out where I am—and yet I am not dying!

Like an architect who finds the lost plans for a house, or the explorer who guides himself with a compass that may be broken, or better still like an animal that's settling into a new lair and trying to remember the one before, I calm down and, relaxing more, investigate where the hospital is, whether the window of my room faces the river, and try to figure out how long I've been here.

Different noises fill my surroundings with their perverse stories. What's that saw screeching early in the morning? Does it chop up human beings? Does it grind their bones to sand? Do they use such material to build houses? And that noise like boiling water coming up from the basement and the ground floor. Is it the sound of lips praying, or the boilers of hell where boiling liquids are prepared for sinners? In a hospital? The voices were like flies buzzing. Are they the same ones? And a roaring like that of wild beasts of the people in the hallways: What will become of it? Will it turn into monsters in distress, or a procession of men with costumes improvised from torn sheets and wet towels, journeying toward the desert, carrying inedible, stinking provisions. So many days of Carnival without a carnival!

These faces appear etched in the darkness. All of a sudden I see them. They can be distinguished from the furniture but seem to be of the same material. They are doctors' faces. They have hands but no bodies or souls. Crowding together they draw near. It is they who suffer. They are the next victims. Those who suffer, suffer less than those who watch their suffering.

Suddenly they turn on a light, as if wanting to surprise me in the middle of some unspeakable sin. One of them, a cross between a god and a locomotive, has a light on his specialist forehead.

They sit me down, hit me, uncover me, shout at me, poke me, stick a thermometer in me, push their fingers into my abdomen until I cry out, tickle me with a blood-pressure gauge on my arm.

"Breathe," they tell me. "Don't breathe," they say, until I turn purple.

How many patients must have died in the hospital because of examinations! I don't even want to think about it. Such violent treatment could kill perfectly healthy people, but perhaps it would save them because it would keep them from falling asleep. After all, sleep foreshadows death.

Because of the many interruptions, time stretches out. The clock looks at me, its face round and ashen. It is eternal like the sun: its hours don't shoot out like bolts of lightning. Eight visits a day by the doctors turn a day into a year. Should we be grateful that something so unpleasant allows us to measure time?

The serum falls drop by drop. An hourglass egg timer, a water clock in a lost garden in Italy, would be less obsessive. There is something feverish about the falling sand, the falling water. The needle stuck in the vein turns into our vein. I don't look at it.

I don't like the gray steel veins of the machines. I am like a machine, but human veins are a different color. Blue, blue. Ink, blood. Blue ink and red blood look alike.

There are floods in Buenos Aires. I know because I can feel it. I know from the newspapers (without reading them): I can hear them crackling in the next room.

It's the birthday of some queen. It's nighttime. I can hear the

drums celebrating the event. People gather in a square with improvised altars and play the famous symphony for winds. How odd that
I had never heard it before! Band music comes from the direction of
the river, ever more excitedly intoning a sublime melody. I would
prefer not to use the word "sublime" for a piece of music. But what
other word could be used to describe that? On the highest notes,
that enter all ears as if they were long needles, people are so disturbed
that the tremulous sound vibrates, endlessly prolonged . . . How is it
possible that I never before heard such a well-known melody? There
must be many recordings of it with different symphony conductors,
modified with different rhythms.

The deaf children in the square, as if they recognize the melody,
swing back and forth frantically. They don't kneel before the improvised altars, they are much too nervous for that. The children are the
lucky ones. The music lasts the whole night. It's like a curse. How
dramatic it is, how long, how endless! At dawn, solitary men on the
terraced pink roofs whistle it, confused by the intonation, since they
don't know it well. I don't know at what solemn, diaphanous moment the last vibration of the music disappears: music at dawn that
keeps the day from ever arriving, just as ejaculation is endlessly post-
poned by yogis. A few hours later, colors, then astonishing visions
burst before my dazzled eyes. Suddenly a yellow hue fills my sight,
one never seen before. Like a neon sign it traces its figure on light
purple water (the purple seeming to indicate water). Inside the yellow zone (representing the earth), groups of motionless, gray, fearful
people are clearly etched, as if carved in stone; they stand beneath
countless parasols, like the Buddha's parasols, and are saving themselves from something. From what? It occurs to me that this is a map
of the world, scattered with monuments.

In the next room someone is reading the news of the floods in the
papers. I once knew a dog that slept on newspaper. The crackling of
the paper, when it moved around or breathed hard, made me think
it was reading the news.

A spot of dampness appears on the wall where the head of my bed
rests. I uselessly look for it in the mirror that faces me. It disturbs

me. I know that it is green, purple, blue, like a bruise, and that it's getting larger. Could it be a symbol of my sickness? The spot of dampness hurts me as if it were inside my body. They call a man to look at it. I wonder if he is a plumber. He carries a little brown bag. The man pokes, bangs on the wall, pays no attention to me. He sighs.

I am thinking of Blake's illustrations to the *Book of Job* and *The Gates of Paradise*.

"There's nothing that can be done," he exclaims, leaving the room smelling of putty. "Every year it's the same. It comes from the house next door," he adds, coming back into the room.

The nurse gives me something to drink. The water doesn't taste like water.

"Enjoy your meal," the plumber says to me.

They call a sister of charity. The sister of charity comes in: she slides along in her dark skirt and her happy, doll-like face as if rolling on little wheels. She is of the opinion that pipes are mysterious. The house will have to be torn down to find the origin of the dampness. She leaves the room with her keys and rosaries.

They used to take presents to the dead. I wonder if I am dead. They bring me a fragrant bouquet of passion flowers, two green nightgowns, candy that is much too sweet, hearts made of chocolate, a bouquet of roses that makes me sick, a pot of cyclamen that I give to the Virgin, a box of cookies, soup that makes me sick.

There are cars in the street, a phone in the room. What time of year is it? Nowadays dead people have everything taken away: their rings and teeth, because they are gold; their eyes, because the cornea is used in other eyes; their skin or hair, because they're used for grafts and wigs. They haven't taken anything from me: I am not dead.

What's going on outside? I have to find out. Trees keep growing, preparing for new seasons. The awful monument with a bronze woman standing on a pink marble pedestal that I can see through the window will no doubt always have those yellow stripes belonging not to the marble but to the urine of passing dogs or nocturnal men with diuretic desires.

"Do you want me to adjust your pillow?"

When I entered this mansion, winter fortunately had already pulled the leaves from the trees and autumn, my favorite season for its golden fruit, had fled.

"Do you want a glass of water?" they ask me.

I can feel, nearby, the smooth, glossy, soft rottenness of the public parks, where men go for fresh air or to masturbate. When the window is open that dirty wind comes in, giving the illusion of cleanliness because it's cold now in winter. There are people who sit down and who are sitting on the benches: women who knit while looking after their own children or those of others; beggar women with bundles of clothing or containers of old bread smelling like oranges; men who press against human beings or plants alike with the same passion to tell secrets; well-cared-for or lost dogs; hysterical cats that copulate, filling the night with electric cries.

"Some fruit juice?" a sugary voice asks.

"How did I get here?" I ask.

"In an ambulance," they tell me.

"And how did they bring me?"

"In the stretcher, on the elevator."

I arrived at night, like a mouse in a basement, without dreaming, stiff, without feeling, still. When I was a girl I played statues, always with the fear of turning into a statue; I played in a dark room (an aphrodisiacal game), afraid of disappearing. You had to close your eyes.

"This time," I am thinking, "I play statues in the dark, but seriously."

The araucaria, sooty and huge, and the unreal rubber tree are nourished on excrement, semen, and glass. Nobody waters them, except God when it rains. All things, even trees, have a will to live, above all and in spite of everything. But if the form of one individual passes on to another, if nothing is lost, why struggle so hard to preserve a given form that, in the final account, might be the most inferior or the least interesting!

"What's your name?" I ask the nurse.

"Linda Fontenla."

Linda Fontenla likes to talk; she also likes the seriousness of the sick. What is a healthy person? Someone boring and useless. For Linda Fontenla life is an endless series of enemas, thermometers, transfusions, and poultices skillfully distributed and applied. If she gets married, she'll marry a sick man, for such a person would be attractive to her, a cluster of hemorrhoids, an enlarged liver, a perforated intestine, an infected bladder, or a heart full of extra systoles.

"Believe it or not, an old man I was taking care of wanted to go to bed with me. Some people have no shame. He offered me everything, even marriage. I told him to go peddle his wares elsewhere. That's why I don't like taking care of men. They're all the same. You can't even apply talcum powder to them; you can take my word for it. They want to enjoy themselves, that's all they want."

"Am I dying, Linda?"

"Dear, what nonsense you talk. Do you want me to bring you the little hand mirror so you can see how well you look? Here you are. Look at yourself. Yesterday you were in bad shape. I was very much afraid."

"But yesterday you told me that I was very well."

"You have to be told that so you'll perk up a little."

I look at myself in the hand mirror, but at the same time look at the nurse's hand. Nurses have painted nails, many more than other people.

"I have a face like a sheep," I hear my voice saying, as if it were someone else's.

"Like a sheep? Your face looks like a sheep face to you? You are so funny!"

"The sheep face that sick people have."

"It's the first time I've ever heard that."

"You must know it, though."

"Don't talk so much. It's bad for your heart."

I look at the palm of my hand.

"They told me you can read palms," Linda continues. "Would you read mine someday?"

"If I don't die."

"Always the same thing! Always death. You should think happy thoughts. Do you want me to tell you a story? When I arrived this morning, a group of women was crying and praying in the entrance hall. I thought to myself, *Rats, my patient died.* It was the man next door, you see? Who would have guessed? Their faces were three yards long from crying. They could have frightened anyone."

"But couldn't they have been crying for me?"

"There wasn't anybody from your family, or any of your friends. Calm down. Are you going to be suspicious now?"

"I don't care in the slightest."

"I know. It was just a joke."

"Turn off the light."

I'm absorbed in my visions. Once again I look at the shadows of the room interwoven with brilliant colors. At first it's a paradise for my eyes. I venture forward with fear, as happens when one is in love. May nobody speak to me or interrupt me. I am present at the most important moment of my life. On the white wall of the room the history of the world unfolds. I have to decipher the signs, at times very complicated ones. The planisphere has formed, with yellow earth, purple water, and groups of people with profiles like bison, sheltered beneath countless parasols. What images await me now? They change as if by magic. I see a head gazing out of a window. The window is composed of four large stones. The head is beautiful, one could say almost angelic, until the stones at the top and the bottom begin to close. The mouth laughs, baring its teeth, like the masks in a Greek tragedy.

The colors fade. An expression of pain appears on the face: the stones are grinding the frightened, frightening face. I wish to see some other vision. I make one up. How? I have a supernatural power, but a limited one. I don't always succeed in seeing beautiful or reassuring things. Don't I like seeing Blake's drawings? These visions seem to come from *The Book of Los* or *The Gates of Paradise*. An endless series of black horses with gleaming harnesses cover the wall. I don't know what carriages the horses are hitched to, nor what distant century they belong to. They dazzle me so much that I can't focus on what surrounds them. Muffled bells mark their slow march. An indescribable joy accompanies them. How sad it would be if these horses never returned! Now they vanish like clouds in the western sky. They were so precise, so clear! Where did they go? These visions must be like certain skies that are never repeated. Now, walking along at the same pace as the horses, as if their limbs were moving in water, four harlequins are spinning around in circles. There are many other harlequins; the room is full of them, but these four catch my attention. I wish they'd never leave! Horses sometimes make me afraid; they are black; at times they are gloomy, funereal. These figures, on the other hand, could never be anything but harlequins, light, happy, immaterial. Looking at them is like making love endlessly, like discovering perfection, like being in heaven. But as I look at them I foresee their disappearance, and that nothing will be able to replace them.

The inside of a room appears, filled with happy characters who form part of some unknown world; then, outside, an enormously tall staircase made of climbing legs appears against the blue sky. And when I'm convinced they will not return, the harlequins appear, moving their bodies so slowly, as can only happen in water. An irrepressible joy seizes me. They come back because I desire so strongly that they do so. Has my supernatural power been perfected? But now they vanish and mystical figures replace them: first the Apostles and then Jesus Christ. Jesus, with a crown of thorns on Saint Veronica's veil, but then the beautiful face of Jesus turns into the face of a monkey and I look aside, to the right. I see a chest of drawers right before my eyes: a shiny mahogany chest I'll never open. The chest changes when I stop looking at it. Now it's an ordinary varnished cedar chest with white spots on it. I don't want to look to my left. Before me I can see a garden covered with huge vines growing up to the sky, and among these vines there are marble statues, also growing skyward. Later I see a mountain of stone gleaming, noticing that the stones are people who are being crushed together, killing one another, people of stone who kill one another with stones. The mountain grows as the dead pile up; the stone men multiply.

A white lion shines, filling the whole wall.

When someone comes into the room and turns on the light, the visions disappear, but the ceiling is covered with the most beautiful roses or with stripes all the colors of the rainbow.

A long-legged dancer is carrying the square glass light fixture in his hands (like a shield); he removes it from the center of the ceiling, but then returns and puts it back in the middle again. I stop looking at the ceiling to admire the roses, prominent against the endless foliage. I've never seen roses stand out against the sky with such intensity. I see them draw closer as if viewed through several magnifying lenses. Then they get smaller, becoming almost imperceptible once again, and more beautiful. The light in the next room goes out. The angel appears. A Chinese garden gradually appears, slowly, as if by a transfer process. I look at this image from every possible angle, as if I were collecting postcards for an album. I am afraid it will disappear. If I could write a date, a name underneath it, I would do so. It disappears. Nothing will console me now that it has vanished. It was a fathomless garden with a pagoda inside. Bamboo was waving back and forth, no doubt in the wind, and there were lakes with shade and rivers with motionless canoes. Everything perfectly still!

I see a golden ship, a million heads looking over the gunwale; it's not moving forward, or if it moves it moves with me on a blue sea. It's a Greek ship. Carrying men's heads as if they were fruit, fruit without bodies, fruit with faces, all the same size, all of them bald.

Now the people have suddenly grown old, the joy turned to pain, the goodness to cruelty, the beauty to ugliness. Why? Nothing lasts. Why? Am I suffering? Is each face a symbol of what I am feeling without knowing it?

There is an angel I am expecting. He is not here; he was not present in my visions. I hear his step, I feel his hand; he gives me something to drink, something to eat. I'm saving images for him, little figures like those that children glue in their notebooks. I hope he likes them! A painting, a book, wouldn't please me nearly as much!

Beauty has no end or edges. I wait for it. But where is my bed, where I can wait in comfort? I'm not lying down; I'm unable to lie down. A bed is not always a bed. There is the birthing bed, the bed of love, the deathbed, the riverbed. But not a real bed . . .

THE BED

THEY LOVED each other, but jealousy (whether jealousy of the past or of the future), a common feeling of envy, and a common lack of trust were gnawing away at them. Sometimes, in a bed, they forgot these unfortunate feelings, and thanks to it they survived. I will tell of one of these instances, the last one.

The bed was fluffy and wide and covered with a pink spread. The center of the headboard, which was made of iron, showed a landscape with trees and ships. The setting sun was illuminating a cloud shaped like a flame. When they embraced, one of them, the lucky one, lying faceup, kissing the other mouth and attracted by the unusual radiance that filled that cloud, could look at it through the fringes of a lamp decorated with red and green tulips.

They lingered longer than usual in the bed. The sounds from the street grew louder and then died down as darkness fell. You could imagine the bed sailing on a sea outside time and space, searching for happiness or for some convincing likeness of it. But they are reckless lovers. Their clothes, which they had taken off, were nearby, within reach. The empty sleeves of a shirt hung from the bed, and a light blue piece of paper had fallen out of one of the pockets. Someone picked up the paper. I don't know what that sky-blue paper had on it, but I know that it produced commotion, investigations, irrepressible hatred, arguments, reconciliations, new arguments.

Dawn was peeking through the windows.

"I smell a fire. Last night I dreamt of fire," she said, in a moment of horror, facing his anger, trying to distract him.

"Your sense of smell is fooling you," he said.

"We're on the ninth floor," she added, trying to look scared. "I'm afraid."

"Don't change the subject."

"I'm not changing the subject. The fire makes sounds like falling water, can't you hear it?"

"Your ears are fooling you."

The room was brightly lit and hot. It was a bonfire.

"If we embraced, only our backs would burn up."

"We'll burn up completely," he said, looking at the fire with furious eyes.

LOVERS

In his plastic wallet he carried a picture of her dressed as a harem girl. She had a picture of him in his conscript's uniform on her bedside table.

Their families, jobs, the schedule of meals and bedtimes, all conspired against their meeting often, but those sporadic meetings were rituals and always took place in winter. First they would buy pastries, and then, sitting under the trees, they would savor them, like children with a snack.

Uncertainty is a form of happiness that works in lovers' favor. Through the labyrinths of their days, of crackly, seemingly endless phone calls, they would always choose Dahlias Bakery as their meeting place, and always choose Sunday as the day, but only after discarding other possibilities. Instead of a coat she wore a shaggy plaid blanket that always came in handy. By the bakery window they would exchange greetings without looking at each other, making a show of their confusion. Those who don't see each other often don't know what to say, no doubt.

"Perhaps in a very dark room or in a very fast car," he thought, "I would overcome my shyness." "Perhaps I would know what to say to him in a movie theater after the intermission, or while taking part in a procession," she thought.

After this interior dialogue, they went to the bakery, as always, and bought pieces of four different kinds of cake. One looked like the Monument to the Spaniards, cluttered with plumes of whipped cream and glazed fruit in the form of flowers; another looked like some sort of mysterious and very dark lace, with shiny decorations of chocolate and yellow meringue covered with sprinkles; another looked like a broken marble pedestal, less beautiful than the others but larger, with coffee frosting, whipped cream, and pieces of nuts; another looked like part of a box, with jewels inlaid at either end and snow on top. After paying, when the package was ready, they would go to the Recoleta, next to the wall of the old age home, where children hide after breaking the streetlights and beggars go to wash their clothes in the fountains. Next to a frail tree, whose branches act as swings and horses for the children who play in them, they sat down on the grass. She opened the package and took out the cardboard tray where the cream and meringue and chocolate glowed, though already a bit squashed. Simultaneously, as if their movements were projected onto each other (mysterious and subtle mirror!), first with one hand, then with both hands, they picked up the slices of the cake with plumes of whipped cream (the miniature Monument to the Spaniards), and lifted them to their mouths. They chewed in unison and finished swallowing each bite at the same time. In the same surprising harmony they cleaned their fingers on napkins that others had left lying on the grass. The repetition of these movements connected them with eternity.

After finishing the first slice they again contemplated the remaining slices on the cardboard tray. With loving greed and greater intimacy they took the second pieces: the slices of chocolate decorated with meringue. Without hesitating, squinting their eyes, they lifted them up to mouths agape. Baby pigeons open their beaks the same way to receive the food brought by their mothers. With greater energy and speed, but with identical pleasure, they began chewing and swallowing once more, like two gymnasts exercising at the same time. She, from time to time, would turn to watch some passing car that was especially valuable, smelling excessively of gasoline, or very large, or would lift her head to watch a dove, the symbol of love, fluttering clumsily among the branches. He would look straight ahead, perhaps savoring the taste of those treats less consciously than she. The abundant whipped cream dripped on the grass, on the folded blanket, and on some bits of trash nearby. No smile would light up their harmonious lips until they finished the contents of the little tray of yellowish cardboard covered with waxed paper. The last bit of cake, crumbled between thumb and index finger, took a long time to reach their open mouths. The crumbs that fell on the tray, her skirt, and his pants were carefully picked up and lifted with thumb and finger to their lips.

The third slice of cake, even more opulent than the others, looked like the material used to build the older houses in beach resorts. The fourth piece, lighter but more difficult to eat because of its sponge-like consistency coated with sugar, left them with white mustaches and white spots on their lips. They had to stick out their tongues and close their eyes to clean their mouths. If they didn't dare to take large bites they missed the best part of the cake, covered with peanuts disguised as walnuts or almonds. She stretched out her neck and lowered her head; he didn't change his position. The chewing followed a regular rhythm, as if they were keeping time with a metronome.

They knew there were other treats left on the cardboard tray. After that first difficult moment, the rest was easy. They used their hands like spoons. Without chewing, they filled their mouths with cream and sponge cake before swallowing.

After finishing the contents of the tray, she tossed the festooned cardboard away and took a little package of peanuts out of her pocket. For several minutes, with the studied gestures of a model, she opened the shells, peeled the nuts, and fed them to him; she saved some for herself, putting them in her mouth and chewing in unison with him. Licking their lips, they attempted a shy conversation on the theme of picnics: people who had died after drinking wine or eating watermelon; a poisonous spider in a picnic basket one Sunday that had killed a girl whose in-laws all hated her; canned goods that had gone bad, but looked delicious, had caused the death of two families in Trenque Lauquen; a storm that had drowned two couples who were celebrating their honeymoons with hard cider and rolls with sausages on the banks of a stream in Tapalqué.

When they had finished the food and the conversation, she unfolded the blanket and they covered themselves with it, lying on the grass. They smiled for the first time, their mouths full of food and words, but she knew (as he did) that, beneath the blanket, love would repeat its usual actions, and that hope, flying farther and farther away on fickle wings, would draw her away from marriage.

THE EXPIATION

for Helena and Eduardo

ANTONIO summoned Ruperto and me to the room at the back of the house. With a domineering tone he ordered us to sit down. The bed was made. He went out to the patio to open the door of the aviary, then came back and lay down on the bed.

"I'm going to perform a show for you," he told us.

"Is the circus going to hire you?" I asked him.

He whistled two or three times and Favorita, Maria Callas, and Mandarin, the little red one, flew in. Staring hard at the ceiling, he whistled once more in an even higher and more tremulous tone. Was that the show? Was that why he had called Ruperto and me? Why didn't he wait for Cleóbula to arrive? I thought the whole performance was meant to show that Ruperto was not blind but crazy; that he would reveal his madness through some show of emotion while witnessing Antonio's feat. The canaries' flight back and forth made me sleepy. My memories flew around my mind with equal persistence. They say you relive your life the moment before your death. I relived mine that afternoon with a detached feeling of panic.

As if it were painted on the wall, I saw myself marrying Antonio at five o'clock one December afternoon. It was quite hot and, when we got home, I noticed with some surprise, as I took off my wedding dress and veil, a canary in the bedroom window. Now I realize that it was Mandarin who was pecking on the last orange on the tree in the courtyard. Antonio didn't interrupt his kisses when he saw I was distracted by that spectacle. The bird's extreme cruelty to the orange fascinated me. I watched the scene until Antonio dragged me trembling to the marriage bed. There, the bedspread, covered with wedding presents, had been a place of happiness for him and of terror for me on the eve of the wedding. The bedspread of scarlet velvet was embroidered with scenes of a journey in a stagecoach. I closed my eyes and was barely conscious of what happened next. Love is also a journey. Over many days I gradually learned its lessons, without seeing or understanding the pleasure or pain it lavished on me. At first, I think Antonio and I loved each other equally, without any problems, except those caused by my innocence and his shyness.

This tiny house and its equally tiny garden are located at the edge of town. The healthy air of the mountains surrounds us: the countryside is nearby and we can see it when we open the windows.

We already had a radio and a refrigerator. Numerous friends filled our house on holidays and on other celebratory occasions. What more could we hope for? Cleóbula and Ruperto visited us frequently because they were our childhood friends. Antonio had fallen in love with me; they knew all about it. He had not sought me out or chosen me, but it was I who had chosen him. His only ambition in life was to be loved by his wife, that she should preserve her fidelity. He paid little attention to money.

Ruperto would sit in a corner of the patio with his guitar and while tuning it would abruptly ask for a mate or, if it was hot, for lemonade. I thought of him as one of the various friends or relatives who form, so to speak, part of the furniture of a house, noticed only when broken or discovered in a different place than usual.

"Canaries are born singers," Cleóbula would invariably say, though she actually detested them and would've killed them with a broom. What would she have said if she had seen them perform those ridiculous tricks without Antonio even offering them a piece of lettuce or a vanilla wafer!

I would mechanically give Ruperto the mate, or lemonade, in the shade of the arbor where he always sat in a Viennese chair, like a dog guarding his territory. I didn't think of him as a woman thinks of a man; I didn't even lightly flirt with him. Many times, after washing my hair and messily putting it up, or with a toothbrush in my mouth and toothpaste on my lips, or my hands covered with soap suds from washing the clothes, my apron fastened at the waist, big-bellied as if I were pregnant, I would let him in, opening the front door for him without even looking at him. Many times, my inattention was such that I think he saw me leaving the bathroom wrapped in a Turkish towel, dragging my slippers like an old woman, or some other sort.

Chusco, Albahaca, and Serranito flew to the bowl that held little arrows made of thorns. Carrying the arrows they eagerly flew to other bowls containing a dark liquid in which they moistened the tiny arrowheads. They looked like toy birds, cheap toothpick holders, decorations for great-great-grandmother's hat.

Cleóbula, who isn't overly suspicious, had noticed that Ruperto stared insistently at me, and told me about it. "What eyes he has," she would repeat endlessly, "what eyes!"

"I have succeeded in keeping my eyes open when I sleep," Antonio mumbled. "It is one of the most difficult tests of my life that I give myself."

I was startled by his voice. Was that the show? What was so extraordinary about it?

"Like Ruperto," I said with a strange voice.

"Like Ruperto," Antonio repeated. "The canaries obey my orders more readily than my eyelids."

The three of us sat in that dark room as if doing penance. But—what connection could there be between his eyes being open when he slept and the orders he gave the canaries? Not surprisingly, Antonio left me rather perplexed: he was so different from other men!

Cleóbula had also assured me that while Ruperto tuned the guitar he would stare at me from the top of my head to the tips of my toes, and that one night when he fell asleep, half drunk on the patio, his eyes had fixed on me. In consequence, I lost my naturalness with him, and perhaps my non-flirtatiousness. To my way of thinking, Ruperto looked at me through a kind of mask on which his animal eyes were mounted, eyes that didn't close even when he slept. His pupils would pierce me, staring at me in a mysterious way, with God knows what in mind, as he would gaze at the glass of lemonade or mate *that I would serve him. Eyes that stared so hard didn't exist in the whole province, in the whole world; a deep blue gleam, as if they held the sky inside them, making them different from all others, from looks that seemed listless or dead. Ruperto was not a man: he was a pair of eyes, without a face or voice or body; that's how I saw him, though Antonio saw him differently. For days on end he would become annoyed at my inattention, and at the slightest trifle he would speak harshly to me or force me to do unpleasant tasks, as if instead of being his wife I were his slave. The transformation in Antonio's character upset me.*

How strange men are! What was the show he wanted to perform for us? The business about the circus was no joke.

Shortly after we were married, he would often leave his job, pretending to have a headache or a strange pain in his stomach. Are all husbands alike?

At the back of the house there was a huge aviary full of canaries; formerly Antonio had always taken care of the birds zealously, but now the aviary was neglected. In the morning when I had time, I would clean it, put fresh birdseed, water, and lettuce in the white bowls, and when the females were about to lay their eggs, would help them prepare their little nests. Antonio had always busied himself with these things, but he no longer showed any interest in doing so nor in my doing it.

We had been married for two years! With no children! On the other hand, how many young the canaries had borne!

An aroma of musk and cedron filled the room. The canaries smelled like chickens, Antonio smelled of tobacco and sweat, but lately Ruperto smelled of nothing but alcohol. They told me he drank. How dirty the room was! Birdseed, bread crumbs, lettuce leaves, cigarette butts, and ash covered the floor.

Since childhood, Antonio had devoted his spare time to taming animals. He first used his art, for he was a true artist, on a dog, then on a horse, then on a skunk that had had its glands removed, which he carried for a time in his pocket; later, when he met me, he decided to tame canaries because I liked them. During the months of our engagement, to win me over, he had sent them to me bearing slips of paper with expressions of love, or flowers tied with a little ribbon. From his house to mine was fifteen long blocks: the winged messengers flew from one house to the other without hesitation. Believe it or not, they would even leave the flowers in my hair or the slips of paper in the pocket of my blouse.

Wasn't it more difficult for the canaries to put flowers in my hair or slips of paper in my pockets than to do those silly things with those damned arrows?

In town, Antonio came to enjoy a great deal of prestige. "If you hypnotize women as you do birds, no one will resist your charms," his aunts told him, with the hope that their nephew would marry some millionaire. As I said before, Antonio was not interested in money. From the age of fifteen, he had worked as a mechanic, earning however much he wanted, and this is what he offered me in marriage. We lacked nothing for our happiness. I couldn't understand why Antonio didn't find some pretext to make Ruperto go away. Any motive would have sufficed, even a quarrel about a job or politics, something that, without their coming to blows with weapons, would have prevented his friend from coming to our house. Antonio didn't let any of his feelings show, though I could tell his character had changed. Despite my modesty, I noticed that the jealousy I inspired was driving a man I had always considered a model of normal behavior nearly out of his mind.

Antonio whistled, took off his shirt. His naked torso looked as if it were made of bronze. I trembled when I saw him. I remember that before marrying him I had blushed before a statue that greatly resembled him. But hadn't I seen him naked? Why was I so shocked by him?

But Antonio's character underwent another change that reassured me in part: his laziness turned into extreme activity, his melancholy into apparent happiness. His life became filled with mysterious occupations, with goings and comings that signified an extreme interest in life. After supper, we no longer had even a moment of rest to listen to the radio or read the paper, or to do nothing, or to chat for a few minutes about the events of the day. Sundays and holidays were no longer a pretext for rest. I, who am a mirror of Antonio, was infected with his restlessness, and came and went through the house, putting closets in order that were already in order, or washing pristine pillowcases, from an irresistible need to take part in my husband's enigmatic activities. A redoubled love and interest in the birds occupied him for much of the day. He set up new props in the aviary; the dry branch in the middle was replaced by another larger and more graceful one, which made the aviary even more beautiful.

Dropping their arrows, two canaries started fighting; their feathers flew around the room, and Antonio's face grew dark with rage. Was he capable of killing them? Cleóbula had told me he was cruel. "He looks like someone who carries a knife in his belt," she explained.

Antonio no longer allowed me to clean the aviary. During this time, he occupied a room that served as a storage space at the back of the house, leaving our marriage bed. On a cot, where my brother used to nap when he visited, Antonio spent his nights (without sleeping I suspect, since I would hear him pacing tirelessly on the flagstones until dawn). Sometimes he would shut himself up for hours at a time in that damned room.

One by one, the canaries let the little arrows fall from their beaks, perched on the back of a chair, and sang a soft song. Antonio sat up and, looking at Maria Callas, the one he had always called "the queen of disobedience," said a word that meant nothing to me. The canaries began fluttering about.

Through the painted glass of the windowpanes I tried to observe his movements. Once I intentionally cut my hand with a knife so as to be able to knock on his door. When he opened it, a flock of canaries flapped out, returning to the aviary. Antonio healed my wound but, as if perhaps suspecting that this was a pretext to get his attention, treated me with coolness and suspicion. It was about that time that he went away for two weeks, in his truck, I don't know where, and came back with a sack full of plants.

I looked at my stained skirt out of the corner of my eye. Birds are so tiny and so dirty. Exactly when had they soiled me? I looked at them with hatred: I like to be clean even in the darkness of a room.

Ruperto, ignorant of the bad impression his visits were making, came with the same frequency and always behaving the same way. Sometimes when I left the patio to avoid his glances, my husband would find some pretext to make me return, as if he actually enjoyed what gave him such displeasure. Ruperto's glances now seemed obscene to me; they stripped me naked in the shadow of the arbor, forcing me to do unspeakable acts when a late-afternoon breeze caressed my cheeks. Antonio, on the other hand, never looked at me, or he pretended never to look at me, according to Cleóbula. One of my most burning desires was to have never met him, to have never married him and known his caresses, but rather to meet him anew, discovering him for the first time, giving myself to him. But who can recover what has already been lost?

I sat up; my legs hurt. I don't like being still for such a long time. How I envy the birds their flight! But canaries make me sad. They look like they suffer in their obedience.

Antonio didn't try to stop Ruperto's visits: on the contrary, he encouraged them. During Carnival, he went to the extreme of asking him to spend the night when he stayed especially late one evening. We put him up in the storage room that Antonio was occupying at the time. That night, as if it were the most natural thing in the world, we slept together again, my husband and I, in our marriage bed. For a moment my life returned to its old pattern; or so I thought.

I glimpsed the famous doll in a corner, under the bedside table. I thought of picking it up. As if I had made some gesture, Antonio told me, "Don't move."

I remembered the day during carnival week when, as punishment for my sins, while straightening up the bedrooms, I discovered the burlap doll on top of Antonio's closet: its large blue eyes of soft fabric even had two dark circles in the middle for pupils. Dressed as a gaucho it would have made a funny decoration in our bedroom. Laughing, I showed it to Antonio, who looked annoyed, pulling it out of my hands.

"It's a memento from my childhood," he told me. "I don't like you touching my things."

"What's wrong with touching a doll you played with when you were a boy? I know boys who play with dolls—does it make you ashamed? Aren't you a man by now?" I said.

"I don't have to explain anything. Please shut up."

In a foul mood, Antonio once again put the doll on top of the closet and didn't speak to me for several days. But we embraced tightly as in happier days long past.

I touched my damp forehead with my hand. Had my curls come undone? Luckily there wasn't a mirror in the room, otherwise I wouldn't have been able to resist the temptation to look at myself instead of looking at those stupid canaries.

Antonio frequently shut himself up in the back room, and I noticed that he would leave the door of the aviary open so that some of the birds could come to the window. Out of curiosity, one afternoon I spied on him by standing on a chair to look through the very high window (which of course I couldn't look through when passing the courtyard).

I saw Antonio's naked torso. Was it my husband or a statue? He accused Ruperto of being crazy, but he was perhaps even crazier himself. How much money had he spent on canaries, instead of buying me a washing machine!

One day I caught a glimpse of the doll lying on the bed. A swarm of birds surrounded it. The room had been turned into a kind of laboratory. A clay bowl held a bunch of leaves, stems, and dark pieces of bark; another, some little arrows made of thorns; another, a shiny brown liquid. It seemed to me as if I had seen those objects in my dreams. To express my anxiety I described the scene to Cleóbula, who said, "That's what the Indians do: they use arrows dipped in curare."

I didn't ask her what curare was. I didn't know whether she was telling me this out of scorn or wonder.

"They devote themselves to sorcery. Your husband is an Indian." When she saw my surprise, she asked, "Didn't you know that?"

I shook my head with irritation. My husband was my husband. I had never thought that he could belong to a race or a world different from my own.

"How do you know?" I asked with some vehemence.

"Haven't you looked at his eyes, his protruding cheekbones? Haven't you noticed how cunning he is? Mandarin—even Maria Callas—is more honest than him. His reserve, his way of not answering when you *ask him something, his way of treating women: Isn't it enough to show you he's an Indian? My mother knows the whole story. They kidnapped him from a settlement when he was five years old. Perhaps that's what you liked about him: his mystery that makes him different from other men."*

Antonio was perspiring and the sweat made his torso shine. He was so handsome and yet how he wasted his time! Had I married Juan Leston, the lawyer, or Roberto Cuentas, the bookseller, I would surely not have suffered so much. But—what sensible woman marries from self-interest? They say that there are men who train fleas— what good is that?

I lost my trust in Cleóbula. No doubt she was telling me that my husband was an Indian to upset me or to make me lose confidence in him; but one day, while looking through a history book that had illustrations of Indian camps, and Indians on horseback swinging boleadoras, I noticed a similarity in appearance between Antonio and those naked men adorned with feathers. At the same time I realized that what had attracted me to Antonio may have been the difference between him and my brothers and their friends, the bronze color of his skin, his slightly slanted eyes, and that air of cunning that Cleóbula had mentioned with perverse delight.

"And the show?" I asked.

Antonio did not answer me. He looked fixedly at the canaries, which had started fluttering again. Mandarin separated himself from his fellows and remained alone in the darkness, singing a song similar to that of a lark's.

My solitude was increasing. I had nobody to talk to about my worries.

For Holy Week, for the second time, Antonio insisted that Ruperto stay as a guest in our house. It rained, as it usually does on Holy Week. We went to church with Cleóbula for the Stations of the Cross.

"How is the Indian?" Cleóbula asked me rudely.

"Who?"

"The Indian, your husband," she answered. "In town everyone calls him that."

"*I like Indians, and even if my husband weren't one, I would still like them,*" I answered, trying not to interrupt my prayers.

Antonio stood as if in prayer. Had he ever prayed? On our wedding day my mother had asked him to take communion; Antonio refused.

Meanwhile, Antonio's friendship with Ruperto was becoming closer. A sort of camaraderie, from which I was in some way excluded, linked them in a way that seemed fine to me. At that time Antonio made a show of his powers. To amuse himself, he sent messages to Ruperto, to his house, via the canaries. People said they played truco in this way, since they once exchanged tarot cards. Were they making fun of me? I felt upset by the games of those two grown-up men and decided not to take them seriously. Did I need to admit that friendship was more important than love? Nothing had estranged Antonio and Ruperto; on the contrary, Antonio, quite unfairly, had become estranged from me. With my woman's pride, I suffered. Ruperto kept on looking at me. The whole drama: Was it all just a farce? Did I miss the conjugal drama, that torture inflicted on me by the jealousy of a husband who had gone mad for days at a time?

We continued to love each other, in spite of everything.

In the circus Antonio could earn some money with his shows, so why not? Maria Callas nodded her head to one side, then to the other, and perched on the back of a chair.

One morning, as if he were announcing that a house was burning down, Antonio entered my room and said to me, "Ruperto is dying. They called me to come over. I am going to see him."

I waited for Antonio until noon, distracted by the housework. When he returned I was washing my hair.

"*Let's go,*" he told me. "*Ruperto is in the courtyard. I saved him.*"

"*How? Was it a joke?*"

"*No, not at all. I saved him by means of artificial respiration.*"

Hurriedly, without understanding anything, I put up my hair, got dressed, and went out to the yard. Ruperto, motionless, was standing by the door, looking at the flagstones of the courtyard without seeing them. Antonio pulled up a chair so that Ruperto could sit down.

Antonio didn't look at me; he stared at the roof, seemingly holding his breath. Suddenly Mandarin flew by Antonio and stuck one of the arrows in his arm. I applauded: I thought that's what I should do to make Antonio happy. And yet, it was a silly show. Why didn't he use his gift to cure Ruperto?

That fatal day, when Ruperto sat down, he covered his face with his hands.

How much he had changed! I looked at his cold, inert face, his dark hands.

When would they leave me alone? I had to put the curlers in my hair while it was wet. I asked Ruperto, trying to hide my annoyance, "What's happened?"

A long silence lengthened in the sun, heightening the song of the birds. Ruperto finally answered, "I dreamed that the canaries were pecking at my arms, my neck, my chest; that I couldn't close my eyelids to protect my eyes. I dreamed that my legs and arms were as heavy as bags of sand. My hands couldn't scare off the monstrous beaks that were pecking at my pupils. I slept without sleeping as if I had taken some drug. When I awoke from that dream, which was no dream at all, I saw darkness; however, I could hear the birds sing and the normal sounds of morning. With a great effort I called my sister, who came over. With a voice that was not my own, I told her, 'You must call Antonio to come save me!' 'From what?' my sister asked. I couldn't utter another word. My sister went running out, and came back with Antonio half an hour later. Half an hour that seemed like an eternity to me! Slowly, as Antonio moved my arms back and forth, I regained my strength but not my sight."

"I'm going to make a confession to you," Antonio whispered, slowly adding, "but without words."

Favorita followed Mandarin and stuck an arrow in Antonio's neck, then Maria Callas flew over his chest, and quickly stuck in another little arrow. Antonio's eyes, staring at the roof, changed color, so to speak. Was Antonio an Indian? Do Indians have blue eyes? In some ways his eyes resembled Ruperto's.

"What's the meaning of all of this?" I mumbled.

"What's he doing?" Ruperto said, since he saw nothing.

Antonio didn't answer. As still as a statue, he received the seemingly harmless arrows that the canaries were piercing into him. I went up to the bed and shook him.

"Answer me," I said. "Answer me! What's the meaning of all of this?"

He didn't say anything. Crying, I embraced him, throwing myself on him; losing all shame, I kissed him on the mouth, as only a movie star would do. A swarm of canaries fluttered about my head.

That morning Antonio looked at Ruperto with horror. Now I understood that Antonio was guilty twice over: so that no one could discover his crime, he had said to me and to the whole world, "Ruperto has gone crazy. He believes he is blind, but he sees as well as the rest of us."

Just as light had left Ruperto's eyes, so love left our house. You could say that those glances were a necessary part of our love. Gatherings in the courtyard lacked life. Antonio fell into a dark sorrow. He explained to me, "A friend's madness is worse than death. Ruperto can see, but he believes he's blind." I thought with indignation, perhaps with jealousy that friendship was more important than love in a man's life.

When I stopped kissing Antonio and drew my face away from his, I noticed that the canaries were about to peck at his eyes. I covered his face with my face and hair, which was thick as a blanket. I ordered Ruperto to close the door and windows so the room would become completely dark, hoping the canaries would fall asleep. My legs hurt. How long was I in that position? I don't know. Then I gradually understood Antonio's confession. It was a confession that bound me to him in a frenzy, in a frenzy of misfortune. I understood the pain he had needed to withstand in order to sacrifice—in such an ingenious way, with those tiny doses of curare and with those winged monsters that obeyed his whimsical commands as if they were orderlies—the eyes of Ruperto, his friend, and his own, so that they both, poor things, would never be able to look at me again.

ICERA

WHEN ICERA saw the set of doll furniture in the window of that enormous toy store at the Colón Bazaar, she wanted it badly. She didn't want it for her dolls (she didn't have any) but for herself, because she wanted to sleep in the tiny wooden bed, the frame of which was decorated with garlands and baskets of flowers, and to look at herself in the mirror of the wardrobe, which had tiny drawers and a door that locked. She wanted to sit in the little chair with a woven cane seat and a turned back, and face the dressing table, where there was an extra bar of soap, as well as a comb to tame her rebellious hair.

The head of the doll department, Darío Cuerda, took a liking to the girl.

"She's so ugly," he would say, by way of explaining his interest in her to the other employees.

Icera considered the dolls as rivals; she wouldn't accept them even as presents: she only wanted to occupy their places. Because she was stubborn, she stuck firmly to her ideas. This peculiarity of character, more than her height (she was much shorter than average), called attention to her. The girl always went with her mother to look at toys but not to buy them, since they were very poor. The head of the doll department, Darío Cuerda, let Icera lie down in the little bed, look at herself in the little mirror of the wardrobe, and sit in the chair, before the dressing table, to comb her hair, just the way the lady across the street from her house did.

Nobody gave Icera any toys, but for Christmas Darío Cuerda gave her a dress, a little hat, gloves, and doll shoes, all of which had been damaged and so could only be sold at a discount. Icera, mad with joy, went out wearing her new clothes. She still has them.

The little girl caused Cuerda some difficulties with her visits, because if he allowed her to choose a present she always chose the most expensive one.

"Mr. Cuerda is always so generous," the other employees at the store would say to the regular customers.

His reputation for generosity cost him a fair amount of money. The girl liked practical toys: sewing and washing machines, a grand piano, a sewing kit with all the tools, and a trunk with a trousseau, all of which cost a fortune. Darío Cuerda gave her a guitar and a rake; after that, since there were not many cheap toys, he chose to give her soaps, hangers, and little combs, things that made the girl happy because they were of some use.

"Children grow up," Icera's mother would say, sincere yet unhappy. "What mother isn't secretly sorry to see her daughter grow, even though she'd like her to grow taller and stronger than the other girls!" Icera's mother was like all mothers, only a bit poorer and a bit more devoted. "Some day, this little dress will no longer fit you," she would say, showing her the little doll dress. "What a shame! I once was little too, and look at me now."

Icera would look at her mother, who was inconsolably tall. Children grew up—this was true. Few things in the world were so true. Ferdinando wore long pants, Próspera couldn't find shoes her size, Marina didn't climb trees because, given her height (she resembled a giraffe), they were too short for her. A tiny worry gnawed for many days at Icera's heart, but she decided that if she repeated the words "I won't grow up, I won't grow up" over and over to herself, she would halt her apparent growth. Besides, if she wore the doll dress, gloves, and hat every day, she would necessarily continue being the same size. Her faith worked a miracle—Icera didn't grow.

Then she fell ill, and for a month she couldn't get dressed. When she got up she had grown four inches. She felt a great loss, as if that increase had diminished her. And in fact it had. She was no longer allowed to stand on the table; she no longer had her baths in the washtub; they no longer gave her wine in her mother's thimble; the grapes she was given and the purple verbena flowers she gathered in the countryside no longer took up as much space in the palm of her hand. The dress, gloves, and shoes no longer fit her. The hat perched on top of her head. Anyone could imagine the girl's displeasure: just think how annoyed you feel when you get fat, when your feet or face swell, when the fingers of your gloves become wrinkled like raw sausages. But by looking hard enough she found solutions for these problems: the dress became a blouse; the gloves could be made into mittens; by cutting off the heels the shoes could be used as slippers.

Icera lived happily once again, until a rude person reminded her of her misfortune.

"How you've grown!" said a nasty neighbor.

To show that it wasn't true, Icera tried hiding under the ferns in the yard, but three other neighbors discovered her right away and kept on talking about her abnormal height.

Icera ran to the toy store, her place of refuge. Her heart filled with bitterness, she stopped at the doorway. That day only dolls were exhibited in the shopwindow. The odious dolls, with the stiff smell of their hair and new clothes, gleamed behind the glass, among the reflections of admiring passersby who streamed along Florida Street. Some dolls were dressed for first communion, some as skiers, others as Little Red Riding Hood, others as schoolgirls; only one was dressed as a bride. The bride doll was a little different from the one dressed for first communion: she carried a small bouquet of orange blossoms in her hands and was enclosed in a light blue cardboard box, the kind that candies come in. Icera went into the toy store looking for Darío Cuerda. She asked the other employees where he was, since she couldn't find him in his usual place.

"Mr. Darío Cuerda?" (Icera, usually so silent, was forgetting her shyness.) "Would you please call him?" she said to an employee she particularly feared.

"Here he is," the cashier said, pointing to an old man who looked like Darío Cuerda disguised as an old man.

Darío Cuerda was so covered with wrinkles that Icera didn't recognize him. Despite his blurry memory, however, he remembered her because of her height.

"Your mother used to come and look at the toys. She liked the bedroom sets and the little sewing machines so much!" Darío Cuerda said politely, coming forward with a maternal tenderness. He noticed that the little girl had whiskers and false teeth. "These modern young people," he exclaimed, "the dentists treat them like adults."

How wrinkled we all are! Darío Cuerda thought. Later on he imagined that it was all a dream, a consequence of his fatigue. *So many old faces, so many new faces, so many chosen toys, so many sales receipts with carbon copies to write for impatient customers. So many children growing old and old people turning into children!*

"I have to tell you a secret," said Icera.

For Icera's mouth to reach Darío Cuerda's extremely long ear, the little girl had to climb up on the counter.

"I am Icera," Icera whispered.

"Your name is Icera too? That's normal. Children are named after their parents," said the head of the doll department, thinking to himself, *Old age obsesses me: even children look old to me.* (In his mind he amused himself mispronouncing the words.)

"Mr. Cuerda, I would like you to give me the box of the bride doll," Icera whispered, tickling him unbearably on the ear.

Icera had never spoken such a long, well-pronounced a sentence. In her view, that box would assure her future happiness. Getting it was a matter of life or death.

"Everything gets passed on," Cuerda exclaimed, "especially predilections. There is practically no difference between this girl and her mother. This girl speaks better but looks like an old woman," he added, addressing someone he thought was Icera's grandmother, who looked like a ghost.

Icera thought that when she got into that box she would stop growing. But she also thought that she would achieve some sort of revenge against all the dolls in the world by taking away this box, lined with blue lacy paper, from the most important of them all.

Darío Cuerda, straining from fatigue—it was no small job to take something from the display window—untied all the ribbons that held the doll in the box and gave it to Icera.

Just at that moment an unexpected photographer walked by, carrying the tools of his trade. When he saw a crowd of people gathered in the Colón Bazaar, he discovered that Icera, for whom he had been searching for some time, was in the toy store. The photographer asked permission to take her picture, while Icera settled comfortably into the box and Cuerda tied the ribbons over her. He knelt down on one knee, brandished his camera, then moved farther away, then moved closer again as if he were himself a doll. Perhaps the picture would be good publicity for the shop, Cuerda thought proudly. As he smiled, he forgot his wrinkles and those of the little girl, blinded by the flash that illuminated everything.

The photographer, who worked for a newspaper, began taking notes, consulting the old woman who accompanied Icera. This was just a formality, as he already knew the name, address, and age of the girl, her life and its miracles.

"When did your daughter turn forty?" he asked.

"Last month," Icera's mother responded.

Then Darío Cuerda realized that what was happening wasn't the result of his fatigue. Thirty-five years had passed since Icera's last visit to the Colón Bazaar. He thought, confusedly perhaps (because he was in fact extremely tired), that Icera had not grown more than four inches in all that time, destined as she was to sleep all of her future nights in that box, thus preventing her from growing in the past.

THE PERFECT CRIME

GILBERTA Pax wanted to live in peace. When I fell in love with her I believed quite the opposite; I offered her everything a man in my position can offer a woman to persuade her to come live with me, since circumstances didn't allow us to marry. For one or two years we met in uncomfortable, expensive places. First in cars, then in cafés, then in seedy movie theaters, then in rather dirty hotels. Once, instead of asking again, I demanded that she come live with me and she replied, "I can't."

"Why not?" I cried. "Because of your husband?"

"Because of the cook," she whispered, and she ran away.

The next day I angrily asked for an explanation. She went on at some length.

You don't know my house; it's like a hotel. Five people live there with us; besides my husband, there's my uncle, one of his sisters, and her two children. They want everything to be perfect, especially the food; but Tomás Mangorsino, the cook—he's been with us for eight years—started to poke fun at us. Although each dish's appearance was rather pleasing, each day his cooking got worse. If I forgot to cover my hair with a kerchief, it'd smell like grease. I would spend whole mornings pleading with him to cook as well as he did in his prime. Mangorsino would look at me with some compassion, but he'd never listen. One morning when I went to see him, wearing a pink bathrobe and a green plastic cap, the kind you would wear to a dance, he stared at me so insistently that I asked him, "What's wrong, Mangorsino?"

"What's wrong? This morning my lady is so beautiful that I hardly recognize her."

That was when I thought of compromising my duty as a housewife by seducing him. As if he had guessed my intentions, he changed his behavior, but only toward me. He sent me meringue puffs, in shapes that suggested his love and in portions large enough for only one person. When he spoke to me, I could sense repressed tenderness in his voice.

"Make some noodles with a very light dough."

"I'll knead it very well," he said, looking me in the eye.

Or else, "And my favorite empanada?"

"I'll brown it. I know you'll like it."

"And what are you going to make for tea?"

"Meringue kisses."

He said these things while devouring me with his wolf eyes.

I acceded to his demands, but things didn't change much. He would send out a dish, forbidding me to eat from it as it was for the others, cheap ingredients and not so fresh. Then the servant would whisper to me while setting a plate on the table before me, "This is for my lady, whose digestion is a bit delicate."

The situation prolonged itself horribly. While the rest of the family writhed with stomachaches, I ate delicious pastries that, had they not threatened my slim figure, would have delighted me.

"My husband wants to eat mushrooms (I hate them, even in pastry) and my children want turkey," I told him one day.

He almost strangled me.

"They are very expensive," he answered.

Our relationship has become fraught with misunderstandings. When he sharpens the knives, he stares intently at my neck. I am afraid of him, why deny it? When he twists a dishrag, I know he is twisting my neck; when he slices meat, he is slicing me. At night I can't sleep. I'm a slave to his fancies.

"Don't worry," I told Gilberta. "What market does he go to?"

"I have the address in my address book," she told me, "1000 Junín Street. Do you plan to kill him?"

"No, something better than that," I answered.

It was the middle of winter and I went to the country to gather mushrooms. I brought them home in a sack. I asked Gilberta for a photograph of Tomás Mangorsino.

"What do you want it for?" she asked.

"I have an idea," I answered. She brought me the picture.

To carry out my plan, I needed to know Mangorsino's habits. After finding out what time he went to the market, I stationed myself at a corner I knew he passed at seven every morning. A man walked by wearing an impeccable gray suit and a brown scarf. I consulted the photograph: it was Mangorsino.

"Mushrooms, very cheap mushrooms," I cried, with a peddler's voice, "very fresh."

Mangorsino stopped, then stared at my gloves. I didn't want to leave fingerprints, just in case.

"How much?"

"Five pesos," I said, speaking like a foreigner.

"I'll take them," he said, handing me money from a bottomless pocket.

The next day, in the afternoon paper, I read the news. A whole family had died, poisoned by mushrooms bought on the street by the cook, Mangorsino. The only survivor was Mrs. Gilberta Pax.

I rushed to the house, where Gilberta was waiting for me. I didn't tell her anything about what I had done. Such a complicated, subtle crime shouldn't be confided to anyone, not even to the person you love most in the world, not even to your pillow.

She told me that her family felt indignant as they were dying and that they didn't lose their senses: when they felt the first symptoms of the poison they ran, forks in hand, into the kitchen, forcing

Mangorsino to eat the same poisonous mushrooms, thus causing the poor man's death. My crime was a crime of passion and, what is more unusual, a perfect one.

THE MORTAL SIN

SYMBOLS of purity and mysticism are at times more of an aphrodisiac than pornographic pictures or stories. This is why—oh sacrilegious one!—in the days before your first communion, when you were promised a white dress decorated with lots of lace, linen gloves, and a little pearl rosary, you experienced perhaps the most impure period of your life. May God forgive me for that, because in a way I was your accomplice and your slave.

Holding a red mimosa blossom, which you would pick in the countryside on Sundays, and a missal bound in white (chalice stamped on the center of the first page and lists of sins written on other pages), it was then that you discovered the pleasure—I choose these words carefully—of love, so as not to call it by its technical name. You would not have been able to give it its technical name either: you wouldn't even know where to place it in the list of sins you studied so diligently. Not even in the catechism was everything anticipated or clarified.

When people saw your innocent, melancholy face, nobody suspected that perversity, or even vice, had already caught you in its messy, sticky net.

When some girlfriend arrived to play with you, you would first tell, then show the secret link between the mimosa flower, the missal, and your sudden feeling of exhilaration. No friend understood it or tried to participate in it, but all of them pretended quite the opposite, to oblige you, sowing in you a panicked feeling of solitude (stronger than yourself) due to your knowing that your neighbor was deceiving you.

In the enormous house where you lived (from the windows of which you could see several churches, a store, the river full of ships, sometimes processions of streetcars or carriages in the square, and the English clock), the top floor was devoted to purity and slavery: to the children and the servants. (You were of the opinion that slavery also existed on the other floors and that purity was absent from all of them.)

You heard someone say in a sermon, "The greater the luxury, the greater the corruption." You wanted to walk barefoot, like the baby Jesus; to sleep in a bed surrounded by animals; to eat bread crumbs, which you would find on the ground, like the birds, but you were granted none of these pleasures. To console you for not walking barefoot, they dressed you in an iridescent taffeta gown, in shoes of gilded leather; to console you for not sleeping in a bed of straw, they took you to the Colón Theater, the largest in the world; to console you for not eating crumbs off the ground, they gave you a fancy box of silvery lace paper, full of candies that barely fit in your mouth.

That winter the ladies, with their headgear of feathers and furs, only ventured a few times to the top floor of the house, where its incontestable superiority (or so you thought) would appeal to them in the summer, when they wore light clothes and carried binoculars, looking for a flat roof where they could watch airplanes, an eclipse, or perhaps just Venus rising. Then they would pat your head as they passed by, exclaiming in a falsetto voice, "What lovely hair! Oh, what lovely hair!"

Next to the playroom, which was also the children's study, was the men's bathroom, a bathroom you never saw except from afar, through the half-open door. The chief servant, Chango, the one granted the most responsibility in the house, who had nicknamed you "Doll," would linger there much longer than the others, something you noticed as you often crossed the hall to go to the ironing room, which you found pleasant. From there, you not only could see the shameful entrance, you could hear the plumbing run past the countless bedrooms and living rooms in the house, rooms where there were glass cabinets, a small altar with images of the Virgin, and sunset glowing on the ceiling.

In the elevator, when the nursemaid brought you up to the play-room, you often saw Chango entering the forbidden room with a sly expression on his face and a cigarette in his lips. More often, how-ever, you would see him alone, distracted, baffled, in different places around the house. He would be standing up, leaning for long peri-ods on the edge of a table, whether a fancy or plain one (any table, that is, except the marble table in the kitchen or the wrought-iron table decorated with bronze irises in the courtyard). "What's the matter with Chango, why doesn't he come?" Shrill voices could be heard, calling him. He would linger before leaving the table behind. Afterwards, when he did come, they of course couldn't remember why they had been calling him.

You would spy on him, but he also ended up spying on you: some-thing you discovered the day the mimosa flower disappeared from your desk and you later saw it adorning the buttonhole of Chango's lustring jacket.

The ladies of the house rarely left you alone, but when there were parties or deaths (such similar occasions) they would have Chango take care of you. Parties and deaths served to strengthen this cus-tom, apparently preferred by your parents. "Chango is serious; Chango is good. He's better than a governess," they would say in chorus. "Of course, he plays with her," they would add. But I know of one person with the mouth of a viper, the kind that's never lack-ing, who said, "A man is a man, but these people don't care at all, so long as they can save a little money." "How unfair!" the raucous aunts would mutter. "The little girl's parents are generous, so gener-ous they pay Chango as if he were a governess."

Someone died, I can't remember who. An intense smell of flowers rose up through the elevator shaft, exhausting and poisoning the air. Death, with its countless ostentatious demonstrations, filled the lower floors, moved up and down with the elevators, with crosses, coffins, wreaths, palm fronds, and music stands. Upstairs, under

Chango's vigilance, you ate chocolates that he gave you; you played with the blackboard, the store, the train, and the dollhouse. Swift as the dream of a lightning bolt, your mother visited you and asked Chango whether it would be good to invite a little girl over to play with you. Chango answered that it was better not to, because two girls would make a racket. A purple color passed over his cheeks. Your mother kissed you and departed; she smiled, showing her beautiful teeth, momentarily happy to see you acting so sensibly in Chango's company.

That day Chango's features were even more indistinct than usual: we wouldn't have recognized him in the street, neither you nor I, although you described him to me so many times. You spied him out of the corner of your eye—he usually stood erect but was curved over like a parenthesis. He walked closer to the edge of the table and stared at you. From time to time he watched the movements of the elevator—he could see the cables pass by like snakes inside the black metal cage. You were playing, feeling submissive yet uneasy. You could foresee that something unusual had happened or was going to happen in the house. Like a dog, you could smell the awful scent of flowers. The door was open: it was so tall that its opening was the size of three doors of a modern building. But that wouldn't make your escape any easier; besides, you had no intention of escaping. Mice or frogs don't flee the snake that desires them; larger animals don't flee either. Chango, dragging his feet, finally moved away from the table; he leaned over the railing on the stairs and looked down. A woman's voice, shrill and cold, echoed from the basement, "Is Doll behaving properly?"

The echo, which seemed so seductive when you spoke to it, repeated the phrase, bereft of any charm.

"She's behaving wonderfully," Chango answered, hearing his words resound in the lower depths of the basement.

"At five o'clock I will bring up her milk."

Chango replied, "Don't worry, I'll prepare it for her myself," was answered by a feminine "Thank you" and then was lost in the tiles of the lower floors.

Chango returned to the room and gave you an order, "Look through the keyhole while I'm in the little room next door. I'm going to show you something very beautiful."

He stooped down next to the door and, putting his eye to the keyhole, showed you what you had to do. He left the room and you were alone. You kept on playing as if God were watching you, as if you had taken a vow, with that deceptive fervor that children sometimes have when they play. Then, without a moment's hesitation, you approached the door. You didn't need to stoop: the keyhole was at the very height of your eyes. What headless women would you discover? A keyhole acts as a lens on the image that is seen: the tiles sparkled, a corner of the white wall was brightly lit. Nothing else. A slight breeze made your hair blow around and forced you to close your eyes. You moved away from the keyhole, but Chango's voice resounded with a commanding and sweet obscenity, "Doll, look! Look!" You looked again. Bestial breathing could be felt through the door, not just the air from an open window in the adjoining room. I feel such sorrow when I think how horror imitates beauty. Through that door, Pyramus and Thisbe, like you and Chango, spoke their love through a wall.

You drew away from the door and automatically went back to your games. Chango entered the room again and asked, "Did you see?" You shook your head, your straight hair flying around madly. "Did you like it?" Chango insisted, knowing that you were lying. You didn't answer. You pulled off your doll's wig with a comb, but Chango leaned once more on the edge of the table where you were trying to play. With his troubled look he was staring at the mere inches separating the two of you, then slid in quietly next to you. You threw yourself onto the floor, holding the doll's ribbon in your hand. You didn't move. Flushes of red covered your face, like those thin layers of gold that cover fake jewelry. You remembered how Chango had rummaged around the white underwear in your mother's drawer when he replaced the women servants to take over the housework. The veins of his hands were all swelled up, as if full of blue ink. On his fingertips you could see bruises. Without meaning to, you looked carefully at his lustring jacket, which felt very rough when it touched your knees. From that moment on, you would always see the tragedies of your life adorned with tiny details. You missed the delicate flower of the mimosa, your odd weakness, but you felt that this arcane spectacle, brought on by unforeseen circumstances, would accomplish its goal: the impossible violation of your solitude. Like two criminals who were very much alike, you and Chango were united by different objects but were pointed toward identical goals.

For a series of sleepless nights you invented dishonest reports that could serve as confessions of your guilt. Your first communion arrived. You couldn't figure out a modest or clear or concise form of confession. You had to take communion in a state of deadly sin. In the pews were not only the members of your (large) family but also Chango and Camila Figueira, Valeria Ramos, Celina Eyzaguirre, and Romagnoli, the priest from a different parish. With the sorrow of a parricide, of someone sentenced to death for treason, you entered the church feeling frozen, biting on the corner of your missal. I see you pale, unblushing before the high altar, with your linen gloves on, holding a bouquet of artificial flowers, like a bride's bouquet, at your waist. I would journey on foot across the whole world, searching for you like a missionary to save you, if only we had the fortune, which we don't have, of being contemporaries. I know that in the darkness of your room, you heard for a long time, with the insistence with which silence seals the cruel lips of the furies who devote themselves to tormenting children (the inhuman voices, linked to your own) saying: It is a deadly sin, my God, it is a deadly sin.

How were you able to survive? Only a miracle can explain it—the miracle of mercy.

THE GUESTS

FOR WINTER vacation, Lucio's parents had planned a trip to Brazil. They wanted to show their son the Corcovado, the Sugarloaf, and Tijuca, and to admire those places afresh through the child's eyes.

Lucio fell ill with German measles; nothing serious, but with "face and arms covered with splotches like grits," in his mother's words, he couldn't travel.

They decided to leave him in the care of a maid, a very kind old woman. Before leaving they told her to buy a cake and candles for the boy's birthday, which was coming up, even if his little friends couldn't come and enjoy it for fear of catching his illness.

Joyfully, Lucio said goodbye to his parents: he thought that their departure would bring his birthday nearer, a day that was so important to him. To comfort him, even though there was no need for that, his parents promised to bring him a painting of Corcovado made of butterfly wings, a knife with a picture of the Sugarloaf painted on its wooden handle, and a telescope through which he would be able to see the most important sights of Rio de Janeiro, with its palm trees, or of Brasilia, with its red earth.

The happy day, or so it was in Lucio's hopes, was slow in coming. Vast zones of sadness impeded its arrival, but one morning, different for him from all other mornings, the cake with six candles, which the maid had bought according to the mother's instructions, sparkled on Lucio's bedroom table. A new yellow bicycle also shone by the front door, a gift left by his parents.

There's nothing so infuriating as having to wait unnecessarily; that was why the maid wanted to celebrate the birthday at lunchtime, but Lucio protested, saying that his guests would be coming later.

"Cake feels heavy when you eat it in the afternoon, just as an orange in the morning is like gold, silver in the afternoon, and deadly in the evening. Your guests won't come," the maid said. "Their mothers won't let them come for fear of your disease. They already told your mother that."

Lucio refused to listen to reason. After their scrap, Lucio and the maid didn't speak again until teatime. She took a siesta and he waited by the window.

At five o'clock there was a knock on the door. The maid went to open it, thinking it was a deliveryman or a messenger. But Lucio knew who was knocking. It had to be his guests. He smoothed his hair in the mirror, changed his shoes, washed his hands. A group of impatient girls was waiting with their mothers.

"No boys among the guests. How strange!" the servant exclaimed. "What's your name?" she asked one of the girls who struck her as nicer than the others.

"My name is Livia."

The others said their names all at the same time and came in.

Lucio stopped by his bedroom door. He already seemed older! He greeted them one by one, looking them in the eye, examining their hands and feet, stepping back to look them over.

Alicia was wearing a very tight wool dress and a knit cap, the traditional kind that is back in fashion. She looked like an old woman and smelled of camphor. When she took out her handkerchief, mothballs fell out of her pockets; she picked them up and put them back where they had come from. Doubtless she was precocious, showing a deep concern with everything around her. Alicia's concern was for her hair ribbons, which the other girls pulled on, and a package that she grasped tightly under her arm and didn't want to let go of. This package contained the birthday present: a present that poor Lucio would never receive.

Livia was exuberant. Her glance would light up and then darken like those dolls with batteries. As affectionate as she was exuberant, she hugged Lucio and took him off to a corner to share a secret: the gift she had brought him. She spoke no words to communicate; this detail seemed unpleasant to all but Lucio, and seemed like a joke to the others. In the tiny package that she unwrapped herself, because she couldn't stand the slow pace with which Lucio unwrapped it, there were two crude magnetic dolls that couldn't resist kissing on the lips, their necks stretched out, as soon as they were within a certain distance of each other. For a long while the girl showed Lucio how to play with the dolls in ways that made their positions more perfect or more unusual. Inside the same package there was a partridge that whistled and a green crocodile. The presents, or the girl's charms, captivated Lucio's attention totally. He paid little attention to the rest of the group, instead hiding in a corner with Livia and the presents.

Irma, who had clenched fists and pursed lips, a torn dress, and scrapes on her knees, infuriated by Lucio's reception, by his deference to the presents from the exuberant girl who was whispering with him in the corner, hit Lucio in the face with the strength of a boy, and not satisfied with this, crushed the partridge and the alligator on the floor with her foot, while the mothers of the girls, all a bunch of hypocrites according to the servant, lamented the disaster that had happened on such an important day.

The maid lit the candles on the cake and closed the curtains so that the mysterious light of the flames would shine more brightly. A brief silence brought life to the ritual. A scandal occurred: Milona stuck the knife in the cake and Elvira blew out the candles.

Angela, who was dressed in an organdy suit with lace hems and other details, was distant and cold; she didn't want to try even a little icing from the cake, or look at it, because at her house, according to her, birthday cakes had surprises inside. She wouldn't try the hot chocolate because it had a layer of scum on it and when they brought her a strainer she became offended, saying that she wasn't an infant, and threw everything onto the floor. She didn't notice, or pretended not to notice, the fight between Lucio and the two girls who had crushes on him (she said she was stronger than Irma), or the scandals provoked by Milona and Elvira, because according to her only stupid people go to silly parties, and she preferred to think about other happier birthdays.

"Why do these girls come to parties like this if they don't want to talk to anyone, if they sit off to the side alone, if they disdain the delicious things that have been prepared with love? Since they were little girls they have been party poopers," the offended maid complained to Alicia's mother.

"Don't get upset," the lady answered, "they're all the same."

"How can I not get upset? They have a lot of nerve: they blow out the candles and cut the cake even though they aren't the birthday boy."

Milona was very pink.

"I don't have any trouble getting her to eat," said her mother, licking her lips. "Don't give her dolls or books because she won't even look at them. She wants candies and pastries. Even ordinary quince jam drives her mad. Her favorite game is eating."

Elvira was very ugly. Greasy black hair covered her eyes. She never looked at anything directly. A green color, like olives, covered her cheeks; no doubt she had a bad liver. When she saw the only present that was still on the table she let out a shrill laugh.

"Girls who give ugly things should be punished, right, Mother?" she told her mother.

When she walked by the table she managed to make her long tangled hair knock the two dolls onto the floor, where they kept on kissing.

"Teresa, Teresa," the guests called.

Teresa wouldn't answer. She was as indifferent as Angela but didn't sit up as straight; she barely opened her eyes. Her mother said that she was sleepy, that she had sleeping sickness. She pretended to be asleep.

"She falls asleep even when she is having fun. It's a blessing because she leaves me in peace."

Teresa wasn't completely ugly; at times she even seemed nice, but she was a monster when compared to the other girls. She had heavy eyelids and a double chin that were not in keeping with her age. At times she seemed like a very good girl, but she wasn't: when one of the girls fell on the floor because of something Teresa had done, she didn't come to her aid, and sat stretched out on her chair, groaning, looking at the ceiling, complaining that she was tired.

"What a birthday party," thought the maid after it was over. "Only one guest gave a present. And better not to even think about the rest of them. One ate almost the whole cake; another broke the toys and hurt Lucio; another went off with the present she had brought; another said unpleasant things, the sort of things that only adults say, and with a doughlike face didn't say goodbye when she left; another sat in a corner like a lump without blood in her veins; another—God help me!—I think it was the one named Elvira, had the face of a viper, something that brings bad luck; but I think that Lucio fell in love with one of them (the one with the present!) just out of self-interest. She knew how to win him over without even being pretty. Women are worse than men. They're hopeless."

When Lucio's parents returned from their trip they couldn't find out who the girls were who had visited him on his birthday, and they thought their son must have secret friendships, which was, and probably still is, true.

But Lucio had now become a little man.

MEN ANIMALS VINES

WHEN I fell I must have lost consciousness. I only remember two eyes staring at me and the airplane rocking back and forth for the last time, as if a huge nursemaid were rocking me in her arms. A boy likes being rocked. I closed my eyelids, wandering around unknown worlds. Then a deafening noise and a hard blow brought me back to reality: the hard crash to earth. Nothing brought me in touch with earth except for the feeling of a bonfire going out, leaving gray ashes so much like silence. I don't understand what form the accident took: suddenly I was here, alone, in the jungle with all the provisions but without any sign of the plane in which I had traveled—all so strange. Someone will come looking for me; I trust the skill of the airmen who besides looking for me and the rest of the crew and passengers will come looking for the plane. They will find me by accident; accidents happen and sometimes they are fortunate. These provisions, if guarded carefully, will last for three weeks. My count may be inaccurate.

Besides, some rodent, some bird, some animal could devour the provisions that aren't adequately wrapped, which would reduce my supply considerably. In that case I would only have the jelly and the little tinned crackers that taste like cardboard, smoked meat, tongue, dates and prunes, repulsive cashews, peanuts.

But those eyes, where were they?

Three weeks is a long time, almost a month. Provisions for three weeks, what more could I ask for? Sharing them—would I have this privilege? I don't remember where I read about some monks who survived for a long time on two or three dates a day. The bottles of wine will also help me stay healthy and strong.

But those eyes that were staring at me, what will they drink?

No animal could be interested in wine: Why? And speaking of animals, I think about the possibility of predators.

Sometimes I hear branches creak and I think it smells of predators, but I understand that if I let my thoughts go I will go mad, so I throw myself down on the earth, kiss it, and try to imagine a world full of sheep, like in the prints we got for first communion, and of butterflies, like in a child's first readers. My bed is so comfortable that after sleeping for eight hours I wake up calm, thinking that I am at home. I stretch one arm out, confidently trying to turn on the light on my bedside table, dwelling in this illusion for a while. If the night is very dark I am seized by great anguish, but if there is a moon I look at the light that shines on the leaves of the trees and the trunks covered with moss and imagine that I am in a tended garden. That image, so silly in reality, makes me feel calm, though I always preferred woods to gardens. That's why I always wandered around with my hair unkempt, why I let my beard grow, and why at times my clothes are less than spotless. Now that I am surrounded by vegetation that grows at random, would I prefer to be surrounded by well-kept plants? No, not at all. My thoughts go back to the city that I hated, to the city's surroundings that I scorned. I angrily remember its smell of gasoline, mothballs, drugstores, sweat, vomit, feet, basements, old people, insecticide, urinals, newborns, spit, shit, kitchens. I don't commit the mistake of redeeming the image of the city with the image of beloved people. I try not to miss the toilets or the sinks. I adapt to this life. One adapts to anything: that's what Mama said, and she was right.

I don't know what sort of climate this place has; I do know that I am disturbed by my ignorance. It would be difficult to find out without anything that could guide me: no barometer, no geographical sign, no botanical or climatic study. Due to a storm, the plane went off course, so I have no idea where it fell. I could consult the sky, but I don't know much about the stars either. I fear making a mistake. I think this place is damp because there are some vines and a variety of honeysuckle that grows in damp places. I don't know whether the heat I feel is tropical or just summer. Beneath the trees there are some ferns piled up among the moss.

What color were those eyes? The color of the marbles I picked out at the toy store when I was a boy.

At night there are fireflies and deafening cicadas. A soft penetrating perfume seduces me: Where does it come from? I don't know yet. I think it's good for me. It comes from flowers or trees or herbs or roots or from all of those at once (maybe from a ghost?); it is a perfume I never smelled anywhere in the world, an intoxicating yet soothing perfume. Smelling like a dog—will I turn into a dog?—I tear at the leaves, the plants, the wildflowers that I encounter. I study the leaves, searching for the perfume. I tear at the bark of trees and taste it. At last I discover what perfumes the air so thickly: a vine, one with insignificant flowers. Nothing about its appearance distinguishes it from the others except its impetuous foliage. While I look at it I think it's growing. I feed myself methodically in accordance with the daily amounts of food that I have decided to eat so that the provisions will last until the plane, or helicopter, arrives, something I expect via men or God. Several times a day I eat small amounts of food. There are some wild fruits that enrich my diet. I am filthy. Why do I take such care of myself? Less than a month ago I thought of committing suicide; now I am methodically eating, trying to rest, as if I were taking care of a child. There are people who only find out who they are after a long time. The song of birds at midnight (at what I guess to be midnight) becomes deafening. I could have made a slingshot out of the elastic bands that I have on the waistband of my anorak and two branches that I have cut. Why hunt a bird? I ask. The natural thing would be to kill and eat it. I couldn't. My will weakens, perhaps. I sleep a lot. When I wake up I take pictures of the trees, of my hand, of my foot, of the foliage; what other photographs could I take? I don't have an automatic shutter to take a picture of myself. Besides, I don't know if my camera is working because it fell hard. Sometimes I pronounce my name over and over, giving my voice different tones. Am I afraid of forgetting it? I discover that there is an echo in the jungle. Nothing frightens me so much as that. Sometimes I hear, or think I hear, the motor of a plane: at these times I search the sky desperately.

Where could those eyes be that stared at me so persistently? What might they talk about? Could they have fallen into the sea, attracted by their own color? What if they were to come all of a sudden?

Little by little I get used to this life. I prefer to sleep: it's what I do best, sometimes even too much. If a predator were to attack me while I slept, I wouldn't be able to defend myself. Every day I commit the foolhardy act of sleeping deeply after lunch; of course I don't know what time it is, because my watch has stopped and for the first time I have lost all notion of time. The sunlight reaches me indirectly through the trees. After losing the thread of time, if I can put it that way, it would be difficult to orient myself using that light. I don't know whether it is fall, winter, spring, or summer. How could I without knowing where I am? I think the trees around me don't lose their leaves. I don't dare go deeper into the jungle; I might lose my provisions. This has become my home. The branches are my hangers. I miss soap and a mirror so much, scissors and a comb. I begin to worry about the question of sleep. It seems to me that I sleep almost all the time and I think it's because of the intense perfume of the flowers. Their harmless aspect is deceptive: they form an arbor that on closer inspection is diabolical. In vain, I rip them up out of the soil; they grow back with even more force. I try to destroy them by burying them but I don't have any digging tools. I try to use a short piece of wood but it is too difficult. Poor Robinson Crusoe, or rather, lucky Robinson Crusoe who knew how to handle the tasks imposed by solitude. I am helpless in a situation like this. In vain I try to destroy the flowers because they climb up into the trees and cut me off from the sky. I couldn't destroy their scent in any case, since this place is like a locked room. Sometimes while falling asleep I've noticed a branch with two or three flowers; when I wake up I see that the same branch has nine more flowers. How long have

I slept? I don't know. I never know how long I sleep, but I suppose that I sleep the way I did when I had a normal life. How could so many flowers bloom in such a short time? I think these things will drive me mad. I observe the flower that is guilty of making me sleepy: it looks like a trumpet flower and it is sweet (I have tried it). The branches that emerge are weaving strange little baskets. I never observed a vine so closely. It curls around trunks and branches, making such a tight weave that sometimes it is impossible to pull it off. It is like a lining, like a cascade, like a snake. Thirsty for water, it comes looking for my eyes. Now I am afraid of sleeping. I have nightmares. I've been dreaming the same dream several nights in a row: the honeysuckle confuses me with a tree and starts weaving a net that takes me captive around my legs. I don't think I'm in bad health. Quite the contrary, I think that I'm perfectly fine. Nevertheless, this state of sleepiness doesn't seem normal to me. Sometimes I ask myself: Have I lost all sense of time? Am I sleeping more than is normal for a human being, or do I believe that I am sleeping more? Is it the perfume that makes me sleepy? At the hour that it is most intense, I begin to nod off, my eyes close, and I fall into a lethargy that frightens me when I wake up again. The progress the vine made up the tree served as my clock for several days. Like a weaver it tightened its grip around each branch. When I woke up I could calculate the time I had slept from its knots but right now it seems to be speeding up. Is it me, or time? Jumping from one idea to another without any order is one of my normal habits, but the truth is that I never had so much time or so much physical inactivity. I never believed that I would find myself in such a situation. Besides, abstinence always horrified me. Yesterday—was yesterday yesterday?—I drank several bottles of wine to relax, and after wandering drunk through the jungle I fell asleep, who knows for how long.

I dreamt that I was saying, Where are those eyes that stared at me so intensely? What would they drink? There are people who are hands; others, mouths; others, hair; others, a chest that you can lean on; others, a neck; others, eyes, just eyes. Like her. I tried to explain it to her while we were traveling on the plane but she couldn't understand. She only understood with her eyes and asked, "What? What did you say?"

I woke up far from the provisions, thinking that I wouldn't ever be able to find them again. I scolded myself harshly. I argued with myself. I found my way back, guided no doubt by divine grace, back to the place of my salvation: my food. What an irony of fate! Depending on food when I was one of those men who boasted of being able to fast for twenty days, who used to laugh at hunger strikes! Now, for a date or a repulsive cashew I would sell my soul. No doubt all men are the same and they would all react in the same way. I don't move, am enclosed as if in a prison cell. I never imagined that a cell and a jungle could be so alike, that society and solitude could have so much in common. Inside my ear a million voices are arguing, getting angry at one another, devoting themselves to destroying me. Tra ra ra ra, I am sick of this.

My God, may I never forget those eyes. May their irises live in my heart as if it were of earth and the irises were plants.

Those contradictory voices (the voices that I hear in my ears) are devoted to destroying me.

Love one another. Never before was it so hard for me to follow that precept. Though one shouldn't scorn solitude. One day the world will be so densely populated that my present lair will no longer be isolated. Thinking about transformations makes me dizzy. With my eyes closed I think about all those crazy things, which isn't prudent of me: the vine takes advantage of my distraction and wraps around my left leg, weaving a fine net around each toe. The baby toe makes me laugh. How skillfully it wraps around it. To say nothing of the big toe that looks like a vessel to sprinkle holy water. The vine does its job in various ways; for the smaller toes it uses a stitch that looks like the slats of modern wicker chairs, for bigger surfaces it uses a strange mixture of arabesques that imitate plastic car seats. I pull the web off my food with some difficulty. I remember a vine at my house called wallflower, with little clawed feet that stuck onto the walls. I remember as a boy pulling off some of the leaves that were like kittens that didn't want to let go of their prey. This vine doesn't have little feet like that wallflower. It is the better for it. It tirelessly goes around weaving knot after knot. Poor trees, poor plants that fall victim to its claws! *Lucky the tree that is barely sensitive.** I recited that to someone (I no longer love) to impress her. The line has stayed with me. I'm not so sure about that "barely sensitive" stuff. At night I think I hear the trees complaining, hugging, rejecting one another or sighing, kneeling before other members of the family or before those who have succumbed to the vine. I entered this vegetal realm in complete ignorance. The only tree I knew, besides the willow, was the *tipa* tree. Once Mama told me while we were crossing San Martín Square, "What beautiful *tipas*!" At that moment two horrible *tipas* walked by.

"Why are you laughing?" Mama protested, looking at the foliage of the *tipa* trees, adding, "Now one can't even admire the trees?"

"What trees?" I asked.

"The *tipas*, silly. Don't know what *tipas* are?"

"Oh, the *tipa* trees," I answered with the due surprise, "I thought you were talking about those ladies."

"You don't know what you're saying. You should go to the jungle to chat with the monkeys."

Poor Mama, she must be regretting that insult now. Sometimes I'm kept awake by that memory, unable to avoid it. I look at the *tipas* in the dark. They had yellow flowers; they made Mama's dress look even bluer. And will I always have the gray face I had in Buenos Aires?

What are those eyes looking at?

A doughlike face—that's what the seamstress who came to sew for my sisters at our house said about me, always thinking I was twelve years old even though I had just turned twenty. What a drag to be twenty! I don't miss my house at all, but a mirror is all the company I have now—for better or for worse—and there I had a

---

* *"Dichoso el árbol que es apenas sensitivo,"* a famous line from Rubén Darío's poem "Lo fatal."

mirror that was as round as the moon. I have fallen asleep this time more deeply than ever, more than the day I got drunk; it's clear that I can't be sure if I'm mistaken.

Where are those eyes? Could I be forgetting them? I can't remember the shape of the corners of those eyes.

Sometimes you fall asleep for five minutes and it seems like you've slept the whole night. Last night I fell asleep, waking up at the break of dawn. Could I have only slept for five minutes? I have proof that that's not the case: the vine had time to wrap itself around my left leg and to reach my thigh: it has my thigh! And as if that weren't enough, now it's started on my left arm. This time I pulled it loose with great difficulty, with less force than before, calling it stupid, like one of my girlfriends says about me in jest. I have resolved to change my location. I lift up my provisions and leave, searching for a place without vines; but I can't find one, and the walking exhausts me. Sometimes I think that years have gone by, that I am old, but if that were the case I wouldn't have any provisions left. Now I have stopped in a place that may be worse, but I don't have the strength to go back to where I was. This whole jungle is a huge vine. Why should I worry? I should only worry about things that have solutions. The perfume will still intoxicate me, making me sleepy. The vine will go on twisting. Now I usually wake up to find another web around my arm or my leg. Yesterday it reached my neck. I was quite upset. It's not that I was afraid, not even when it wove itself around my tongue. I remember that when I was dreaming, I shouted, imprudently opening my mouth. It's weird. I never thought that a vine could find its way so easily into my mouth.

"Pervert. Who do you think you are? A person can't trust anybody anymore," I told it.

I'm amused when I think about how my friends will laugh at this anecdote. They won't believe me. They won't believe my lack of laziness either. Lately I have tried weaving knots like the vine does around the branches: it's a very difficult experiment but an interesting one. Who can compete with a vine? I am so busy that I forget those eyes staring at me; understandably I have forgotten to drink and eat. Human gender, oh so changeable! I, suddenly female, wrap the pen in my green fronds, like the pens that prisoners wrap with silk and wool thread.

LIVIO ROCA

HE WAS tall, dark, and quiet. I never saw him laugh or hurry for any reason whatsoever. His chestnut eyes never looked at anything straight on. He wore a kerchief tied around his neck and always had a cigarette in his mouth. He was ageless. His name was Livio Roca, but he was called Dumbo because he pretended to be deaf. He was lazy, but in his periods of leisure (he didn't think of inactivity as laziness) he fixed watches that he never returned to their owners. Whenever I could, I'd escape to visit Livio Roca. I met him during summer vacation, one day in January at Cacharí. I was nine years old. He was always the poorest member of the family, the most unhappy, according to his relatives. He lived in a house that resembled a railroad car. He loved Clemencia—she was perhaps his only consolation and the main subject of gossip in the town. Her velvet nose, cold ears, curved neck, short, soft hair, and obedience were all reasons to love her. I understood him. At night, when he unsaddled her, he would delay saying goodbye to her, as if the heat of her sweaty body gave him life, taking it away from him when he left. He let her drink deeply, prolonging the farewell, even when she wasn't thirsty. He hesitated before bringing her into his shack to sleep at night, under cover, in the winter. He hesitated because he feared what would later in fact happen: people said he was crazy, completely crazy. Tonga was the first to say it. Tonga, with his embittered expression and needlelike eyes, dared criticize him and Clemencia. Neither could ever forgive him. I loved Clemencia in my own way, too.

Grandma Indalecia Roca's silk bathrobe was kept in a room full of trunks. The robe was a sort of relic that lay at the feet of a Virgin, painted green, with a broken foot. From time to time, Tonga and the other members of the family, or some visitor, would place unlucky flowers or little bouquets of herbs that smelled like mint, or sweet bright-colored drinks, at her feet. There were times when a crooked, multicolored candle would tremble, its flame dying at the feet of the Virgin; for this reason, the robe was adorned with drops of wax the size of buttons. Time eliminated these rituals little by little: the ceremonies happened more and more infrequently. Perhaps for this reason, Livio dared to use the bathrobe to make a hat for Clemencia. (I helped him do that.) I think that's what caused the misunderstanding with the rest of the family. Tonga called him a degenerate, and one of the brothers-in-law, a bricklayer, called him a drunkard. Livio put up with these insults without defending himself. Only some days later did the insults start bothering him.

He couldn't remember his childhood except how unhappy he had been. He had scabies for nine months and conjunctivitis for nine more, according to what he told me while we were sewing the hat. Perhaps all of that contributed to his losing faith in any kind of happiness, never to regain it. At the age of eighteen, when he met his cousin Malvina and became engaged to her, he may have had a foreboding of disaster at the moment he gave her the engagement ring. Instead of being happy, he was sad. They had grown up together—from the moment he decided to marry her, he knew the union would not be a happy one. Malvina's friends, who were numerous, spent their time embroidering sheets and tablecloths and nightgowns with her initials on them for her, but they never used those things, embroidered with such love. Malvina died two days after the wedding. They dressed her as a bride and put her in the coffin with a bouquet of orange blossoms. Poor Livio couldn't look at her, but in the darkness of his hands, where he hid his eyes the night they held the wake for her, he offered her his faithfulness in the form of a gold ring. He never spoke to any other woman, not even to my cousins, who are so ugly; when he went to the movies he didn't look at the actresses. Many times people tried to find a girlfriend for him. They would bring prospects over in the afternoon and sit them down on the wicker chair: one was blond and wore glasses, and they called her the English girl; another was dark with braids, and a flirt; another, the most serious of them all, was a giant with a pinhead. It was hopeless. That's why he loved Clemencia with all his heart, because women didn't matter to him. But one night, one of those inevitable uncles, a mocking smile on his lips, decided to punish him for the sacrilege he had committed with his grandmother's robe, and shot Clemencia. Together with Clemencia's neighing, we could hear the murderer's loud laughter.

THE DOLL

EVERYBODY says, I am such and such, I am so-and-so, except for me, who would prefer not to be who I am. I'm a soothsayer. At times I suspect that I don't merely see the future but that I cause it. I began my apprenticeship in Las Ortigas. I have an office in La Magdalena. Clouds of dust, the police, and my clients all pester me.

According to the doctors' official reports, my identity papers declare that I am twenty-nine years old. My mother died the day I was born, that much they all agree on. They also told me something I will never forget: that someone found me one January night in the pastures by Las Ortigas. Throughout my life, the reports they have given me about my birth have varied widely. I have no reason to believe in some of them more than others. Nevertheless, I prefer to imagine being born in those pastures, next to a lagoon surrounded by willows, rather than at the door of the shed where corn and wool were stored under a corrugated iron roof. The lagoon has many birds and a bottom of white sand; the willows cast trembling shadows that resemble flocks of sheep or horses that look like Eriberto Soto. The shed is full of cats and sheepskins. At night the cats wail and jump up on the scales. There are fleas, lots of fleas, and red ants.

In one version of my birth, my mother was Polish, wore a new dress and a pair of black patent-leather shoes; in another, she was Italian, wore a threadbare dress, and carried a bundle of firewood; in another, she was just a schoolgirl who carried a notebook and two books (one geography and the other history) under her arm; in another, she was a filthy gypsy who carried tarot cards and gold coins in the pocket of her red skirt. There was even someone who gave me a fake photograph of my mother. For a time this image excited my filial feelings. I put the photograph at the head of my bed and for days on end directed my prayers to it. Later I found out the photograph was of a movie star and that someone had cut it from an old magazine to make me happy or to torment me. I still preserve it along with a bouquet of dried flowers.

Throughout my childhood, which felt very long to me, people used to tell me the story of my birth to entertain me. Miss Domicia enlivened her story by drawing cups and houses in a graph-paper notebook. When she took off her glasses to clean them with a white handkerchief, she would always speak to me of a lagoon where there were many willows and where birds filled the morning. My eyelids, the door to sleep, would close. Miss Domicia was methodical. For the two years I lived with her, before our fight that I will describe later on, she would enter and leave my room at the same time every day. She would tell me the same story in the very same words. On her belt, she carried a bunch of keys, which fascinated me. Her dark hair was dry, straight, and long; she always wore it braided, coiled around either side of her head. Miss Domicia was a sort of head maid, resented by the other servants. During her tenure, the house was fresh, clean, orderly, or so Mr. Ildefonso, who was a little afraid of her, assured her. The sets of sheets edged with hemstitches according to her instructions were never mixed with the napkins and embroidered tablecloths, as they had been in other periods. The bedspreads were not torn or stained with coffee or rust. Miss Domicia was the guardian angel of the cupboards, of the pantry. With a ringing of keys, she would open the huge doors of the cabinets where soap, jam, wine, dried fruit, tea, coffee, cookies, and sweets were kept, along with those that held white clothes with lace and embroidery, edged with hems.

Miss Domicia wasn't fond of me: she would wash my hands with boiling water; she would twist my toes when she put on my socks; when she rubbed my face with a handkerchief, she would squash my nose so hard that tears would well up. If I mention her prominently, it's because she was the one who discovered my gift of second sight. I remember a rainy day in January as if it were today. We were not allowed to go out and play on the covered porch. From the living-room windows we watched the branches of the trees being whipped by the wind. Suddenly, in the midst of my games, I announced the arrival of Kaminsky the engineer.

Mr. Kaminsky had visited the ranch only once. His name and his height had made a vivid impression on me. With a careful pantomime I described his arrival, which occurred several hours later. Miss Domicia, her hands hard and dry, pulled the damp hair from my forehead, looked at my eyes with her spiderlike eyes, and said to me, "You scamp, you must be a witch." What was a witch? I guessed that she was saying something awful about me. I suddenly pulled her hands away from my forehead. She insisted on brushing my hair, even as I struggled, kicking and screaming to avoid the touch of her hands. How long did the fight last? I don't know. It seemed to me that it filled the whole of my life, that it would continue to fill it. We ended up shut in the bathroom. I had been injured. Miss Domicia wet my head and eyelids with cold water and punished me. She promised never to touch me again, a promise she kept religiously. On numerous occasions she said that it would have been better for everyone if the old woman at Las Rosas had taken care of me. She also said that my presence at the ranch bothered the adults and perverted the children. I tried not to hear her words or look at her face, a face that seemed to me like that of the devil. By mistake, a shameful mistake in my opinion, against all the teachings I had received, I imagined the devil as being female and not male (as she was dressed accordingly in illustrations, looking like a bat with a black cape instead of wings).

The old Las Rosas woman—that's what they called Lucía Almeira because she lived at the cattle station at Las Rosas—took me in, or so they told me, the night I was born, and kept me in her house until I was three. Perhaps I'm confusing my memories with the stories I was forced to listen to. I don't know. A room with a dirt floor: a sheepdog and five chickens and their chicks were lodged with me at Lucía Almeira's house.

Lucía was thin, wrinkled, and dark. I never saw her sitting down. She was constantly moving from one side of the room to the other. She was so poor that her shoes had no soles. Why had she taken me in? How did she feed me? No one ever found out. Some people said that she planned to raise me to join the circus in town; others said that she loved children madly and that by taking me in she was realizing one of her dreams. In her hands, wrinkled and black, I remember the bits of bread she gave me; I also remember the straw mat with which she covered the open window to help me sleep, and the flatness of her chest where I could hear her heart beating.

Those silent days, days in which my memory barely glimpses a few tiny details of the world around, Lucía Almeira took zealous care of me—everything I've gathered agrees on this point. She took me to the Rivases' three times a week when she went to do the washing. While she washed, I would play with torn old rags, pinecones, cats (until one of them gave me an awful scratch). Playing with the children in the house, I learned to walk. They got so used to seeing me that at nightfall, when Lucía said goodbye and picked me up to take me home, some of them would cry.

Lucía Almeira consented to my spending one night, on Christmas Eve, at the Rivases'. She allowed me to do so again on later occasions when the other children begged her. Little by little she grew used to what had once seemed impossible for her: letting me go. Perhaps the illness that was later to cause her death had so weakened her that it took away her desire to keep me and take care of me as if I were her daughter. Perhaps Esperanza's enthusiasm for me made her jealous. Once, she didn't come for me. After a long consultation, Mr. Ildefonso convinced her it was better to let me stay on forever at the ranch.

Esperanza liked my company. Mr. Ildefonso thought my stay at the house would make his daughter forget the puppy that she never parted from. Instead of playing with the dog, Esperanza would play with me.

Esperanza forgot the dog, and I forgot Lucía.

I don't remember when I came to that yellow house. I feel as if I've always known it. Esperanza showed me its most secret corners: the attic and the mouse room, which is what we called a sort of dark cell where empty bottles and sacks were piled. The house had an enclosed courtyard and a cistern, a corridor with blue flagstones, and Gothic arches over the front door, a door decorated with panes of glass with white designs like lacework. The trees that surrounded it, mostly eucalyptus and Australian pines, were very tall and tangled.

Esperanza and I were the same height and the same age. When we ran races she always beat me, because she managed to cheat in some quick, tricky way. When we climbed trees she would insist that the highest branch I reached was much lower than hers, even when mine was much higher than hers.

Esperanza's arms were covered with freckles. She was cheerful and bright; when she shouted, the veins in her neck would stand out and she would turn very red. She liked scratching. The marks of her fingernails were etched in my skin in purple lines that would last for days. Many times I thought she belonged to the cat family, and that that was why her favorite dog was so overjoyed when it was rid of her. I never could love her. I liked boys, no matter how boorish and unpleasant; they seemed superior to girls to me.

My bedroom was located in the wing of the house that faced the front. I slept with a nursemaid, Elsa, who would wake me up to ask if I had remembered to recite the Lord's Prayer. She took care of me only at night.

Across from my door, on the other side of the courtyard, was the boys' room. Before they went to bed, they would try to scare us by banging on our windowpanes and imitating the hoots of owls. I often cried for fear, while Elsa stood before the mirror slathering her face with cold cream and curling her hair around slips of paper. Often I buried my tears in the pillow as I watched her close the shutters, after opening them just slightly to peer out.

For me, the stormy nights were the only calm ones. It seemed to me that the house, like Noah's ark, was floating on water, and that nobody would come to trouble the sleep of a crew composed of evil men and good animals. I had forgiven the cat for her scratches, but I could never forgive Esperanza or Miss Domicia for their evil and devious deeds.

Ever since the day I had announced Mr. Kaminsky's arrival, some people started treating me with respect. Soon I began predicting the weather, announcing early in the morning whether or not letters would arrive that day, whether the rabbits would die. One day, when Mr. Ildefonso was leaving for market, he asked me if his calves would sell for a good price. Without a moment's hesitation, I gave an answer that later turned out to be the truth.

Mr. Ildefonso was stocky, his hair thick and black, and his green eyes would shine with extraordinary brightness; he wore a reddish straw hat with a leather strap and the top of which was full of little holes. He spoke in an emphatic way, pronouncing the last syllables of each word as if they were a threat. He always wore a handkerchief knotted around his neck and a tiepin with a little pearl set in gold. Everything about him indicated an orderly, neat, domineering person. I often heard people talking about him in respectful terms, terms much more respectful than those I heard applied to his wife, Celina, whose ill-apportioned acts of charity earned her some of the local people's lasting resentment. Mrs. Celina seemed distant to me, like a portrait. Her precarious health forced her to get up late, to go out only briefly with a parasol, to take long naps, and to go to bed early. She always dressed in long white skirts, and looked very tall. Sometimes she covered the upper part of her face with a blue veil; on those occasions, her mouth, with its sweet smile, would receive all of my attention. Mrs. Celina allowed me to approach her without fear. She always wore gray gloves and took them off only to close her parasol. After closing the parasol, she would straighten her ring so that the blue stone would show, then she would pass her bare hands over her forehead, as if the hands or the forehead were not her own. She would absentmindedly kiss her children one by one, and me, too, not without some feeling of aversion. Horacio, who was always the last one, would merit the longest, quietest kiss. I never knew whether that pause was intentionally directed to Horacio or whether it was part of an absentmindedness that automatically turned the last kiss into the longest one. Motionless, I always watched that kiss, a gesture that remained deeply engraved on my memory. It seemed to me that a secret form of voluptuousness always presided over such moments: it was a morning of sunshine and ripe fruit, an evening when the grass was covered with dew.

Celina Rosas incarnated all the virtues of sweetness and refinement for me. Her room, where the blinds were almost always shut, was a sort of altar forbidden to the rest of us mortals. When I passed the sometimes half-open door, I used to glimpse the floral patterns of the curtains and the mysterious bronze bed where she slept. I thought her life wasn't in contact with other lives.

Esperanza and I ate in the pantry; Juan Alberto, Luis, and Horacio ate in the dining room. After meals, while they were serving the coffee, we would play cops and robbers, London Bridge, and tag.

During one of those lazy periods after dinner, while Mr. Ildefonso was smoking his cigar and Mrs. Celina was looking vacantly out of the window, with one cheek resting on her hand, a scene revealed the falseness of the calm that ruled over that house.

Mrs. Celina's absence didn't seem to sadden Horacio. It surprised me that those long kisses in the morning and evening had not left a greater mark on his heart. Horacio, with his penknife and his dog

Dardo, was in the habit of going on outings in the morning. He would barely glance at me, and if he did so it was to demand something of me or scold me for something. His attitude, rather similar to that of Juan Alberto and Esperanza, didn't offend me to the same extent. I admired him. After many subterfuges I managed to dress in a way that brought me luck. The clothing consisted of some short, baggy trousers of the kind the gauchos wear, a linen shirt, and some rubber boots I'd been given. One day, during Carnival, feeling the need to dress up, I put on that male clothing, which stood out more than Esperanza's disguise as a gardener. Horacio began treating me as if I were one of his male friends. To treat me as one of his friends was at times to mistreat me badly. He would often invite me to go horseback riding. When he needed to pee, he would do so right in front of me, without hiding at all, while we watched the lines of ants going by. We had conversations we would never have dared to have in front of other people. Two or three times we went swimming in the round metal tank without telling anyone. To seem manlier I stripped to the waist. At naptime, in the afternoon, I would escape to his room to tell him and his brothers about the conversations I had overheard in the kitchen and to describe to them what Elsa did at night by the mirror before going to bed. I never thought that my intimacy with Horacio would prove so costly to me.

Juan Alberto said that dogs were like people: when one was harmed, all the others would pounce on him to finish him off. Luis said that dogs were much better than people, but that people were like monkeys imitating one another. Horacio said that each person resembles some animal, or that each animal ends up looking like a person, and that it was ridiculous to compare monkeys and dogs. Miss Domicia resembled a camel; Elsa, a rabbit; Mr. Ildefonso, in profile, a buffalo; Kaminsky the engineer, a donkey. Esperanza became indignant and, after some protests regarding her parents, said that men all resembled owls because they hissed at people at night to silence them. I said the only thing I could think of, that men were like cicadas, but

I couldn't explain why. Then, when nobody heard me, in the middle of all the shouting, I said that they resembled cicadas because they were so noisy.

The boredom I felt when I was with Esperanza made the time seem longer. I often felt that I was about to faint when Mlle. Gabrielle would take us to her favorite place under the trees to give us our lessons. There, in the shade of a linden tree, she would open a knitting bag and take out balls of yarn, pieces of fabric, cookies and thread, a broken book. Everybody knew that Mlle. Gabrielle was untidy: wherever she went she left behind bits of thread, fabric, wool, cookie crumbs. When she scolded us for dropping something she would blush, feeling she had no right to demand of others what she failed to do herself. She was good, blond, pale, and had a mustache. She taught me to read; she taught me some rudiments of French and mathematics; she also taught me some fables, which she forced me to recite for Mrs. Celina's birthday.

Mlle. Gabrielle made us take turns reading aloud from a book she herself had illustrated. The days I had to endure these readings were unlucky ones for me. Some disaster always happened, the direct product of my ill humor or disaccord. One such day I intentionally destroyed the diary of Juan Alberto, who thought of himself as an adult, someone worthy of respect, simply because he had a diary. In the tiny pages I had read the ridiculous notes: *January 22nd, I bought five packs of cigarettes and a tennis racket; January 23rd, had a shot of rum; January 24th, Luisita looked at me when I went past her door; January 25th, having a tooth pulled is horrible.*

When he found out I had destroyed his diary he didn't say anything, but I guessed his intentions by looking in the depths of his eyes: he intended to wait for the right moment and then take his revenge in some nasty way. All day long I tried to be friendly to him, to agree with him about everything, but I knew that whatever I did to avoid his vengeance would only help bring it about.

Juan Alberto was eleven years old. I think boys are the crudest at that age; girls start much earlier, at eight or nine, an age I hadn't reached yet.

We awaited the arrival of Mrs. Celina. A telegram had announced her coming. I had not dared to say that she would return, something I had foreseen long before the telegram arrived. They began waxing the floors early in the morning. Mlle. Gabrielle, Esperanza, and I went to get flowers and peaches from the orchard. We put the peaches on a blue porcelain plate and the prettiest flowers in a crystal dish. We took advantage of the occasion to eat peaches, nuts, and two or three squares of chocolate, the kind that Mlle. Gabrielle had ordered several bars of to make the desserts that were such a success.

Those exceptional days, when one could eat at times other than regular meal hours, you might have thought I was crazy about any kind of food; it seemed as if food contained something that made me drunk, since when I ate I started laughing without being able to stop, with a high nervous laughter. The joy of seeing Mrs. Celina again manifested itself in numerous acts of absentmindedness, in the plates of food, and in the flowers that Mlle. Gabrielle picked.

To anyone who was willing to listen I described a doll I had imagined, with brown curls, blue eyes, a straw hat, and a light blue organdy dress. It said "Mommy" and "Daddy" over and over.

At siesta time I took advantage of the state of confusion that filled the house to escape with Horacio. Without our hats on, we walked beneath the afternoon sun toward the round metal tank where we were planning to swim. Horacio took off his sandals, his trousers, and his shirt; I had also stripped, but still had on my sandals and a handkerchief that I knotted around my head like a hair band. We climbed up on the corrugated metal to enjoy the dirty water before diving in; all of a sudden Horacio said he saw a snake and said that he would kill it. He jumped down to the ground, and I let myself fall down after him. The snake glided away and disappeared in the weeds. We searched for it on our knees. For some time

Horacio had been looking for a coral snake to capture in a bottle: the one that afternoon was the first coral snake he had ever seen, besides those illustrations he had admired in books. We peed, I squatting down on a slope and Horacio standing next to me; then, squatting in the grass, in the same posture that Horacio said attracted reptiles, we waited to capture the snake. Suddenly, we heard a voice above us, "Here they are." We turned around. There was Juan Alberto, and a little farther off under a black umbrella was Miss Domicia. Motionless, without realizing what was happening, we looked at each other. Juan Alberto pointed at us and said, "They're always up to the same thing." Miss Domicia, whose face was hidden by the fabric of the umbrella, gave a sort of grunt and turned around, telling Juan Alberto to follow her. The solitude and the heat embraced us once more. Horacio shrugged and went back to looking for the snake. I got dressed, watching the dark threatening clouds in the sky. Without speaking to Horacio, I went running to the house; I went to my room and threw myself on the bed. I was unable to think about the doll!

A big storm was gathering. I felt relieved when I heard the first thunder. "Perhaps the flood will come once and for all and I'll be saved from my shame," I thought. I heard a lot of running around the courtyard, then the rain and the banging of shutters. I heard the bell at four o'clock, then the sound of teacups and spoons, announcing it was teatime. I didn't dare leave my room. After a time that seemed an eternity to me, Mlle. Gabrielle came looking for me. I looked at her in terror. I soon saw that she wasn't unhappy with me; I got off the bed to follow her, after combing my hair and getting dressed as fast as I could. In the pantry Esperanza was sitting at the table. I sat down without speaking to her; to calm myself I imagined I had dreamt the whole scene that afternoon. There were just a few more hours until Mrs. Celina would arrive. Mr. Ildefonso, Juan Alberto, and Luis would go to meet her in a carriage. I drank my tea meekly.

After tea, when I was crossing the courtyard, I heard them talking about Horacio and then talking about me in connection with him. The story had passed from mouth to mouth and would reach Mrs. Celina's ears and she would stop protecting me with her distant smile.

"We'll have to tell her," Miss Domicia was saying.

"Do you dare?" Doña Saturna responded.

"I couldn't rest if I didn't do it. I'd have it on my conscience."

"And who'll pick up the pieces?" Saturna asked.

"I don't know. I don't care," Domicia said. "This will teach her not to collect what isn't hers. They already have enough children without looking for more. I wash my hands of it all."

The sound of a carriage, in the midst of the rain, interrupted the dialogue. The horses stopped before the entrance to the courtyard of the house. Mr. Ildefonso, wearing his glasses and holding an open umbrella, prepared to greet his wife. Esperanza ran to her mother's arms before anyone else. Juan Alberto and Luis came out, banging the doors behind them. Horacio came last of all. I stood behind a column, watching what I thought was the beginning of a tragedy. All of them took the traveler's cardboard boxes, packages, and suitcases out of the carriage, while she stepped on the footboard of the carriage wearing a green rubber raincoat. Mrs. Celina looked hard at the house, up and down, as if she were seeing it for the first time. She kissed her children, pausing to remove a glove, smooth her hair, and shake her wet raincoat.

When she kissed Horacio she saw me behind the column and called me. I slowly approached her to receive her kiss. She handed me a cardboard box, asking me to open it and see what was inside. Surprised that I was not provoking the aversion I expected, I opened the box and found the doll with brown curls, blue eyes, a straw hat, and a light blue organdy dress. I shook it. The doll said "Daddy," "Mommy" in a soft moan. They advised me to take it out of the box by removing some strings that held it in place like a prisoner. Since I didn't dare to do it, Mrs. Celina pulled it out of its prison herself.

"Witch," Mrs. Celina told me.

"*Sorcière*," Mlle. Gabrielle told me.

Both of them recognized the doll I had described.

That was how they pointed me toward the difficult art of sooth-saying.

CARL HERST

CARL HERST had a very broad face, prominent cheek and jaw bones, and sunken eyes. My brother wanted to buy a dog from him. He lived in Olivos and we went to see the dog. When we arrived at the house, Carl Herst himself opened the door. He made us go straight to his study. There we sat down and drank cold beer; he spoke to us at length about his breeding program, how much work was involved, the animals' pedigree, and the importance of proper feeding.

He went to the back of the yard in search of Fulo (that was the name of the dog he wanted to sell to my brother) and we stayed behind looking around the room. On the walls, there were photographs in golden frames, all of them of dogs; the picture frames on the tables had photographs of hairless dogs, hairy dogs, dogs in groups, by themselves, midgets, very tall ones, long ones like sausages, pug-nosed ones with moonlike faces, mothers and children, siblings, all ages. In a half-open album I glimpsed collections of snapshots, also of dogs: in the countryside, in the city, running, sitting, lying down. When Carl Herst arrived with Fulo, my brother and I were laughing, but I soon stopped laughing because the animal scared me. He had a huge jaw and cold, round eyes.

"Is he fierce?" I asked.

"He's very good," Herst answered, "and very loyal."

After discussing the price, my brother decided we would come back the next day.

The next day there wasn't anybody home when we arrived, but a neighbor told us that the gentleman had said we should walk around to the backyard if we wanted the dog. We went to the end of the yard where there was a cyclone fence and, inside the fence, a large and well-appointed wooden doghouse. Trembling, I followed my brother. We went in through a little iron door with peeling paint. The dogs looked at us in a friendly way, and Fulo came running over. Then he went into the doghouse, and my brother followed. I peered in from the outside. My eyes rested on a picture hanging on a white wall. I looked at it intently: it was a photograph of Carl Herst.

On the other walls there were plates hanging with inscriptions such as, "What dog is like a friend?" "Love men, take care of them, they are part of your soul." "I have a friend—what else matters?" "When you feel alone don't seek another dog." "Man won't betray you, a dog will." "A man never lies."

THE MUSIC OF THE RAIN

THE PEBBLES on the road sang beneath the wheels of the stage-coach. In the awakened garden it was impossible to confuse the slow rhythmic sound of a horse-drawn coach with the dry quick sound of an automobile. That day everything seemed musical: the wheel of the well that brought up the bucket, voices, coughs, laughter.

"Who has arrived?" some shrill voices asked.

"Octavio Griber," a deep voice answered.

"Who?" insisted the impatient questioner.

"The pianist," answered the deep voice.

"In a stagecoach? It's raining. Couldn't they come by car?"

"The pianist is crazy for horse-drawn carriages and rain—he says they are musical. At least the horses were neighing."

The people were sitting in the living room, in armchairs that were probably too comfortable, so comfortable that after a while it was hard for some of them to get up, making their posture look permanent. In the garden, from time to time there was a lightning bolt, followed by thunder, which lit up the room.

The owner of the house, who knew how to play the piano, stood next to the window. He was so used to wishing for his picture to be taken in that romantic pose that he adopted it frequently.

Illuminated by the lightning, the pianist finally entered. No shyness softened his face. He greeted all of the guests with a nod that left his hair in disarray. When he saw the enormous mirror next to the piano he ordered that it be covered up. (This demand caused a fuss. They didn't have anything to cover it with. They finally found a flowered coverlet and fit it as best as they could over the mirror.)

Then the pianist walked with great ceremony to a corner where there was a screen decorated with ears of corn, bunches of grapes, and doves, took a velvet jacket out of his satchel with golden clasps, and, after taking off his overcoat, shoes, and socks, slipped on his jacket.

At the pianist's request, various hands with rings on their fingers opened the piano lid. The pianist took tiny pieces of white silk paper out of his pocket and carefully put them, one after another, on each of the felt hammers inside the piano, which he had examined before like a doctor examines a patient. The owner of the house concealed his anxiety when he saw all of the little pieces of paper on the hammers, but then could no longer contain his impatience and exclaimed, with an unexpected voice, "He is an eccentric." And he warmly asked the pianist's mother, "Why does he do this?"

"It's a new system that makes the tones of the piano daydreamy. It sounds like a clavichord."

"Sounds like, or dreams? One system cannot ever be any newer than another, since no system is new. The clavichord is an old instrument. What advantage can there be in using modern effects to achieve old ones? But what I especially dislike is his touching the insides of the piano. Enough moths have already gone in there."

Octavio Griber looked severely at the owner of the house, lit a cigarette, and said, "I don't play anything without the silk papers." He continued to carefully insert his slips of paper and murmured in the direction of the owner of the house, "They have told me that you are a great pianist. Will you share some of your repertory with us?"

"Yes, but I don't play with my feet," answered the owner of the house, abruptly.

He was very jealous. When he became that way, his beard gave him away, turning so rough that no one would kiss him, no matter how much Brylcreem he put on.

"After these encounters, I feel older," he whispered in my ear.

I noticed for the first time that he was cross-eyed from looking at his beard so much, and this trait, in fact, was the secret of his intelligent appearance.

The rain in the garden grew more intense. It could be heard hitting the windowpanes like stones instead of raindrops. That was when the programs were distributed, written by hand with neat handwriting. Various compositions of Liszt were included: "Beside a Spring," "Saint Francis of Paola Walking on the Waves," "The Fountains of Villa d'Este." The names of Debussy, Ravel, Chopin, Respighi were written in green ink. The papers flew from one hand to the next.

When the programs stopped flying around they were used as fans. The pianist sat down at the stool, placed his burning cigarette on the edge of the piano, and swung around several times in order to establish the correct height. He looked at his feet, the pedals, his feet, the pedals again, and then started playing scales with one of his big toes. The notes poured out in a most unusual staccato. The guests didn't know whether to applaud or laugh.

"How funny," someone said. "I could do that too."

"But why can't he play like other people, with all of his digits," said a woman's voice, sharp as a pin.

"Because that would be difficult. He would have to be an acrobat to play with all five toes."

"I meant with his fingers, for God's sake. Why does he play with his feet?"

"There are people who paint with their feet or their mouth. What's wrong with that?"

"But they are handicapped."

"It is his way of playing—sometimes he only plays with his big toe. And he's always faithful to the first composition he ever played, and likes to repeat it. The beginning of his career was brilliant. He never followed any teacher's advice," said Mrs. Griber, slowly, ecstatically. "When my son began studying he would say, while looking at his toes, 'Why so many toes?' It was useless for the teacher to give him orange, lemon, or raspberry drops, or even chocolate candies, which gave him a rash. He refused to touch the piano with all of his digits. He would play exclusively with his big toe. After that first experience he started using the slips of silk paper so as to achieve what he proclaimed were more natural sounds. A piano tuner revealed all the secrets of the instrument to him. He was in the habit of exclaiming, 'I will make it out of tune in C flat and D minor.' Nobody knew what he meant. Perhaps he himself didn't know, but the sounds he produced were so extraordinary that once someone from the apartment below came up us to ask which of Wanda Landowska's records we were playing because they had never heard anything so wonderful. Here he doesn't dare, but in other homes he uses irregular tunings. It's useless to debate with geniuses," said Mrs. Griber.

Octavio Griber, who had switched to playing with his fingers, suddenly twisted around on the stool and looked at the audience as if to say, "Who dares to speak when you are here to listen?" Nodding his head without a word, he imposed silence for them to listen to his interpretation of Brahms's "Ballade in B minor."

"This piece of music has nothing to do with water," someone chimed, who understood the liquid nature of the ballade down to its smallest details.

"With lightning," answered Octavio, imperiously.

Debussy's "Gardens in the Rain," "The Sunken Cathedral," "The Goldfish," Ravel's "Water Games" acquired a perfect sonority despite being muffled by the silk paper. When he played the song "At the Water's Edge" by Fauré, another of his countless original ideas, he hummed the melody so softly that he provoked loud applause; Chopin's "Raindrop" prelude was an even greater success. Without a doubt, the contact of the virtuoso's bare feet on the keys influenced the interpretation of every work. They all agreed with the review that had appeared the day before in the newspaper; they had to admit his genius, just as the audience had applauded the last concert at the Colón Theater.

"But all of the pieces he plays are by French composers," protested one lady.

"Chopin isn't French, nor is Liszt, nor for that matter is Respighi."

"Van Gogh was the first painter to paint the rain. Isn't that strange?"

"What does painting have to do with music?"

"Van Gogh associated music with painting. And the first composer who made the rain sing was Debussy."

"That's not correct."

"What isn't?"

"That van Gogh associated music with painting. If he did it was during one of his fits, like when he sent his ear all wrapped up as a present. Besides, he wasn't French. Handel, Grieg, Schubert, even Wagner in *Das Rheingold* were all inspired by water."

"But that's orchestral music, not piano music. *Das Rheingold*, what a strange idea."

"What piece was that by Chopin?" a young man asked.

"Didn't you read the program?"

"One of the études, the 'Raindrop.'"

"Who has dropsy?" asked a lady who was sitting on the other side of the room.

"It's a piece of music," they answered.

"That's the height of perversity, to be inspired by a disease."

The piano resounded with a fresh mystery. Nobody was listening to it except for one woman who exclaimed, "There are melodies that kill!" She began to sob, her face in her hands. "I have never been able to listen to 'Gardens in the Rain' without weeping."

Behind the windowpanes it seemed as if the trees in the garden were growing. Suddenly the performer stopped. He asked that the windows be opened and said, "At the very least I want the trees and the rain to listen to me."

He saw a thousand beautiful eyes with tears, or rather tears with eyes. He smiled. If he could have gathered those tears in a test tube, he would have gathered them like orange blossom oil, as a bitter. "'The Bride's Tears,' my next composition, will bear that title," he thought. But they brought him some cold orangeade and a platter of strawberry tartlets. He drank the orangeade and ate the tartlets as if in a hurry. After every gulp he sucked on each of his fingers as if sucking on candy. They offered an embroidered silk napkin for his hands, brought on a tray. He looked at the tray, then took the napkin and stuffed it quickly into his pocket. He spun the stool around and set his hands on the keys again, looking at the ceiling as he had once seen Paderewski do at the Rino Bandini Theater. A woman approached him, took him by his chin, and said, "What a precocious boy: he's as smart as his great-grandparents!"

When the music resumed, something disturbed him. He inclined his head until touching the keys with his ear. He crouched down to look at the pedals. One note was louder than the others. He stood up, examined the inside of the piano, discovered that one of the hammers had lost its slip of paper. Octavio Griber asked for a piece of silk paper. They looked for paper all over the house with flashlights because it was dark by now and the upper rooms were inaccessible without light. Finally they found some apples wrapped in green paper and brought them to the living room on a tray. Would this paper do, even though it's not fine paper?

Octavio Griber put the strips of paper in the place where they were missing, carefully tested the notes and immediately recognized the superiority of paper used to wrap apples.

"Water Games" resounded once again on the piano, sounding as it had never sounded before, thanks to the new addition of the green paper. Sometimes lightning, followed by thunder, shook the fringes of the chandelier, but nothing shook the people who listened, speechless, to the sounds from the piano. The applause, cautious at first, filled the room with enthusiasm. Octavio, trembling with emotion, asked two young men who were near him to open the piano again. He indicated exactly what they were supposed to do. He took out of his pocket what looked like some small pliers, but it was a diapason; he came up to the young men who were energetically opening the insides of the piano.

"It will just take a moment," said Octavio to the piano, as if about to do a surgical operation.

Someone protested, but shame overtook the protester. How could anyone prevent a genius from expressing his originality? To distract him, someone took the owner of the house to the foyer to look for some silverware that was needed. Octavio tightened or loosened some of the piano strings. At last he managed to detune the instrument completely.

It was impossible to recognize Schumann's "Carnival" or Debussy's "Gardens in the Rain" or Ravel's "Water Games." Each piece had become something different that he alone could play.

The storm didn't let up. The rain beat against the windowpanes.

After the Spanish-style hot chocolate and pastries of various colors and shapes were served, and after asking the owner of the house to play his repertory, Octavio Griber, sighing, took off his velvet jacket in the same corner where he had put it on and packed it into his satchel, changed his clothes, smoothed out his hair, and put on a fresh pair of socks and then his shoes. When he looked at me to say goodbye, I showed him my album to get his autograph.

"What's your name?" he asked.

"Annabel," I answered.

He wrote, "To Annabel, from her admirer Octavio."

The carriage was waiting for him at the door.

The owner of the house dashed off to retrieve something and returned with an envelope and a miniature piano and pianist.

"For our little Octavio," he said bitterly, as if repeating a lesson he had learned by heart.

"No," whispered Mrs. Griber, holding him back. "You might offend him. He doesn't like to be called 'little.'"

"The Japanese give toys to adults. Besides, he's not of an age where he should be easily offended," said the owner of the house, stroking his beard, rough as a piece of felt.

"Some of us were born to be offended," exclaimed Mrs. Griber.

"But how old is your son, ma'am?"

"That's a secret. He says he's younger than he is, even young as he is. He has never looked at himself in a mirror; maybe that illusion preserves his youth. Once at age five he told me, when I insisted that he look at himself, 'Music isn't visible in the mirror.' Does he look old to you?"

"Not at all. He plays the piano like a five-year-old."

The owner of the house gave the envelope to Mrs. Griber, who was getting into the carriage, and the little piano to Octavio, who was standing by the door in the rain. Octavio looked at the toy, wound it up, and placed it on the ground. The tin pianist started to move and the little music box played the opening of a waltz. Octavio picked up the toy, wanting or not wanting to hear the music, wanting or not wanting to look at the tin pianist. Then, suddenly, he threw the toy away and climbed into the carriage. When the carriage turned a curve in the road, Octavio looked out from behind a black rubber curtain and stared outside—the rain and the trees were listening to the Brahms waltz interpreted by the toy pianist.

SHEETS OF EARTH

"GARDENER. Arborist. Landscaper. Available. Besares 451." She smiled. For more than a year this ad had been buried in mothballs in her sweater pocket. She crumpled the paper in her hands and threw it on the floor. Resting her head on the back of the rattan chair, she gave a sigh of relief and told her husband, "How lucky we are to have a good gardener." Her husband looked at her over the top of his newspaper. "A real gardener," she went on, "who treats plants with tenderness and who truly loves them as if they were his little children," and when she said these words, she felt the fullness of her joy: her children were healthy, it was a beautiful day, she had found a good gardener. Sitting on the terrace, wrapped in the whiteness of her dress, she felt what all women dressed in white must feel on a beautiful day—she felt transparent and impersonal like the day itself, surrounded by crowds of flowers awaiting her. She put on her gloves, retrieved the shears to cut some flowers, and went down to the garden, protecting herself from the sun with an umbrella. The image she saw in the mirror was very attractive.

The smoke of the trash fires filled the back of the garden and dyed the sunlight a milky blue; it clung to the gaps among the vines, clouding the sky of foliage. It was the most beautiful time of day, which I can say without fear of being contradicted because during the daytime in a garden, each moment can be the most beautiful, something we don't notice when we are inside and always surprises us as if we were never aware of it.

The mower caused the birds to sing louder. The gardener moved as if he were inside a sort of great parade, moving ceremoniously from plant to plant, picking off insects. His arms, even at moments of rest, remained in a steady curve, weighed down by invisible hoses, scythes, hoes, and rakes. He smelled intensely of dry leaves and wet earth.

In the course of his life, the gardener had planted millions of trees for different families. He had worked on islands in the Paraná River, in the area near Tandil, in the province of La Pampa; he had even worked in the southern regions of Río Negro, and in the north to Iguazú, always with the same bundle of clothes and the same wife with indistinct features. The same hardworking wife and no children. Smelling of dry leaves and sweaty earth, he wiped his perspiration with a large silk handkerchief that had purple and green stripes. He lived at the back of the garden in a little one-room house.

The gardener turned over the earth with a large shovel; then he broke up the clumps of earth until it was silky and pliable. His hands were so connected to the earth that he had trouble pulling out the weeds. Every time he touched the earth it was as if he was slowly and repeatedly planting his hands; they were covered by now in a kind of dark bark like that of tuberoses, capable only of growing in earth or in a glass of water. For that reason he avoided washing them in water, and instead cleaned them on the grass; he also tried to avoid plunging them too deeply into the earth, and used a long thin trowel to pull out the weeds. But that day, in a moment of carelessness or hurry, he dropped the trowel off to one side and stuck his hand deep into the earth to pull out some unwanted plant. Kneeling at the bottom of the garden he made desperate attempts to pull out first the plant and then his hand. But footsteps drew near, making the pebbles sing. His hand didn't want to come out of the earth. He raised his eyes and encountered that special smile the woman displayed when cutting flowers, and heard her say, "I am delighted. I have never had so many flowers." She took off her cap with her left hand and said thank you three times, with a feeling of respect that could be seen in the movement of her head. She went on, "I would like to plant some bushes, some decorative plants near the gate. Which ones would you recommend?" "There are so many varieties," said the gardener, feeling his hand growing inside the earth, "there's *Euonymus japonicus, Euonymus microphylla* or *pulchellus, Photina serrulata* or Japanese laurel; all of those bushes are evergreen and resistant. There's also *Philadelphus coronarius* or archangel angelica, commonly known as angelica; it is covered with white flowers in the spring- time." "Yes, yes, angelica is one of the plants that I like best; it has dark leaves, and its flowers grow in neat fragrant clumps." She went on walking, spinning the handle of her umbrella. Her children ran around her, round and round. They stopped for a moment to look for pebbles on the path; then they came running back to where the gardener was. "What are you doing?" they asked, sitting down on their haunches. The man answered them patiently, "I am pulling out weeds." The children wouldn't leave; they had lost a coin or a pencil that they kept looking for until they got tired, then they went gal- loping off making noises like a locomotive.

The night was quietly falling, unfolding the usual sounds. The gardener heard the woman calling him; she was walking along the path from the house to the gate. He didn't move. In the darkness he could only see the light-colored benches; he knew that the woman wouldn't be able to see him. He sat down on the ground, took the striped handkerchief out of his pocket, always using his left hand, and wiped his brow. He was starting to feel hungry. Cooking smells came from the kitchen and an equally delicious sound of plates and silverware. He called his wife, first with a weak voice, then louder, until finally he made himself heard. His wife came running and asked him if he had hurt himself. "No, I'm not hurt. I'm hungry," the gardener answered. "Then why don't you stop working? It's time for dinner." "I can't," and he pointed to his hand. "But why don't you pull on it harder?" "I've tried as hard as I can." "So," said the woman, "will you have to spend the night here?" "Yes," the man answered; then, after a pause, "Bring me my dinner. Be careful that they don't see you." The woman hurried off and returned a little while later with a bowl of soup, a salad, and a piece of bread. She had forgotten to bring him a glass of wine. The man ate eagerly. The woman looked at him in the darkness, guessing at his expression. "Should I bring you a blanket?" "No," the man said, "it's not cold." He finished eating and lay down on the ground. The woman wished him a good night.

After being there alone for a while, he remembered that he hadn't had anything to drink. He wanted to call his wife, but his voice trembled in the wind like a very thin piece of onionskin paper. Also the door of the little house was closed, the lights were off, everything indicated that his wife had was already asleep.

Thirst grew like huge expanses of sand; the gardener crossed them in his memory until he reached a pine forest in Patagonia. He was walking, carrying an ax and a saw. The trunks were thick and covered with moss. They were very tall but it was necessary to prune them to keep them under control. The pruning was hard; it lasted for days and days. The branches stuck out like unexpected snakes. The forest sighed amidst the liquid sounds of the saws. The sudden expulsion of birds and animals that lived in the branches made the night wake up completely. The trees were bleeding with a wonderful smell—their wounds open, striped with red and blue. The forest became a huge hospital of wounded trees, without arms and without legs. He felt thirsty that day, the same thirst he felt now, a thirst mixed with the smell of resin.

A fine drizzle was falling; there were no pines, not a single pine tree. How strange it was that the garden didn't have sugar pines or other conifers. The lights in the big house were still on. There were visitors and after eating they strolled in the garden with the lady of the house.

He knelt down on the ground again. She saw him in the darkness. Somebody cried from far away, "Still working!" The cry sounded like that of a grateful swimmer, diving back into the water.

The gardener felt his hand opening inside the earth, drinking water. The water rose slowly through his arm to his heart. Then he lay down among endless sheets of earth. He felt how he was growing long hair and green arms.

The night was long, very long. At the surface, various animals brushed against his buried arm; it felt like the light contact of indifferent worms. A caterpillar slowly climbed up his back just before dawn. Never before was dawn so slow, struggling to make its way through the branches, setting out the morning. The gardener heard them calling him. He wanted to bend down and pick up the trowel from the ground but his waist lacked elasticity. From that day forward he lived according to the laws of Pythagoras; the wind and the rain busied themselves with erasing the traces of his body from the bed of earth.

AND SO FORTH

LOVING someone isn't enough. Perhaps out of fear of losing the one you love, you learn to love everything that surrounds him. The scarf he wore, his shirt, his handkerchief, the pillow with its faux vanilla beans where you both lay your heads, the torn flower bud in a vase, the window curtain always half open, the carpet beneath your bare feet, the bathroom, a mirror that should be thrown out but never is, there on the street by the house where we stopped and heard the strident chords of a piano, or where we took in a lost dog, or the little abandoned garden with a stucco statue representing Bacchus, or a battered mermaid that sprays not water but mud out of its tiny serpent mouth, or the sky that is never the same forest of buildings and inscrutable faces. This whole world is a monument to our fidelity, because what is ours will never be found elsewhere without all the visions I have listed, symbols of the love that enslaves us. And if you go in search of a world without memories in order to forget, there is nothing that will block our eyes or our ears. Our skin is wide awake and covered with eyes, although others think that we only have two eyes, and ears, although others think we only have two ears. Certain key places in our bodies connect us to those aspects of spirituality, of sex, that cannot be confessed, like the palm of the woman's hand, the inside of her elbow, or the vulnerable flesh of his ear and the curve of his foot.

If you seek a world without memories, often it's abandoned to snow and snowy peaks, so out of reach, listening for a nightingale in your dreams to announce spring, or for the bells of a sleigh—happiness. You go searching, and after taking many shortcuts, come to the sea, to the sea's edge, because sand is the place of sacrifice and of the finest games. There are tamarinds on the coast. God doesn't want any memory of their fragrance or form to survive, those poor plants by the sea. They're good for hanging clothes on, offering shade to the water that moistens hair, eyes, feet, bent knees, as we pray not to feel the water's form, trembling, trying to forget! Later, searching for the hot sand, closing your eyes, showering in the droplets that mark the edges of the picture of the clouds above the beach, a lighthearted custom in fathomless air. Sleep doesn't come to you there because the sand burns as if it were proclaiming a swift act of retribution. Then the one who wants to sleep kneels down shouting, gathering sand with two hands, to shape something yet unknown, wanting to make an absolute void with something unknown. She caresses and molds the sand with a chef's art, an art learned in childhood, while speaking to someone who is standing next to her, more indifferent than the rocks and even less attractive, and the sand becomes a mysterious mouth, linked to the first lava tubes of the volcano.

The sun is dropping. The sea grows calm, but when it is at its calmest it comes back with force, colder than ever. "Where are you, oblivion? Where could your form have gone, a form that escapes mine? Where could you be, you who makes nothing resemble itself? What sort of Eumenides are you, shaping the sand?"

Nothing answered, not even the sand, which opened its lips when the water arrived to kiss it. The sun was dropping, lighting the waves and the seaweed, each curve illuminated from a low angle. Something was moving with humanlike energy. Why human? If what you were looking for is what is not human, the beach was empty. Two boys passed by and stopped to look at the mountain of sand that resembled a mountain, making your soul feel the size of a fly. It seemed as if they didn't see him. One of them knelt down and rummaged around for something in his pocket.

"Is there a piece of paper?" he asked, looking around. "A little piece of paper."

In one of the tamarinds two pieces of paper attached to the branches were trembling. The taller boy pulled the pieces down and scrunched the paper into a ball, carefully sticking it into the hole that tunneled through the mountain. He took a box of matches out of his pocket and stooped down to light the paper, using several matches. It took a while for smoke to rise out of the hole. The smell of fire mixed with the smell of the sea impresses you, pushing away the supposed forgetfulness. He asked the boy, "What are you doing?"

The boy didn't answer or look at him.

"How can you know if you're dreaming when everything seems so real?" he asked. "By waking up," he said, answering his own question. "And how can I know, when I wake up, that I am truly awake?" And so forth. Talking to yourself is the last subterfuge. The smoke was making a picture. He covered his eyes so as not to see what that picture was, just as he covers them now so as not to see what he has written. A man's lust is infinite. Nothing can hold him back from desiring to be what he wants or doesn't want to be. But if he writes his name on the sand, if he shapes a statue or a volcano on the beach, he can't let go of them and must carry on with them. Proud sand, how many buildings did you erect, as if the last were first and the first last? How many masks did you make? It isn't possible to sweep them away with shovels or rakes from the edge of the sea.

Boredom afflicts those who are the saddest, and this man, who was the saddest of all, ran toward the sea without anything in mind, not even intending to dive into the water, water that was turning opalescent. He had left his clothes hanging on a tamarind branch but was still wearing his sandals, and around his neck hung a towel displaying the head of a tiger. When he walked against the wind the tiger's jaws moved as if it were devouring something. Ignoring the bizarre impression that he was making, he ran along the beach brimming with joy. The tide was coming in. Sometimes the waves carried pieces of wood, sometimes floating debris, the strange forms of which attracted attention, like omens of storms. The promontory of sand in the shape of a volcano was no longer visible, and neither were the boys, who had hidden themselves, nor the tamarinds. Why worry about lost footprints if what you really want is to lose them, and thus construct your identity? He plunged into the water the way seabirds do, following the line of the breaking wave. Suddenly he saw something that he couldn't believe: a body half submerged in the sand at the very spot where the last wave receded. There, submerged in water up to its waist when the waves crashed, he could see part of a torso and a headful of hair as messy as a mass of seaweed. This secret being, neither human nor animal, triggered a sense of fear, and yet it seemed an animal beyond any doubt. By what certainty was this thing that so resembled an animal not an animal? He remembered when he was a boy and asking his mother where he could find a mermaid. His mother had answered, "Mermaids don't exist, my child. They exist in fables, in stories, in poetry, but they don't exist in reality." The boy had answered, "I know they exist." "How can you be so sure?" asked his mother. "Because they are in the dictionary." This statement brought no answer. The boy found an engraving of a mermaid in an enormous encyclopedia. It was the same image that was lying there on the sand. Approaching it was imprudent, because fear of unknown creatures is so powerful. Drawing near, with a hesitation that gave him courage, he knelt down next to the unknown being, unsure at first if it was male or female.

"Hello. Who are you?"

Not being able to say anything is very sad for someone who takes an interest in someone else.

"Are you cold? The sun has set."

The head nodded slightly. No words were spoken, but they understood each other.

The being had two eyes, one green and one blue. This was the only difference between the being's eyes and those he was used to dealing with. As for the curly hair, its bright color perhaps due to the light of the sunset, it wasn't braided or gathered together, but it wasn't completely loose either.

He whispered, "What beautiful hair. Doesn't the seawater spoil it?"

Instead of answering, the being's eyes grew bigger.

He held out his hand to help it get up. The gesture was not warmly received.

"Shall I bring you a towel?"

He looked all around for his towel, but it wasn't there; he couldn't even find his footprints.

What could he do now to forget her? The eyes he was seeing, one blue and one green, cannot be forgotten. Where could he hide to forget them? Where could he hear that silence? But she spoke.

"And my hair?" she said. "Don't you like my hair?"

"I love your hair and your eyes."

"That's all?"

"For the moment that's what I know for certain because it's all I know. Later on we'll see."

"We'll see?"

A light shot out of her eyes like fire from a volcano.

"Why are you angry? A supernatural being doesn't get angry. I cannot imagine what I will do to forget your eyes, this beach, this sky: Why has all of this happened to me? Doesn't the rest of my life matter? I will see you again! I haven't lived until now. Do you understand?"

"We'll see," she said, and without getting up she dove into the water and disappeared into the depths of the sea.

That night he couldn't fall sleep. All night long he kept asking himself whether that sentence—"We'll see"—was an insult or an invitation. He went back to the tamarinds to sleep and watch the sunrise, staring at the fixed point where he had watched her disappear. He spent the whole day waiting for the same hour, since it seemed to him like the time when there might be another encounter.

He went into a coffee shop by the breakwater. He sat down at a table. He saw that the floor tiles were blue and green. It was impossible to forget the color of those eyes. He ordered something to drink. The glass they brought him was green, but filled with liquid it turned a bluish green. He noticed in the center of the table was a vase of centaureas. Why did he remember that suggestive name? Had his mother taught it to him? Or had an illustrated catalog revealed it to him? The stamens of those flowers seemed like blue eyelashes to him. Pursued by that color he returned to the beach with the sensation that he had run all the way around the world. It was not due to a preference for aerobic exercise, but those who saw him run by thought that he was competing in a race. Timidly, he suddenly slowed down when he saw that he was the object of admiration.

After the long day had come to an end, she arrived. The conversation they had was so similar to the previous one that it doesn't bear repeating, but their love was growing, and the brilliant blue and green of her eyes had taken possession of him.

He contemplated the world around him. It was flooded with salt, iodine, love; he studied the coast, the lichens, the seaweed, the breakwater, the rocks. He heard the unforgettable screech of the seagulls. He bought a camera. He took a picture of his beloved. He kept that picture. He felt loved, utterly faithful. He slept with her in the water. That's not as hard as it sounds. Not even impossible, the lover declared. And what about her? May someone answer from the depths of the sea.

A DOLL'S SECRET MEMORIES

FOR A LONG time life has treated me like a girl treats her doll, paying me no attention except when playing. I am how I am, inside my cell, because I live in a cell where no one else can enter, just me with my countless demands, some of them impossible, others as easy to fulfill as those of a girl. My life passes like a nun's life, but without suffering, without pain or sadness. That doesn't mean that I am indifferent to the beauties of love or of sweet friendship. I would like to be clear when I recount my life and tell of my heart's sensitive nature. Many people believe that I am a being different from everyone else who lives in this unfashionable world. I hope they can learn to see me rationally, without any flirtatiousness. Solitude has made me totally sincere so what I am writing seems unbelievable to people who live in a closed society. I am independent, free to think and feel as I do, without the slightest shame. Some day, perhaps, I will emerge from my secret, happy to imagine other worlds, brighter and bolder ones that would astonish anyone, expressing the depths of my confidence. I am what I want to be for the whole of undisturbed eternity. Nothing belongs to me here in this house. I want to describe its geometry. An enormous, hexagonal hall joins the rooms. A hallway leads to each bedroom. I have an altar with saints, a little kitchen with pots, spoons, knives, and forks. I live in a world in which water covers the earth. For a week it has been raining without end and this area of the city is completely flooded. The electricity doesn't work, there isn't any drinking water in the houses, and the floodwaters are filthy. This makes me happy because nobody can bathe me. The telephones don't work, nor do the gas stoves. "You have to resign yourself," says an old woman who feels happy. For her, resignation is the only form of hope. Resign ourselves? What does that word mean? I've heard it in a dream where what they were looking for was never found and they were saddened because they couldn't find it. I think it's like hope, although spoken in a different tone of voice, one that reminds me of the strange emphasis with which men spoke in my childhood. Could I have been a child once? I don't have little dresses or little shoes or little hats that would prove that I was a child, and I don't have tiny furniture sets or cars either. My toy is the computer. Nevertheless, I was a girl, so tiny that nobody could see me. When they didn't look at me or celebrate my straight blond hair or my haircut or my dress or my way of speaking, I witnessed a flood. I was sleeping on water as if on a very soft, almost drinkable waterbed. Lifting my feet, I saw the houses submerged in the liquid, my head raised so I could breathe. Someone shouted in the street, "It's an angel! Look at the angel!" Someone I can't name, because I have learned that people are perverse and may misinterpret my words, saved me from the water where I had been floating for several hours. It was near Olivos, down by the river, where there were willows and blue hydrangeas. The person who saved me carried me in her arms without finding out what boy or girl owned me, because a doll is like a dog and belongs to someone in a very intimate way. She took me to a house below the bluff from which you could see the river. She ran to the bathroom in search of a towel and napkins; she dried my feet with a light blue towel and my hair with a white lace napkin. She took off my dress, ironing it I think, then put it back on me very carefully. In her arms I heard her voice telling me, "Barbara, your name is Barbara, don't forget, and you will be mine."

Two or three days went by without anybody bothering us. She knew me, I knew her. "My name is Barbara," I said to her one day, "but what is your name?" "My name is Andrómaca," she said, holding her breath. "It's a very odd name, but it has been mine since my baptism and I hope it will still be odd when I die." "You won't ever die," I answered. "I would have to die first." So we waited for a spring day to cut flowers and put them in vases around the house. Jasmine, hydrangeas, chrysanthemums, bridal wreath—the names were familiar, and she taught me to recognize flowers and perfumes and colors. She sat down in a chair and told me, "I am going to cover you in candies and dresses and toys, but don't tell anyone." Then she kissed me, putting her tongue in my mouth. It was like a freshly cut strawberry. "You will sleep with me in my bed, okay? Don't fuss like a baby or close your eyes when I am speaking to you."

The first day we took our naps together. It was strange waking up in that house that was so different, in a world full of unknown people and of strange birds in gilded cages. "I hope you love me the way I love you, otherwise I'll kill you." She closed her eyes when she spoke these words just as I opened mine. "Don't be afraid, I won't ever kill you because I am sensible. Take a good look into the depths of my eyes." I looked at her and she at me. But happiness never lasts. Lightning and thunder filled the sky. Something happened that stormy day. The bad weather returned. It was nap time. In her room, as if in a dream, I discovered a doll that was different from all the others; she was dressed like a sultan's wife, moved, closed her eyes, shouted. She was in Andrómaca's house. She was so beautiful that I didn't dare look at her, and I kissed her and she me. But Andrómaca swept her up and rocked her until she fell fast asleep. "Do you know what Andrómaca means? Happiness in marriage," she explained. I protested, "But you're not married." "I am going to marry right now." "But that's not possible," I said. "Yes it is—here is the ring." The day darkened and I fainted. I didn't regain consciousness because the room disappeared.

Readers will think that I am lying and that Andrómaca never existed. These words are inside my body. "Open me up if you dare. Maybe today, maybe tomorrow, maybe never, I will throw myself out of this window." She approached the window, opened it, and looked around. "Watch me," she said. She jumped and fell into the air. She dissolved like a sugar cube. All that was left was the blue of her eyes lost in the extraordinary solitude of jealousy.

But my life didn't end there. Life goes on without a body, entering plants, smelling the perfume of every flower. Life goes on with its odd surprises. It turns into a detective. I went back to Andróma-ca's house at night. I snuck into her room. She was hugging the doll that wasn't an odalisque but a sultan's wife. Both of them were sleeping. A duo of snores held my attention before the thrushes sang; I forced myself to listen to the snores so as to forget my sadness, and felt utterly disenchanted. When the lightning bolts made them visible I threw myself on the ground to see them better and when the last bolt of lightning hit the house I screamed with a dull scream. It seemed we were rising out of the center of the earth, in the place where all three of us had been struck by lightning—I without a body, the two of them with their bodies full of hope, without any future, without heaven or hell, in the eternity of my consciousness.

CORNELIA BEFORE THE MIRROR

I AM SAYING goodbye to everybody in writing, except for you. The house is empty. At eight o'clock Claudia locked the front door. Cornelia! My name makes me laugh. Why not? Sometimes at the most tragic moments I laugh or light a cigarette and lie down on the ground and look at you as if nothing bad had to happen. Certain postures make us believe in happiness. Sometimes lying down makes me believe in love.

"I am a mirror, I am yours. Since you were six years old, because of me you wanted to be an actress; your father, with his face of a national hero, your mother, with her face like that of the republic, were against it. How silly respectable people can be. When you put furs and felt in mothballs your despair is reborn; in fact the people who oppose our vocations, like moths, have to be fought every day, every year."

"That's right! But don't mention moths or mothballs or furs or my family; don't even mention my name. It seems so ridiculous to me. They could call me Cornice—that would amount to the same thing. I have written it on the bathroom walls when I undressed to shower before going to school; I have written it on the garden arbor in San Fernando when I learned to write; I have written it on my left arm with a golden needle. We live as if we could live for a thousand years, brushing our hair, taking vitamins, cutting our nails and eyelashes, choosing and choosing as if we were at the Gath and Chaves department store."

I have known you for a long time, from the time I was a few months old, no, maybe later when I had uneven bangs and had ribbons in my hair that were the color of my dresses. For the last few days, as soon as I see you appear, as if I were seeing you for the first or the last time, my heart beats faster. You are a compendium of all the people I have loved. You are surrounded by an atmosphere that is liquid, as if you were inside water, in the light in which fish swim, in the deepest reaches of the sea or on the surface of a still lake. Your voice alone makes me love you. I live in an opaque material world, airless, a world of factories; you must understand that instead of dreams I sometimes have nightmares.

"Greed, with its philosophical face ..."

"I was never greedy!"

"You were, but in an original way. Pride, with its emeralds full of gardens."

"My mother is proud, not me!"

"Lust, with its kids who are smarter than their teachers. Lust! How often have you looked up that word in the dictionary, smearing jam on the pages. You were precocious: when you were eight you had twenty orgasms a day."

"I was even more precocious when I discovered your navel. Sloth, with its dreamy feeling of resignation. I am lazy."

"Gluttony, with its golden cookbooks."

"The most horrible of the sins!"

"It seems horrible to you because it makes you fat. Envy, with its dark velvet, with its inexplicable whims."

"Am I envious? I don't know whether I am or not! Jealousy and envy are hard to tell apart."

"Wrath."

"Wrath? When?"

"The day that you threw your mother's jewelry on the floor; the day you ripped that fancy dress. Wrath, with glassy eyes like a hyena's, all of its enchantments are embodied in you."

"Now you want me to examine my conscience? You helped me disguise myself to beg for forgiveness. Forgiveness from whom? From God and from my ancestors. I always pretended to be someone other than who I am. Naturally that moved you. Your defects, your conflicts are mine. When I stole Elena Schleider's gold cigarette case, in that country house that smelled of floor wax where they invited us to spend a summer, there, at the end of the bedroom, your eyes, like two stars, guided me to steal the case all by myself. You knew why I was stealing it, for whom. I thought you were a hypocrite, but I don't bear you a grudge. In a golden frame, with me, you loved and hated Elena Schleider. When they punished me I suffered because I couldn't see you, because I couldn't touch your hands, wrapped in a sort of jellylike mist, a mist that is so peculiar to mirrors. Your mouth is as smooth as a spring and as cold as the blades of scissors. Hateful mirror! In a few more moments you will not see me anymore. I promise you. I am in the habit of lying, but never to myself."

"That skirt you use, that green linen blouse looks good on you. I hope they embalm you for posterity. Don't smoke so much. Your teeth used to astonish me but now...they look like ivory, like common ivory."

"You were my only friend, the only one who betrayed me after getting to know me. Sometimes, many times, I saw you in my dreams, but I didn't feel the blue pressure of this glass when I touched you. We are twenty-five years old. That's a lot, too much."

"I have seen old people who have no wrinkles, my dear, with purple hair, decrepit old people who look like they are in disguise, and I have seen very ancient children, deathly pale, who pretend to be children. They would come to visit."

"I always looked for you to laugh. When I cried, I would hide behind the painted wood screen so that you wouldn't see me, next to the heater in the dining room, where things smelled of fried food and oranges. I knew that you didn't like my tears. You liked to see me laugh, with a hat made out of a sheet of newspaper, a hat with donkey ears, an admiral's hat, or a regular hat. That was the one I liked best. I was always fascinated by plumed hats. I dreamt that I was dancing 'The Death of the Swan' in a plumed hat. When she was eleven my mother saw Pavlova dance 'The Death of the Swan.' Ever since then I have dreamt about a plumed hat and death. I could be forty; in make-believe years I could be forty, an age I will never attain, and have a deeper voice, self-confidence, composure, greater dignity."

"You will always have an endless variety of voices, from the deepest to the highest. With your dyed hair, even five silver hairs annoy you. Your impeccable fingernails are pink, but they break; you need more calcium."

"Tomorrow I will consult Dr. Isberto."

"You can do all the harm you want without anyone noticing. Everyone believes you are a saint, not just because you hide in the darkness of inner rooms but also because your eyes are very far apart from each other, which gives you an expression of innocence and of exuberant happiness."

"I could be very poor, end up living in misery, beg in passageways, never see you, my angel, wander from door to door until I finally end up going to a house to offer my services as a laundress, despite the fact that I don't know how to wash clothes. Then you would see me kneeling, my universal mirror, with a rag in my hand washing the floor, because the owners of the house would take advantage of my lack of experience to have me do all sorts of tasks. You would see me seducing the men, any man who came to the house, the milkman, the shop assistant, the plumber, because women who work in these jobs have a kind of beauty in their unkemptness, a natural beauty that other women with their makeup don't have. Look at me with my messy hair, my rosy cheeks. You don't like to see me in the arms of a man because you are as jealous as I am. Men are monsters; love transfigures them. But I don't let them seduce me. In my hands, which smell of soap, I hide my innocent whims. Why? I don't know. They are like the precious stones in the workings of a watch—those rubies are necessary! I will be able to sweep the flowers, darn the socks, clean the carpets so long as your smile watches over me. I am virtuous. The poor, when they are wretched, are virtuous; if they are wretched they must have a reason for being so. I have very short fingernails, which is why my hands look like those of a stone statue and not like those of a prostitute or a married lady. Now it's all over: the performances, the scenery, the theaters with their seats, grudges, acts of obedience, the fear of obesity, bribery, condescension."

"You never let me come too near to you, you always keep me at a distance, that's why we are so sick of each other. I share all of my memories with you. How I enjoyed the bread we ate together! The cup of coffee with milk, each sip flowing down your mysterious throat, trembling slightly! Sometimes you set down the cup to look at me. Sometimes, when you gathered your straight hair and braided it with ribbons, paying no attention to the passing hours, we would lose ourselves in a sort of landscape where your knowledge of geography didn't matter because you invented all of the places we visited. How you enjoyed the rain that chilled your face almost like mine!"

"How I enjoyed not just what was pleasant but also what was awful and terrible, that pain in my gut, in my ecstatic shoulders, that venality in my body that you repeated! In my childhood it took me an hour to take the castor oil that my mother served me with warm orangeade. I don't know what this drink will taste like. Before I have it I will taste pure water once more."

"How cold, how soft, how new, how pure! If you went into a cave some summer night with a bunch of jasmine in your hand, you wouldn't feel such coolness!"

"Here's a remedy they use for anemia in small doses. I stole it from the lab where Héctor worked. Am I dreaming? I hear noises inside the house. I am not afraid of you. I didn't want to throw myself under a train or into the sea, the beautiful sea, because that way I couldn't take you with me. I came to this house because it's the only place we could be alone together, but I forgot that there are ghosts. You can't imagine how long it took to find the keys to this house—nobody trusted me. My aunt thought that I wanted to meet up with some lover of mine."

"Tastes, like smells, have great importance for you. Your taste buds are very sensitive, but today the taste of the poison doesn't matter to you."

"I think you share my indifference. Today, now that you are looking at me with greater attention than usual, I love you and hate you more than ever. If someone were to see us what would they say? For example, if my father were to see us, 'What are you up to with your doughlike face? Do you think you can deceive the mirror?' That's what he would say, surely thinking that I am the most beautiful woman in the world even though I resemble my mother, in the oval shape of my face for instance, in my chin, in the unusual appearance of my eyebrows. I have lived in this house for so long! I can take a mental inventory of the things I like: the greenhouse that fascinated me and where I used to hide, and the room used for ironing that is now a storeroom. Everything has turned into a boutique. This show-case was the living room. What difference is there between a show-case and a living room? I was stifled when I came here. I feel strangled by the hands of all the people in the paintings on the wall, staring at me, and in the dining room, with its chandelier and silverware, and the bedrooms, the one with red curtains where my brother Rafael was born. I would have gone to hell in order not to see them! Luckily my aunt bought this house to store hats. The sale of the house was dramatic. My father needed money and my mother couldn't forgive him for that. I will have a drink before I swallow the contents of this glass. People always say that it's best to drink down awful things in one gulp, things like castor oil, milk of magnesia, though I usually drink them slowly. My dear, don't look at me with such pity! Do you remember the day I brought you that dog that was crying? I thought it would get better in your arms and I called you. You laughed be-cause the dog had a bandage around its head, it looked like a Turk, and when it saw itself in your arms it growled like a wild animal. I didn't know it was dying. Do you know what is happening to me now? Why don't you laugh? Is my death more important than that of a dog? I see the red and blue colored glass in the windowpanes that looked out on the patio in my childhood. Behind the glass, among the leaves that knocked against it, I would hide to do naughty things. Later I would run to see you: I would give you my face and my secrets. That brought us together. The governess was knitting a purple shawl that smelled of smoke and she let me play with the spools of yarn; afterwards she would wash my hands in a basin with flowers where she would spit when she was sick. How strange. The front door was closed; I am sure there was nobody inside the house. I have chosen this place because my only witnesses are the hats, the astonished faces of the mannequins with faces and voices like ladies, yes, but that are benign when they are by themselves. Wait: someone has moved the doorknob. I am sure I saw it move."

"But nobody could be coming at this hour. My aunt is at home, sick. Claudio doesn't have a key and even if he had one he wouldn't come at this hour. Claudio, my childhood friend! What will he say when he finds out? Two in the afternoon. I am nervous, no doubt. Who is it? Answer. Nobody frightens me, not even the devil. Angelic beings sometimes frighten me. What are you doing here?"

"Who are you? How did you come in?"

"The door was open."

"Why did you come in?"

"To see the dolls."

"What dolls?"

"The dolls with the hats on."

"What is your name?"

"Cristina."

"Just Cristina?"

"Cristina Ladivina, from the Green Rose."

"My name is Cornelia. Where is the Green Rose?"

"On Esmeralda Street."

"You are a ghost, a lost girl, with emeralds and green roses. Do they let you go out at this hour?"

"They let me whenever I like."

"Even at night?"

"Night is like day; darkness is just like light."

"How old are you?"

"Ten."

"You are pretty. Look at yourself in the mirror. Do you see my reflection? Yourself?"

"No."

"Haven't you ever seen yourself in a mirror?"

"In the water, in the mud next to rivers, on the edge of a knife."

"You scare me. And how did you get into this house?"

"The man let me in."

"What man?"

"The man who showed me the dolls in the shopwindow."

"You are a ghost. Do you know what a ghost is?"

"Someone who is alive yet is not alive. Are you a ghost?"

"I don't know."

"You came in to scare me, didn't you? Am I dead already? Did you come to take away my soul? You are that aunt of mine who died of measles when she was ten, the one named Virginia. Did you come to take away my soul?"

"No. I came because of the dolls."

"And who is the man you were talking about? Where is he?"

"Over there."

"Nothing scares me, not even a man with such a face."

"Are you alone?"

"I was with that girl who just came in."

"Who were you talking with?"

"Before the girl came in? I was speaking with myself in the mirror. You don't believe me, right?"

"Where is the person you were speaking to?"

"Here in the mirror. Look at her."

"Tell me where she is."

"Look around the house if you like. And the girl?"

"Are you the owner?"

"No. And I don't want to be. I am the servant. The owner's niece."

"I don't believe you."

"Do I look so serious? So important? So respectable that I would lie to you? Don't butter me up, please; besides, you don't know what I like, so you wouldn't know how to please me."

"They are all the same."

"Who are 'they'?"

"Women. They all lie."

"I am different, I assure you."

"I don't believe you."

"Have you met women who have given you opportunities like this?"

"Shhh, don't shout. I'm not deaf."

"I am speaking in my normal tone. Who is that girl who came in with you? Is she really a girl, or is she a dwarf disguised as a girl?"

"I don't know."

"Do you use children as shields? Tell the truth. I don't want to think ill of you, but there are some things that don't seem right to me. For example: to use a ten-year-old girl to protect yourself. Besides, don't you know that children are very wise? They are detectives, tiny detectives."

"Be quiet. Don't speak in such a loud voice."

"I am speaking in a low voice as if I were in the confessional. Do you ever confess?"

"Answer and don't ask questions. Is there anyone in the house?"

"Why do you look at me like that? Don't you consider me a person?"

"Is there someone besides you? Shhh, be quiet."

"Don't be afraid. There is no one. Just me and the mirror. Sometimes I think there are ghosts in this house. Today I thought there was one, but when I found out it was you and that girl who looked like a ghost I calmed down. 'No matter how bad a man is, he is a man,' I told myself."

"Shhh. I forbid you to speak."

"I won't speak."

"Where are the house keys?"

"If you tell me not to speak, how can I answer?"

"Don't be silly."

"Which keys? There are so many keys."

"Any key."

"Don't you know which keys you want? There are many keys: the one to the big chest of drawers, the one to the storeroom, the one to the pantry, the one to the trunks, the one to the iron safe. Which one do you want?"

"The one to the iron safe."

"Here they are. My aunt is very imprudent. She doesn't look rich."

"Give me the keys."

"And then what will you do to me? Do you intend to kill me?"

"That would make sense."

"How do you intend to kill me? With that knife? Do you think I can't see it?"

"Are you scared of it?"

"A little. I don't like weapons. Do you have a revolver?"

"I have everything I need."

"That knife is hideous. Do you know if it's sharp, at least?"

"It's rust-proof. It slides right through."

"But with the blade against the throat? That first icy contact with the steel... And then... The blood running and staining the floor... making spots on the rugs and the curtains... Doesn't it make you sick?"

"I won't kill you with this knife."

"How then? With a bullet?"

"With a razor blade."

"With one of those pencil-sharpening blades? Isn't it more practical to use a knife? After all, a knife is used more than a razor blade for such purposes."

"It's a matter of habit."

"I would use a knife or a revolver. A sword is too long. How crazy. A revolver, of course, isn't a good idea because it's noisy. The sound hurts my ears. I have to cover them when I hear a shot, which is why I could never go to a shooting range, even though I consider myself a good shot. I didn't try committing suicide with a revolver. Do you know how to shoot? Did you win any prizes? Men know how to shoot. It's no use—that's why men go to war and women stay at home or in hospitals tending to the wounded. I'm always behind the times. Women were born to stay quietly at home, men for great adventures, for dangerous enterprises."

"They are brand-new. These razor blades are brand-new."

"I know you're a very good man. You have a kind face. All the faces in the mirror are kind. Of course a face doesn't say anything. In the papers there are pictures of men with the faces of murderers though they are saints, while there are others with the faces of saints though they are actually murderers. Will you promise to murder me? Promise."

"I promise. Give me the keys."

"And where will you attack me?"

"That's easy. I will cut the veins of your wrist, and then your blood will flow out. If it takes a long time I can submerge you in a hot bath. Is there a bathtub in this house?"

"There's a bathtub, but there isn't any hot water at this hour. Please begin. I have a great desire to die. You are very good, but what do you intend to do with my body? Do you intend to cut it up in little bits and spread them across the province of Buenos Aires? Do you intend to carry me in a sack, like people carry coal or potatoes? Or just leave me lying on the floor? Do you know there are mice in this house that could disfigure me? It would be a shame. Do you hear them? Do you know of any poison to kill them? My aunt is worried: the other night they pulled the feathers off a hat along with two cherries tied on with a velvet ribbon. Traps are no good. What if they decided to eat off my fingertips? If they were to bite the back of my neck or my throat? Can you imagine the pain I would feel?"

"The dead don't feel pain, miss."

"Is that what you think, sir? The dead are very sensitive. They feel everything. They think more clearly than we do. If you offer them meat or wine they won't appreciate it, but offer them music or perfume and you'll see. They are never absentminded. They see ultraviolet colors like doves do. They are refined and sensitive. Otherwise, how else could you explain that they are given so many flowers? That people spend so much on flowers, statuettes, masses, hearses? How should I know?"

"That is an old custom. Which key is it?"

"Customs have a reason for existing. The dead see the flowers, they know where they are buried and who killed them. They see the hearse, the black circus horses, the white initials on the black cloth that covers them. Dear sir, couldn't you throw me into the sea? I love the sea. I hate ceremonies, candles, flowers, the whisperings of prayers. I am bad. Nobody loves me."

"The sea is far away. Which key is it?"

"Don't you have a car? You could rent one. Or maybe your brothers or your uncles have one? Surely some friend does. You prop me up in the car as if I were alive and take me to the sea. It's so easy, and the sea is so beautiful. It would be a nice trip for you. Don't you like the sea?"

"Bodies float, miss. They float ashore."

"You could put rocks or lead weights on my feet. Haven't you read in a newspaper or novel that they throw bodies into the sea? Don't you ever go to the movies? It's so poetic."

"Give me the key."

"It's one of these. Don't disturb the papers in the safe. My aunt suffers a lot when there is anything messy in the house. Don't let your cigarette ashes drop on the floor please. Afterwards I will have to sweep up."

"Don't move."

"I won't move. Can you open it? My aunt always has trouble with that, too. She can never open a locked drawer or door. It's one of her misfortunes. Why don't you take off your gloves?"

"You will open this door right now, you scorpion."

"Who are you talking to?"

"If I turn to the left you twist to the right; if I turn to the right you twist to the left, you bitch."

"Are you talking to the keys?"

"Don't you talk to the mirror? What difference is there between a key and a mirror?"

"The mirror answers me."

"These answer me, too. They see you are a liar."

"I swear I'm not. Do you want me to open it?"

"You are lying."

"I don't lie. Safes are hard to open, but any thief can open them. Aren't you a professional thief, my dear friend? Tell me about your life. It must be interesting, a life so full of unexpected things. Are you married? No. You are too young. Were you ever engaged? Are your parents alive? Do you have any sisters? Have you traveled? Where did you spend your childhood? Do you have photographs of yourself as a child? I would like to see them. Have you traveled in Argentina? I haven't ever left Buenos Aires; I never traveled. Can you believe it? A woman my age. When I think that China exists, India, Russia, France, Canada, Italy, Italy above all, that makes me desperate. Few people like me. Because women don't like an ambitious woman. In my adolescence I stole a golden cigarette case and sold it for a hundred pesos. You have to be brave to commit a robbery. Those who let others rob them are fearful, don't you think? My aunt, for example: every night she looks under her bed to see if there's a thief. I, on the other hand, am afraid of ghosts. In this house they say there are ghosts, a ghost dressed in red. Did you notice the color of the walls when you came in? Maybe you didn't see them because it was dark. Well, the ghost is dressed in that same red color, an orange red, the color of bricks. She is a little girl, I saw her with my own eyes. It's so hot. Aren't you hot with that scarf on? Why do you wear that scarf? Doesn't it bother you? You have a scar on your forehead. Are you deaf? Why don't you answer me?"

"What a night!"

"Are you thirsty? Do you want to have a glass of water?"

"Water is for fish."

"It's good to drink water when it's hot."

"I don't do what's good. I do whatever I feel like."

"You're right. I would do the same if I could. But I am not so impolite. I have no willpower. Do you want a glass of whiskey or gin? Some Argentine brandy? Sherry? Here in this cabinet we have some bottles. When we finish working we sometimes have a little drink."

"I don't care about drinks."

"Don't you want anything? Nobody dies from a glass of whiskey."

"Don't insist, miss."

"What luck! This poison is mine; I want it to be mine. How it glows in the mirror!"

"Here's another key."

"I'm confused. It's surely this one. It finally opened. Now will you find what you were looking for? Nothing. Your hurry only lasts a minute. You are very original. You don't throw anything on the ground. There's nothing that you think is valuable, but each person has different ideas about what is valuable."

"Now I am thirsty. I could drink a whole demijohn of water. This one isn't cold enough but I'll drink it anyway."

"Now you have to kill me."

"I changed my mind. I didn't find what I was looking for here."

"You aren't looking for anything. You are a poor crazy person. You have to kill me. Did you hear me? To redeem yourself you have to kill me. If you don't keep your promise I will inform the police about you. You will die of shame. Look at yourself in the mirror!"

"If you want to inform on me go ahead. I burnt churches, I donated blood in the hospitals, I have a universal blood type. I don't like to boast but I don't want you to think that I am good for nothing. I did a good job. Now they have asked me to kill—"

"To kill whom?"

"That's a secret."

"You are tired. Why do you speak like that? Are you tired?"

"I am perfectly fine. Secrets are meant to be told in a low voice."

"They asked you to kill me."

"No. I tried to kill you to practice. It seemed easier to me to start with a woman."

"And why did you open the safe if you were only thinking about killing? And why do you wear gloves? And why do you keep your face covered? Aren't you scared of being sent to prison?"

"I asked you for the keys out of curiosity, to pass the time."

"Do you know why you wear gloves and cover your face? I'm going to tell you: so you don't leave fingerprints and so your comrades won't suspect that you are a coward, a good-for-nothing, a poor devil who is incapable of killing. So now you have to kill me—that's the punishment you deserve. What difference is there between killing me and decapitating Saint James the Apostle and his horse? You decapitated them, right? If you killed my image in the mirror you would kill me, too. Why are you afraid now though you weren't before? We human beings are as unreal as images. What church did you burn?"

"As many as I could. I don't know their names. Don't think it was easy. Some of them wouldn't burn."

"How many virgins and saints did you hit?"

"None. At the very moment—"

"Tell me. I'm not going to look down on you any more or have less pity on you."

"At the very moment I was going to cut off the head of one, my hand let go."

"Why?"

"I don't know. I have rheumatism. She looked at me with her gypsy eyes, as if she were going to say a blessing. She was the smallest one. Just this tall and I couldn't hit her. The other guys laughed at me."

"And wasn't there an inscription on the pedestal?"

"No. I am sorry that I didn't cut off her head. Now I see her everywhere. As if she were a soothsayer, she keeps looking at me."

"She was a soothsayer. Saints are all soothsayers. You have to kill me. You have drunk some of the contents of this glass. In it there was an expensive poison that was very hard to obtain. You are going to kill me. Haven't you ever prayed? There's still time. You have to kill me immediately. If you don't I will spit in your face and call all the mice in the area so they come and eat your tongue and your hands. If you prayed such unpleasant things wouldn't happen to you like the ones that I am promising. Do you hear me? I am going to scream. Help!"

"Who are you?"

"What is going on?"

"Nothing, nothing. This man was supposed to kill me: he promised me and now he denies having done so. He is going to die in a few moments—and he doesn't want to redeem himself because he is a coward!"

"Sorry for interrupting. I heard screams, saw the door was open, and came in. I'm not from the police—don't worry. What's going on here?"

"This man came to kill me, making me believe that he was looking for something. He opened the safe and scattered everything about. He doesn't need to steal—he's a wealthy man. I don't know what he wants; he doesn't either."

"What should I do? Please tell me."

"Don't get upset."

"We've let him get away. That's awful."

"Why?"

"What would they do to him, with his huge body? Can you tell me?"

"What he deserves: punishment. We should chase after him."

"Impossible. He's going to die. I heard a noise. Something has fallen on the floor below. It's him! He has died like a dog. But don't you understand—he has died! He drank some poison."

"I don't understand at all. First let's close the front door. Please. Let's see if the man isn't hiding somewhere in some corner of the house."

"I can't see anything. I'm going to turn on the light."

"Don't worry, there are men who have nine lives like cats. Didn't Rasputin get poisoned a thousand times and yet he survived? What should I do?"

"You should do what that man didn't do: kill me."

"Kill you?"

"Yes, kill me. For the last three nights I haven't been able to sleep because I've been looking for a way to kill myself. Yesterday, I acquired this poison and I was about to drink it in the silence of this house when I heard bizarre noises."

"And the criminal appeared at the door, just like in the movies or the theater."

"No. Instead of the criminal a little girl appeared, very quietly, stopping at the threshold."

"A little girl? I hear noises."

"That's the mice—lots of mice. They walk like men."

"And this girl came in with the man?"

"According to her, the man forced her in."

"What for?"

"To see these dolls. These mannequins were huge dolls according to her. I asked her what her name was."

"And did she tell you?"

"Yes. She told me her name was Cristina Ladivina."

"Ladivina or *La Adivina*, the soothsayer?"

"Ladivina or Ladvina, I'm not sure. It must be a Russian name. When I asked her what her last name was she answered, 'Ladivina from the Green Rose.' When I asked her where the Green Rose was she said, 'On Esmeralda Street.'"

"The Green Rose is nearby. It's an empty coffee shop where the waiters sleep instead of taking care of the customers."

"That I would never have guessed! Everything seemed so strange to me. In the mouth of that girl the word Esmeralda wasn't the name of a street but of a precious stone. When I saw her I felt afraid. And I was so disturbed, so very disturbed that when I saw myself in the mirror with her, I couldn't see her image reflected next to mine. And now that I think about it, instead of seeing the whole room in the reflection, I saw something strange in the mirror, a dome, some sort of temple with yellow columns and, way in back, inside the niches of the far wall, some divinities. No doubt I was the victim of an illusion. These days I have been hearing so much talk about churches in flames!"

"And could you tell me why you want to die? Do you have a date with someone in the other world?"

"And you—why do you want to live? Can you tell me that?"

"If you let me think for a while I would tell you."

"Is it so hard? Do you have to think about it in order to tell me?"

"I am not as spontaneous as you are."

"Don't be afraid of making a fool of yourself."

"I am aware of my limitations, but happiness, and the lack of obstacles, don't seem indispensable for me to live."

"Me neither. Sometimes you make a decision and fulfill it even though the cause that has made you decide to do it no longer exists."

"Then you operate on the basis of selfishness."

"No, not selfishness but rather out of impulse, a seeming fidelity to myself."

"Do you want to tell me why I want to live? I don't think that this is the moment to think about personal matters. Why are you laughing?"

"I'm not laughing. All men say the same things, they speak about personal matters as if they were a disease."

"They are a disease."

"I always think about personal matters, it's true. Do you look down on me? That wouldn't bother me. You can sit down if you like."

"When we passed by the house, the window of this room made me curious, as if I had a foreboding that something was going to happen tonight."

"Maybe we've seen each other sometime in the street."

"Not likely, because I usually walk looking down at my shoes, not seeing the people around me."

"Everyone needs to speak to someone who isn't a person—I with the mirror, the criminal with the keys, Cristina with the dolls, you with your shoes. I look at everything without seeing anything. That's my habit. People think I'm nearsighted. In a certain sense I am."

"Do you live here?"

"No, I work here."

"What do you do?"

"Do you see these hats? I make them. At night I study and during the breaks I read. This is my library, my dressing room. And what do you do?"

"I am an architecture student."

"Ribbons, flowers, feathers, veils—these are for me what buildings must be for you."

"That waltz you can hear is Brahms's love song. When I hear that melody I get angry with the chatter of the ladies who come here to buy hats. And my aunt waits on them fastidiously. The shrillest ones talk like this, 'How lovely, oh, but oh how lovely' and 'I like big hats.' They are awful, my dear, just awful. Look at yourself in the mirror. Seeing yourself—doesn't that scare you?"

"Ribbons, Matilde, they drive me crazy."

"And will cherries come back in fashion as adornments for hats?"

"Italian straw is out."

"This hat is very flattering—through the veil your face is visible as if in a bell jar."

"Too expensive, much too expensive."

"A person can no longer afford to buy anything, anything at all."

"I told you so."

"Why are hats in fashion? Sometimes I ask myself that. Because of the sun, the rain, the wind?"

"It's our only act of modesty. We use them to cover our faces, like the sultan's wives with their veils, to protect ourselves from those who look at us shamelessly."

"That's not true. Beneath the brims they kiss us fervently, or use them as a screen."

"Do you think they have velvet hats?"

"Velvet isn't for this time of year, right? It's too hot. I want one of yellow straw. One that brings good luck."

"I have a beautiful one."

"What would be ideal would be a hat made of moss. I hate straw; it makes my neck itch. I am allergic to it."

"Where will I find the right hat?"

"Let's go, ladies, it's late. Ma'am, could you please bring me a washbowl and some soap?"

"Do you want to go to the bathroom?"

"*I am too tired and don't feel well.*"

"*I will go look for a washbowl.*"

"*Are you angry with me? Why did you ask me for a washbowl?*"

"*My feet are very dirty. I'm going to wash them if that's okay with you.*"

"*Get up and look at the hats. There are lots of them. There must be one you—the one made of moss, perhaps?*"

"*In that hat I will dance 'The Death of the Swan.' When I was eleven my mother saw Pavlova dance 'The Death of the Swan.' Since that day I have dreamed of a plumed hat and of death.*"

"*She has fainted.*"

"*Don't wake her up, she's asleep.*"

"*She has turned into a swan, a true swan.*"

"*And where is Leda?*"

"*I am Leda.*"

"*Rise up, swan, and prepare yourself for your death that draws near.*"

"*Hats change, they change like we do.*"

"*People aren't polite. We're in a hurry. We're embarking on the Augustus next month. We will reach Paris in the middle of winter. Will they be wearing something practical and pretty, elegant even, something in the shape of a turban, or a crown, or a cloche?*"

"*We will be away for a year. This girl was dreaming about Paris. She has some little friends there, but we are planning to go to Italy, and of course to England.*"

"*Blessed are those who can travel. I would like to always travel back and forth, back and forth, like Englishmen. I know Italy, Venice, ah, Venice—there I have been for all my honeymoons.*"

"*I like Florence, with those museums and palaces; raw silk shirts, blouses, ties that you can buy for almost nothing, and the perfumes.*"

"*I wonder what the first hats in the world were like.*"

"*You are beautiful and everything fits you well. The oldest hat must be of Greek origin. Do they conspire in this house? Is there some plot? Be careful. The Greek hat is called* petasus *in Latin; it is a small light hat, which was tied on with a string. It was used for travel or in the country-*"

side, and Romans wore it to go to the theater or to greet one another. In China, during imperial times, the use of certain hats was an official obligation. And not only women used decorations like that on their hats: Philip the Third, in his Pragmatics of 1611, allowed men to wear chains, headbands with gold decorations, adornments with cameos, or strings of pearls on their hats. Do you know the story of the top hat? The top hat was invented in 1782, no, in 1797, by the Englishman John Hetherington, who was taken to court and fined for having dared to go out on the street with a tube of silk, tall and shiny, on his head. The fine was imposed because several women fainted and some children were injured by the crowd that ran up to see that strange and terrifying object."

"How interesting! All the models are at your disposal."

"I like this one. The one with tiger skin."

"It's a cat. How cute."

"I am worried. Don't you think that we should chase after that man, find out whether he has died?"

"A person who is about to die tries to forget about everything unpleasant, such as crime and the police. You didn't believe me, did you? You thought that man was my lover. Clear your mind of that lie! I was going to kill myself. I should have been dead by now. By some miracle, because of that man who came here to kill me, you are talking to me. Do you see that glass? It contains a little bit of poison. At the moment I was going to drink the poison the man entered and I left the glass on the table. The man promised to kill me in a manner that wouldn't be too painful: with a razor blade. He asked me for the keys to the safe. I gave them to him. At first I thought he couldn't open it, but later I realized he didn't care. His feigned anger inspired terror in me and I tried to poison him. I offered him some water. He drank a little. After he opened the safe he told me that he was going to pardon me. I protested in vain. Now I think that man has nine lives like a cat, which makes me sorry. He confessed to me that he had set fire to the churches, that he was guilty of, or pretended to be guilty of, murders."

"But he is a dangerous man."

"Aren't all the dangerous men free and all the good ones prisoners? I don't want them to put us in jail. I don't want to postpone my death. Show me the revolver."

"Be careful."

"But it's a toy! Do you always use a toy revolver?"

"No. Only when I'm with you."

"It looks real. But would the man have gone through with it if it weren't for this revolver?"

"Kill one of the two of us, and if we're really lucky, both of us. He was scared. Fear is sometimes original."

"He was a coward."

"Do we have to be afraid of cowards?"

"When I spoke to him about the mice and the ghosts he trembled."

"But that isn't a symptom of cowardice. I am afraid too."

"Of what?"

"Of lots of things."

"But tell me of what."

"Of being with you, for instance, here in this house."

"Do I seem so terrifying to you?"

"Yes."

"So could you promise me something?"

"Anything at all."

"Will you promise to kill me?"

"I promise, so long as you tell me your life story first, without omitting a single detail."

"Telling my life to a stranger doesn't seem so absurd to me. At other moments in my life I would have sought out a person who seemed nice to me or who was very attractive, but now—do you want me to tell you the truth? I would like to debase myself so as to die in peace."

"You aren't very detached from life."

"Why do you say that?"

"I notice the way you play with that ring. Are you very fond of it?"

"I am."

"Who gave it to you?"

"Nobody. I myself. Objects fascinate me."

"In order to die you have to let them go. Why don't you give it to me?"

"I would never give it to you. You have a very violent character."

"How do you know?"

"By the form of your hands."

"Do you devote yourself to palmistry? As I said, you are far from letting go of life."

"You don't know anything or understand anything. But I will tell you the story of my life, if it can be called a life: a long time ago I dreamt about the theater, about escaping from my house. I couldn't tear myself away from the mirror, where I practiced how to move like an actress. That's why I have such a huge variety of voices! I could imitate the voices of my aunts, of my friends. I was eleven, maybe not the most important age, but for me it was because that's when I saw Pablo for the first time, in San Fernando. I almost fainted; it was at Elena Schleider's house, and I adored her. Elena was a friend of my mother's and she invited us to spend the summer. Since I was very girlish, all of the visitors treated me as if I were a baby girl. However Pablo's attitude was different with me. Pablo studied engineering but he was interested in literature. Sometimes he would read me passages from a novel he was reading or would hide with me in the kitchen so the visitors wouldn't see us, or he would seek out my foot or hand under the table, during the meals, to join me in making fun of one of the guests. He used to stare fixedly at me in order to hypnotize me. During the hot days of January, at siesta time, when everyone was lying down or was trying to cool off with fans, we would ride to the river on bicycles. Sometimes we would rest under some tree and talk about Elena Schleider. Pablo would ask me to imitate her voice. How the cicadas sang! And the grasshoppers at night! Now, when I hear them, I feel as if I'm reliving that period. Pablo would say to me, *They are going to punish you.*"

"*I don't care, I don't care, and I don't care.*"

"*It's 1:04 and you should be having a siesta.*"

"*I know. Who invented the siesta? I could kill him. On the other*" *hand, I would hug whoever invented ice cream. Do you want to try some?"*

"I hate strawberry ice cream."

"I hate lemon ice cream. I want you to try mine," I would say to him, imitating Elena's voice, 'Hypnotize me!'"

"Treat me with respect. Don't lick it."

"I wonder what Elena is up to. She is probably dressed all in sky blue. It's her favorite color. Everything sky blue, sleeping under the mosquito net."

"Her siestas are very long."

"Sometimes she comes out of her bedroom at 6:30 in the afternoon, when the visitors have just finished having tea."

"Do you love her a lot? More than your aunts?"

"I don't love my aunts."

"Why do you love Elena so much?"

"I don't know. She has so many little bottles of perfume in her bedroom, and necklaces and flowers and little ornamental combs that look as if they're made of caramel, along with lots of books and photographs. She isn't like other people. When I go into her bedroom she lets me touch everything and gives me things. But it's not because of those presents that I love her. My aunts give me presents. It's a matter of affinity."

"More than affinity. It seems like you admire her deeply."

"Deeply? That's true. I admire her. I wonder why I admire her. It's as if I were in love."

"Could it be because she plays the piano?"

"I admire her for nothing in particular and for everything. Because she inhabits herself as if she were inside a house. Because she is shameless. Because she doesn't have any pimples or marks on her face."

"When you are older you will be the same way."

"I don't want to be."

"You are shy. At your age you should blush at anything."

"I am not shy. I've always been this way."

"It's finished!"

"What's finished?"

"The ice cream. It doesn't last long enough."

"Would you eat some more?"

"Five more scoops, all different colors."

"Strawberry and caramel? Do you want me to go get more? I will sacrifice myself."

"Five of caramel and five of strawberry. All the different colors except the color of snow. That awful lemon ice cream. I want to go to the United States so I can eat ice cream every day. No. Don't leave. Hypnotize me!"

"I'm going to get the ice cream."

"I'd rather you stay. I have so much to tell you."

"The only reason you want to go to the United States is to eat ice cream?"

"In the summer, just for the ice cream. The rest of the time I would study theater. Hypnotize me!"

"You will be a great actress."

"Do you think so?"

"Of course I do."

"In what respect can you tell that I'll be a great actress?"

"Your little monkey face."

"How funny."

"In your way of moving, in your way of sitting or speaking when you are sad or happy."

"Do you know when I am sad or happy?"

"Of course."

"How happy I am! I thought nobody understood me. Elena doesn't understand me."

"Now you know that someone does."

"It didn't seem possible to me, Pablo! Do you think that someday I will be a great actress?"

"I am certain of it."

"When I told Elena that I wanted to be an actress she answered by saying that my mother would be against it. And it was true. She can't stand my talk of theaters or actresses."

"Your mother is very severe."

"She hates me. Hypnotize me!"

"Don't say silly things."

"She hates me, you'll see. For her, her moral ideas come first, then me second. Besides, she is blind. She's a close friend of Elena's."

"What do you mean by that?"

"That Elena doesn't have the same moral ideas that my mother does but my mother doesn't realize it."

"How do you know?"

"I overheard the woman who does the ironing and the gardener."

"What a young lady you are!"

"The woman who does the ironing and the gardener both love me. How many days are left before the summer comes to an end? Hypnotize me!"

"You are already counting."

"That's the day when my happiness always dies. How much is left?"

"Let me count—part of January, all of February, and part of March: sixty days. How strange you are, Cornelia! So girlish in some respects and so much like an adult in others."

"And how stupid you are."

"Thanks."

"They're calling me."

"Can't your mother buy you better shoes?"

"That's how I spent the first days of my adolescence: adoring and waiting like an idiot for the arrival of summer, for Elena Schleider, for Pablo with the gardenias, the magnolias and the sharp cry of the birds. During the winter I would see them from time to time. It took me a while to realize what ties existed between Elena Schleider and Pablo. Elena Schleider was so serious that nobody thought her capable of committing adultery. Besides, she looked like the supposed portrait of Lady Talbot by Petrus Christus. On one occasion there was talk that Elena Schleider didn't want to go on a business trip to Europe with her husband. It was said that she was sick, but during that whole summer, her cheeks shone brightly, which suggested to me that fever makes people more beautiful. For a long time I kept one of her hairpins. I remember when they moved me that summer from one room to a different one that Pablo didn't meet me during the siesta as he had been in the habit of doing. On several occasions he told me that I should wait for him in the shade of the willow tree that was some distance away from the house, near the riverbank. I would look impatiently at the water. One day I decided to return to the house to reproach Pablo for his behavior. The front door, however, was locked. I climbed up to the balcony, found the door open, and entered. I walked on tiptoe to Pablo's room. Nobody was there. Then I went through the house, room by room, until I reached Elena Schleider's. 'You are all that I have in life,' murmured Elena Schleider's voice, transformed. In the twilight at first I couldn't see anything, but then, like Bluebeard's wife, upon entering the forbidden room I drew back in horror. Pablo and Elena Schleider, like some mythological monster, were embracing on the bed. They were talking about a golden cigarette case, in a low voice, as if they were in confession. It was a present that Pablo had given Elena. I rushed out into the garden in horror, went down to the river and hid among the plants."

"Why don't you go on?"

"I don't know. It seems like I'm speaking for nothing."

"Please! You make me forget the horrible world in which we live, its tortures."

"Tortures?"

"Yes, tortures. Go on."

"That night they came looking for me with flashlights and they found me quite late, disheveled and with a torn dress. I said that a man had raped me. I made up that story. A little later, when I had gotten undressed for bed, Elena and Pablo came into my room to see whether I had stopped crying."

"Have a little coffee. Finish it. It will do you good," Elena told me.

"Please, a little more."

"Now you need to tell us what happened. Can't you speak to us?"

"Don't make us suffer so. For an hour we have been begging you to talk to us."

"I won't tell anyone. You can be sure of that."

"Me neither. Nobody. Be reasonable. Talk is cheap."

"It was a man, a horrible man. He tried to rape me."

"Where did you learn that word?"

"I didn't learn it. I knew it already."

"Cornelia reads a lot. Besides, she is a young lady. We always forget how old she is."

"But what happened?"

"He tore my dress."

"Don't cry. Don't cry. Maybe there's a misunderstanding. Why did you go out at night?"

"I got lost. I was gathering jasmine blossoms from the garden fence. It got dark; it was a very dark night."

"You shouldn't wander far from the house."

"No, at that hour I don't plan on going out again."

"You scared us so much. My head hurts. I'm sick. You are thoughtless. I'm going to bed. I'll leave you with Pablo. You have more trust in him. Don't be upset. Don't think. Tomorrow we will talk more calmly."

"I'm scared."

"Of what?"

"Of his coming back. I heard footsteps in the garden."

"Wait. I'm going to put out the light. There's nobody here. You are nervous."

"No."

"You said that the night was very dark. Maybe you were dreaming? Look how bright the moon is up there."

"I haven't dreamed. I'm sorry I didn't die."

"You are saying that to punish me."

"I am saying that because that's how I feel."

"Don't cry. You are a little girl."

"I don't feel well. I'm going to faint."

"Cornelia, Cornelia, answer me. I'm going to call a doctor."

"No. I'm feeling better. Don't move. Aren't you superstitious?"

"No. Why?"

"Did you hear the hoot of the owl?"

"*Yes.*"

"*Do you hear it? When someone is about to die an owl will hoot. Maybe I'm about to die? I committed a deadly sin.*"

"*What sin?*"

"*Not just one!*"

"*All deadly ones? I will go to hell. When I think of the fires of hell I feel cold.*"

"*Don't shiver. I will save you from hell.*"

"*You aren't God so you can't save me.*"

"*I can protect you.*"

"*Nobody can protect or save a sinner.*"

"*You have repented.*"

"*I haven't.*"

"*You are nervous. I'm going to give you a tranquilizer. Take it.*"

"*I don't want to, and I don't want anyone to dominate me.*"

"*Nobody means to dominate you. Don't be a little girl.*"

"*Being eleven is worse than being a slave.*"

"*Aren't you happy? Aren't you ever happy? Come on, don't play the victim. I want to see you smile.*"

"*You don't understand me. I won't be able to sleep. That man, that horrible man.*"

"*Don't cry. Try to sleep. Calm down.*"

He held me in his arms. Silence and darkness entered me. I told the truth: a man raped me that night. What do you think?

"I am listening to you."

"The next day, as if nothing had happened, Elena Schleider and her guests took me to the movies in the afternoon. Elena Schleider said something about how deathly pale I was, about the need to cut my hair and teach me better manners. I hated her the way you can only hate someone you've loved. That's when I made a plan to get revenge. The next day I stole the golden cigarette case and shortly thereafter I sold it to buy Pablo a ring. I had to wait for the right moment to give it to him. Elena Schleider was out shopping. All the guests were playing cards except for Pablo. Trembling, I approached him and said to him: *I know that you hate me and I can't keep on living like this."*

"But my dear, how can you think that?"

"Then if you don't hate me I'll give you this ring, which I got you after making many sacrifices. Will you wear it? Answer me. Do you hear me?"

"What are you saying? Forgive me. I am studying a very difficult subject."

"With much sacrifice I got this golden ring and I want you to wear it. Will you wear it?"

"I couldn't, it's impossible. I've never worn a ring, nor will I ever wear one. Besides, it looks like an engagement ring."

"What does it matter if it's an engagement ring?"

"It matters a lot. I don't like symbols."

"If you don't want to wear it on your ring finger, you can attach it to your key chain."

"That's silly. Who puts rings on key chains? What do you want to say to me? You have strange ideas!"

"You'll be sorry for the rest of your life."

"Are you going to cry again? Cornelia, my patience has limits."

"If you don't attach it to your key chain I'm going to kill myself. Today, right now."

"Don't shout. The whole house will hear you. If that's what you want, fine, give me the ring. Are you satisfied? Did you have some candy? The ring is dirty."

"No."

"What do you want me to do now? Kill myself? What do you want? Are you going to cry again?"

"I have to tell you something."

"Tell me right away. Don't torture me."

"I'm going to have a baby."

"What you're saying surpasses my comprehension. You are crazy. I am crazy. Perhaps we are all crazy. But I think you're lying."

"I am telling the truth. Always the truth. Do you want me to leave?"

———

"Pablo, can you hear me?"

"I was studying. In this house it's very difficult to study. Almost impossible."

"I saw Cornelia leave with her eyes red from tears. What's the matter with that girl, can you tell me?"

"She's a child. You know what that misfortune is like. You were one once."

"I was always happy. As happy as a bird."

"There are girls who suffer when they are eleven."

"Why at eleven? I don't understood, please explain."

"If you don't know, I can't explain."

"You think that I'm unfeeling, right? You think that my joy is a bit absurd, a bit cold."

"Don't say things you don't feel. You know I adore you."

"When there are people with us you are different. Horribly different."

"Don't be childish. You are more beautiful than ever. This is the first time I've seen you dressed in yellow."

"It's the color of jealousy, the color of broomstraw."

"Don't be jealous. In your room, in your hair, in your hands, there's the smell of broomstraw, even though the time of its flowering has passed."

"I was broomstraw in another incarnation."

"Broomstraw or jasmine?"

"Broomstraw and jasmine."

"I had hidden myself to listen to the conversation. Elena Schleider found out about the ring. Furious, she told my parents, who have many children and are very religious. Because of my impassivity, they threw me out of the house. The story about the baby was a lie, but thanks to that lie my aunt wanted to protect me, so she hired me as an employee in her boutique on the condition that I forget about becoming an actress. Elena Schleider threatened to kill me if I saw Pablo. Instead, as part of my revenge, I pretended to fall in love with another boy, but this turned out badly because I really did fall in love and Pablo started to pursue me. In a luxury car!"

"And are you still in love?"

"No. Have you always had a mustache?"

"Only when I go out. When I am at home I take it off."

"Take it off now."

"Why do you want to kill yourself?"

"Why do you wear a false mustache?"

"Why do you want to kill yourself?"

"It doesn't matter why. Now you have to kill me."

"You have told me part of your life. Perhaps the most important part? The rest is missing. Weren't you once five, six, seven, eight, nine? Didn't you have smallpox or German measles? Weren't you afraid of the dark? Didn't they ever tell you stories?"

"Do you want my life to turn into the *Arabian Nights*? The people we hate the most are the ones we have entrusted with all of our secrets. When we are in their presence we can't change our soul. They are always there to remind us what we were like."

"I give up. For me to keep my promise you have to keep yours."

"I can't continue right now. I am dead. I would like to go to the Green Rose and give Cristina the mannequin. I would like to know whether the man has died. That is my last wish."

"Let's go together. Could we drop by my house to get the revolver? A real revolver."

"Do you think someone might chase us?"

"The revolver is for killing you. I prefer being armed. I could strangle you or cut open your veins, but the revolver is more impersonal. And that letter?"

"It's my letter of farewell."

"Give it to me. Everything that has to do with your death belongs to me."

"I am repulsed by your behavior."

"Why do you kiss your reflection?"

"Because it inspires in me the desire to kiss it."

"And don't you have to repress your desires?"

"No. My image in the mirror is the better part of myself. Let's leave. I hope you turn out the lights. But what is that light visible through the blinds?"

"The light of the moon. Buenos Aires is my only unknown city. It's always the port where I have just arrived."

"Mirrors are very important. They are the soul of a house. Roman mirrors were small, designed to be held in your hand."

"I don't like to see my profile. One side is cruel and the other is stupid. I would break all the mirrors."

"Hasn't anyone heard of the burning lens? That's what they were called in the Middle Ages: concave or parabolic mirrors that gathered the rays of the sun into a point called 'the focus,' where the heat was so great that things caught on fire. How wise I am! Don't you admire my knowledge of history? Didn't Archimedes burn the flotilla of Marcellus in Syracuse; and Proclus, the engineer of the emperor Anastasius, wasn't he the one who burnt Vespasian's flotilla in Constantinople with mirrors? In the sanctuary of Demeter in Patras there is a sacred spring that feeds a pool in which, when combined with a mirror, it's possible to practice divination."

"I too believe in magic, in cards, in the transmission of thoughts, in human telepathy."

"In a temple near Megalopolis, Pausanias says that those who look at themselves in the mirror will see very confused images or nothing at all, but the images of gods and their shining thrones will be seen clearly. What a strange pink light is coming through the window. I thought I was in Megalopolis. I thought that it was dawn. How intimate streets are in the summer, even if we feel like intruders. I forgot about the mannequin."

"I forgot about the mustache."

"Why do you disguise yourself?"

"So as not to recognize people."

"I don't know anything about you. I think that trust should be mutual. Why don't you talk to me? Why don't you tell me about your life?"

"I know important parts of your biography, don't forget."

"The events of a life don't shape the character of a person."

"But doesn't people's behavior with regard to those events give an indication of their character?"

"Not at all. There are people who are very hard to know well."

"I know you. I haven't gotten to know anyone else so closely. In the final analysis, you want to hide yourself, to hide your true personality. Why don't you tell me about your dream from last night?"

"What obligation do I have to tell you?"

"It's normal a thing to share. How reserved you are!"

"Men are very reserved."

"And women are very distrustful. I don't believe what you tell me."

"And why should I lie to you?"

"To get to know me a little better than you believe you know me."

"I don't lie to you. I dreamed that you were killing me."

"Do you want me to believe that we had the same dream? Let's see—I killed you. And what else?"

"You took the knife that I was about to stab you with away from me. Then while I embraced you, you stabbed me instead."

"You behaved like some sort of vulgar queen, in her nuptial flight. And the black man? That black man who had a child in his arms—who was he? Why was he wearing a mask?"

"That was Claudio. But he was also the pyromaniac."

"I wonder what desires of yours were expressed in that dream."

"How absurd you are. To think that I went by the Green Rose every day and that I thought that Esmeralda Street was a common emerald. How many days have gone by since yesterday!"

"To think that you passed by every morning of my life, without seeing me, and that I didn't see you either. Why did we come to this place? I would prefer a prison to this little window next to a wall with piles of hatboxes."

"We couldn't have stayed here for good. The mice would have eaten us."

"I came to feel at peace with the mice in this house. They have such a funny way of behaving, like the mice who obeyed Saint Martin of Porres."

"I am afraid."

"What are you afraid of?"

"I don't know."

"You must be nervous because you haven't slept. You are afraid of the man. Are you afraid that he is dead or that he isn't dead?"

"It's not that."

"You are afraid of meeting people."

"No. I am afraid that Cristina is not alive, that she has never been alive."

"I exist. You exist. The kiss we shared exists."

"We never kissed. If you think we have kissed it's because you've kissed a ghost."

"The piles of boxes exist, as does the storeroom of hats, with the adornments and all the felt."

"Everything seems so unreal. I would have to hurt myself to discover whether I exist."

"Don't be in such a hurry. There is always something that hurts us."

"But I am referring to a wound of the kind that bleeds, a wound made by a knife. For instance, if I had a knife I would cut myself."

"You haven't slept. You are nervous."

"You have no imagination."

"But I have a memory. We had the same dream. My life is very poor. If I were to tell it to you, you wouldn't keep telling me yours. There's no time for so many confessions. In Native American secret societies, the only initiates who are admitted are the ones who have had certain predetermined dreams. We had the same dream..."

"That's true. Perhaps we have been having the same dreams since we were born. Tell me yours. You must have dreamed a lot before you met me. And I always dream about myself. When I was a little girl, I had conversations with my own image. I spoke to it a million times. At night I dreamed about this mirror. Perhaps it was the influence of reading *Alice in Wonderland*, which fascinated me. They say that at the moment of death one remembers all the incidents of one's life. When I was preparing to die tonight, I relived the feelings of my childhood before this mirror."

"Don't you agree with Stendhal when he says that 'love is the miracle of civilization'?"

"Do you still have illusions?"

"Yes."

"What's your name."

"Daniel."

"Daniel. That's my favorite name. In religion classes I imagined Daniel a million times in the den of lions. Your eyes are so light that they make me believe in the truth. It's a pity that we only met on the last day."

"The last day?"

"The last day of my life."

"Nobody could imagine that we just met, or that for that reason you must be totally indifferent to me, or me to you."

"Would you give up everything for me?"

"I would die for you. And you—would you live?"

"We haven't known each other long. And now this whole matter of suicide—it's absurd, isn't it?"

"Why did you promise to kill me?"

"To avoid a suicide. Who is Cristina?"

"A ten-year-old girl."

"And why could a ten-year-old girl matter?"

"It's a mystery, and besides she is ten, a fairly mysterious age. We don't know what she's up to or whether she exists."

"And what is the girl going to do with the mannequin?"

"She likes it better than a doll. Why don't you tell me your secrets?"

"I will tell them to you if you agree to live. Do you agree?"

"How can I agree to things that are none of my business? Blessed are those who died or lived at a time when mirrors didn't exist. Nothing kept them from killing themselves, as I would like to do with the contents of that innocent glass. Leave. I want to look at myself in the mirror. What I most adore in the world is water: drinking it, looking at it, imagining it. In this glass I am holding some of it captive, even though it's mixed with that other thing that is less pure. Mirror, I will approach you and kiss you. How fresh, how pure, how unlike anyone you are! I press my lips against yours as if no one could ever separate us. All the photographs are mirrors of what we were, but not of what we are or of what we will be. Let me look at myself. I am the only thing I don't know. I am going to drink something better than life itself. Luckily I know everything that is not me. I approach the mirror. I want to kiss myself. Nobody will prevent me from kissing myself. Nothing will prevent me from kneeling. No distance keeps us apart, not even the glacial cold of the flat surface. I am going to die right now. I will undress and be totally naked. Totally naked. If anyone comes near, they should leave right away, leaving me to see myself for the last time. What a strange noise. Where is it coming from? What I hear is coming from up above, as if something were being broken. I arrived at this house so long ago and I've never heard that before. Could the mice have slipped behind the mirror? Or maybe something is loosening in this huge tower. Why am I so afraid of you, oh mirror? I wasn't afraid of you before. Before I would approach, but now I am drawing away. Are you going to kill me? Will you dare? I will die beneath your glass. I will kneel at your feet. I will cover my head with my arms so as not to see the cascade of falling glass. What garbage you are. I will look for myself in all of the fragments of you: an eye, a hand, a lock of hair, my feet, my navel, my knees, my back, the beloved back of my neck, but I will never be able to piece them back together."

"I don't have much voice left. Those who are looking for me are the worms, the mice, dust. The death of a person isn't like the death of a mirror. I never believed I would have the luck to die with you."

(COM)PASSION

No one noticed the passion that dominated her until after her adolescence: the desire to inspire compassion. The desire was so strong in her that she voluntarily contracted various diseases and put herself in situations surrounded by severe illness in order to awaken a deep feeling of compassion in those around her. I will try my best to give a brief account of her actions that allowed me to understand her motives.

This is how I fell in love with her: I spent summer vacations at a beach and her tent was near mine, allowing me not only to talk to her and share ocean swims but also to hand her a towel so she could dry her hair, a mirror so she could brush it, invite her to have a sandwich, and take a picture of her completely nude among the tamarisks. Then one brilliant night perfect for a swim, she returned disheveled and in a terrible state, with blood on her lips, saying that five young men had raped her among the tamarisks. I tried to console her. She was upset with me because I had taken a nude picture of her. Even if nudity was in fashion, she said, the young men weren't used to such permissiveness, and seeing her naked had incited them to rape her. She cried so much that I had to accompany her to the eye doctor the next day.

"Nobody will want to marry me," she whispered, sobbing.

"But are you a virgin?"

"Yes, even if you could care less," she answered, weeping even more.

"But today virginity has no importance," I told her. "Besides, you could easily recover your virginity with the help of a gynecologist."

"I would never deceive the man I love," she answered.

I fell in love with her because her beauty was so imperious and I couldn't resist her charms. No matter how incomprehensible her feelings and words were to me, there was the fact of her green eyes, her mouth, her angelic profile, her sensitive hands, her ears, all willing to tell the truth. Will I be happy with her someday? I asked myself. Will we have children? Will we live in a house with a garden? She was a rich young woman who lived in a fancy house, but I never thought about her wealth when I imagined marrying her. Nor was any interest in improving my social position part of my desire to marry her. I am poor, but I don't envy people who have more than I do. Leaving poverty behind actually frightened me when we were about to marry. I sleep with my dog, but she didn't like it; I have a canary, but she hates that pet, too. I eat raw onions, which disgusts her, and she criticizes me for being messy. I prefer to wear the same style of blue-colored shirt but she makes me change into a pink one. I don't wear a tie to the movies but she insists that I wear one. I cut my hair once a month but she wants me to cut it four times a month. "You are a pig," she said once, while I was eating a sausage. Not eating sausage seems impossible to me.

It's better not to get married if you don't share the same tastes with your spouse. Besides, love can be expressed with the same passion whether you are married or single if the one you love gives herself fully to you.

Through a long series of conversations, the most significant aspect of which were the goodbyes, I gradually came to know her. I cannot forget that afternoon during Carnival when she dressed up as a Dutch peasant woman. The flannel outfit was very warm, with three skirts, one on top of the other, and two jackets, one of white cotton and the other of velvet. Two braids of yellow wool completed her stylish hair. She sweated so much that she didn't want me to touch her. In the middle of the party she fainted, falling to the ground like a bolt of cloth. The whites of her eyes showed when she had her eyelids closed. I thought she was dead. With a weak voice she said, "I feel that my life is leaving me ... I hear distant voices as if from some other world and everything looks blurry—it's like the day of the apocalypse that I read about in the Bible."

I was surprised that she could utter such a long sentence in the state she was in. I cried in desperation, from a feeling of impotence. For an instant I thought I could see a smile of satisfaction on her face, but I quickly attributed it to the blessedness of dying. I took care of her until five in the morning, giving her drops of coramin and little cups of coffee that I prepared for her in the kitchen along with cups of verbena tea. Then, as my distress increased, she suddenly seemed to improve. I told her that I loved her with all my heart, something that I had never told her or felt the need to tell her. Life changed for me. I thought seriously about marriage.

"How sad this world is," she said, while being dressed in her bridal gown. As she combed her bangs, she tore the veil they had sewn and made everyone cry. "It's a bad omen," she exclaimed, picking up some of the orange blossoms that had fallen. "We will never be happy," she said, looking into my eyes.

"Why are you so superstitious?" I asked her. "Don't you think that only attracts misfortune?"

"If you don't attract it, it will come anyway," she replied, and smiled with the same smile that I had seen with surprise when she saw me weep.

After the wedding, among other calamities—a bad fall while ice-skating, the loss of a valuable ring—she became ill.

She said she was diagnosed with a contagious virus, but she never let me accompany her to the doctor. Her illness was strange, as she swayed from the heights of euphoria to the deepest depression, accompanied by nausea and headaches. She was in bed for a week, not allowing anyone to open the blinds so that the sun wouldn't disturb the clarity of her vision or ruin the silk curtains. When she finally recovered she seemed even more lovely and delicate. I took her for a ride around the lakes of Palermo Park. We stopped next to the Andalusian patio, where we had ice cream. The passing tourists stared at us. I attributed it to my criminal appearance.

Living together turned out to be difficult. We trusted each other.

There was a desk where she kept her papers. She didn't mind if I read the letters which I confess filled me with curiosity. One day I found a little envelope that intrigued me because of its shape and color. I opened the envelope and read the letter inside it:

Dear Baby Jesus, Christmas is approaching and I am very sad. I hurt my knee on a piece of glass and the pain is like being in hell. The biggest cut I have is on my knee. To make me feel better from this pain I would like to have a dollhouse with an ambulance and nurse, as well as a first aid kit. I am signing with my own blood. Felicia. Christmas 1955.

"How old were you when you wrote this letter? Seven?"

"I didn't write it. My aunt did."

"But did you sign it?"

"Yes, with my blood."

"And did Baby Jesus bring you everything you asked for?"

"Everything except the ambulance, which cost too much when you added it to the expense of the dollhouse, which was already quite expensive."

TRANSLATOR'S NOTE

I FIRST met Silvina Ocampo in 1978, when I visited her husband, Adolfo Bioy Casares, at their apartment, wanting to interview him for some research related to my dissertation. The writer José Bianco invited me to dinner the same night, telling me that Ocampo had phoned him every few minutes while I was there, asking about me, commenting on my youthful appearance. A few days later there was a dinner at Bianco's apartment, the other guests being Borges, Bioy, and Ocampo. At one point that evening, she retrieved a book from Bianco's shelf—a copy of her story collection *Las invitadas* inscribed with a dedication to Bianco—and added a new dedication to me. On subsequent visits to Buenos Aires we met often and became close friends. I remember her reading my palm and my aura, and I still have a portrait she drew of me. During our many conversations, the idea for this book was born. Ocampo insisted that we choose her cruelest stories, and we corresponded frequently about details of the translation. Eventually, Penguin Canada accepted a selection for publication, though by the time the book appeared in 1988, Ocampo's mind had already gone, and five years later she passed away.

I am grateful to Jeffrey Yang and New York Review Books for giving our book a second chance in a considerably revised and expanded form. To the previous collection we've added the magnificent novella *El impostor*, published in *Autobiografía de Irene* (1948), and a selection of early stories from *Viaje olvidado* (Forgotten Journey, 1937) and from the last two collections Ocampo published in her lifetime, *Y así sucesivamente* (And So Forth, 1987) and *Cornelia frente al espejo* (Cornelia Before the Mirror, 1988). Ocampo's reputation has grown tremendously in the two decades since her death, and a whole range of unpublished works—stories, a verse autobiography, aphorisms, a novel—have appeared in Argentina, in careful editions by Ernesto Montequín, who has also produced new editions of Ocampo's previously published books. Critical work on Ocampo in Spanish, English, and French has also thrived—as it happens, the languages she also spoke and wrote in—and some of her stories have been adapted to the theater and the screen.

For me, Ocampo's most accomplished short stories are still the ones we selected together those many years ago, from *La furia* (The Fury, 1959) and *Las invitadas* (The Guests, 1961). Brilliant and chilling, these stories are also thoroughly strange, not only in narrative content but in their wild syntax and language. Revisiting my old translations I have tried to preserve the oddness of the language, even as I have revised to pull the English syntax a bit farther from the Spanish. Argentina is more familiar to English readers now than it was a quarter century ago, so I have restored some place-names in Spanish, keeping the original accents and spellings. In one case I added a footnote to clarify a reference to a line of poetry that wouldn't be familiar to English readers, but I have held back from explaining the world of secret references in these mysterious, fantastic tales.

I dedicate this new translation to Silvina, in fond memory.

—DANIEL BALDERSTON